Land of my Dreams

A Home for my Heart

Norma Gail

Lighthouse Publishing
of the Carolinas

LAND OF MY DREAMS BY NORMA GAIL
Published by Lighthouse Publishing of the Carolinas
2333 Barton Oaks Dr., Raleigh, NC, 27614

ISBN: 978-1941103173
Copyright © 2014 Lighthouse Publishing of the Carolinas
Cover design by KillianGroup, www.thekilliongroupinc.com
Interior design by Thomas White

Available in print from your local bookstore, online, or from the publisher at:
www.lighthousepublishingofthecarolinas.com

For more information on this book and the author visit: www.normagail.com

Brought to you by the creative team at LighthousePublishingoftheCarolinas.com:
Brian Cross, Amberlyn Edwards, Rowena Kuo, and Eddie Jones

Library of Congress Cataloging-in-Publication Data
Holtman, Norma Gail Thurston
1st ed. Land of My Dreams/Norma Gail Thurston Holtman

Printed in the United States of America

To Dirk, the love of my life.

Thank you for your patience, your encouragement, your belief in me,

and for holding my heart gently within our circle of golden bands.

CONTENTS

ACKNOWLEDGEMENTS

When I look back on the journey to publishing *Land of My Dreams*, I am amazed at the number of people who have helped and encouraged me along the way. This book would not exist without the help of so many people who gave of their time to help me realize my dream. I have been blessed by their honesty, candor, encouragement, and prayers. They all deserve credit for what this book has become and whatever it accomplishes, for without them, it might not exist.

When I broke my right foot in 2008, ending up in a wheelchair, I needed something to occupy my mind, and thus began *Land of My Dreams*. Now, in 2014, I am seeing the hard work become reality. I want to thank the many people who helped me.

My husband Dirk, children Ian and Amy, daughter-in-law, Lissa; my mom, Nell Thurston; and my mother-in-law, Hester Holtman; put up with years of me talking about dead relatives from my genealogy research. Then they had to put up with years of me starting conversations about my imaginary friends, the characters from my book. They don't necessarily understand, but they love me anyway, and overlook my strange affinity for make-believe worlds.

Dirk has offered his encouragement, his opinions, and his recommendations about how a man would respond in various circumstances, and how the fishing scene should go. That's true partnership in a marriage. He has attended writer's conferences as my support and encouragement, working from the room while I attended workshops, and enduring meals while listening to writers talk about their books.

Next are my friends who read and critiqued the earliest manuscripts: my childhood friend and high school writing buddy, Brenda Parrish; Jan

Montgomery, my former Teaching Leader in Bible Study Fellowship who risked our friendship to be honest; my best friend and spiritual encourager, Jeni Civerolo; my dear friend, Roseanne Pennington; and our wonderful family friend, Billie Waters. The second-round readers, two of whom, Brenda and Roseanne, came back for a second dose; Sharon Finch, Laura Galbraith, and Helen Duncan, all gave such valuable input. The women in the Bible studies I lead at church have encouraged and prayed for me all along the way.

Angela Breidenbach did the first critique at my very first Colorado Christian Writer's Conference, even meeting with me over lunch, and said from the beginning that *Land of My Dreams* was publishing material. Cindy Sproles accepted my first devotional submissions to ChristianDevotions.us, and further helped me believe I could write. Linda Evans Shepherd taught the Continuing Session for Beginning Fiction Writers at my second conference, and encouraged me that my book could be published. Marjorie Vawter showed me how valuable editing is and further encouraged my dream.

After putting me into shell-shock at my second CCWC, when he turned a 15 minute appointment into 30 minutes of rewriting the beginning of the book, Eddie Jones, the Acquisitions Editor of Lighthouse Publishing of the Carolinas gave me my chance by offering me a contract. I am forever grateful. He helped me learn to take the tough stuff and keep going to make it happen.

My editor, Amberlyn Edwards, is a blessing. She took the book on when another editor dropped out and really got things moving. She is a terrific encourager and a tough, but gentle teacher. I have loved working with her!

Amy Drown, my Scottish content advisor, gave me so many excellent pointers and worked so hard to make things the best they could be, even beyond the Scottish references. Her knowledge of piping was invaluable and her editing suggestions were insightful. Thank you, Amy!

The beta readers who gave of their time to correct mistakes and let me hear the opinion of readers, and the influencers who helped promote the book have my everlasting gratitude.

My thanks would not be complete without thanking Tim Burns of Visible

Platforms who set up my website and took me through the book launch.

Thank you, one and all, for your willingness to work with me, love me, and encourage me when my belief in myself wavered. God bless you abundantly.

Land of My Dreams

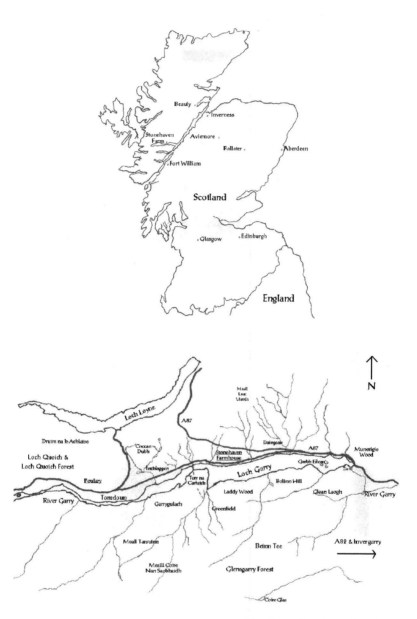

Glen Garry & Stonehaven Farm

"He has made everything beautiful in His time. He has set eternity in the hearts of men, yet they cannot fathom what God has done from beginning to end."
Ecclesiastes 3:11

CHAPTER ONE

GOODBYES

Bonny Bryant knew it was crazy to even think about a man when she was headed for Scotland. The Albuquerque International Airport was the first stop in her quest for a new life. Nonetheless, she paused to look at the tanned, trim man in the business suit as he came down the escalator. There was no harm in appreciating a handsome man while she waited for Kari, but then the familiar lump formed in her throat and she turned away, searching for her best friend.

Where was Kari, anyway? She had paused to speak to some old friends of her parents, and Bonny went on to check her bags. The bottom of the escalator was their designated meeting place. A glance at her watch showed only ten more minutes before she would have to go on. She swiped her hand across her eyes. *Hurry, Kari, I can't leave without a hug. You're all I've got.*

The tall man stepped off the escalator, a few feet away, and Bonny clasped her hands and closed her eyes, forcing herself to close her mouth. The similarity of his build and appearance to Adam gave her a jolt. Why did she have to be reminded of him right now?

Forcing her thoughts to the present, Bonny looked around the familiar chaos of the "Sunport" with a feeling of nostalgia. Massive wooden *vigas* carved and painted with bright Native American symbols provided a unique New Mexican flair, undiminished by the varied origins of the travelers. She would miss the distinctive culture of her hometown.

The frantic fluttering in her chest stopped when she spotted Kari Anderson hurrying through the crowd. "I'm sorry, Bonny. They wanted to know all about the wedding plans and how Dan is doing. It took longer than I intended."

"It's okay. Walk with me to security."

"I hate that you had to stand here alone all that time. Let me take your carry-on. You'll be handling it alone long enough. There's so much I want to say to you."

Relieved of the backpack, Bonny grabbed Kari's elbow. "Slow down, will you? I want to remember everything—the sights, sounds, and smells, all the things that make New Mexico unique. I'm glad you suggested bringing frozen green chile along. It will be nice to have a taste of home."

Kari put her arm around Bonny's shoulders as they made their way down the crowded hallway. "I'll send you care packages when you get homesick, just like I do for Dan."

"Not quite the same, I hope. I can do without the socks." Bonny set the pace as she continued her sentimental farewell, sniffing the delicious odors of New Mexican food from a nearby café and savoring the distinctive flavor of the Sunport. She had never lived anywhere else. From this point on, everything would be unfamiliar. No reminders of home or of Adam. *Whoa girl, one step at a time.* Too much time dwelling on it and she might panic.

The glass doors leading to the security area meant the time for good-byes had arrived. She leaned into her friend's shoulder, knowing nine months stood between them and the next hug.

"I wish—"

"No, don't." Bonny didn't want to listen again to all the reasons why moving to Scotland was a bad idea. Sidestepping to allow a group of businessmen to pass, she held Kari at arm's length. She looked into her friend's watery blue eyes, taking in her tall, willowy build, jet-black hair, and casual elegance. "I'll be back for your wedding in the spring. Let me leave with the memory of my best friend wishing me well."

Kari nodded, shaking the shining waves of hair behind her shoulders and pasting on a smile. "I'll be lonely with Dan in Afghanistan and you in Scotland. I hope you find what you're searching for."

Bonny tried to swallow the lump that lodged in her throat once again. "I'll be fine."

She stretched to kiss the freckle-sprinkled cheek of her much-taller friend. Squaring her shoulders, she stepped through the doors toward her future, whatever it held.

After clearing security without a glitch, she paused to look up at the imposing sculpture of an Indian shaman grasping the feet of an eagle in flight. It seemed appropriate. "Here I go, stepping off into the unknown. Good-bye, New Mexico."

Chapter Two

A New Beginning

Twenty hours later, give or take the half hour in the parking lot practicing driving on the wrong side of the road, Bonny eased the car into gear and joined the traffic whizzing by. She was on her way from Inverness to Fort William. Her father's instructions for driving in Great Britain echoed in her head. *Look right, turn left, look right, turn left.*

"Okay, Dad," she whispered. "Here I go. I wish you were with me. I'm living our dream."

She pulled out onto the street toward the A82. After months of looking at maps, she was driving the highway that would take her through the Great Glen, past Loch Ness, and on to Fort William Christian College.

Once free of the city traffic, she began to relax a little. Maybe with some distance from reminders of her own loss and the preparations for Kari's wedding, she could find peace again.

The honking of a car horn brought her back to the reality of the fast-paced traffic around her. The beauty stole her breath away, and shivers tingled up her spine with the inexplicable feeling of belonging she had felt from the moment she stepped out of the airport terminal. For the first time in three months, she had hope.

◌ঙ৶◌

As she rounded a curve in the road, the imposing hulk of the ruined Urquhart Castle came into view, silhouetted against the dark, mysterious waters of Loch Ness. *Deliberately destroyed to thwart the enemy.* Bonny pulled into the crowded parking lot, remembering the history from a travel book. Seeing it in person created an intimate identification with the castle's Grant Tower, standing defiant and proud against the choppy waters of the loch and the leaden gray of the clouds. She was in Scotland—alone.

Recognizing a kindred spirit in the ancient edifice, she looked across the loch to the trees and farms on the other side. The peaceful pastoral scene caused her eyes to blur, and she stepped back into the car. As she fumbled in her purse for a tissue, she determined to set her mind on building a new life. *No one here has to know. Stand proud.*

Easing the leased red Vauxhall Astra into gear, she headed back out onto the highway, anxious to reach Fort William Christian College and her new home.

Once, she would have thought God agreed with her desire for a new life. But now, she no longer believed God involved Himself with people's daily lives. Gazing around her, she imagined such an incredible place had the potential to help anyone start over—and she would.

Dwelling on the negative led to a dead end. She wasn't about to start feeling sorry for herself now. She popped a CD into the dashboard player, glad she had thought to bring her favorite Celtic music. It was impossible to keep from tapping her foot to the perfect soundtrack for the symphony of sights unfolding around each bend in the road.

Bonny gaped at the green mountains with their rocky summits shrouded in clouds and the cotton balls of mist floating past. Graceful waterfalls plummeted down steep hillsides, and the deep, glacier-carved lochs captured her in their spell. In her mind, she saw a kilted figure standing high on a mountainside, the haunting melody of his bagpipes beckoning her. This land of legend and myth had enchanted her since childhood. She was fourteen the last time she visited with her parents, and the verdant green of Scotland had come to symbolize the haven of peace she longed for.

An hour and a half later, a high mountain, which had to be Ben Nevis, rose into view. She gazed up at the rocky face and farther up to the rarely-seen summit. The dark sky had cleared, leaving a sky as blue as the Scottish flag. The highest mountain in Great Britain towered over her new home in Fort William, filling her with a sense of protection and permanence in the same way Sandia Peak did back home. She had grown up in the mountains, and all the best times in her life were somehow related to them. She pictured the log and stone house, once a welcoming home, standing quiet and empty, the family that once inhabited it reduced to only her. The family she hoped would someday fill it as nebulous as the swirling clouds which had greeted her arrival in Inverness.

Turning into the first major parking lot after entering Fort William, she turned on her cell phone. "Janet, it's Bonny Bryant. I'm finally here, in the parking lot of the Nevis Bank Inn."

"I'll see you in five minutes. *Fàilte gu Alba*, welcome to Scotland. And Bonny, Scots call it a car park."

"Thanks. I'm certain you'll find plenty to teach me."

"*Guid*, cheerio."

When a blue car pulled up, she recognized the pretty blonde with the warm smile and striking, lavender-blue eyes. The photo on Facebook did her justice.

"*Feasgar math,* good afternoon. I feel as if I know you already from our e-mails." Janet's hug was a warm and encouraging welcome.

Bonny laughed and hugged her back. "What a delightful greeting. I guess I'll begin to understand sooner or later."

"Don't worry. I'll translate. You'll want to learn some basic phrases since you're living here." Janet's warmth and enthusiasm quickly set her at ease.

"I noticed the traffic signs give both English and Gaelic names. And everything is even more beautiful than I remembered."

"Ach, that's *guid*. I would hate for you to travel so far and feel disappointed. How was your trip?"

"The flight went fine. Once I got enough courage to leave the parking— car park and drive on the wrong side of the road, the trip from Inverness was spectacular. I love it here." She waved her hand at the surrounding scenery.

"Dr. Cameron said to stop by anytime for the key to your office."

Bonny couldn't help clapping her hands in eagerness. "I'm anxious to see him and the school. Let's go now."

"Oh, aye, you can follow me to the college, and then to your house." Janet motioned toward the cars.

The college lay on the outskirts of town. Passing through the tall, wrought-iron gates, Bonny read the lettering, "Fort William Christian College, 2005." Tall trees and colorful flowerbeds lined the circular drive. She stepped out of the car, gazing up at the stately, three-story, granite building with its high-pitched and gabled slate roof. "This dignified old building gives a sense of decorum you wouldn't expect in a new school."

"Aye, it does. An old gentleman with no heirs donated it for the express purpose of providing students easy access to a Christian education. The estate was much larger, but they sold some of the land to create an endowment for renovations and provide for the future."

Rose bushes and holly trees lined either side of wide steps leading to the double front doors with oval, leaded-glass windows. Bonny held her head high as she followed Janet. Eager as she was to begin her new life, she felt a twinge of sadness for all that would never be.

They approached a desk to one side of the large, round foyer, the centerpiece of which was an ornate staircase branching off to either side. Moments after the receptionist announced them, Dùghlas Cameron rushed out of a nearby office. His dark hair was thinner on top, but he still projected the contagious energy Bonny remembered.

"Uncle Dùghlas, how good to see you."

He approached her with a gentle hug, kissing her on both cheeks. "Welcome, Bonny. I wish you were here under happier circumstances. I hope we can bless you and help you to heal." His welcoming embrace brought unwelcome tears to her eyes. He pulled a handkerchief out of his pocket and handed it to her. "I thought you might need that today, so I brought two. I trust you had no problems on the way over. I expected you to rest before visiting me."

His strong Scottish burr brought back pleasant memories of his last visit to Albuquerque. It was comforting to find one familiar face in this new place. "Thank you. Right now, I'm running on adrenaline, but I was anxious to see you and the school."

Janet followed as he hooked Bonny's arm through his for the short walk to his office. "Arriving in July should help you feel quite at home by the time school begins in September. Mairi wanted me to invite you for dinner this evening, but I told her you needed to rest. Please consider us your family while you're here."

She swiped at her eyes as they misted over again. "How about tomorrow evening?"

"Perfect. I so anticipated spending time with Andy again." He looked down, shaking his head. "The friendship your father and I developed at university remained strong, in spite of the years and distance between us."

Bonny cleared her throat. "I miss him. Everything happened so fast."

He patted her shoulder. "I do too. Why don't you rest and settle in? Give me a ring when you're ready, and we'll talk about your classes. Of course, your father and I discussed it, but you'll have your own ideas. Janet will give you the tour, and don't hesitate to ask Mairi or me if you need anything." He handed her the paperwork and keys. "Cheers, Bonny. I hope you'll be happy here."

She stood on tip-toe to kiss his cheek. "With my parents gone, I'm glad I have you and Aunt Mairi to lean on."

Janet shut the door behind her and steered Bonny down the hall. "He really is like family to you, isn't he?"

Bonny nodded. "My parents were both only children, so their best friends were the aunts and uncles I never had. I'll have to remember to call him Dr. Cameron when people are around. It's hard to break old habits. But tell me about the school."

"It's a lovely place. Let me show you around a wee bit."

In her eagerness to explore, Bonny felt a burst of energy. "Thanks. Does Unc—Dr. Cameron show such concern for the entire faculty? He's still the whirlwind of enthusiasm I remember."

Janet laughed. "Aye, he's keen on meeting the students and sets a strong example of living to glorify God. He's out among the students and faculty almost every day."

Bonny cringed, remembering her deception about her faith. "This will be very different from a large secular university where the president doesn't even know my name."

The marble floors, mahogany wainscoting, and high ceilings gave evidence of what a fine home it had once been. Though the classrooms boasted new desks and modern whiteboards, the old building lent a sense of antiquity. She wondered if the wide windows overlooking the broad green lawns, towering trees, and lush beds of colorful blooms would make it difficult to keep students' minds on their lessons.

"The pictures you sent didn't do it justice. What a place to go to school." Bonny inhaled the essence of old wood and time.

"We'll take a more detailed look around when you've rested. Let's get you settled."

They got back into their cars, and she followed Janet out the main gate and around the corner, stopping in front of a small stone cottage with green and white trim and a red front door. The only word that came to mind was amazing.

"This charming cottage is for me? I never expected anything so pretty."

"Aye, it's lovely." Janet's smile showed satisfaction. "It served as the caretaker's house for the mansion. We want things home-like for our visiting professors."

"It's a fairytale cottage with all the beautiful flowers and hedges."

"All you have to do is enjoy. The groundskeeper will care for the gardens. Come inside and see what you think."

Crossing the threshold, Bonny felt as if she had stepped into a Scottish version of *Better Homes and Gardens*. The flowered couch and tartan armchairs in front of a fireplace, flanked by bookshelves, created an inviting atmosphere. She paused in surprise at the sight of her own family photos on the piano, then looked around, recognizing her books on the shelves and a few familiar knick-knacks.

"You unpacked for me? Thank you for making everything warm and comfortable."

"It's just a wee bit o' Scottish hospitality. I left your clothing for you to unpack, and you don't have to leave things where I put them. As to the decorating, Mairi Cameron did most of that."

Bonny wandered through the house, sinking into one of the chairs by the fireplace as jet lag began to take over. "You thought of everything. The bright colors and fresh flowers ... just seeing my own books on the shelves makes me feel welcome. It's like finding old friends waiting for me. You don't know what it means to have such a cozy, restful place right now."

Janet's eyes were full of questions as she shook her head. "You'll need a wee rest after your long trip. If you want, I'll bring dinner 'round about seven, and we can get better acquainted. Unless you'd prefer the evening to yourself."

"How thoughtful. I would appreciate that, and you're right. A little rest will do me good. I feel I have a friend already." Bonny stood and hugged her.

"Aye, you do. There are basic groceries in the cupboard. We can shop for anything else you need tomorrow. We'll tour the town when you're ready. Back a' seven." Janet let herself out.

Bonny explored the quaint house again after Janet left. Her luggage sat in the larger of the two bedrooms, and she lay down, intending to rest. When she closed her eyes, however, her mind filled with the reasons she left home—reasons unaltered by the change in scenery.

From somewhere down the street she heard bagpipes.

∞

Out of a fog of sleep, Bonny awakened to someone knocking at the door and calling her name. Feeling a little disoriented, she looked at the clock on the nightstand and discovered three hours had passed. She got up and rubbed the sleep from her eyes as she went to let Janet in. They sat at the kitchen table, sharing traditional Hotch-Potch while they peppered each other with questions.

"You're brave to move this far from home by yourself. I'm not certain I'd have the courage," Janet said.

Bonny took a deep breath, closing her eyes and remembering her well-practiced response. No one needed to know she was escaping not only the loss of everyone dear to her, but painful humiliation, the destruction of her dreams, and even the happiness of friends. She cleared her throat and tried to sound convincing. "My parents died within six months of each other. My dad died in April. I had no responsibilities, and the adventure was too good to pass up."

"I can't imagine losing your parents so close together."

"I felt overwhelmed by reminders everywhere I turned. It made the move very attractive." Bonny clenched her hands into fists and swallowed hard, willing herself to maintain control.

"You'll receive a warm welcome. The students and faculty are eager to have American History and Literature added to the course list. I'm teaching a full load or I'd sign up myself."

Janet's change in the direction of the conversation came much to Bonny's relief. "You'd take the class?"

"A lot of the faculty is interested. Don't be surprised if a few pop up in your classes. Just because I'm a forty-year-old professor doesn't mean I quit learning."

Bonny swallowed a sip of water. "I never expected such interest. It's a great opportunity to teach the curriculum Dad and I wrote together. I was supposed to come over and co-teach the Civil War sections, but then with his cancer ..."

"It must feel good to fulfill his dream. You mentioned your friends Kari and Dan in your e-mails. There's no one special in your life?"

Bonny winced. "Not anymore. And you?"

"A long time ago. Right now, I think you need a good night's sleep."

After Janet left, Bonny opened the suitcase containing the things she needed for the night. The rest could wait until tomorrow. No prayers had crossed her lips in a long time, and tonight was no exception. She refused to let the past prevent her from living in the present.

co80

Opening the door of the large, old, granite-block house, Dr. Cameron ushered her toward the fireplace. "Welcome, Bonny. Come in and dry off. It's a *dreich* day. Our Scottish weather must seem quite different after a lifetime in New Mexico."

"I love it. The rain and mist are a nice change," she said, laughing. "Thank you for putting Janet and me in touch. She's gone out of her way to make me feel welcome."

"Oh, Bonny, I'm so glad to see you." Aunt Mairi crossed the room to give her a warm hug. "It's difficult to believe how things have changed in the five years since we last visited you."

Aunt Mairi gave her a gentle hug and motioned toward the dining room. "Our dinner will be ready as soon as I take the rolls out of the oven. I hope lamb is all right."

"Of course." She hung back for a moment, examining the banner on the wall. Sporting the Clan Cameron coat of arms, it was bounded by the clan tartan and set in an antique wooden frame. It brought back memories of being a fourteen-year-old girl feeling as if she were visiting royalty. The house, like the college, smelled of old wood, but with the added aromas of roasting lamb and Uncle Dùghlas' pipe.

After the blessing, he said, "Friendships as special and long-lasting as I had with your father are rare. Though we spent only those two years together in Edinburgh, we never lost touch."

"He was looking forward to teaching here. It all happened so fast ..."

Aunt Mairi reached across the table and laid her hand on Bonny's arm. "How can we help you, dear?"

"It's difficult at times. Just being away from all the reminders helps. I can't thank you enough for asking me to come here." There came the tears again. Uncle Dùghlas rubbed his eyes with his fist. He was struggling too.

"I understand. Will you come to church with us on Sunday? Going to worship always comforts my heart," Aunt Mairi said.

Uncle Dùghlas smiled. "Yes, what a lovely idea."

"Thank you, but Janet already invited me." Janet had mentioned it in passing, but she did invite Bonny first.

"Yes, of course. Andy and I used to discuss the Bible for hours. Remember, Mairi?"

She nodded. The moisture in the corners of her eyes was a poignant sign of her own treasured memories. "Beth and I developed a strong friendship also. We must value precious people when we have the opportunity. Life changes in ways we least expect."

Uncle Dùghlas lay his hand on Bonny's arm. "Your father was very proud of you. It pleased him that you shared not only his love of history, but his faith as well. He said your teaching abilities put him to shame—quite a compliment, I must say."

Bonny sat silent, unable to find her voice or stop the tears from welling up in her eyes.

"Yes." Aunt Mairi dabbed her eyes with her napkin. "I will miss them both."

The evening wore on too long. Bonny was ready to escape the memories by the time dinner was over, but of course, staying to visit a while was necessary. At nine o'clock, she made a graceful escape, pleading exhaustion.

After only one wrong turn on the way home, Bonny stepped into her little house, grateful to be alone. Her emotions were on edge after an evening of memories. She headed straight for her bedroom, cracking the window enough to smell the fresh scent of rain. Once in bed, she burrowed under the blankets, enjoying the unfamiliar, but welcome, cool of a Scottish summer night. Sleep evaded her, as memories circled in her head like vultures, each one waiting to grab a piece of her—and they succeeded.

CR&C

One week following her arrival, Bonny crossed the college compound for her first faculty meeting. She arrived early, but faculty members were already gathering in the lecture hall.

"Welcome, Bonny," Dr. Cameron said, ushering her in. "Everyone wants to meet you."

Janet had already introduced Bonny to a few fellow professors they'd met while shopping. "Our colleagues are more of a family than co-workers."

Bonny agreed as she watched the constant stream of laughter, hugs, and good-natured camaraderie. A man across the room drew her eyes like a bee to heather. Standing over six feet tall, he looked as solid as Ben Nevis. He stole her breath away. The only way to describe him was rugged and outdoorsy. He wore a plaid shirt tucked into riding breeches, which were tucked into tall, brown leather riding boots. He looked as if he belonged out in the hills rather than in a classroom. His eyes were a brilliant blue, and his hair was a mass of barely-under-control, reddish-blond curls.

With blood pounding in her ears and a fluttering in her stomach, she leaned toward Janet. "Who is he?"

"Kieran MacDonell, a math professor and a friend. He owns a large sheep farm north of here. *Wheesht.*" She held her finger to her lips. "Dr. Cameron is speaking."

Bonny studied the powerful man whenever he wasn't looking her way. Sheep farming explained the physical strength he exuded. His eyes met hers once, acknowledging her with a brief nod and an expression impossible to decipher, before he turned away. He spoke little and appeared somewhat disengaged from the general life and laughter of the group. Her pulse had begun a steady increase from the time she first noticed him. She had never experienced such a strong reaction to any man, but memories made her cautious.

"Did you bring something to wear to the faculty party?" Janet held the door open after the meeting. "It's a lovely event. The men wear their kilts, and the women wear evening dress. We change tables between courses. You'll meet people from all the different departments."

"I'll show you the dresses I brought and see if any of them will work."

"Janet will make certain you meet everyone there."

Bonny turned at the sound of a deep voice to find the big sheep farmer behind her.

"Kieran, meet Bonny Bryant." Janet nudged her, making her aware of her open-mouthed stare.

He reached for her hand, engulfing it in his own large one. "Welcome. I hope you're settling in all right." His wide smile and sparkling eyes were warm and friendly.

"Janet is taking good care of me."

"She's the best. I have to rush. I'm meeting a sheep broker at the farm. *Feasgar math*, ladies." With a nod, he headed toward the stairs, leaving the scent of an unfamiliar, but very masculine, aftershave in his wake.

Bonny's eyes followed him, wondering if the intriguing Professor MacDonell might attend the faculty party.

CRED

The distinctive skirl of bagpipes filled the air as Bonny returned from her walk. A green Land Rover was parked down the street near the gate of a cemetery. She listened for a moment before opening her front door. She was too far from the center of town to hear the pipers who played for change on the street corners. Just like the day she arrived, the music came from the cemetery she had discovered on one of her walks.

The next day, she and Janet climbed a hillside above the town. "When does the heather bloom?" She surveyed the scene spreading out before them. A virtual sea of the abundant plant covered the steep, round-topped mountains.

"The peak comes in September and October. The hillsides will be covered in purple."

"It's incredible now. I can't imagine anything prettier." Bonny took a sip of water from the bottle hooked to her belt, remembering her question from the day before. "I heard bagpipes last week when I arrived and again yesterday. Are they for funerals?"

Janet met her eyes. "It's Kieran. On Fridays, he stops at the flower shop and then goes to the kirkyard, the cemetery, where he visits the grave of his wife and baby. He plays his bagpipes for her."

"What happened?"

"Ach, such a terrible thing, it's still impossible to believe. Bronwyn died in childbirth two years ago, and the baby with her. It gets lonely on his isolated farm. I think he began teaching again to have more interaction with people. He loves farming the best, though. He's a rare one—gentle, kind, and considerate."

His warm welcome and romantic way of dealing with such devastating loss caused her eyes to mist over. A man like that was one she could care for, but it was too soon to think of another relationship.

CHAPTER THREE

KIERAN

Kieran MacDonell felt as dreich as the weather. He stood at the window of his office in the old stone farmhouse on Loch Garry. Hillsides dotted with sheep spread out before him in the heavy rain. Two years ago that very day, his dreams died in one horrific instant. Now, the house was silent, empty of the joy and laughter so anticipated then.

A knock interrupted his reverie, and his housekeeper, Eleanor, entered with a fresh pot of tea. He wiped his eyes on his sleeve in a futile attempt to hide his tears. Bronwyn's photograph clattered to the floor from the window ledge where he'd placed it when Eleanor knocked.

She set the tray on the desk, crossed the room, and laid her hand on his arm. "Bless you, lad. I miss her too. It's a *sair fecht*, but dwelling on her death rather than moving forward with your life does not honor her."

He laid his hand on her small, work-worn one. "I know you're right, but how can I put it behind me?"

"Leave the past in the past, Kieran. There's more to life than sheep. You're but forty. You've a long life ahead of you." She squeezed his hand, then turned and walked out, closing the door behind her.

The night before, he had visited the bedroom he once shared with Bronwyn, fleeing back to his own room after only a few moments, pursued by myriad emotions raised by visiting their private sanctuary. In that room, they had shared love and laughter and conceived their son. He tried to face the future, but guilt and grief stopped him. Her life ended too soon. Liam, who would be a busy two-year-old by now, never had a chance.

Sipping his tea, he recalled the moment he spotted Bonny Bryant at the faculty meeting. He had been preoccupied by thoughts of her ever since. Petite, she lacked Bronwyn's classic beauty, but was pretty with a vital energy. The softness of her small hand and her sweet smile lingered in his mind. She impressed him as strong, yet somehow vulnerable. No woman except Bronwyn had ever affected him with such intensity. One of the other professors had explained to him how she came to be there, and it signaled courage worthy of admiration.

He'd known a professor was coming from America. But he hadn't anticipated this sensation of standing on a precipice, ready to plunge into the unknown.

C3∞

Kieran noticed Janet's office door standing ajar when he entered the faculty office wing the following afternoon. Though classes didn't begin for a few weeks, she sat at her desk, surrounded by textbooks and lesson plans, unaware of his presence until he cleared his throat.

She startled, then smiled, shoving aside her papers and motioning toward a chair. "I don't remember the last time you visited my office."

He looked at the floor, searching for the right words. "Janet, you're my oldest friend. My life feels empty and void of purpose. I spend more time with sheep than people. I can't move on."

He sat down and she reached for the hand he laid on the desk. "Ending one chapter doesn't mean your life is over."

"Ach, Eleanor says the same thing."

"It pains me to see you still hurting so."

In frustration, he stood and walked to the window. "I have no one else to talk to. I need a change." It was difficult to find adequate words to convey his feelings. "I know what you're thinking, but church isn't the answer. God abandoned me two years ago, and nothing since then has shown me He cares."

"I know better than to suggest church to you." Coming up next to him, she nudged him in the ribs. "Besides, if you know what I'll say, why ask for my advice? Every time I suggest anything, you tell me I'm meddling."

Her gentle chiding made him laugh. "You don't give up, do you? You're a good friend."

"I'd better head down to the car park." She pointed out the window at the small figure below, the unmistakable red hair shining. "Bonny's finished with her walk. You should get acquainted. You share some rather similar experiences."

He felt a stab of pain near his heart, along with a familiar sense of panic at the thought of caring for a woman other than Bronwyn. He turned toward the door. "I—not today."

"Stubborn Scot. I knew it was a waste of breath." She began to gather her belongings. As he headed down the hall, she called, "Why don't you come to the faculty party this year?"

CB&O

Kieran dug the steel blades on the toes of his boots deep into the damp earth, lifting the twenty-two-pound hammer to his shoulder. He swung his arms around and around and let fly the stone with its wood handle. It whooshed through the early morning air.

Birds called in the thick woods surrounding the meadow. He peered through the mist, hearing the hammer land with a thud in the damp grass. He checked the distance against the markers set up in his practice area—118 feet. He picked up another hammer from the pile. Six more today and then he needed to check on the South pastures.

Bronwyn's voice echoed in his memory. Her encouraging cheers had urged him to the all-around championship at both Cowal and Braemar, the two most prestigious of the Highland Games. When he cut back to only two events, she had cheered as loudly as ever. "126 feet, Kieran, love. Give it your best, now."

The image of Bonny entered his mind as he dug in again. He swung the hammer around with determination and let it fly—125. Better. He sent another soaring through the air, then another, and so on until he exhausted the pile and himself.

His morning ritual complete, he recorded his throws in a notebook as he piled the hammers and stones into a wagon he kept in the barn. Ten throws of the light and heavy hammer, followed by ten more for each of the stones. The Ballater Games were one week away. Janet had attended his competitions since Bronwyn's death. She had cheered him on, providing the moral support of someone special in the sea of faces. Maybe she would bring Bonny along. *Now that was a random thought.*

He replayed the conversation in Janet's office as he stretched to cool down. Deciding who was right for him was none of her concern. He didn't even know if he wanted a woman in his life. An isolated sheep farmer in Scotland had little to interest an American only in the country on a temporary basis.

He stretched with care. The shoulder injury from three years ago at the Lochaber Games still flared up on occasion. He felt guilty contemplating showing off his strength for a woman other than Bronwyn, but …

Dragging the wagon behind him across the uneven ground, Kieran wondered if Bonny would come. The games were ancient, and Janet was a thorough tour guide.

Taking the back stairs two at a time, he sought refuge in his room before Eleanor's sharp eyes could detect the frustration he never managed to hide. He flexed the muscles in his arms as he washed the sweat of the workout from his upper body. Then, he shrugged into a thick, brown sweater. Yes, a Highlander in his kilt impressed women, Americans in particular. She appeared somewhat younger, but he wasn't in such bad shape for forty.

He pulled on tan riding breeches and rubber Wellies for his rounds of the sheep pastures. Perhaps he should rub lanolin into his hands. Hard and calloused from farm labor, they felt as rough and scratchy as heather in winter. They were not the hands to impress a woman.

By the time he reached the pasture, he'd made up his mind. He would consider attending the party.

CRBO

A driving rain pelted the windshield, the wipers swishing back and forth in a brisk rhythm as Janet drove along the winding, two-lane road. "It's a dreich day. We'll be *drookit* by the end of it."

Bonny laughed. "I keep hearing those terms. Definitions, please?"

"Dreich is damp and rainy. Drookit is soaking wet. No self-respecting Scot lets rain stand in her way. You'll enjoy Ballater, a lovely village in Aberdeenshire, about a half-day's drive from Fort William. The area is known as Royal Deeside, near Balmoral, Queen Victoria's favorite vacation place. Sorry, we'll have to tour it another time. The royal family spends the month of August there."

Dressed in warm clothing, with her rain suit ready, Bonny marveled at the serene beauty. This was their first weekend excursion, and Janet had promised plenty more. Green hillsides, curtained in mist and sprinkled here and there with a farmhouse or castle ruin, held her rapt attention. "Thanks for your willingness to show me around. The pastures look like a painting with the white sheep on the green grass and all the dry-stone.

Janet agreed, never taking her eyes off the road. "Aye, it's lovely, but it's also harsh and unforgiving. Not long ago, surviving in the Highlands required tremendous strength of constitution and character. It's still tough for those who work the land. As for showing you around, I'm glad for a travel companion. I enjoy weekend outings."

Constitution and character—the words created a definite contrast between Kieran and Adam. She had no delusions as to the type of character the latter possessed. *Why did he hold my attraction for so long?*

The big Scot had such masculine appeal. He had filled her thoughts since she first saw him in the faculty meeting. She was eager to watch him demonstrate the skill Janet talked about. It was too soon for another relationship, but it gave her a warm feeling to discover he had qualities beyond the good looks which had first attracted her attention. Paying too much attention to appearance had been part of her problem where Adam was concerned.

Even before they reached Ballater, Bonny was captivated by the thick forests and heathered hills surrounding the quaint town. The forest floor was grassy and free of debris. Large groves of ferns flourished under the majestic trees, their towering trunks bright green with moss.

The crowded, curving streets created the sensation of stepping back in time. The old-fashioned granite block buildings captivated her, as did the wood-sided train station, painted pale yellow and trimmed in red.

They found a parking place on a side street, and loaded up with umbrellas and backpacks. Janet's quick pace hurried Bonny along the uneven sidewalks. She stopped to stare into the window of a sporting goods shop displaying curling stones and a butcher shop exhibiting stacks of canned haggis. The little, unexpected cultural differences provided the kind of refreshing change that distracted her from the reasons for her uprooted life. She pictured Kari's fiancé, Dan MacDowell, laughing if she sent him a can of haggis in honor of his own Scottish roots. Maybe she should. A Marine serving in Afghanistan needed a little humor to brighten his day.

"We'll look around tomorrow." Janet pulled her along. "In the train station there's a lovely display of Queen Victoria's last visit. You can see her private suite and the dogcart her family used to travel from here to Balmoral. Right now, we need to hurry over to Monaltrie Park. We don't want to miss anything."

"I didn't expect such a beehive of activity." Bonny surveyed the variety of activities as they paid their fee and entered the park. "It's similar to a county fair back home."

Delightful aromas from the food booths filled the moisture-laden air, making her mouth water. Vendors displayed their produce, fresh meat, crafts, and clothing. The light, misty rain, which Janet referred to as *mizzle*, didn't seem to affect the crowd.

Janet directed her attention to a track with a grassy field in the center, surrounded by benches with people standing three and four deep behind them. A covered grandstand stood at one end. "Dignitaries and officials sit in the grandstand. The chief of Clan Farquharson and his wife will attend. There's a MacIntosh in his ancestry, making him a distant relation of mine. You'll see the Highland dancing contest under the tent and bagpipe competitions over there. Track events for various ages alternate with pipe bands marching around the field. There's something different everywhere you turn."

Bonny heard Janet's obvious pride in one of the grand traditions of her homeland. Then she pointed out a strapping Highlander. "There's Kieran, changing his shirt. I try to attend his competitions since his wife died. He needs a friend."

Bonny sucked in a deep breath at the sight of his rippling muscles as he pulled on a faded blue T-shirt sporting a red lion, and reading "Scotland— The Tartan Army." His blue and green kilt came almost to his knees, his legs showing sturdy and strong below it.

"They compete in kilts?"

"Tradition."

"What does the slogan mean?"

"Our national football team. You call it soccer."

Bonny couldn't take her eyes off the series of events Janet called "the heavies," which required both strength and skill. But when Kieran took the field, she found herself ignoring the others. When he wasn't competing, her eyes searched for his glowing red-blond hair in the area where the contestants stretched out on the wet grass, warming themselves with sweats and blankets while waiting on other events. She hadn't felt this way since high school when she had a serious crush on the quarterback of the football team.

Janet provided a helpful commentary. "Watch his intense concentration. Kieran's one of the older athletes, competing only three or four times a year now. He's had his turns at Braemar, though. He was national champion more than once."

Remembering an article she'd read on the Internet, Bonny asked, "Isn't Braemar the final competition to determine the overall winners?"

Janet raised her brows, with a nod of approval. "Aye, but the older you get, the more difficult it becomes to compete. He's cut back his events to throwing the hammer and putting the stone. The light hammer and stone weigh sixteen pounds, and the heavy weighs twenty-two. He loves it too much to quit. He tossed the caber better than anyone."

"How much does it weigh?" Bonny kept her eyes on a young giant, grunting with effort as he hefted the massive pole.

"It's nineteen and a half feet tall and weighs around 175 pounds. That's Brennan Grant, one of our local athletes."

Bonny turned back to the field, where the young man failed to tumble the enormous caber end over end. She glanced at the math professor again.

Fascination didn't come close to describing her feelings. It didn't hurt to know he was also kind and understood what it was to lose the most important people in your life. How ridiculous to spend so much time thinking of someone she knew so little about.

The weather felt like autumn, but the hearty Scots appeared to be enjoying their summer weather, ignoring the constant drizzle punctuated by periods of pelting rain.

"Thanks for suggesting the rain suit. I'm not used to this." She smiled at the sight of children in sleeveless shirts and shorts, and a dapper-looking older couple strolling along in their tartans, licking ice cream cones and declaring it "a lovely day."

Bonny regarded the varied group of contestants gathering on the track, already dripping wet. The rain was coming down in buckets. "They're going to run up that mountain in this?"

"Aye, it's tradition. They go around the track, down Bridge Street, across the River Dee, up the trail visible through the trees to the top of the mountain, then back. They'll have a muddy mess today."

The crowd cheered with enthusiasm for their favorites while teams from towns, fire departments, and clubs competed, sliding in the mud, pulling and straining.

Bonny laughed as a tug o' war team lost its battle, sliding into the mud. She raised her voice over the cheering crowd and boisterous yells of the participants. "Tug o' war must be a big thing here. At home you only see it at picnics and kids' birthday parties. The grunts and groans make it sound serious."

Janet pointed to a group finishing their round, calling back and forth with threats of a sound thrashing in the next round, though the smiles and good-natured handshakes belied anything serious. "Everyone enjoys it."

Hungry and cold at the end of the day, they stopped for an early dinner at The Rowan Tree, a small restaurant on Bridge Street. Scottish folk tunes played in the background as they ate steaming bowls of hot cream of mushroom soup, thick and full of chunky, delicious mushrooms. They followed it with haggis, a traditional Scottish pudding. Bonny found the mixture of sheep's pluck—the heart, liver, and lungs, minced and mixed with oatmeal and various spices—to be palatable. Instead of the traditional sheep's stomach, it came in a plastic baking bag with large, metal staples at the ends. A tiny china thimble of Drambuie, a potent 160-proof Scotch whisky, sat on top.

With a grimace, she downed the potent liquor. "To new friendships."

⌘

Driving toward their hotel, they saw Kieran ambling down the street, carrying a duffle bag and bundled in sweats. Janet pulled over. "*Co-ghàirdeachas*, old friend. You outdid your young competitors again."

"Aye, it's more difficult every year, though." The hair curling in damp ringlets around his face fit better with the tender side Janet portrayed in telling about his wife and infant son than with the brute strength he exhibited in competition. Bonny wondered how it would feel to run her fingers through those curls. *Get ahold of yourself, girl. You don't even know the man.*

"Do you want a ride to your car?" Janet asked.

"Thanks, but I'm parked 'round the corner." He pointed a short distance ahead. "I'm driving to Beauly to visit my parents."

Janet grasped the hand he held out. "Tell them hello. I thought Brennan Grant looked like he might carry on the grand tradition of champions from Fort William. He's a tough competitor."

Kieran shook his head. "Brennan's a nice lad, but he'll never replace me as the greatest champion ever to come out of Lochaber."

"That seems a bit presumptuous. Janet said it's only his first year in competition." Bonny hadn't intended to say it out loud. His high opinion of himself sounded just like Adam. Did a big ego always have to accompany the good looks and athleticism she found attractive?

Janet turned and glared at her with narrowed eyes. "I've been explaining the games to Bonny all day."

"Dr. Bryant." He bent to peer farther into the car. "I wasn't aware you were an expert on our Highland Games."

"I'm not, but it seems you would be glad to see a young competitor from your part of the country following in your footsteps." Bonny felt the heat rising to her cheeks.

"Just because he'll never best me doesn't mean I don't think he's a decent competitor. I just don't see the same fire in his belly I had at his age."

"You have to admit he did himself proud with the caber today." Janet spoke up to Bonny's relief.

"Aye, he's passable. He doesn't have the stomach for hard work, though. He's been working on the farm part-time. I should know." Looking right at Bonny, Kieran grinned, apparently enjoying their little *tete-à-tete*.

"You seem to have a very high opinion of your own accomplishments, Dr. MacDonell." Just like Adam. Well, she needn't waste any more time dwelling on him, no matter how much she was attracted by his physical attributes. Never again would she allow what met the eyes to blind her to the man inside.

With a loud boom of thunder, the sky opened up again. Kieran smiled, his gaze meeting Bonny's. "It was nice talking with you, Dr. Bryant, Janet." He paused, nodding at each one as he spoke. "I'd better head to the car before I'm drookit. *Guid eenin.*"

Janet rolled up the window and turned to Bonny before she headed up the street. "What was that about?"

Bonny shook her head. "He may be your friend and a great competitor, but I prefer a man with a less-exalted opinion of his abilities."

"He's not like that at all, Bonny. He's sweet and humble, and he's right." Janet steered through the crowded street in the direction of their hotel. "Brennan isn't the competitor Kieran was, but he's the best Fort William has at the moment."

"Have you known Kieran long? You two talk as if you were good friends."

"Oh, aye, since we were children. He's a dear friend. I sometimes think he'll spend the rest of his life alone. He still grieves and only someone special will succeed in breaching the fortress he's built. All the women envied what he and Bronwyn had. A love like that is worth waiting for."

"I envy people who find their soul mates, as if they're two halves of the same person. I don't believe a love like that is out there for me." Bonny turned her face to the window, trying to control the emotions warring in her mind. Kieran was an attractive man, but she would just as soon not spend time around him after what she just heard.

"You came down kind of hard on him. I think you two would discover a lot in common if you ever got to know each other."

"He reminds me of someone I prefer not to think about anymore. That's all."

Turning into the car park at the Deeside Hotel, Janet said, "I hope you don't mind sharing a room. There aren't a lot of hotels in these small towns."

"Oh, no problem." *As long as I don't have to listen to her talk about Kieran all evening. I got that out of my system.*

Janet set her suitcase under the window, turned down the spread, and curled up on the pillows at the head of her bed. She crossed her arms and cocked her head to one side. "You mentioned there had been someone special once. Would I be prying if I asked what happened?"

Bonny busied herself straightening her suitcase. "In one year, my life changed much more than it did when I moved to Scotland. I can heal and grow stronger here, away from the reminders. Right now, I need some sleep." She pulled her nightgown over her head. "I'll tell you about it another time."

Climbing into bed, she pulled up the blankets, feigning sleep. Images of the handsome Highlander kept playing in her mind. Until today, she had pictured him as a gentle giant of strong character and commitment, able to love someone other than himself, a man worthy of her respect. It was disappointing to discover he was no different than Adam.

The next morning, Bonny discovered a missed call on her phone. A cold lump settled in her stomach when she recognized Adam's number. She deleted the voicemail without listening. He had shown no qualms about destroying her world. It was over.

CS&O

The sight of the new American professor seated next to Janet emblazoned itself in Kieran's mind. He had not experienced such an intense desire to show off his skill and strength to a woman in many years. He wished he could still toss the caber, but at least he'd triumphed in both of his competitions.

The notion of Bonny watching threatened to make him lose his concentration altogether. Long-forgotten emotions roiled deep inside, his mind filled with her shining russet curls and large emerald eyes as he drove to Beauly. Their brief conversation showed her to be a woman with spirit and fire. He liked that.

Once at his parents', he went straight to bed, conjuring up the memory of her smile. For the first time in two years, thoughts of a woman penetrated his long-fettered heart, making his loneliness a prison. She had challenged him, but looking back, he had sounded egotistical. *What a fool.*

The next morning, he awakened sore from the competition and tired from a restless night. In his dreams Bonny beckoned him, but in the background, Bronwyn held their son, pleading for his help.

"Kieran, whatever is the matter?" When he lumbered downstairs, half-asleep, and seated himself at the table for breakfast, Maggie MacDonell laid the back of her hand against his forehead. "You're all *peely-wally*. Perhaps it's time to retire from the games."

"Mother, it's normal to feel *wabbit* the day after a competition. I had trouble falling back to sleep, and then dreamed of Bronwyn and the baby." He shrugged, avoiding her eyes by staring at the plate she placed in front of him.

"It's been two years, *mo mhac*." The worry in his mother's voice was obvious as she laid her hand on his shoulder.

"It's just a dream, Mother. They're not unusual." He shoveled a spoonful of haggis into his mouth and picked up the morning paper, ending the conversation. He understood her concern. He still feared the debilitating depression he had suffered off and on since Bronwyn's death. It reared its ugly head now and then, threatening to deprive him of a productive life, even steal it from him altogether. He had never given serious consideration to falling in love again, but that was before he met Bonny Bryant with her feisty attitude and eyes the color of a pasture in springtime.

CHAPTER FOUR

CHANGES

In Scotland, a sunny day with a hint of mist in the air was too good to waste. Pulling on her sweats and running shoes, Bonny set off at a brisk pace. She breathed in, savoring the damp morning air on her desert-acclimated skin. She slowed her pace on top of a tree-covered hill with a view of the town below.

The fluffy white blanket of low clouds over Loch Linnhe slowly dissipated while the blue sky shone bright above it. Toward the southeast stood Ben Nevis, over forty-four hundred feet tall and half-covered in clouds—beautiful Ben Nevis, the Mountain of Heaven. The sight must have overwhelmed the ancient Gael who named it. She needed a friend to explore its slopes with. What fun she, Kari, Dan, and Adam had on all those hikes up the La Luz Trail at home. Sandia Peak might be taller, but "The Ben" looked quite challenging.

Returning home, she showered and dressed for lunch and shopping with Janet. Her new friend had proved invaluable when it came to teaching her how to do things the Scottish way. Driving on the wrong side of the road wasn't the sole difference. The currency, and even grocery shopping, referred to as going "*awa' fir the messages*," were all confusing in their own way.

"Do Fort William and the college meet your expectations so far?" Janet headed toward the center of town.

"I love it. Compared to the five hundred thousand people in Albuquerque, less than eleven thousand is small. I live in the mountains, near small towns, but drive into the city to teach. When I first saw Ben Nevis towering over Fort William, it reminded me of home. I enjoy the outdoors. I'm going to love a country where walking is a national pastime. Coming early to get used to things before school began was a wise choice. Two more weeks of play and then down to work."

The town did feel home-like. Fort William sat on the shores of Loch Eil and Loch Linnhe, the longest loch in Scotland, connected to the sea by the Firth of Lorne. She was excited to discover some of the last undeveloped beauty in Europe right outside her back door.

The patio of the Georgian-style No4 Restaurant, in the center of town, was surrounded by a charming garden. It felt old and very European, almost as if she had gone back in time.

"I told you, I began my career at the University of Edinburgh. When they opened an evangelical Christian college in Fort William, I knew God wanted me here, so I moved home." Janet's placid blue eyes conveyed feelings quite the opposite of the dread arising in Bonny's heart. This wasn't a topic she wanted to discuss.

The meat pie filled with chicken and mushrooms didn't seem as appealing anymore. She steeled herself, searching for the words to make Janet understand. "I've struggled with my faith since my parents died. I believe in God and Jesus Christ. I believe He created the world and died for my sins, but I doubt His involvement in my daily life. I won't tell the students how I struggle. I will be able to teach a biblical worldview because it makes more sense than anything else." She had to go to church, since it was required of the faculty, but she couldn't believe as she once had.

She could sense Janet hesitating. "I can see your hurt runs deep. I've experienced loss and betrayal too. When I was sixteen, I came home from school to discover my dad had died from a heart attack at work. I married a captain in the Army when I lived in Edinburgh. Five years later, he had an affair while stationed in Sri Lanka, and we divorced. He married her and still lives there."

"I had no idea. Sometimes I forget I'm not the only one." Bonny reached across the table and laid her hand on Janet's arm. She had the perfect opportunity to open up about Adam, but the words wouldn't come.

Janet continued in a soft and steady tone. "The hurt of betrayal consumed me until I learned to seek my comfort and refuge in God. When you discover there's no peace without Him, you'll find God there waiting for you."

Bonny remained silent, and Janet continued, "Enough. We're supposed to be enjoying ourselves. Let's have some fun."

Bonny had a gnawing hunger to put the anger and pain behind her and move on. Someday she would question Janet, but not yet.

Janet shielded her eyes from the sun when they stepped out of the restaurant after lunch. "It's too lovely a day to waste feeling down. We need a change of mood. Let's do some shopping."

A backseat full of packages later, they headed home. As Bonny stepped out of the car, Janet said, "Why don't you come to church with Mum and me on Sunday? It's small, so it's easy to meet people."

"I'll think about it."

"Guid, I'll see you in the morning." Janet waved as she drove off.

Bonny stood amidst the flower beds, staring after her. *Oh, Adam, even 4600 miles isn't enough to escape you. I might have an easier time forgiving God for my parents if I still had you.*

⚜

When Kieran left his office, he saw Bonny standing behind her car, her foot tapping and shoulders sagging. "Can I help you, Dr. Bryant?"

She startled, and he realized he had been so intent on watching her that he had failed to give warning of his approach. The eyes that met his sparkled, their brilliance drawing him like a treasure hunter to a prize emerald. She was a lovely woman.

"Dr. MacDonell, hello. I've changed flat tires before, but these lug nuts won't budge."

He checked the urge to brush a smudge of dirt from her cheek. "It's Kieran, and I'm glad to be of help." He forced himself to ignore the nervous pounding in his chest and the urge to run. He was alone with the woman who had filled his mind day and night from the moment she had walked into the room.

"I'm Bonny, and thanks."

"I'll take that spanner off your hands."

"Spanner? Oh, you mean the lug wrench, of course." She held it out to him and smiled.

He took a deep breath. Her smile reminded him of sun breaking through a Scottish mist. His fingers brushed hers as he took the large spanner, and he realized how small her hands were, like his mother's finest china. Dainty and delicate.

Something about the patient way she watched caused his uncertainty to subside. Rescuing a damsel in distress wasn't a bad way to meet. Tossing the caber was no longer possible, but he knew how to change a tire. She stood near enough for him to smell her perfume—feminine, like a rose garden.

When he stood up from putting on the spare, he realized how he towered over her. Her head didn't even reach his shoulder. She seemed, not fragile, but vulnerable. He couldn't leave her with a flat tire. "Why don't you follow me to my mechanic? He'll fix your tire in no time."

She reached into a duffle bag in the back of the car and offered him a towel. "Here, for your hands. I've missed my hike, but I'd like to thank you with dinner." When he gave the towel back, she offered her hand in thanks.

He was surprised at the warm feeling her touch evoked. "You don't need to repay me. But it will still be light for hours this time of year, and there's nothing more lovely than roamin' in the gloamin'. If you want, I can show you a path near your house."

He felt like a teenager on his first date, shy and uncertain, but he longed to bring pleasure to those tantalizing green eyes. This was new territory. Eleanor, Janet, and the students he tutored were the only women he'd been alone with in two years.

"Thank you. I—I put stew in my slow-cooker this morning. It's nothing fancy, but I guarantee it's good." A blush tinged her cheeks an even brighter shade as she continued. "I hope you don't mind the green chile. I needed a taste of home."

"I've never eaten green chile. How spicy is it?" One glimpse of her smile, and the quivery feeling in his stomach returned. He was as unsure of himself as the first time he asked Bronwyn out. Then, he had known life would never be the same. Was that the case now?

"You'll notice the bite, but I make it even hotter at home." Her grin was mischievous.

He discovered he was eager to spend time getting to know her. "I would enjoy trying it. Follow me." He held her car door as she got in.

After dealing with the tire, they parked the cars at her house. Bonny said, "My hiking boots are just inside the door. Can you walk in those?"

He looked down at his brown leather riding boots. "I have hiking boots in the back of the Land Rover. Do you need to change?"

"These jeans are fine, but I'll grab a sweater. It's a lot cooler here than at home."

When she reappeared, he pointed down the street to where a trail began in a grassy field, and she fell into step beside him. It led down to the shore of Loch Linnhe—easy, winding, and with plenty of room for two.

An uncertain silence hung between them as they stopped on the shore of the loch, where they stood watching the waves lapping at the sand. The clouds on the horizon turned to brilliant shades of pink and orange under the rays of the sinking sun. The water became a shimmering lake of multicolored jewels.

"How long have you been teaching?" She startled him by breaking the silence.

He kept his focus far across the water. It would be easier to speak of Bronwyn if he wasn't looking at Bonny. "I taught twelve years at the University of Glasgow, then I returned to my family's sheep farm to help my parents. A few years ago they moved to Beauly. Then my wife died two years ago. I started teaching at FWCC last year to get out and around people a little more." His voice caught in spite of his attempt to keep it steady.

"I'm sorry. I didn't mean to bring up something upsetting."

"I can't put it behind me." He looked down at her, hoping to gauge her reaction.

"I understand." She glanced up before turning her eyes on the horizon and hugging her arms to her chest. "I'm an only child. My mom fought a brain tumor for two years. She died last year. Six months later, I lost my dad." In a whisper, she added, "My fiancé broke our engagement the day after my father's funeral." She turned red, looking out at the water with a frown. Watching her reaction, it was obvious she had not meant to say so much, and he looked away also, offering her the opportunity to regain her composure. When he looked at her again, the sun caught a shining drop on her cheek, and he reached for his handkerchief, which she accepted with a tremulous smile. The brief touch of her fingers sent a tingle up his arm. He felt the heat of anger rising in his face at the idea of someone treating her with such cruelty. Her shoulders seemed too slight to bear such a load.

She sniffled and continued. "Dr. Cameron and my dad did their graduate work in history together at the University of Edinburgh. They stayed close through the years. When my dad told him we had written an American History and Literature curriculum together, he invited Dad to teach it here, with me as guest lecturer on the Civil War. When Uncle Dùghlas—Dr. Cameron— called with condolences, he offered me the opportunity to teach in Dad's place. I'm better here, but there's still an empty house waiting back home."

Kieran's heart lurched at the idea of her struggling with such loss. "I'm sorry. You have no other family?"

"No, my friends are my family now."

"It takes a lot of courage to leave everything behind. I've lost count of the times I wanted to escape. My wife was pregnant when she died. I've had a difficult time going on alone, but the sheep need tending, so I live with the memories." He felt a choking sensation in his throat and paused to gain control. "We should head back." He motioned for her to precede him. "There's a culinary adventure waiting for me."

She turned back the way they came, and Kieran followed, feeling the warm glow of something shared. *The lass is more alone than I am. At least I have my parents.*

When they reached her house, he set the table while she dished up bowls of rich, steaming broth with chunks of beef, carrots, potatoes, and little bits of an unfamiliar green, which he guessed was the chili. He took a small amount on his spoon, blowing to cool it off, and tasted. "Mmm, it's good. I thought it would be hotter."

Bonny's melodious laughter was contagious. "It gets hot enough to make your eyes water and can leave your lips and tongue burning. Not much will quench its fire, though in New Mexico we usually follow it with a deep-fried, bread-like delicacy known as sopapillas. You bite off the end and fill the middle with honey. Mmm ..." She shut her eyes and smiled. "I've never tried them at a lower altitude."

"From the look on your face, it must compare to ambrosia." He couldn't help smiling and realized he no longer felt tense.

"An excellent description." Her eyes glowed incandescent. "Albuquerque is a mile high, so if they puff up there, they should turn out fine here, though they'll cook faster. I live in the mountains outside of town, at about seventy-four hundred feet."

"You live three thousand feet higher than Ben Nevis, but it's desert?"

As their conversation continued, he was surprised at how much they shared in common, despite the differences in background. Both grew up as only children, living in the mountains with doting parents and a deep commitment to God.

"You have horses?" The question popped out so fast it surprised him.

"Three."

"I have four. I enjoy riding when I make rounds of the flocks. Where are your horses while you're here?" The more he found out, the more intrigued he became.

"My neighbors agreed to keep an eye on everything. Their teenage son loves horses." She paused. "I miss them already."

"Perhaps you'd enjoy coming out to ride with me sometime." His heart continued its rapid palpitations. "My farm is only an hour and a half north of here."

"I'd love to. That's quite a commute. How do you teach and manage your farm too?"

"My farm manager has been there since before I was born, and I teach only three days a week. I have good people I can trust. After Bronwyn's death, I discovered I needed to get away sometimes. It's lonely. I enjoy teaching, but tutoring struggling students is what I love. The drive isn't so bad once you're used to it. I'm an early riser."

She nodded in understanding. "I hated being in a big house alone all the time. I find I don't sleep as well as I used to. You really like tutoring?"

"I do. Math is such an important skill. It does something to people's self-esteem when they struggle with it. I teach trig, but I tutor anyone who needs it. There's nothing like seeing the light come on when they finally get it." He paused when she smiled and shook her head as if in surprise. He had to ask. "What are you smiling about?"

She had leaned back in her chair with her arms crossed. Even the slight smile playing over her lips was dazzling. "When Janet and I talked to you in Ballater, you sounded pretty egotistical. I'm seeing a different side of you. Everything you've done today has been compassionate and kind. You went out of your way to help me. When you opened up about your wife and son, I realized you're not like I thought at all."

He felt as if sunshine had come out of the clouds. "That day in Ballater, you were talking to an athlete pumped up on the adrenaline of competition. You're right. I realized later that my ego had taken the upper hand. I wasn't very generous toward Brennan. He's a good lad who works for me part-time on the farm. What else can I tell you to dispel the notion that I'm egotistical and self-centered?"

"I shouldn't have judged. Janet told me I was wrong. She also said you play the bagpipes."

"Oh, aye." He was grateful for her abrupt change of subject. Things were getting too personal too fast. The heat began rising again at the thought of her and Janet discussing him. "I play in the evenings to relax and belong to the local pipe band. They played in Ballater, but I was occupied with the competition. Did you enjoy the games?"

A glow lit her alluring green eyes. "Very much. I enjoyed watching you. It must require incredible strength and constant training."

His already-warm face grew warmer. "I enjoy it. Working on the farm helps me keep in shape."

"I was impressed. Janet isn't exactly an unbiased fan, you know."

When she smiled again, he felt like he'd tossed the caber for a perfect score. "She's as loyal as my mother. It's encouraging to see a friendly face in a field full of strangers."

While they cleared the table, Bonny shared her difficulties learning to drive on the left side of the road. "When I arrived, I drove around and around the parking lot—car park, trying to gather up enough courage to brave the traffic. My dad always said to look right and turn left. I repeat it over and over to myself at corners and roundabouts."

"Aside from the driving, what do you think of our wee bit o' land so far?" He exaggerated his brogue and wasn't disappointed when she laughed. *She's lovely. If only dinner had lasted longer.*

"It sounds ridiculous, but I feel I belong, even after such a short time. My grandmother came from Aberdeen—a Fraser—and my father used to tell me her stories. She met my grandfather near the end of World War II when he was there in the Army. She was eighteen when they married and moved to America. Dad enjoyed mimicking her accent. My name was his idea."

"A perfect choice." He rubbed his forehead, embarrassed at the unintended voicing of his thoughts. "I—I mean it suits you."

"Thank you. There's an apple pie for dessert."

"That sounds lovely." He wandered into the small dining room while she cut the pie and prepared the tea. His eyes were drawn to the bookshelves on either side of the fireplace. A brief glance revealed classic favorites. Walking back into the kitchen, he asked, "Are those all your books?"

She set the pie and tea on a tray with sugar, cream, and fresh lemon. "The ones on the right are. The others were already here."

He drew close to her side at the kitchen counter. "I enjoy Mark Twain, James Fenimore Cooper—my mother raised me on Dickens." Something else they had in common. He realized the unfamiliar eagerness to share things about himself came from wanting to dispel any more false ideas she held onto from their conversation in Ballater.

"Dickens is my favorite. You're familiar with the American authors too?"

"We receive a good education over here." He picked up the tea tray and headed toward the living room. "Our tastes are remarkably similar. Maybe we can share books."

"I'd like that." She motioned him to set the tray on the coffee table and took a seat on the couch. "Is your sheep farm large?"

He chose a chair across from her, and his heart started pounding again. To describe the farm, he had to mention Bronwyn. "It's a moderate-sized farm, compared to some farther north. Stonehaven Farm sits on the shores of Loch Garry, on traditional lands of the MacDonells of Glengarry. My second great-grandfather on my father's side bought some of the traditional clan lands, reclaiming a wee bit of the family heritage. The house and main barn are over two hundred years old, new by European standards."

She didn't need a history lesson on the MacDonells, so he moved on. "My parents didn't want to force me into farming, so I went to the University of Glasgow and majored in math. I chose to go straight into grad school and then studied for my doctorate while teaching." He found it easier to continue when he remembered her losses. "I met and married Bronwyn. When she decided to teach also, we stayed in Glasgow. Starting a family proved difficult. When she finally became pregnant after fifteen years of marriage, we wanted to raise our child in the fresh air and slower pace of the Highlands.

"I enjoy teaching, but my heart leans toward the farming. We raise fine Scottish Blackface sheep and Cheviots. Last year, I added five hundred Kyloe, the hairy Highland cattle. I plan to add more." He paused, surprised at how easy she was to talk to. "Tell me something about New Mexico."

When she laughed, her eyes lit up the room. "Scotland and New Mexico are as different as water and dust. The sun shines about 278 days out of the year. When it rains, the sun comes out as soon as it finishes. It's rarely over one hundred degrees in the summer, and it doesn't stay below freezing for long, yet we have four definite seasons. The altitude is high, the air clean, and you can see forever, from desert to high mountains. One reason I find Scotland captivating is the mountains."

Mountains—something else in common. "It's obvious you love it there."

"It's home, but I needed a change." Pain dulled the gleam in her eyes as she turned away, twisting a strand of hair between her fingers.

Her fiancé, of course. "A change, Bonny, or an escape?"

When her surprised eyes met his, the sadness shadowing her face indicated he'd hit a nerve. She cleared her throat. "More tea?"

He fixed his gaze on hers, holding out his cup. "I'm a good listener."

"I don't doubt it. Another time, though."

"It's hard to put the past behind and move on. No area of my life is untouched."

"I agree. People are uncomfortable with pain and loss. They'll do anything to avoid discussing it."

"That's the truth. Janet's a good listener. We just disagree about how to deal with things."

"Church?" Her tone was tentative.

"Yes." He had to be honest himself if he wanted to learn about her. The subject was not something he felt right about hiding, and since she brought it up … "Since Bronwyn's death, I attend church as little as possible. Dr. Cameron knows I struggle, but he doesn't realize I no longer accept a personal God. You can teach trig without bringing up matters of faith. I teach one class and tutor ten hours a week."

Bonny nodded. "I understand. I believe in God, but I haven't noticed any evidence of His personal interest. I considered just visiting different churches, but Janet insisted I attend with her. I've run out of excuses for not going."

He found himself leaning forward, elbows on his knees. Did he dare? "I won't worship a God who allowed an innocent baby to die while my wife bled to death, without help."

"How terrible." There was a noticeable tremor in her voice, and she dabbed at her eyes with the napkin from her lap. *Were her tears for his loss?*

The electricity flowing between them sparked conversation on a level he had longed for. Someone understood at last. "It's haunted me day and night for two years." *She's easy to talk to, as if we've been friends for years.*

Bonny set her teacup on the tray and settled back on the couch. "Tell me about her."

He struggled to slow his breathing and calm his palpitating heart. "Charming, talented, intelligent, and poised. Her hair was a similar color to yours, but without the curls. She was tall, with eyes the color of sapphires. We met during my time as a graduate assistant, when she was an undergrad. What a superb mathematician, a terrific teacher, a gifted artist, and a talented decorator. She planted beautiful gardens around the farmhouse." He sighed, staring down at his hand where the gold band still bound him to her. "I lost my best friend."

"You loved her very much. I see it in your eyes. I think I would have described Adam's eyes as possessive rather than loving." Her cheeks colored at that, and her words cut to his heart in their honesty. It was easy to see how raw her emotions were. Her deep thoughts kept surfacing before she was ready. She was lonely too.

"Aye, we were soul mates." He paused before plunging into the story of the darkest moment of his life. "I had gone into town for supplies, and Eleanor, the housekeeper, was away from the house long enough to carry lunch out to the men in the lambing barn. Bronwyn was alone when her labor began very abruptly—two months early. My farm sits in an isolated spot with no close neighbors. It's subject to frequent power and telephone outages and the heaviest rain in the UK.

"We knew she had a problem, a partial placenta previa. The placenta covers the opening of the womb, creating a risk of early separation and hemorrhaging. I had seen it with sheep. I knew the dangers." He stopped, swallowing hard. "The doctor put her on bed rest early on. He meant to admit her to hospital the next day. Eleanor called for help, but a storm kept the emergency helicopter from flying. I arrived in time to deliver our son, Liam, but he was stillborn. She bled to death in my arms."

Bonny's cheeks were wet. Her brilliant green eyes never left his face as he continued. "I blamed myself for leaving her, and went into a deep depression. My parents stayed at the farm for months." He spoke no louder than a whisper, but her eyes held the understanding he longed for. "They were afraid I would kill myself—I planned to more than once."

At two o'clock in the morning, he left with a promise to ring Bonny up and invite her to dinner, and then he began his long, dark drive to the farm. The evening was more than worth it though. For two years, he had hungered for the understanding and companionship he felt after one evening with Bonny.

She had told him enough about Adam for him to see her pain. It was disturbing to hear her say she had never seen love in her fiancé's eyes. Bronwyn's love for him had glowed in her eyes as she breathed her last.

Once home, he alternated between tossing and turning in bed and pacing the floor. How lovely it would be to hold Bonny close, to feel her tender lips beneath his own.

CHAPTER FIVE

EDINBURGH

Edinburgh overflowed with excitement and people. Summertime, with the Edinburgh Festival and Military Tattoo, drew thousands. The crush filled the Royal Mile between the Castle at the top and Holyrood Palace at the bottom. People crowded the stands erected on the Parade Grounds of the Castle twice each evening to hear pipe bands from around the world.

"I got the tickets as soon as I found out when you were coming. Everyone should visit Edinburgh during the Tattoo. The sight of the lone piper on the parapets of the castle, near the end of the program, makes me cry."

"And tonight it's Kieran?"

"Aye." Janet opened her program to a list of performers and pointed to a pipe band whose name was a jumble of Gaelic letters Bonny could never hope to pronounce. "The Tattoo used to be exclusively for the military bands, but in the past couple of years they've begun inviting civilian bands. This band is one of the best in the world, and Kieran used to play with them when he lived in Glasgow. They've won the World Pipe Band Championship several times. So when they were invited to play this year, they asked Kieran to join them."

"It sounds exciting." Bonny's cheeks grew warm at the mention of Kieran. She had yet to tell Janet about their meeting, holding it as a cherished secret, too fragile to reveal.

"You'll love the bright-colored tartans, the skirl of bagpipes, and the rhythm of the drums as the bands perform intricate marching patterns." Janet's contagious enthusiasm became Bonny's own. Soon she was tapping her foot, her heart thrilling to each new tune and thrumming in excitement to the ones she recognized.

From their seats halfway up in the stands, she spotted Kieran on the field through her binoculars, standing tall and proud, her pulse quickening every time he was in the arena.

Near the end of the evening, the awe-inspiring melody of his pipes from the torch-lit parapets added to the interest—too soon to call it romance—taking root in her heart.

She believed he felt the same. How it would affect his opinion to know what Adam did? *Will he think something is wrong with me?*

At noon the following day, Janet had arranged to meet Kieran for lunch at the castle. "You two need to get acquainted. Stay here and visit while I get the sandwiches."

"You didn't tell her about the other night?" His eyes indicated surprise, but Bonny heard approval in his voice.

She glanced toward Janet, who was standing out of earshot. "I saw no reason to excite her. She believes we're kindred spirits. It was important to her for us to get acquainted." As she had noticed the other night, crinkly lines started at the corners of his eyes whenever he smiled.

"I agree." His tone was conspiratorial and his laugh contagious. "I enjoy making her happy, so we'll play along for her sake, aye?"

"You mean say nothing?" Bonny asked with a sudden, delicious sense of conspiracy.

His answering smile filled her with warmth, a mixed sense of attraction and being found attractive. "Let her enjoy it. Once I finish in Edinburgh, we'll go to dinner. In the meantime, we don't need rumors starting. It's a small town and an even smaller school."

Bonny nodded, stifling a giggle as Janet returned with their sandwiches. It was fun pretending to get acquainted. Kieran mentioned a couple of new details they hadn't discussed during their late-night conversation. She became more enthralled with everything he said. Her initial judgment had been so wrong. He was a man of strong character. When he excused himself for rehearsal, she found herself daydreaming about the plaintive beauty of his bagpipes, sounding from the torch-lit parapets. Tiny electric shocks twizzled up and down her spine; she hoped her expression didn't hint at her secret.

☙

The Royal Mile was teeming with tourists. Bonny and Janet almost needed to hold onto one another to keep from becoming separated. As they made their way between Edinburgh Castle and Holyrood Palace, Janet caught her breath and sidestepped into an open doorway, dragging Bonny with her.

Sensing her fear, Bonny moved in close behind her. "What's wrong?"

"The dark-haired man across the street—it's my ex-husband, Sean. Stay behind me." Janet's voice quivered.

"He's crossing the street toward us."

Her eyes grew wide with fear, and she clutched at Bonny's arm. "Don't leave us alone. Please."

He crossed the street, shouting a greeting. It wasn't difficult to imagine him sweeping a woman off her feet. His dark good looks were appealing, but Bonny knew from experience to look below the surface.

"*Awrite*, Janet, imagine seein' you back in your old territory. *Hou are ye?*" He laid his hand on her shoulder, and she shook it off, her face reddening with anger, her eyes flashing.

"I've told you to act as if you don't know me."

"Ach, Janet, I didn't plan it. Can't I ask how you're doin'? We were close once, aye?"

"Aye, close—you call marriage close?" Janet's blue eyes turned to steel, her voice harsh. "You have a strange way of showin' you care. If you ever see me, I'd appreciate you pretending we're strangers."

"Have it your own way." He shrugged and marched back across the street, shaking his head. Janet turned her back, biting her upper lip.

They returned to the hotel in silence, where Janet disappeared into the shower while Bonny pretended not to hear the sobs. She had her own dilemma, another voicemail from Adam. She took a deep breath and listened, then rubbed her throat, attempting to eliminate the tight feeling his voice evoked.

"Hi, Bon, I hoped you might answer. I don't have words to say how sorry I am for hurting you. Vanessa is out of my life. I still love you. What I did was selfish and I understand you not wanting to talk to me, but I want you back. Please call me?"

She deleted the voicemail, and then turned out the light, facing the wall, unable to hide her disquiet.

All night long, Bonny heard Janet tossing and turning. When she came out of the shower the next morning, Janet sat reading her Bible.

Janet had drawn closer to God in her sorrow and pain while she had turned her back on Him. Janet leaned on God—she had nothing.

CHAPTER SIX

KARI AND DAN

As much as she hated to admit it, Bonny was avoiding her best friend. She and Kari had been there for each other, in good times and bad, since they were fifteen, sharing everything from Kari's struggles to overcome years in foster care, to breakups with boyfriends. But, the miles between them made it easy to neglect problems Kari reminded her of.

Her delight in Kari marrying her lifelong friend Dan was still tinged with the grief of her own broken engagement. She was supposed to have married first. Watching her friends prepare for their wedding raised the specter of her own shattered dreams, both menacing and crippling.

Following the trip to Edinburgh, Bonny called home for only the second time since arriving in Scotland. "This is potentially the highlight of my teaching career, Kari. My classes are filling up. It's exciting."

"I'm glad you're doing alright," Kari said. "I'm so lonely with you and Dan both away. Since he's been in Afghanistan, it's easy to imagine the worst. I miss my fiancé and my best girlfriend."

"I'm sorry. You've been with me through so much."

Kari sighed. "I hope you find what you're searching for, Bonny."

"It's a challenge learning how they do things here, but Janet's showing me around. I take long walks in dozens of lovely places. I'm glad I came."

"Please, remember your way home."

The sound of Kari's loneliness tightened a cord around Bonny's heart. "I miss home, but for now, this is a good place for me. What do you hear from Dan?"

Kari hiccupped, a sure sign she was crying. "He's fine. He hates it there, but I keep him caught up on the wedding plans."

She heard the resignation in Kari's voice and realized her own selfish mindset was hurting her friend. "He'll be fine. Our Danny Boy will come home to his gorgeous fiancée, and we'll all be together again."

"You're right. Hey, I have another call. I don't want to miss him. Good-bye."

"I love you, dear friend. Bye, now." Bonny believed her choice to come to Scotland was a wise one, but she still felt a sense of guilt for leaving Kari to plan a wedding without her.

∞

Dan MacDermott reached into his bag and pulled out another soccer ball, patting the round-eyed little boy on the head as he handed it to him. Everything in Afghanistan was the same color—the color of the dirt that sifted through the fabric of the tents and coated his skin. If all the good he could do was to bring joy to a child, he had to be satisfied. Bigger accomplishments were up to God.

"Will you look at him?" Dan nudged his best friend, Major Jeff Phillips. "I'll remember his smile when I feel as if the fighting will last forever. Average people over here are faceless to the folks back home. The public doesn't see how we reach out to the locals. When a child approaches me without fear and runs away with a big grin, the whole world feels happier. I didn't know about this part when I signed up for the Marine Corps."

Jeff clapped him on the back. "One good day makes up for a lot of bad ones, right?"

"You bet."

They stood on a spot of flat ground just outside a village of clay huts. How did people manage to sustain themselves in a place like this? Glancing around, he didn't see any signs of industry or business, nothing except some parched-looking plants in what appeared to be a garden.

Jeff pointed to the happy kids surrounding a group of Marines. "Hey, let's join them."

Whoops and yells came from the sun-scorched field. A couple of the guys had started a soccer game—kids and Marines divided between the teams.

Laughing and howling, they kicked the ball and slid in the dirt, no one keeping score. For a while, everyone was happy.

After handing out candy and gum, along with fresh fruit and sandwiches, the Marines packed up to return to the base.

When Dan climbed back into their Humvee, he felt the happiest he had since he arrived in the war zone. "This makes the madness disappear, even if it's only one afternoon."

"Keep your goals small, buddy," Jeff answered. "If you want to see great things, you'll only be disappointed."

Arriving on the base meant back to business as usual, but the afternoon's interlude provided a needed break in the nightmare called Afghanistan. A letter from Kari waited on his bunk, and when he opened it, he found pictures of her and both of their mothers planning for the wedding. She hadn't e-mailed them, knowing he loved to carry pictures in his pockets. She included sample menus for the wedding reception and a picture of his sister in her bridesmaid's dress.

He pulled the phone card from the Blue Star Moms out of his pocket. This precious bit of free time was the perfect chance to phone her. "Hey, gorgeous, your letter and pictures came today. Thank you, and thanks for including my mom and sis in your planning. Wow, I miss you."

"It's good to hear your voice. I miss you too. I talked to Bonny right before you called."

There was a little quiver in her voice, and a muffled sound as if she was clearing her throat.

"How is our adventurer?" He laughed.

"Don't laugh, Dan. I hate to admit it, but I feel jealous when she describes the fun she's having with her new friend, Janet." She hiccuped the way she always did when she cried.

Dan sighed, drumming his fingers on the desk. Home was a long ways away, and it seemed twice as far when the love of his life was upset. It was frustrating to be one of the sources of her sadness. "We've discussed this, honey. Remember, she's running away from our wedding. It has nothing to do with you and everything to do with Adam."

"I'll try." She sniffled. "What's happening over there?"

"I wish every day was like this. We played soccer with the local kids and handed out candy, soccer balls, and dolls for the girls. Keep everyone sending stuff. I'll e-mail you the pictures."

"If I can pass around photos, it helps. My students love them. Have you read over the menus for the reception yet?" Her tone lightened up a little.

It was nice to have something good to tell her. "No, but Mom sent a package with jerky, underwear, red licorice, and dehydrated green-chili stew. It reminded me of the miles between us, and I wanted to hear your voice."

"Describe the kids for me."

He laughed at the afternoon's memory. He had made mental notes of the details that would make his middle-school-teacher fiancée smile. "This one little guy was really cute. He was smaller than the others but unafraid. When I handed him a soccer ball, he took off, happy and smiling. Kids are the same everywhere. It's a morale booster."

"I'm glad something fun happened for a change." Her voice broke, and he took a deep breath and cleared his throat, trying to control his own emotions.

"Yeah, we had a soccer game—kids and Marines together. We laughed and slid in the dirt. It felt super."

"You sound cheerful. I can't wait until you're home and we're together." Her voice was quiet and hollow-sounding, and the sound of her loneliness passed through him like a chill, in spite of the hundred-plus temperatures. It reminded him of basic training, when he was away from home the first time. He hated doing this to her. As soon as this tour was over, he would be out of the Marine Corps and home for good.

He motioned to the corporal, who approached him, holding out a note. "Hey, honey, I need to talk to the colonel."

Kari sighed. "Semper Fi, Marine. Duty calls. I love you."

He hated it when she cried, and wiped away a tear or two of his own. "I love you too. Don't worry, okay? I'll be home in six months."

He walked over to the command tent, thinking about the smiling kids. *If that's all I accomplish today, Lord, let it be enough.*

Half an hour later, Dan lounged on his bunk, remembering his conversation with Kari and thinking how blessed he was to be able to go home someday. The people who lived here had no way to escape. Praying for them and doing his job were the only things he could do.

"Hey, Mac," said a cheery voice behind him. "What's in the care package?"

"My favorite goodies." Dan looked up from the letter he was re-reading and tossed some jerky and licorice toward Jeff. "There's also dehydrated green-chili stew. I'll share if you behave yourself."

His Bible lay on the bunk, and Jeff picked it up. "You don't miss a day, do you?"

"I read from Proverbs every day. It helps me advise my men, changes my attitude, and helps me handle interactions with the locals. My words and reactions are more like Jesus."

"Maybe I should try it. What's the other book?" Jeff reached for a paperback lying next to the Bible.

"A Bible study Kari and I are doing on marriage. We do our lessons alone, then once a week we discuss our answers by phone or instant messaging." Dan handed Jeff the pictures Kari sent.

"Whoo, you're one lucky man, MacDermott. Didn't you finish your premarital counseling before you deployed?" He shuffled through the pictures and handed them back.

"We did." Putting down his pen, he turned toward Jeff. "This helps us stay in touch on a spiritual level. It's opened up opportunities for us to explore subjects we might ignore with me over here."

"I envy you, bud."

"A jewel like Kari is worth waiting for."

"Yeah, you're right. I wonder if something like that might have saved my marriage. She couldn't take it when I deployed to Iraq. Left me for a cop."

Dan sat up straight, giving Jeff his full attention. "You never told me what happened before. That's rough."

"Yeah, I went to church when I was little. My dad was a preacher's kid, but he left my mom for a woman in the choir. My mom had no use for church after that.

I went in the summer when I visited my grandmother, but that was all."

Dan made an effort to keep his voice calm. Perhaps this was the opportunity he'd been waiting for. "I learned about a relationship with Jesus at a Young Life meeting in high school. I was in Sunday school all the time, but hearing it from someone my own age made a big difference. Seeing the class bully change before my eyes made me want what he had."

Jeff reached over and snagged a piece of jerky. "If I was ever going to look into religion again, it would be because of you. You live your faith like no one I've ever seen before."

"I'd be happy to share my story with you." Dan shot up an arrow prayer that this might be the time.

"Maybe someday," Jeff reached for another stick of licorice, standing as he did. "I've got a report to write. See you later."

"Yeah, see you later."

Dan dropped to his knees beside his cot. Prayer helped him focus on God, rather than the unknowns of tomorrow. It had been a good day. He'd made a child smile and there was a possibility he would be able to talk to Jeff about the Lord sometime soon.

Chapter Seven

Views of Loch Linnhe

A thrill tingled its way up Bonny's spine as they entered the dining room at the Highland Hotel. Wide windows provided a stunning view of the sun setting in a blaze of color over Loch Linnhe, reminding her of the evening she and Kieran walked down to the shore together. He hadn't phoned like he said he would in Edinburgh, and she hoped to see him at the faculty party.

As Janet promised, the room was noisy and full of people. The women were radiant in evening gowns, sparkling with sequins and beads. The male professors in their kilts were as bright as peacocks showing off their plumage.

Round tables covered in snow-white linen were set with sparkling silver and crystal, complementing the luster of gold-rimmed china and bright blue napkins. Bonny followed Janet around, hoping to remember the names while keeping an eye out for the handsome Highlander.

"I arranged to be seated with you all evening, even though we'll change tables after every course," Janet said as they laid their purses and wraps at their first table and headed for the hors d'oeuvres. Even in August, the damp, cool Scottish evenings made a warm wrap necessary.

"I don't know how I would survive without you," Bonny said. "I'm glad Uncle Dùghlas asked you to help me acclimate."

As they approached the crowd of faculty members, Janet whispered, "Heads are turning. You're stunning."

Bonny laughed, her eyes still searching. "You're imagining it. They're curious about the American professor, nothing else."

"You're *aff yer heid*. It's a true Highland beauty you look in soft green with your red hair."

"Bonny," Dùghlas separated himself from a group of people, coming to kiss her on the cheek. "You're stunning."

"Thank you." She supposed the floor-length dress of shimmering satin did bring out the color of her eyes and the blush in her cheeks. Thanks to the efforts of Janet's mom, Agnes, her hair cascaded down her bare back in coppery ringlets.

"I haven't seen near as much of you as I would like. Are you acclimating?"

Bonny thought the bold red and green Cameron tartan kilt made him look shorter and stockier than usual. "I'm doing well, thanks to Janet. I love it here."

"Hello there, Bonny, Janet." Aunt Mairi stopped next to her husband. "Are you ready for classes to begin?"

"I can't wait." Bonny hugged her, then stood back and looked at her dress of Cameron tartan. "You look lovely, Aunt Mairi."

"Thank you. Dùghlas, the head waiter has a question for you." With a nod, they excused themselves and headed off to see to details.

Moving through the crowd toward their first table, Janet introduced her to everyone.

She kept searching for Kieran, sighing with pleasure when he entered right after they were seated at the second table. He flashed a smile and headed for his assigned place.

"The main course is the longest sitting of the evening," Janet said as she led Bonny toward their third table a little later.

"I'm already full. If I keep eating, my dress won't fit."

Janet eyed her, laying one hand on her shoulder. "As we say, *dinnae fash yerself*. Don't worry about it. What size are you anyway?"

"A four at home, whatever that equals here."

"Small enough not to worry about it." Janet shook her head in mock irritation. "The sight of fresh broiled salmon and thick Scottish Aberdeen-Angus steaks will change your mind." Waiters in tuxedos were carrying in trays laden with plates of two of Scotland's specialties.

"You're right, it looks delicious." Then she saw Kieran heading their way, a stunning sight in his kilt of bold bright blue and green. The warmth rose upward from her shoulders to her cheeks. She had found it impossible to think of him as egotistical since he had shared his deep concern for the students he tutored and the agony of his wife's death. He was worthy of more than mere physical attraction. To her dismay, they ended up across the round table from each other. She had hoped to be close enough to carry on a conversation.

Janet's prediction proved true. Kieran was quiet in a crowd. When he caught her watching him, he hid his mouth behind his napkin. She could still see his eyes though, matching the brilliant blue in his tartan. They crinkled at the corners like she remembered. The way he looked at her, coupled with the candlelight dancing in his eyes, proved both disarming and endearing. She knew she blushed whenever she caught him glancing at her, and she lowered her gaze, pretending to concentrate on her meal. Speaking to him without betraying her attraction was impossible.

As the main portion of the meal ended, everyone moved to the next table. Janet went ahead, deep in conversation with an English professor. Bonny was so intent on avoiding Kieran's eyes, she collided with him. She dropped her purse, and when she bent to retrieve it, they bumped heads.

He handed the bag to her, rubbing his head. Bonny giggled, and he smiled.

"I didn't mean to ignore you. I think we should become better acquainted before giving people something to speculate about, though. My Aunt Alice heads your department, you know."

"I understand." She moved on with her heart rat-a-tat-tatting, reminiscent of the drums at the Tattoo. His magnetism was undeniable.

Everyone prepared to leave after the dessert course, and the other biology professor engaged Janet in a lengthy discussion. Bonny wandered toward the windows, entranced by the loch, the surface of the water shimmering silver under a full moon. She caught her breath when someone walked up next to her. Glancing up, she discovered Kieran towering over her.

"A grand sight, aye?" She trembled at the deep timbre of his voice.

"However, the woman who captured my attention this entire evening is far lovelier. I haven't forgotten my promise to ring you up soon. I will."

ᙆᔕᙣ

"He said you're more beautiful than moonlight on the loch?" Janet's tone was incredulous. "You don't realize how miraculous it is for him to speak to you at all."

"He said 'lovely,' and he was only enjoying the view and being friendly." Good thing it was dark so Janet couldn't see the flush she felt rushing to her cheeks.

"It's beyond friendly. The poor man lives a solitary life with his sheep, except for a housekeeper, the farm manager, and some hired men."

Bonny took a deep breath. "I'm aware of more than you know. We took a hike, ate dinner, and talked for eight hours one evening before our trip to Edinburgh."

"You and Kieran met without letting me know? What are you hiding from me?"

Oh, dear, what if he isn't pleased? "Okay, but please don't make a big thing out of it. I had a flat tire after work, the week before the Tattoo. He changed it and took me to get it fixed. Then he showed me a new place to walk, and I invited him home for green-chili stew. We talked until two in the morning. We have everything in common except sheep, and I imagine I'll find out they're nice once I learn something about them. Otherwise, you didn't miss much."

"Two in the morning? And you let me introduce you in Edinburgh, knowing nothing?"

"Act like I didn't say anything, please? He promised to call soon."

"You do have a lot in common."

Bonny's involuntary laugh held all the cynicism bottled inside her heart. "Pain, skepticism, and a love of the same literature and music. He's easy to talk to. He'll make a good friend."

"A friend, aye, he'll be that, and loyal to the end. But haven't you imagined anything more? He's but ten years older, and a fine man, kind, and gentle. Both of you deserve the chance at happiness."

Kieran was right about people making more out of their friendship than there was. "Janet, he helped me with a flat tire, showed me a new trail, and ate dinner with me. He's a nice man."

Janet shook her head. "You don't know what you need, and Kieran's every bit as daft. Mum asked if you were coming to church with us tomorrow. Will you? You have to stop visiting around sometime."

Bonny remained silent, struggling to answer. "I don't know what I believe anymore. Kieran's life proves the same thing. Since I have to go, I'll see you in church. Thanks for picking me up. I enjoyed the evening."

"You can't hang onto your anger at God forever, and neither can Kieran. You both look for help everywhere except the one place you can find it. Once you hear Graeme preach, you won't regret it."

Bonny readied for bed, reflecting on the changes in her life. Once in bed, she lay awake, staring at the ceiling and thinking. Her parents' faith had been so strong. The way the three of them used to pray together, she always felt comforted afterwards. She longed to experience the peace she had felt then.

Still puzzling over the choices before her, she arose at six for a hike to sort out her thinking. The wound from Adam's betrayal was still fresh, but she felt drawn to Kieran in a way she couldn't deny. Doing nothing and becoming a caricature of Miss Havisham in Dickens' *Great Expectations* was a less-than-comforting prospect.

Janet's comment emphasized the difference in their reactions to their severed relationships. Once again, she determined that Janet handled it better.

∽∾

Bonny approached the small stone building the next morning, still contemplating her conversation with Janet. Faith Chapel met in a former office building on the main road into town from Fort Augustus. She arrived early and found Janet and Agnes already seated in metal folding chairs halfway down the aisle.

It seemed that everyone who came in knew Janet and Agnes, and they introduced her to them all.

A half hour later, during a short pause in the praise and worship time, Janet leaned over and whispered, "You have a lovely voice."

"Thanks. I've sung in choirs or on the praise team since I was little. I didn't realize how much I missed it."

The pastor, Graeme McDholl, preached on the prophet Elijah running away after Jezebel threatened his life. Bonny could identify with the disillusioned prophet as he hid in a cave. She'd seen no more signs of God in the stormy winds that had lashed her life than Elijah did as he watched from the mouth of the cave. Her world had been devastated as surely as the earthquake and fire he experienced without God revealing himself. God showed himself to Elijah at last, in a gentle whisper.

"What did you think of Graeme's sermon?" Janet questioned Bonny over lunch, following the service.

"It made me consider subjects I'd prefer not to deal with. But he's very good."

She caught herself listening for that whisper, but God didn't speak to her anymore.

The following Sunday, the worship leader, Jamie, approached her. "Janet suggested I convince you to audition for our Christmas program. We're doing a musical production in the auditorium at the college this year, and we need more strong voices. Auditions are next week."

❧

The following afternoon, Kieran appeared as Bonny was sitting on a bench under one of the spreading old trees, changing into her hiking boots. "Congratulations. I hear they're adding another section for your class. I need to apologize for avoiding you the past couple of weeks." He sat down next to her. "I'd enjoy becoming better acquainted—if you're interested."

She narrowed her eyes, hoping the look she gave him was as chilly as the water in Loch Linnhe. "When you never called, I thought you'd changed your mind."

"I—I know it must have looked that way. I haven't spent time with a woman since my wife died. It took time to get my courage up."

"You didn't seem to have a problem the night we talked until two a.m."

"You're not going to make this easy for me, are you? You seemed fine at the faculty party."

"That was before you made me wait a third time. First you were in Edinburgh for the Tattoo. Then I didn't hear from you until the party, and now it's been two more weeks. If you don't want to see me, Kieran …"

"I wouldn't say I wanted to see you if I didn't."

"I wasted years with a man who took advantage of me at every opportunity. I won't ever let that happen again." She stood so that she was looking down at him.

"That's one reason it took me so long. Bonny, I would never want to hurt you. The longer I waited, the more I wanted to be with you." He sounded sincere; but then, so had Adam.

"You're certain?"

"I'm not like Adam."

Now he was reading her mind. She took a step back. He was honest and kind—well worth giving another chance. "I was going for a hike. Do you want to join me? We'll see how things go."

He nodded, his whole face lighting up with a smile that created a warm, melty feeling inside of her, similar to what she remembered from schoolgirl crushes, only stronger. "Aye, I hoped you might like company."

"I'd enjoy it."

He stood and gestured for her to proceed. "Lead the way."

They walked along in silence, enjoying the cool, crisp afternoon with a slight mist in the air, the scent of early fall, damp, with the first of the decaying leaves underfoot. Already, Bonny had come to agree that a light mist wasn't worth acknowledging compared to the constant rain of most days. The sky was a pale blue with thin clouds, the mist seeming to arise from nowhere.

It was an afternoon worthy of a postcard. The winding path led through tall pines and trees beginning to clothe themselves in the brilliant yellows, oranges, and reds of autumn. The cerulean loch below glimmered in the afternoon sunlight, creating a dazzling view.

They walked half a mile before Bonny broke the silence. "Did you really plan to walk with me?"

"Oh, aye, I wanted to ask you to dinner later in the week."

The shiver passing through her wasn't due to the light breeze. "I'll let you know after our walk."

"I'm in town three days a week for class and tutoring. I thought Friday evening would work. Are you afraid, or just making it difficult?"

"Both." She tried to imagine a love like Janet had described between Kieran and his wife. She would settle for nothing less.

An hour later, they stood overlooking the shimmering lochs below. Kieran moved close enough for her to feel the heat from his body as he blocked the chill breeze blowing from the water. "The view from here is one of my favorites."

Bonny laughed. "I can't get used to so much water. We don't have this much in the entire state of New Mexico."

"Whoo," he let out a breath of air, shaking his head.

She laughed, bending to pick a wildflower, thinking how fragile she felt when it came to men. "You think I'm kidding."

"I can't imagine the desert. I've traveled around Europe, but I haven't seen anywhere without water."

She laughed again. "I'll show you pictures sometime. Albuquerque gets less than ten inches of rain a year. The mountains get more, but it's minuscule compared to here."

He shook his head, grinning down at her. Then he took the flower and tucked it behind her right ear. "It sounds like the Sahara."

"Not at all. It has its own beauty." She did enjoy his company.

"Say yes to dinner on Friday. If you don't want to see me again, you can tell me after that."

"All right. One thing at a time."

His eyes crinkled at the corners. "I'll pick you up at six."

When they reached the parking lot, he held her car door, lingering a little longer than necessary.

She checked the rearview mirror as she turned onto the street. He stood still in the same spot, watching her drive away. Reaching up, she touched the flower still tucked behind her ear, wondering if it was a promise of good things to come.

☙❧

Kieran climbed out of the Land Rover to get a closer look at the tracks leading into the heavily forested area on the south side of the loch known as Greenfield. From up ahead where a ruined cottage had been built into a shallow cave, he heard the sound of voices.

Expecting someone either lost or sightseeing, he slogged through the mud, his Wellies sinking up to his ankles in spots. "Hello?"

At his call, the voices stopped. The only way across the loch was by the bridge just west of the house. They could have come from the direction of Tomdoun, but it bore further investigation.

"Hey there." A man sat on a stone fallen from the long-derelict chimney. He looked up as Kieran approached.

"Brennan? I thought you were off today."

The tall young man with shaggy hair stood up, his deep brown eyes bright and alert. "Yes sir, I am. I was just hiking around a bit. I heard there used to be a town here and thought I'd have a look."

"The people left here in the late 1700s. It's been empty and neglected since." Kieran walked to the door of the cottage and looked in. "Nothing much here, just a few stones. The people who called it home moved north to Caithness and then to Canada, victims of the Clearances."

Brennan kept looking over to the right where a quad-bike sat spattered in mud. "I heard they lost their lands to the MacDonells."

"The Greenfields were MacDonells also. They took the name Greenfield to remind them of their home, when they went to Canada. It wasn't unusual for lower-ranking clansmen to be evicted by more well-to-do members of their own clan who sided with the English."

Brennan glanced over his shoulder, giving the impression he was listening for something.

"Is someone else here, lad?"

His eyes reminded Kieran of a startled deer. "No—no, I came alone, just curious. Do you have a problem with me being here?"

Something caught Kieran's eye near the quad bike. Sure enough, two sets of footprints leading from there to the cottage, then one set leading into the woods. The boot prints looked the same, but one set seemed a wee bit smaller. "There are two sets of footprints and I thought I heard voices. I don't mind if you have someone with you."

"I said I was alone. I was talking to a squirrel that startled me when I went to look inside the cave." He edged toward the bike. "How did you come to own the land? You're not a Greenfield."

"No, I'm a Glengarry MacDonell. My second great grandfather bought the land comprising Stonehaven Farm. I inherited it. I own land on both sides of the loch." A rustling in the bushes sounded like something larger than a squirrel. "You're welcome to be here, as long as you don't disturb anything."

"Thanks, we—I won't."

"Fine." With a look he hoped left no doubt who was boss, Kieran turned and headed back to the Land Rover. As he backed down the muddy track, a flash of red caught his eye in the trees. He would make certain to tell Angus and Seumas to keep an eye on young Brennan Grant. He had the feeling something was up. Why should a Grant care about the long-ago ancestors of the MacDonells? Something didn't fit.

⁂

Janet drove Bonny home from her first choir practice the next night, and they sat in the driveway talking. "I think you could do each other some good. I also think you need a dress for the Fort William Charity Ball. If your dinner goes well, Kieran's bound to ask you." She smiled as if her prediction had already come true. "The pipe band will be performing, so he won't miss it. Everyone wears their tartan. Bryant is a corruption of O'Brian or MacBrian, and not a recognized clan, so they don't have one. We can use the Fraser's, for your grandmother's side, though, a soft red with a bold plaid of blue and dark green. You'll win his heart in a minute."

Bonny ducked her head to hide her warming cheeks, the curse of a fair complexion. The idea sounded more appealing than she wanted to admit. "Who said I wanted to win his heart?"

"You blush whenever his name is mentioned," Janet teased.

The next morning, she remembered dreams of dancing with what Janet called "a *braw and bonnie* Highlander." Her heart fluttered at the thought of his booming brogue. Only once, she whispered his name, "Kieran," and there was magic in the sound.

Chapter Eight

Thoughts of Home

Bonny's heels made a thwacking sound as she walked across the marble floor of the college foyer, disturbing the quiet of the almost empty building. She'd awakened early with a heart heavier than her briefcase full of books. It was five months to the day since her dad's death. Her mind still had a hard time processing all the changes. If the God her parents had believed in did exist, how did He fit into it all?

"Bonny, I have updated class lists for you." A voice called from behind her.

Yanked back to the present, she turned and walked back a few steps to the office she had just passed. Leaning on the half-door, she forced her thoughts back to the real world. "Thanks, Lorna. How do things look?"

The energetic genie of the registrar's office, as Janet called her, was a perpetually smiling friend to every professor at the college. "Your elective course has attracted more students than we planned for. We've moved you into the larger lecture hall on the second floor and opened two more sections, as Dr. Cameron mentioned. I have your new class lists ready."

Bonny took the papers, ruffling through them with a feeling that was both joy over the success of the class and sadness because her dad wasn't there to share it. "Janet told me you work magic. She was right."

The tiny woman, a few inches shorter than Bonny, blushed to the roots of her shining silver hair. "It's the most popular course we have right now. The waiting list extends to next term."

"Thanks. I don't know how you keep track of everyone so well. See you later."

"Stop by this afternoon in case there are any more changes."

"Okay, see you later."

There was a tug o' war in her heart between pleasure and pain. The method she and her dad had developed for combining history with biographies and literature of and about the time provided a different view of America than the modern media offered. Statements of faith by the Founding Fathers proved to be a valuable tool in helping students understand what incited the men and women of the former British colony to risk everything in their fight for freedom. She was finding they challenged her as well.

Giving the same lecture five times in a row kept her mind off the more poignant aspects of the day. By the time she flicked the switch on her computer and sat down with a re-heated meat pie to check Facebook, she felt exhausted from holding in her emotions all day. Her heart leaped when she discovered Dan was available for instant messaging. After the initial greetings, she decided to lay it all out to the friend who had shared her ups and downs since their days in the church nursery:

It's all so bittersweet, Danny Boy. I'm having success, but Dad isn't here to enjoy it with me. And—I find myself examining the personal spiritual lives of America's Founding Fathers in more depth. Pastor MacDholl is talking about the basis for real faith. As I prepare lessons and grade papers, I realize how much my view of the world is rooted in the Bible. So why isn't my personal life subject to scripture anymore? Here, away from the familiar routines of home, I'm re-examining issues I've ignored for a long time.

He answered back:

Bonny, you're avoiding the inevitable confrontation between the anger you cling to and the challenge to renew your faith in God. We're to go on faith, not feelings. You forgot that somewhere along the way.

☙❧

Waking up to find the sheets pulled loose at all four corners, Bonny remembered vague dreams about Adam. On second thought, perhaps nightmares were a better term for them. She wasn't free yet. That being the case, was she ready to have dinner with Kieran, if he called? After debating all through her morning walk, she picked up the phone and called Kari.

"Hey stranger, I thought maybe you didn't have phone service to the rest of the world."

Her best friend did know how to lay on the guilt.

"Kari, I'm sorry for not calling more often." Bonny felt the heat of shame, even though Kari was far away. "I've been busy with classes starting—it's crazy. How are you?"

"Everything's fine." Kari sounded more upbeat than the last time they talked. "I started a Bible study for middle-school girls. It's fun and fills my time."

"You have such a gift. I've never known anyone who loves kids like you do."

"They make me smile. What's up with you?"

Bonny hesitated. "I'm adjusting. Janet's a lifesaver. Her mom invites me over for dinner every week. I've attended church with them the past three weeks. She put the choir director onto me, and I'm singing again—and enjoying it."

"That's great. Your voice is like my love of kids. There are some things it's a sin to waste."

It was now or never. She needed Kari's input if she was going to start spending time with Kieran. "I'm feeling challenged and confused. The pastor, Graeme MacDholl, is someone I could open up to."

"New friends and a good minister. It sounds like you're doing well."

Bonny watched the rain sliding down the windows and dripping off the eaves. Her eyes joined in, raining droplets on her jeans. "I love it here, until I remember I have the same empty house to return to."

"Oh, honey, I don't know what to say. Have you met anyone to socialize with?" Kari sounded so concerned, Bonny felt like a child hiding stolen candy. The empty house wasn't the source of her fear. It was the thought of spending time with a man again, especially a handsome one with an accent capable of charming all common sense right out of her head.

"I'm starting to." She hesitated a moment, anticipating the reaction. "There's a math professor, Kieran MacDonell, a real Braveheart kind of guy, even at forty years old. Janet and I watched him compete in the Highland Games and heard him play his bagpipes in the Edinburgh Tattoo. We've taken a couple of short hikes together, and we're having dinner Friday night."

"Forty years old and a hunk? Do those terms belong in the same sentence?" Kari's voice rose in pitch, and Bonny laughed, imagining the expression on her face.

"In this case, yes. He helped fix a flat tire on my car. So, as a thank you, I invited him over for green-chili stew. We talked until two in the morning. What a Scotsman—rugged and handsome. His voice makes me feel all melty, like butter, and his eyes are the color of a loch in the sunshine. His wife died in childbirth when the emergency helicopter failed to reach their farm in time due to a storm. The baby was stillborn and Bronwyn died in Kieran's arms."

"Oh, Bonny, how terrible. Don't get too involved with someone in Scotland." There was the anticipated caution. "You'll end up with your heart broken again."

"We're only eating dinner. I don't know if I'm ready for a relationship yet." Time to end the conversation before Kari criticized too much. "Hey, it's getting late here. I still need to check a couple details before class tomorrow. I didn't find out your latest wedding plans."

"It's okay," Bonny heard the quiet monotone of disappointment in Kari's voice. "I'm fine. We'll visit again soon. Just take things slow, all right?"

When they hung up, Bonny sat, watching silvery streaks of rain slide down the darkened window glass in the lamplight. The anticipation of spending time with a man again was somewhat terrifying. Kari's warnings were well-intentioned, but then she didn't wake up alone day after day, and she hadn't met Kieran.

⊗⊗

A few days after her messaging session with Dan, he emailed her, explaining how much Kari missed them both. "I hesitate to mention this, but Kari's hurting too. I realize you have problems with the whole wedding thing right now, but she needs you."

After chiding herself all night over the self-centered conversation, Bonny phoned Kari again the next day. "Bring me up to date on your wedding plans. I love my dress, by the way. It only needs shortening to fit perfectly. Yours is gorgeous."

"Oh Bonny, the pictures don't do justice to the lace. It's everything I ever wanted." She heard the wistful note in Kari's voice. "It brought back memories of the homecoming and prom dresses we shopped for together. I miss you."

Kari then launched into a narrative of her latest plans, making Bonny glad her tears weren't visible over the phone. It dredged up reminders of the day they had stumbled across her never-worn designer bridal gown mislabeled in the bargain section. Kari startled her out of her day-dream. "Are you still there?"

"Yes, you're a dream. Wait until Dan sees you."

"Hey, I should say good-bye. I want to write to him tonight. I love you, friend. God bless you, and thanks for calling."

"Good-bye, I love you, too." Bonny hung up the phone, sitting still in the silence. She had thought her relationship with Adam was as loving as Kari and Dan's. When she took time to listen to Kari, it became obvious she hadn't felt the excitement and longing over her marriage to Adam that Kari felt for Dan.

When home is so far away, why does everything still hurt so much?

Chapter Nine

The Farm and Other Things

The Old Pines Hotel near Spean Bridge was a brief, scenic drive from Fort William. Bonny's first impression was that the unassuming exterior was too new to deserve the name "Old Pines." Once inside, she was surprised by the sophistication of the restaurant, which had wood paneling, a low ceiling, and modern Scandinavian-style tables and chairs with stark, straight lines. The charming, laid-back atmosphere was perfect for exploring her growing attraction for Kieran.

His interest in everything she said, and the soft glow in his eyes, made her feel attractive, something she hadn't felt in a long time.

He held her chair and sat down across the table where the hostess placed his menu. "The talk around campus is that your class is 'pure dead brilliant.' That's quite a compliment from college students. How do you feel?"

"The students are enthusiastic, and I'm enjoying teaching a curriculum I helped write. My dad would have been pleased."

She watched in fascination as he angled the narrow chair to a place where he had more room for his long legs.

"Are you settling in, then, learning your way around?" His soft tone sent fingers of warmth from her toes right up her spine.

"Starting to, but I need advice on handling a student. Do you mind?" His cologne, reminiscent of woods and spices, took her thoughts in a thousand directions, none of which had to do with school or students.

"I'd be happy to help." His wide grin teased. "What's the problem? If a lad of eighteen has a crush on the professor, I can't blame him."

Her cheeks grew warm when he moved the vase of purple flowers and leaned closer. "If only it were such a small problem. I haven't dealt with anything this serious before. I prefer to try handling it myself if I can, rather than taking it to Dr. Cameron. It's a woman, probably in her mid—"

Approaching from behind Kieran, in the white blouse and black skirt of a waitress, was the student she was about to describe.

"Good evening, Dr. Bryant. Can I get you anything to drink?"

"Deirdre, I didn't know you worked here. Water, please."

"Still or sparkling?"

"Oh, sparkling, please. I'm still not used to ordering that way."

She was a pretty brunette, though almost as large as Kieran. "What can I get you, Dr. MacDonell?" The look in Deirdre's eyes when she turned toward him was nothing less than sultry, and her voice took on a flirtatious tone.

Here we go again, Bonny thought, falling for a man who seems to appeal to every woman who sees him. A smile flickered across his lips, and the corners of his eyes crinkled. "Still, thanks. Have we met?"

Deirdre smiled, turning her back on Bonny and leaning one hip against the table. "I'm in Dr. Bryant's history class. I've seen you around campus. I'll be right back with your water."

"You're not in my trig class. I would remember."

He knows she's attracted and he's enjoying it, even with me sitting right here. Oh, why does he have to keep doing things that remind me of Adam?

Deirdre paused, her lashes fluttering, drawing attention to eyes that were an unusual amber in color. "No, I'm in algebra, but I've requested you as my tutor. I heard you were the best."

She was interested in more than just math, and he was playing along. Were all men like that?

"Deirdre? I'll look for you on my schedule." That smile of his could dazzle any woman.

"Yes, Deirdre Adair." Her right cheek even dimpled when she smiled.

"Good. I'll see you next week."

The laughing blue eyes turned back to Bonny, stirring the butterflies in her stomach into action. It was obvious he felt the admiration of them both and was enjoying it. "Shall I order for both of us? The venison loin is excellent."

"Yes, please."

Her thoughts were roiling around in such a state of distraction that she would never make sense of the menu. When a man recognized the effect he had on women, it could only lead to trouble. Adam had strayed. Did she want a relationship with someone who enjoyed attracting the attention of every woman in sight, one who would flirt with another woman with her sitting right across the table? It didn't fit with what Janet had said about him, but she couldn't know everything.

Distracted by her own thoughts, and lulled by the deep timbre of his voice, with its rolled r's and musical, even spellbinding, accent of the Highlands, Bonny jumped when Deidre walked away, and he addressed her again.

"Bonny, is something wrong?"

"Umm, no, sorry. I was admiring the restaurant. It's very nice."

"You were saying something about a student before we were interrupted."

"I don't know if this is the place to discuss it."

His eyes narrowed and he leaned even closer, just as Deirdre returned with their water. He moved out of the way, but his eyes remained fixed on Bonny's with an intensity that made her giddy, failing to even acknowledge Deirdre. When she walked away, his voice grew softer, and the joking tone was gone. "This has you concerned, aye?"

His fingers brushed her hand where it lay on the table, and she reached for her water glass, swirling the sparkling water until it formed a tiny whirlpool, anything to distract her from his closeness. Leaning forward, she whispered, so as not to be overheard. "It's a little awkward. Deirdre is the problem."

"Yes?"

"She wrote a paper on the Salem witch trials, which took place in the late 1600s. It demonstrated no understanding of the history. Instead, she compared it to the so-called 'inappropriate fear and unfair outrage' Christians today express toward anything pagan. She also referred to the 'English oppressors,' *Sassanachs*, she called them, plaguing Scotland. It ends with the words '*Saor Alba*.'"

Kieran's eyes widened and he sat back, crossing his arms and lowering his voice. "Free Scotland, in a paper about American history? I gather her viewpoint wasn't within the scope of the assignment?"

"Not even close. I moved it to the bottom of the pile until I can decide what to do."

"Give it back and make her to do it over—as assigned." He swallowed the last of his water, his eyes never leaving hers. "Set a deadline and stick to your requirements."

"She's so—threatening."

"She doesn't seem very intimidating to me, but if you need help, I'll turn up to intimidate her." His smile was back.

"Thanks, I hope that's not necessary. I only wanted to confirm it with someone with more experience dealing with students."

"The plates are hot." Deirdre set their dinner on the table, looking only at Kieran.

"Thanks." He gave her a brief nod, looked back at Bonny, and winked.

Attempting to return to safer territory, Bonny remembered a conversation with Janet from a few days ago. "Janet told me your parents have a Bed and Breakfast in Beauly."

"They do. The Heather Hill Inn is one of the top B&Bs in the Highlands. My mother thrives on serving high tea and hosting guests as if they were family friends."

As on the evening he changed her tire, the conversation flowed between them with ease. When he paid the check, she realized she remembered little of the meal, only a deep sense of pleasure in his company.

He stood to pull her chair out. "Shall we go back to your house? There may not be a student making eyes at you, but I happen to have a crush on the professor and a date to view snaps of New Mexico."

She preceded him out of the restaurant, her cheeks hot from his confession. "Watch yourself, professor. You're still on probation, remember? I haven't said you were off the hook for making me wait so long for your call. And what's the deal flirting with Deirdre?"

The red began at his collar and spread up to his hairline. "I-uh, wouldn't worry if I were you. She can't begin to compete."

∽

Bonny clicked through the photos with her laptop plugged into the television. Explaining and describing as Kieran questioned, they drifted closer together until their shoulders were touching. Even that small amount of contact heightened her awareness of his charm.

She included pictures of her parents and Kari and Dan, places they visited and activities they enjoyed. She had managed to edit Adam out, hoping to ignore him altogether, until she slipped. "Adam and I—"

When she tried to avoid looking at him, Kieran scooted to an angle facing her, one elbow resting on his leg, chin in hand. "Bonny, there's nothing wrong in mentioning Adam. It hurts sometimes, but he and Bronwyn are a part of who we are."

She caught herself twisting her hair and, remembering her mother's aversion to the bad habit, she tucked her hands under her thighs. "Whenever I think about what he did, I wonder what I might have done different."

His arm rested on the back of the couch, and he moved it down, placing it around her shoulders. The intensity of his gaze made her feel as if her heart lay bare before him. "You think there's something wrong with you because of what he did?"

At his touch, a thrill of electricity surged through her, and for a brief moment, she imagined his strong arms surrounding her. She shook her head, turning away from the piercing blue gaze. "It's a long story. We'll save it for another time."

"I'm a good listener." He squeezed her shoulder and withdrew his hand. "Nothing he did will ever change my opinion of you."

His tender eyes, gentle voice, and the masculine scent of his aftershave were intoxicating. The place where his hand rested on her shoulder still felt warm, and she remembered Janet's words. *A love like that is worth waiting for.*

"Do you want more tea?" She stood and headed for the kitchen, hoping for a moment alone.

He followed, and her heart rate increased until the dishes on the tray rattled.

"How about coming out to the farm to ride on Saturday?"

"I'd love to. I miss my horses." The words were out before she realized it. She was eager for more than the riding. Thinking about seeing his home and learning about his life made her glad she had already set the tray down. She somehow managed to put more water on to boil without spilling any.

When they returned to the living room, she sat across from him, attempting to keep his overpowering physical presence at a safe distance. She felt drawn to him like a parched traveler to a land full of water, yet she hesitated at such intimacy.

At three a.m. they said reluctant good-byes. Leaning against the door after he left, Bonny closed her eyes. She remembered the warmth of his hand on her shoulder, the brief touch when he took the tray from her, and the way it made her mind whirl when he looked into her eyes.

What am I doing? He seems more sincere than Adam, but the similarities are disturbing.

CᔥꙄꙄ

As the beauty of summer gave way to the cooler autumn air, Kieran recognized healing taking place in his wounded heart. The same appeared to be true for Bonny, if her more relaxed attitude was any indication. At first, they had only walked in the gloaming after an early dinner, enjoying the peace of the hour right before dark. Now, they walked at lunch or after classes, spending evenings with books, music, and conversations that grew deeper and more personal daily. They rushed to grade papers and prepare their lesson plans in order to spend weekends together.

The following Saturday, Kieran stood just behind Bonny at the famous overlook to Loch Garry. Below them, the forest-lined loch shimmered silver under the high clouds. He had lain awake the last few nights, imagining this moment.

The warmth of her hand penetrated the sleeve of his tweed jacket. "Where is Stonehaven Farm?"

With one hand, he pointed, and then rested his other hand on her shoulder.

"It's hidden by the trees. See the bridge across the narrow part of the loch? Just a wee bit this side of the bridge is the clearing where the house stands. From this angle, the loch looks like a map of Scotland."

"It does. It's hard to believe there's a farm in there. When you said 'heavily wooded,' you weren't kidding." She placed her hand on top of the one he rested on her shoulder, small and cool against his skin.

He held still, wondering how long she would let him remain so close. "Yes, but to the northwest, the forest thins out. Loch Garry begins over there to your left, where you can see the dam. The Munerigie Wood and the Gleann Lauogh Forest, my favorite childhood haunts, lie beyond it. There, near the turnoff from the main road is Daingean, the ruins of a village abandoned during The Clearances in the late 1700s. Reforestation covered it over after World War II, and they didn't find it again until 1999. It's so small that even old maps of the MacDonell landholdings failed to show it."

She turned her sweet face up to his, and he thought she must hear his heart pounding. "Kieran, it's amazing. The mountains around my home are beautiful, but nothing can compete with the green and the lochs."

"I'm glad you like it." It felt natural to take her hand as they headed back to the car. Once on the road again, Bonny stopped questioning, her head turning from side to side as if she was trying to take in both sides of the road at once.

He appreciated her silence after they turned off the A87 onto the single-track road running along the north shore of Loch Garry. There was an emotional reaction in bringing a woman to the home he had shared with Bronwyn for the first time. It had become very important for Bonny to love it.

The single-track road required a certain amount of concentration to avoid oncoming traffic or slow farm equipment. He couldn't help laughing when they paused for a herd of Highland cattle blocking the road. "These are not mine, but cattle and sheep are a frequent road hazard in the Highlands."

"I don't mind. It's superb. The mountains, Loch Garry, the forests—I love it. It must be magnificent in summer."

"I hoped you'd be keen on it." The slow thud of his heart changed to a fluttering in his chest.

"I know I'll love everything about Stonehaven Farm. Tell me more."

"Aye, gladly." Seeing the rapt attention on her face, he took a couple of deep breaths to slow his heart. "They call this road the longest, most beautiful dead end in the UK." He mimicked a travelogue, drawing a giggle from her.

"It's single-track and steep in spots, with sharp turns. You need to pay close attention. You'll find few passing places and lots of rugged hills and old stone bridges, though the roughest spots lie beyond the farm. Sheep are one of the few things this harsh land can support."

Her cheeks glowed an attractive shade of pink. "This isn't rough compared to the four-wheel-drive roads my dad and I explored in our Land Cruiser."

Her enthusiasm was exhilarating.

"Are you truly as interested in everything as you seem?"

"It's fun. I've never been around sheep."

Her energy and enthusiasm were a drastic change from the listless melancholy which had threatened to overwhelm him the last two years. "For generations, my father's family has maintained a strong herd of Scottish Blackface sheep and Cheviots. We produce wool, mutton, and lamb. It's a good life."

Rushing, gurgling burns tumbled toward the loch on every side. When they reached a patch of meadow at the crest of a hill, the two-story stone house came into view. He watched her face as she surveyed his home. The rapture in her eyes lifted the pall of grief a little. He tried to see his home through her. Screened by forest and overlooking the loch, the old, ivy-covered house stood surrounded by tall pines and large flower beds. Sheep grazed on the lawn, paying them no attention whatsoever.

"This is home."

"Oh Kieran, what a perfect place to live." Her wide eyes moved from the house to the loch and back again. "I can't imagine leaving this for trigonometry."

Easing the Land Rover into gear, he turned into the drive. "I can't imagine it now either, but as a young farm boy I was eager to experience city life."

When he came to a stop in front of the house, Loch Garry lay below them, obscured in part by a tangle of trees. A pack of barking, tussling dogs appeared from behind the old stone barn to greet them, barking and jumping around in play as Bonny petted and laughed.

"What are their names?"

"The border collies are Corrie and Bruce, the English sheepdogs are Wally and Una, and the Labs are my hunting dogs, Mary and Darnley."

"I love their names."

He laughed, a rare occurrence since Bronwyn's death, but even more so at the farm, where he seemed perpetually sad.

She gave him a quizzical look and walked toward him. "What are you laughing at?"

He placed one hand on her back; his heart hadn't felt so light in two years. "The way you throw yourself into things with your whole heart. I haven't enjoyed a woman's company so much in a long time."

"This is fun. I want to see it all."

"You've got it. The trees you see are almost all the result of reforestation. The Highland Clearances, in the late 18th and early 19th centuries, stripped it bare. The wealthy landowners not only cleared the land of the people who worked it, but they cut the trees to create more room to graze their sheep as well." He fought the sudden urge to put his arms around her. He was surprised she had let him put his hand on her shoulder. She seemed to pull away whenever he touched her for more than an instant.

"How many MacDonells?"

"Close to five thousand. The MacDonells of Glengarry claimed this area around the middle of the sixteenth century. Some survived The Clearances, but their descendants lost their towns and farms under the waters of Loch Garraidh when it was dammed for hydroelectric power after World War II. It's become a haven for wildlife preservation, fishing, and reforestation, though. Only a few estates remain, making wildlife management one of my biggest concerns. I don't employ a gamekeeper or *ghillie*. I enjoy taking care of it myself. There's been a lot of poaching lately. I have to make certain no part of the farm goes long without being inspected."

"You have quite a legacy, but what a shame. The Clearances changed the entire history of Scotland, didn't they?"

He started toward the house. "Aye, they cleared the land of people and trees in favor of sheep. By the way, it's Eleanor's day off, so we're alone." Bonny Bryant seemed like everything he could want in a woman, and Eleanor thought he should be trying to move on. However, something made him want to keep things just between him and Bonny for the time being.

When she stopped again, he pointed down the loch to the West. "The bridge you can see, there, to the West, crosses over to Torr na Carraidh, commonly known as Tornacarry. The majority of houses on the far side of the loch are summer homes. The road leads to the forests on the south side, and a large burn, Allt Coire nan Saobhaidh. I'll point out the mountains to the North on our drive back. Stonehaven Farm consists of large pieces of land on both sides of the loch."

She giggled. "You're not going to test me on place names, are you? Does anyone else live here year around?"

Her smile and laughter created a warm feeling in his heart where a cold, hard knot had been. "The people at the salmon farm do. The others serve as hunting and fishing lodges or vacation rentals."

Bonny pointed across the loch. "What spectacular mountains. Have you climbed them?"

"The ones you can see from here. Let me show you the house, and then we'll take that ride I promised." He guided her through the downstairs, showing her the family crest above the fireplace, pointing out heirlooms, antiques, and paintings of flowers and local landscapes. He couldn't take her upstairs. That seemed too close to Bronwyn, too close to something he couldn't let go of yet.

She stopped in the center of the room, turning in a circle. "I always wanted a library." When she paused, she faced the case where awards from Highland Games, bagpipe competitions, and agricultural shows were displayed. "Are all of those yours?"

"Not all, but a good number. I told you I was the champion of Lochaber." It was meant as a joke, but he sensed her stiffening, saw her eyes narrow and her jaw clinch. "Why do my achievements offend you so much?"

She turned bright red then and lowered her eyes. "It—it's just that Adam is, well, competitive. He plays golf, soccer, racquetball, basketball. He's interested in politics, always trying to get ahead at the law firm, and has, well, no humility at all. When I became a burden rather than a trophy he moved on."

She faced him with a sort of half smile. "It's a charming home, Kieran, really beautiful."

He was surprised at how important it was to him for her to like his home, and himself. At the same time, he was experiencing an astonishing conflict of emotions over bringing a woman into Bronwyn's home.

She stopped in front of a painting of wildflowers with the loch in the background, one of Bronwyn's. "You weren't kidding—she was talented. For an old house, it's full of light and color. The gardens must be magnificent in full bloom."

"Yes." He closed his eyes, remembering. "She was—one of a kind."

The dogs joined them again as they walked toward the barn. He enfolded Bonny's hand in his, and was pleased she didn't pull away. Its small, delicate coolness created a welcome contrast to the hard, lonely ache he had become accustomed to.

"The wind in the pines and the sheep baaing in the pastures give me a calm, tranquil feeling." Bonny closed her eyes and breathed deep. "Everything is so picturesque. It must be even more spectacular when the sun shines."

Kieran eyed the high, silvery clouds. "Ach, lass, we call this a sunny day in Scotland."

Bonny laughed then, leaning her face against his arm as she turned it upward in a move that caught him off guard. "I wasn't complaining. It's just so different from home, especially the cool, cloudy weather; but I love it here."

"I want you to." He put his arm around her shoulders, stifling a strong urge to kiss her. Instead, they ambled down the lawn toward the gate leading to the water. "We have our own kelpie."

"In Loch Garry?" She stopped and turned to face him, her tantalizing eyes as green as the surrounding forest.

"You can't have a loch without a water horse." He laughed, pulling her close as a gust of wind blew off the water. "According to the legend, seven children played along the river. One touched it and his hand stuck to it. When the others tried to help, their hands got stuck also, and it dived under the water, taking them with it. Nothing was ever seen of them again, except for their hearts, floating in the water."

"I usually like your stories, but that's awful."

He grasped her hand, tugging her with him. "It kept me from wandering too close to the water when I was young."

She laughed and didn't pull away. "I can imagine."

Kieran pointed across the clear, rippling water of the loch, where a mountain stood surrounded by forests and smaller hills. "The mountain to the South is Beinn Tee, in the Glengarry Forest."

They stood side by side, enjoying the peaceful scene, when a large bird snatched a fish out of the water in a graceful swoop. Bonny's mouth opened in surprise. "Is that …"

"A bald eagle. Their grace and power amaze me, no matter how often I see them."

"It's paradise." She shaded her eyes, watching the eagle soar overhead with its catch as they walked the last few yards to the barn.

"Aye, you'll see eagles, falcons, hawks, and owls. We have everything from rabbits and squirrels to red deer and osprey. Let's mount up so you can see as much as possible." If he could have her around all the time, perhaps the lonely longing for what he had lost would subside.

Bonny let the large gray gelding in the first stall sniff her hand before stroking him between his ears and patting his neck. "What's your name, handsome?"

"Storm is mine, and the best horse I've ever owned." Kieran patted the horse on the neck and turned to introduce her to a gray mare in the next stall. "I call this one Misty. You'll be riding her. I haven't had her long, but she's sure-footed and gentle. I bought her from a hunting guide in Tomdoun whose daughter moved to London when she married."

"What a nice-looking dapple gray. Misty and Storm, huh? Was that planned?"

"No, but it's suitable. Hello, Kelpie." He pulled a wisp of hay from the mane of the small black mare in the next stall. His mother sometimes rode her, but it seemed wrong to put Bonny on Bronwyn's horse. "Water horses can turn themselves into either a horse or a woman." He granted the horse an extra measure of oats as she nuzzled his shoulder.

"What an unusual combination."

"Ach, I simply tell the stories. I didn't make it up." He guided her on to the next. "The gelding there, Selkie, belongs to my Da."

"He's gorgeous."

"Have you heard of selkies?" He gave her a handful of grain for the black horse nuzzling her hand.

Her beguiling eyes shone with curiosity. "No, you'll have to further my education in Scottish folklore."

He leaned one arm on the stall gate. "A selkie is a seal, usually a male. Once every seven years, they shed their skins and come up out of the water. They possess amazing beauty, and the stories are often tragic. They fall in love with a human, but in time, they must return to the sea. However, if the human hides their skin, they have to remain. Their haunting voices tempt people and lure ships to wreck in revenge for the killing of their fellow seals."

Bonny's smile created a warm feeling he hadn't felt in two years. "Your folklore is fascinating. Do you know more?"

"These are just the thorn on the thistle."

She fed Misty from her hand, rubbing her nose and face before moving to her mane and back, speaking in a quiet tone. Once he pointed out which tack to use, he went to saddle Storm, watching her out of the corner of his eye. The way she tightened the cinch a little bit at a time and then cleaned the hooves of debris proved she was as experienced as she said.

Kieran didn't meet many women, but this American who'd entered his life without warning was unique. Once again, he wondered at Adam's behavior. "You do know your way around horses. I noticed you let her sniff you before you started groomin'."

"My dad made certain I knew how to care for my horse."

Riding around the lower part of the farm, Kieran was seeing his home with new eyes. The fresh air, the soft breeze, and the beauty by his side made the land itself seem different.

When the often-skittish sheep failed to come to Bonny, Kieran quelled her disappointment by catching a ewe lamb for her to pet, and came up close beside her. "You'll smell like sheep and horses, and everyone will stay away from you, including me."

"They look softer from a distance. Their wool is full of grass and burrs, and they're oily." She wrinkled up her nose, laughing as he captured one hand in his. "Besides, I'll bet you smell the same, except when you come to town. I've been meaning to tell you how nice your aftershave is."

"Arran Eau de Quinine, from the Isle of Arran, in the South."

She leaned close and inhaled. "Quinine? It's—woodsy. It suits you."

A glow of pleasure spread through him. "Thanks, as long as the quinine doesn't make you think of the plague or something."

The sheep continued to crowd around, as attracted to her as he was. "Lanolin comes from the oil. These sheep are prized for their strong and supple wool."

Bonny laughed as one young ewe nudged her leg. "So petting them will make my hands soft?"

Catching the other hand, Kieran held them to his cheeks. "It's impossible for your skin to be any softer."

With a smile, she moved on toward a patch of heather, the way a bee flits from flower to flower. She seemed so comfortable with everything, so genuine in her excitement and interest. Could hope overcome sadness and open the way to a new life?

They headed back to the house at noon. Eleanor had left a simple lunch of Forfair bridies, and Kieran and Bonny sat across from each other at the big table in the farm kitchen.

"I didn't see any pictures of Bronwyn." Bonny paused in between bites of the meat pie.

He hated to admit the truth, but he had promised never to lie. "There are two snaps in my office upstairs. During the worst of my depression, I found it easier if I didn't see her face. It's no different than you editing Adam out of your photos."

"But it is different." She pushed a crumb around with her fork. "You and Bronwyn shared a good life. I refuse to allow Adam to steal more from me than he already has. The photos remind me of the important part Kari and Dan play in my life. They're my family now."

After setting the dishes in the dishwasher, they headed back to the barn, where the well-watered horses awaited. "I noticed a lot of crosses decorating the house. They don't bother you?"

He turned away, clearing his throat. "Bronwyn collected them. I haven't altered much of anything belonging to her. I guess it's ridiculous to keep them when they don't mean anything to me. When I try to change things in the house, the depression becomes worse, so I stopped trying." He turned away again. Would she accept his problem or see it as weakness?

"I suffer from something similar myself. I refer to it as 'Miss Havisham Syndrome.'" Her voice was soft with understanding.

She laid her hand on his, pulling him back with her touch.

"You mean from *Great Expectations*?"

"Exactly."

He let her precede him into the barn, marveling again at the compassion in her eyes as he had the first night. "Adam professed to believe in God. He convinced me that he was serious, too. However, his actions weren't consistent with his words. It's been hard to make myself move on. Sometimes I feel stuck in time."

"Bonny, I won't lie to you—ever. Will you trust me with your story?" He softened his voice, reaching over and tilting her face toward him with his finger under her chin. "Holding onto it allows him to keep stealing from you over and over."

She remained silent for so long, he expected her to refuse, but she sat down on a hay bale and began. "We met as undergrads and dated through his law school and my doctoral dissertation. He's ambitious, interested in politics."

Her voice quivered with emotion. Her expression looked as if she were preparing to leap off Ben Nevis. "We became engaged while my mom was having chemo for a brain tumor. She died two months later and we postponed the wedding. My dad needed me, and I needed time to grieve. Seven weeks after she died, my dad found out he had pancreatic cancer. He died six months after my mom." She wiped her eyes on her sleeve. "Our entire engagement was under the shadow of their cancer and deaths."

Bonny paused, and he offered his handkerchief. When he bent down to hand it to her, the sweet scent of her perfume filled his nostrils, in sharp contrast to the barn's tangy odor of manure.

"Adam wasn't supportive when they were dying—when I needed him the most. I excused it, convincing myself he couldn't handle being around sick people. But, the day after my dad's funeral, with the wedding invitations addressed and ready to mail, he broke our engagement. At least I learned the truth before I married him."

He sat next to her, placing one hand in the middle of her back, noting once again how small she was. His hand covered most of her back, and he softened his tone, not only because of her pain, but because of the overwhelming desire to protect her. "You're as crippled by your pain as I am."

"He dumped me for an attorney in his office." She stood, turning her back to him. Her words rushed out like flood waters on the Garry, and he sensed shame mingled with pain in the torrent. "He claimed he was a Christian, but he began dating behind my back when I was busy caring for my parents. I don't understand why he stopped loving me. I felt so worthless, as if I wasn't important enough to wait for until the difficult times passed. What was I to do? I had to care for my parents. I needed his support ..."

When Kieran stood and wrapped his arms around her, she buried her face in his chest, her hot tears wetting his shirt. He had forgotten the tender, protective sensation of comforting a weeping woman, the helpless feeling of wishing he could make things right. "Wheesht," he murmured, smoothing the shimmering silk of her hair. "Bonny, only a *dunderheid* would make you feel worthless. It reflects on him, not you. The first time we talked, I realized you were special." *And if he had married you, I would never have met you.*

"But he chose Vanessa over me, after all those years …" Her arms slid around him, making his mouth go dry and his heart beat faster. "Everyone offered advice. I was humiliated. Returning wedding gifts was a nightmare. The dress still hangs in my guest room closet." When she looked up, tears were sliding out from under her eyelids, black streaks of mascara cascading down her cheeks in their wake.

On impulse, he blotted the tears from under her eyes with his finger. It felt right to hold her, to have her seek comfort in his arms. "He was cruel, and you're not at fault. I can't imagine—the person you love continuing on with someone else. There's no need to feel ashamed."

She massaged her throat, a nervous gesture he'd noticed before. "One reason I came here was to escape, but he keeps calling. He left a message once, but I recognized his number. Kari wants me to block him. I can't …"

He pulled her close again, an instinct to shield her from more pain surging through him. "Don't allow him to harass you, Bonny. Let me block it for you. Or better yet, change your number."

Gratitude showed in her eyes when she looked up. "Thank you, but I need to take care of it myself. I refuse to let him keep a hold on me. I—I was afraid you'd think there was something wrong with me if you learned he left me for someone else."

"Never." He rubbed her back, his arms still around her. "The problem was him, not you."

Could he be certain about that? They hadn't known each other very long.

Mounting up again, they headed toward the bridge across the loch. Bonny pointed at first one thing and then another, questioning him about everything. He hadn't laughed so much in a long time.

"It's so beautiful here." Her face was glowing. "In spite of what The Clearances did to the land and the dam filling the glen, it's pristine, timeless, as if it has lain untouched forever."

"Aye, but civilization made its mark here long ago and continues to this day. In spite of the preservation and reforestation, they're preparing to build the largest hydroelectric dam in Scotland up the slopes of Meall Coire nan Saobhaidh. They'll dam the *burn*, turning a small loch on the upper slopes into a large reservoir. The powerhouse and tunnel facilities will be underground to avoid destroying the views, but the view from the top of the Beinn will change forever."

When she shook her head, a small shaft of sunshine caught the highlights in her hair. "Wow, coming from a place where reservoirs look out of place wherever they are, I can imagine why people here would find that upsetting."

"It's home, and changes in the scenery are difficult. I'm grateful so much will be underground." They headed across the bridge toward Torr na Carraidh and Greenfield.

"The woods across the loch are the result of reforestation?" She tried to see everything at once, and he imagined her head turning in circles like an owl.

From the center of the bridge, nothing obstructed their view of the loch. "Yes, with native conifers and broadleaves." Her enthusiastic response to his home increased his desire to rid his life of loneliness and share it with someone. "To the left is the Laddie Wood, one of my favorite places as a wee boy. I know it like my reflection in the mirror. Over to the southeast is Bolinn Hill, home to a group of MacDonells and Stewarts until their eviction in the late 1700s. A remnant stayed on, but by the early 1800s they headed to Glengarry County in Canada. Very little remains, though it's a popular place to hike. They're restoring an oak wood that once stood there."

She cantered ahead, waving one arm around as if taking in everything at once. "I can't wait to explore it with you, on horseback, hiking, fishing—did I tell you I used to hunt with my dad?"

"Is there anything you don't do?"

She stopped her horse and cocked her head to one side. "Hmm, I can't toss a caber."

He stifled a laugh, and in the most serious tone he could manage, said, "I'll teach you if you like."

The sound of her laughter reminded him of music, and he joined her. It felt good, happiness rather than the depression that frightened him. Perhaps it wasn't too late.

He cleared his throat and took a deep breath. "I started to say that one of these days I could take you out fishing in the boat. We can also wade the River Garry, since you fly fish."

"I already e-mailed Kari to have her send my gear. She was shipping over some clothes I wanted anyway. I'll need help, since I'm not familiar with Spey casting."

For a brief moment, he pictured himself standing in the river, his arms around her, his hands on hers, helping her master the technique. The thought was intriguing. "Your hands are too small to handle a Spey rod. The cast itself is merely a two-handed technique for a large roll cast, when there's no room to back-cast."

He hated for the day to end, but the sun was low in the sky. "We need to feed the horses and head back to town before it's too late. I'll take you to dinner."

"Race you back to the barn," Bonny shouted as she prodded Misty in the sides, taking off at a gallop.

"You can't win." He prodded Storm in the sides, passing her with no problem, halting near the barn.

A few minutes later, she rode up laughing. "I should make certain I can win before I start a race."

"Aye, and have a horse capable of winning. I expected a fine horsewoman like yourself to judge the capabilities of your mount with more accuracy."

"I only wanted to laugh and have fun. You did, didn't you?" She was out of breath. "We both need more laughter in our lives, Professor."

Then perhaps you'll decide to stay, and I won't always feel sad and alone. The unspoken words surprised him, but she was everything his heart longed for. "That we do, Professor."

CʒʘʘO

Kieran looked up from his desk at the sound of Deirdre's cheerful hello, and smiled. She was pretty enough and made it obvious she was interested in him. It made him uncomfortable, and not just because of Bonny.

"Did you pass your test?"

Her glossy red lips curved into a flirtatious smile. "A perfect score, thanks to you." She sat down and scooted the chair close to him, laying her hand on his forearm.

"I do my best. You still have to know it when it comes to the test. You've put in a lot of work. You deserve it." He reached for his algebra book. "So let's move on to the next chapter."

"That's what I hoped you'd say." She moved her chair a little closer.

"What are you talking about?" Her perfume filled the small office. Bonny had said it was Beyonce's Midnight Heat.

"I want to invite you over for dinner to thank you for all your help." The neckline of her dress was too low, especially for a woman of her generous proportions. Coupled with the cologne, he found it distracting.

"That's nice of you, but unnecessary. I get paid for tutoring."

She frowned. "I know, but you go above and beyond, Kieran. I appreciate you."

"Thank you, Deirdre, but I don't date students. Now let's begin on page 150."

She laid a well-manicured hand on his arm again, red lacquer glistening on her fingertips. "Kieran, I simply won't take no for an answer," she crooned. "I could go to another tutor, so I'm not your student. My grades might suffer some, but we could be together." Her voice had taken on a seductive tone. "Tell Dr. Bryant we're having an extra tutoring session."

"You're still a student at the college where I'm on faculty, Deirdre. I can't."

"If you change your mind, the offer stands. That rule doesn't have to apply to you and me." She leaned against his arm.

"Let's do the math. I'm here to be your tutor."

When she left an hour later, he heaved a sigh. Every week he wondered if he had said something to encourage her. He was supposed to have dinner with Bonny, so he took a deep breath and dialed her number. "How about if I take you out for dinner tonight?"

"Sure, if you want to. Any special reason?"

"No, I just thought you might have had a long day too, that's all."

CHAPTER TEN

OF TROUT AND RAINBOWS

Kieran realized he was staring with an open mouth when Bonny came through the kitchen door, dressed for fishing. "You belong on the cover of an Orvis catalog."

Her eyes were the green of his mother's antique beryl brooch, and soft clouds of mist formed in the cool, damp air every time she breathed. "I told you I had everything I need and more. Kari and Dan love fly fishing, so she knew what to send."

An olive green shirt peeked out from under an Aran wool sweater and waterproof jacket. She even made chest waders look feminine. Wearing a wide-brimmed hat of olive drab sporting a large bow, she was the most appealing fishing buddy he'd ever had. He noted with approval the wicker creel, her net, a vest with flies, and assorted paraphernalia. Once again, he thought how unique she was, so feminine he ached for the scent of her, a touch even as small as his hand on her back. Everything with Deirdre was just playing around. With Bonny it was becoming serious. But how could he reconcile his love for Bronwyn with this intense longing for the company of another woman?

He took Bonny's rod and creel, catching her free hand tight in his own. It made him feel like he could scale Ben Nevis in one giant leap. "I put a fighting butt on a regular rod. It should work like a Spey rod, but fit your hands, allowing you to play a good-sized fish for a while." He gave her the rod, her exuberant smile filling him with an odd sensation of floating down the river, weightless and without a care. "You'll learn fast. The technique is identical to a large roll cast."

She gave him a sweet smile and squeezed his fingers. "Okay, let's head for the river."

The Garry snaked its way between Loch Quoich to the West and Loch Garry, rushing and tumbling over rocks and between tree-lined banks that were lush and green. The air was pleasant and warm for autumn, and the white, fluffy clouds showed no sign of rain. He stepped in first, reaching for her hand as she came down the slippery bank.

"I haven't fished since my mom got sick. I'll need a refresher course. Will you stand behind me to help?" Her thick, auburn lashes fluttered as she met his eyes and he almost dropped the poles.

"Are you flirting with me, Dr. Bryant?"

"What do you think?"

He stepped back, feeling a rush of warmth. "Let me watch you cast."

She performed a very poor roll cast, and he felt certain she was setting him up. From the snaps he had seen, she knew how to fly fish. The thought of her teasing to entice him to put his arms around her was delightful.

He stepped up close beside her, noticing again how well she fit right under his shoulder. "I'd better help."

"Those pictures of Dad and me on the San Juan River were from before my mom's cancer. It's been three years."

He encircled her with his arms, feeling a rush of warmth as he placed his hands on hers. When she looked back at him, her face was aglow, and he had to force himself to remember they were two wounded people who needed to take their time.

"Let me place your hands in the correct position." The soft, silky curls that escaped from under her hat and blew across his face smelled of citrus. Holding her this close, fishing was the last thing on his mind.

"How's this?"

Her hands weren't positioned right at all, but playing along was too much fun. "Ach, Bonny, keep your hands shoulder-width, put the bottom hand on the butt, and the top hand at the top of the cork." Once again, he reached around her, placing his hands on hers.

She moved further back into his arms. He had never considered fishing a contact sport, but the idea was appealing. "Move your top hand up and down until it's comfortable."

They practiced holding the line against the rod with the top hand, stripping it off the reel and locking it in place with her middle fingers, and then shooting the line. After about ten minutes, he stood back with reluctance to watch her cast on her own. It was perfect.

He heard the crack of a twig breaking, and caught a flash of blue through the trees. Someone was watching them. Whoever it was had disappeared when he turned for a better look, and then Bonny was shouting.

"Whoa, Kieran, I caught one. Come help me." She was whooping as he came alongside. The air surrounding her was electric with excitement. She knew what she was doing and was good at it too. Watching her play the small trout, there was no doubt she had played a game to get his arms around her. The rush of elation was akin to winning the Highland Games.

"Oh," she squealed as there was a flash in the water and her fish disappeared. "What happened?"

He doubled over laughing, holding his sides.

"Did you see that?" Her mouth opened wide in surprise. "It took my fish. What was that?"

Kieran struggled to catch his breath. "One of the larger trout from the loch must have swum up the river. It ate your fish." He couldn't stop laughing.

"It ate it?" They waded to the bank, plopping down side by side. When one stopped laughing, the other started again, on and on until both held their sides and lay back, breathing heavily.

"You said we needed to laugh more." A curl had come loose, and he reached over, tucking it behind her ear.

"We certainly did." She giggled again. "That was so strange."

"I've fished these waters since I was a boy, and it's a first for me. The bigger browns live deep in the lochs and eat smaller fish. They grow quite large, and anglers catch them with lures from boats. They've been known to swim up the river on occasion." The joy of the shared experience made him choke up with longing. "I never expected to feel this happy ever again."

Her eyes connected with his.

"I feel it too." Her voice was soft as a whisper as she looked away, fiddling with the scissors hooked to her vest. She stood and walked over to where her rod lay on the grass. It seemed as if every time he got too close, she made a move to avoid deeper intimacy. There was a small ache near his heart as he watched her step back into the water. He could strangle Adam for wounding her so deeply.

"Come on, I want trout for dinner." She motioned him toward the water.

He had to move with care. His loneliness made him eager, but she needed time.

As they fished their way down the river, he turned back to check her progress, nodding with approval. "I must be an excellent teacher. You've mastered it."

"You are, if my full creel is any evidence."

He needed to spend more time with her. "Let's clean our catch, and we'll have a lovely dinner by candlelight."

Bonny reeled in her line with a smile that made him feel dizzy. "Candlelight, fresh fish, and you? Let's go."

As fast as she had moved away, she came closer again.

ଔଠ

"Come see this." Kieran and Bonny stood atop Grant Tower at Urquhart Castle, overlooking Loch Ness. For her, it was a place of poignant memories. He pointed to a rainbow arching from one side of the loch to the other as she moved into the crook of his arm. "Now, down there."

She stood on tiptoe and looked to where he pointed, at the base of the tower.

"Step onto that ledge and I'll steady you."

The warmth of his hands around her waist contrasted with the chill wind. She shivered and leaned close enough to hear the stubble on his chin scratching against her raincoat. "The rainbow enters the water at the foot of the tower. Another fifty feet, and it would form a complete circle. Amazing."

His arms tightened around her. "No more so than the woman in my arms."

She kept silent. Did he feel it? What could be more romantic than a rainbow all their own?

"No one else sees it."

His warm breath tickled her ear, and she leaned against him, wrapped in a sense of wonder and delight. No one even wrote things this perfect. "Just we two."

Kieran bent over her, his lips touching hers, tentative and searching. She leaned into his arms, her heart leaping in her chest as she allowed her lips to reveal her readiness to move forward. The scent of him was becoming so familiar. The taste of him was even sweeter.

He moved one hand to the back of her head, tangling his fingers in her hair. "I've wanted to kiss you since the first night we talked."

She traced his lower lip with her finger. "Mmm, my gallant Highlander."

"My bonnie lass." His voice was barely above a whisper, and a little hoarse. He smiled and smoothed the damp curls away from her face with a big, callused finger, his touch as tender as his kiss.

She cupped his cheek in her hand. Somehow she had to let him know she was ready for a relationship. "The day I arrived, I stopped up there in the parking lot and cried. The ruins seemed to symbolize the wreck of my life. I never imagined how fast it could change."

His reply was to pull her to him again, and she turned her face up to his in eagerness. It began as soft as the mist surrounding them, but as the rain intensified, so did his kiss, neither caring if they got soaked to the skin.

The rain lessened as they descended the tower steps. By the time they reached the Land Rover, the sun was shining enough for a picnic lunch. In between bites, Kieran asked, "Did Deirdre ever finish that paper?"

"She got angry and said she expected me to handle the class with a more open mind. According to her, the entire faculty is a bunch of bigots lacking in understanding and tolerance."

His hair and eyebrows burnished gold in the sun, making his eyes a more brilliant blue. "Judgmental people frequently accuse those they disagree with of being more judgmental than themselves."

"She refused to rewrite it or discuss why it failed to meet the requirements of the assignment. I gave her the points for historical references, lowering her grade from pass to third class honors, and handed it back." Bonny longed to smooth the tangled mess of curls at the back of his neck, but she lacked the courage, in spite of the closeness developing between them.

He frowned, his eyes narrowing. "Is she rude in class?"

"She sits in the back with a surly expression, but says very little. It will be interesting to see what she does for the final paper about America's influence in the twenty-first century. Her test grades are excellent, so unless she blows her final paper, she'll pass."

Frowning, he stroked the back of her hand. "Bonny, I don't want you to talk to her alone again. If she confronts you somewhere, say you need to do something in administration, head to where there are people."

As he gripped her hand hard, his eyes changed to a steely-blue. After Adam's self-centeredness, she found his protective nature endearing. "You think she's dangerous?"

The hair at the back of his neck reminded her of a bush turned reddish-gold for autumn. He twisted his fingers through it, and frowned. "I can't say, but don't risk it. She tried to get me to have dinner with her when she came for her tutoring session the other day. She wasn't happy when I refused, and wanted me to lie to you about it. Protect yourself."

"I promise I will." The impulse to smooth his hair was too difficult to resist. The thick curls felt soft and springy. He turned red from the neck up, and then caught her hand, pressing his lips to the back of it, his eyes crinkling into a smile.

CRO

Bonny answered the phone with an eager "Hello," without looking at the caller ID. Kieran often called around eight on nights he wasn't in town.

"Finally you answered, I was afraid you never would."

Adam. She sat straight up on the edge of her chair, every muscle in her body tensing as she felt a familiar quickening of her pulse. "I didn't look before I answered, or I wouldn't have. But now I can have the pleasure of hanging up on you."

"Bonny, please?"

Begging, that was a tactic he hadn't tried before. "Give me a reason why I should listen to anything you have to say."

"Because I love you and want you back in my life."

"No. I'm over you. Now hang up and never call me again." She turned the phone off and threw it to the other end of the couch.

There would be no more grading papers tonight. In spite of her curt answer, the familiar sound of Adam's voice evoked emotions she didn't anticipate. His betrayal had changed her life even more than her parents' deaths. If not for that, she never would have met Kieran. Why did a thrill of excitement run through her when he said he loved her? She was over him—wasn't she?

CHAPTER ELEVEN

DIFFERENCES

The pleasant, sunny weather at Loch Lomond and the picturesque town of Luss made for a romantic day. Multi-colored leaves of red, orange, and yellow shone as bright as summer flowers in the cooling autumn air. Bonny and Kieran hiked up a hill through the peaceful woods, along a path by a quiet, clear stream, where the beauty of the loch spread out before them. They meandered through the streets of small shops and stone houses, laughing and reveling in each other's company.

Later, in a borrowed boat, they floated in silence among the small islands dotting Loch Lomond. He sang her the plaintive ballad as if it were a love song, in a hushed, deep baritone. "By yon bonnie banks and by yon bonnie braes, where the sun shines bright on Loch Lomon', where me and my true love were ever wont to gae, on the bonnie, bonnie banks o' Loch Lomon.'"

They drove home after dark, holding hands across the console of the Land Rover. Bonny squeezed his hand, endeavoring to glimpse his expression in the dim light of the car's display. "Kieran, come to church with me tomorrow?"

"You weren't going to pressure me." He withdrew his hand and put it on the steering wheel.

"I didn't mean to, but I enjoy sharing things with you." She regretted it at once, sensing a shadow fall over their perfect day. This was such a magical time of discovery. They were breaking free of the cocoons holding them captive and learning to trust the calling of their hearts. They were testing their wings, hoping to soar again.

With a pang, she realized something of the utmost importance was missing, and a sense of panic arose, along with a memory of Adam, refusing things that were important to her. She would not ruin this. "I'm sorry."

They drove the rest of the way in silence. Kieran walked her to the door and put his arms around her, whispering into her hair, as soft as a kiss. "It's as if I've been struggling through a long nightmare, and awakened to the lovely sunshine in your eyes. Our similarities are more than our differences. We mustn't allow this to come between us."

The warmth of his embrace eased the sense of fear gnawing at her insides. If he was falling in love with her, she was not going to mess it up. "It's fine, really. How about lunch instead?"

⋐⋑

Kieran was waiting when Bonny got home after church. They ate sandwiches and soup before driving out to Glen Nevis for a hike. "In the middle of church I found myself longing for the warmth of your arm around me." If only she could take it back. She had promised not to do this, even if it was the truth.

He crossed the room and set his plate down on the kitchen counter with a clatter. "You may miss feeling close to God, but I don't."

"Will you at least come when I sing my first solo? Seeing you in the audience will encourage me." Bonny set the plates in the dishwasher and closed it too hard.

His eyes sparked with blue fire. "Ach, I'm there for you when you need me, but you understand my feelings."

She knew how to be demanding too. "No wonder they say Scots are stubborn. It's my first solo here, and you attend Dr. Cameron's church sometimes."

"Only to keep him satisfied. Coming to hear you isn't the problem. We agreed on matters of faith, but if you change, I'm afraid it will ruin everything." He walked into the other room.

She called after him. "I didn't say I believe everything, but faculty members belong in church, and I love to sing. I wasn't asking you to commit yourself. I understand it's difficult."

When she carried in the tea, his *crabbit* mood had vanished. The new word she had learned was very appropriate.

"Bonny, do you keep a journal?"

"Why?" The abrupt change caught her off guard.

He slumped in one of the chairs by the fireplace, his hands gripping the arms. "You have so much passion. History and Lit professors mull things over, and they often write. I want to know everything—to see into your heart and mind." He accepted the cup of tea she offered, his eyes roving toward the sticky toffee pudding.

"And if it's not what you expect?" She felt taken aback and embarrassed.

"It will be."

She was at a loss, trying to decipher the expression in his eyes, but it made her stomach flip-flop in expectation.

"It's more of a notebook." She served him a large piece of the pudding. "I write volumes and volumes, the feelings I can't share with anyone. It's therapeutic. I've written poetry too, but I don't claim it as mine alone."

He set the teacup down, his eyes forming question marks. "I don't understand. If you wrote it, it's yours. What do you write about?"

"God and my feelings—I can't explain it. Words rush into my head, and I'm compelled to write them down." She watched him inhale a forkful of the pudding. "At the time, it felt as if God was comforting me. A poem sometimes popped into my mind, and I was compelled to stop what I was doing and put it down on paper. When I finished, they came out within a word or two of their final form. It was uncanny, but they're the best I ever wrote. I still journal sometimes, but I haven't written poetry since ..."

"Can I read them?" He held his fork in mid-air, his eyes and voice bright with anticipation.

"I—I guess. I don't know what you'll think." She headed for the bedroom.

"I'm sorry. It's too personal a request. I'm no literary critic. I just want to understand you better." He put the bite he held on his fork into his mouth, closing his eyes in delight. "Mmm, is this recipe from Agnes?"

"Yes, Janet gave me her mom's recipe." She went to the bedroom and rummaged through a box in the back of the closet. She took a moment to compose herself before she walked out, hugging the notebook. "Letting you read them is a big step. I've kept personal feelings to myself for a long time."

"You don't have to let me if you'd rather not." He apologized. "It's okay if you feel they're too personal."

"No, I want you to."

◌౩౪◌

Kieran propped himself up in bed, reading late into the night. There weren't many poems in Bonny's notebook, but the depth of emotion and clear articulation of feelings astonished him. It was no exaggeration. God spoke through her pen. They spoke to him also. He brushed damp droplets from the neat pages as he recognized issues he had struggled with for two years. Overwhelmed by the dimension of her personality, and variety of her gifts, one thing became clear—he wanted Bonny Bryant for his own.

When they went hiking in Glen Coe on Saturday, she asked, "Have you read my poems?"

How do I explain they haunt me? "More than once, and each time I see the lovely woman who wrote them more clearly. The one you named 'My Refuge' draws me again and again. I can't identify with the faith, but I can with the pain. I can't imagine how you believed with your heart torn in two."

Bonny's eyes widened, and her jaw tightened. "Before my dad died, my beliefs were stronger. He was such an example and encourager. After I lost him, then Adam ..." She paused, her long lashes shadowing her cheeks. "No one has ever read them before. It's humbling to discover something so personal can speak to someone else. My heart was speaking, and perhaps my spirit."

"Would you read my favorite out loud to me? I want to hear it in your own voice, please?"

"I'll try." When they returned to her house, he asked again, and she complied.

My Refuge

I have asked the Lord many evenings
Why my days seemed filled with pain,
I have begged and pleaded with tears on my face,
And over the years His answer came:

Land of My Dreams

"I have another path for you
Than some of my children trod;
It won't be easy; you'll not always see,
But you will learn to know your God.
I may lead you through the desert
On a road of shifting sands;
But there's joy at the end of the journey
If you never let go of My hands.
Sometimes the way may be rocky;
It will bruise and scrape and shred,
You'll feel that you can't take another step,
But My strong shoulder will cradle your head.
There are dark caves and many shadows,
But in My presence you will always be,
For the only way through the darkness
Is to take strong hold of Me.
"Yes, my child, others' paths may seem easy,
It may appear that I shield their pain;
But there's no greater joy in the sunshine
Unless first you've been through the rain.
Your Savior was made perfect through suffering,
He had a heavy Cross to bear;
I won't allow pain and struggle
Without the promise that His glory you'll share."
So if it seems you're walking in darkness,
When the enemy seems to win;
Take your refuge in the arms of Jesus,
Heavenly Savior and earthly Friend.

They sat close together in the waning light of the afternoon, their emotions stinging like raw, open wounds.

Kieran walked in darkness. Bonny offered the first light in two years.

A renewal of her faith in God changed everything, unless he pulled off a convincing imitation. Keeping her was worth doing anything.

CHAPTER TWELVE

A NIGHT TO REMEMBER

The recent tension did nothing to diminish the increasing attraction Kieran felt for Bonny. He drew an involuntary breath at the first sight of her, dressed for the Charity Ball. The soft red of her strapless, Fraser tartan gown made her skin glow, white, and soft as rose petals. Her long skirt looped up at one side to reveal yards of frothy, white tulle beneath the tartan. She was the image of a lovely Highland lass.

"Beautiful doesn't come close to describing you." The love, loneliness, and longing overwhelmed him, making it impossible to find words.

Bonny lowered her head, peeking up at him through her thick lashes. "You're rather dashing yourself. I'll have the most braw and bonnie Highlander at the Ball as my escort."

He laughed. "I'm forty years old, Bonny. My braw and bonny days are far behind me."

She turned a bashful shade of pink. "I disagree. You're the bonniest man I've ever met."

She turned for him to help her on with a hooded cloak of black velvet, his lips grazing the tempting spot at the base of her neck. "You could be a lady of old Invergarry castle."

"Thank you, milord." Bonny curtsied, and then inspected him up and down, front and back. "I find a kilt and sporran very romantic. I feel as if I went to sleep in one time and awakened in another."

He bowed, and tucking her arm through his, guided her to the car. "M' lady, your carriage waits."

Once inside the ballroom, Kieran escorted his diminutive jewel of a lady around, his giant hand covering her back, his ears attuned to whatever she said. He saw the rapture on her face at the skirl of his bagpipes when he performed with the pipe band. In a short time they had shared a deeper level of communication than he had ever experienced with anyone. Words were only a small part of it. They understood each other on a level many married couples failed to achieve.

His triumphs in the Highland Games had made him famous. Respected and congenial as he was, women had attempted to catch his eye since Bronwyn's death. His appearance at a ball he had avoided since then was creating a stir, as he anticipated. He heard the murmurs as he guided Bonny around the room, introducing her to old friends. He must convince her to stay with him. She was his one hope to escape the darkness.

CR&BO

Graeme MacDholl offered a prayer before dinner. Though not handsome, his warm brown eyes and crooked smile were welcoming and friendly.

Janet arrived unescorted and sat with Kieran, Bonny, and the university faculty. Bonny watched as Graeme stared at Janet from his place at the head table. She pointed it out to Kieran as they danced later. "They're perfect together. She's so lonely."

"Aye, that she is."

"You're such good friends, did you ever date?"

"We did, in secondary school, but there's no spark. It lasted a month. Why, are you worried about rivals?" He laughed, his straight white teeth lustrous in the dim light, his cobalt blue eyes dancing.

She felt the heat creeping up, and in a strapless dress there was no hiding it. "No, but it's easy to overlook someone close to you. She and Graeme make a perfect couple, but she insists on remaining alone."

He shook his head. "Aye, they do, but she won't change."

Moments later, he nudged her. "Perhaps they're figuring it out themselves. Look." Graeme stood next to Janet while she conversed with a group of women.

Kieran steered Bonny in their direction in time to hear the pastor say,

"Hello, Janet. Are you enjoying your evening?"

Janet turned to face him. "I am. Graeme, will you join us?" She motioned to an empty chair and turned toward the orchestra. "Oh, the Blue Danube Waltz. It's one of my favorites."

"W—would you care to dance?"

Graeme's nervous expression made Bonny smile. "I'm glad. They're both lonely."

Kieran leaned close to her ear. "I believe the Bible when it says man shouldn't be alone."

C800

Halfway through the evening, Kieran excused himself. Bonny watched him approach the director of the orchestra, and whisper something. Her heart quickened, expecting him to request a special dance. Instead, he retrieved her cloak and led her out for a stroll on the grounds of Inverlochy Castle.

Queen Victoria had said that the castle, built in 1863, was a lovely and romantic place, and Bonny agreed. Though the thirteenth century castle lay in ruins, the impressive home built nearby, now a hotel, was romantic and picturesque. She was Cinderella dancing with her prince, a prince in the guise of a rugged and handsome Highland sheep farmer.

Torchlight played across his face, creating highlights of bronze in his hair. The damp air was heavy with the scent of late roses. Her life had become a romantic novel, and she waited to see what adventure the next page contained.

As they approached the garden, right outside the windows nearest the orchestra, he paused. "I don't need to ask if you're enjoying yourself. I see it in the glow in your cheeks and the light in your eyes. You're radiant."

The strength of his arms and the deep, accented tone of his voice caused her heart to beat faster as he drew her close in a firm embrace, which came close to lifting her off her feet. "You've brought me back to life. Bonny—I'm in love with you."

His eyes searched hers, and she breathed deep, taking in the fresh night air. Unable to raise her voice above a whisper, she said, "I love you too, Kieran."

As if on cue, the orchestra began to play.

"There is no more romantic waltz than 'The Rosebud of Allenvale.'" He rested his forehead against hers, his arms enfolding her, warm and strong. "When I first saw you tonight, your shoulders reminded me of a rose petal, so creamy and soft. May I have this dance?"

She managed to mouth "yes," before he captured her lips, communicating a sweet urgency she had no wish to deny. The taste of his kiss and the scent of his cologne created fanciful thoughts of what it might be like to spend her life in the security of his arms.

As they began to waltz in the play of the torchlight, he whispered, "*Tha gaol agam ort*. It's the Gaelic for 'I love you,' and I do love you, my bonnie lass."

"I love you too, Kieran."

Any hesitation between them disappeared when they returned to the ballroom. They danced every dance, whispering words for each other alone.

When they reached her house after the ball, he stepped inside out of the cold. One lamp glowed in the darkness, leaving them wrapped in the dream-like haze of newly confessed love.

"Since your grandmother was a Fraser, you should know our clans fought each other at one time." His eyes glimmered with mischief. "A hint of friendship between us would have led to our deaths."

"When?" The light joking did nothing to change the mood of the evening. His voice and his touch were the only sensations penetrating the aura surrounding her, enveloping her in a thick cloak of romance and dreams.

"The Battle of Shirts took place in 1544 between the MacDonells of Glengarry and Clan Fraser at Loch Lochy. An ancestor of mine, Ranald Gallda, was in line for clan chief, and the Frasers became involved when Ranald married a girl from Clan Fraser …"

"Oh, so there's a history of romance between our clans." She felt giddy and light as air. He loved her.

"Aye, lass, are you sayin' it's in our blood then, to fall in love?" His eyes danced with fun, his accent strong, and his eyes ardent with emotion in the dim light.

"Maybe." She raised her lips to his, full of exhilarating, all-encompassing, new love. "I'll see you tomorrow for our hike, *oidhche mhath*."

"Excellent, you're learning. *Beannachd leit*, my Bonny. *Tha gaol agam ort*."

"I love you." She leaned against the door after he left, overwhelmed by the gift she had been given.

CR80

Bonny looked up when someone knocked at her office door. It stood open, and Uncle Dùghlas stepped in.

"I need to talk you, my dear. Do you mind if I close the door?"

She nodded, sliding the papers she was working on over to one side. "Is something wrong? I've never seen you in the office wing before." He sat down, the chair squeaking as he scooted closer to the desk. "I wanted to talk to you, and when I saw your car outside, I thought I would come in."

"Is Aunt Mairi doing all right? She looked beautiful at the ball last night."

"She's fine. It's Kieran I wanted to speak with you about." He stuck a finger behind his tie, loosening it a little.

"Kieran? Why?"

"Bonny, he is a great math professor, and I consider him a friend. However, he leaves something to be desired where his walk with the Lord is concerned." His voice was kind and concerned, fatherly, and it almost brought tears to her eyes.

"He's struggling. I have had struggles of my own." How much could she say without getting reprimanded for not being truthful?

"Did you think I wouldn't notice? I thought it best to give you some time. Your pain is still so fresh, and your father would want me to be gentle with you." He took out his handkerchief and blew his nose.

"You knew?" She sat back in her chair, waiting to see what he would say.

"Your father told me he thought you were struggling with your faith the last time we spoke. I would have known the night you had dinner with us, even if he had said nothing."

"You never said …"

"You needed time. I'm pleased you're going to church with Janet. Graeme is a good pastor. You were raised in the truth, Bonny. Your parents taught you well. You'll come back to it, given time. Just be careful. Guard your heart well." He leaned forward, his voice serious and low.

"I love him, Uncle Dùghlas, and he loves me. We've discussed this. I believe he will change in time."

He reached across the desk to pat her hand, then pushed back his chair and stood to go. "You can talk to Mairi or me, dear. Go slowly."

Bonny stood and walked around the desk. "Thank you. You're a good friend, a good uncle. My father knew you would be. I'm so glad I came here. I promise I'll go slow."

"True love never asks us to compromise, Bonny. It makes us better than we were alone. Take your time." He walked out and closed the door behind him.

⋘⋙

As she removed the mail from her box when she got home, Bonny paused to examine a plain white envelope. Her address was typed, but it had no return, and bore an Albuquerque postmark. Communication with friends and colleagues took place via email. The one page missive within was also typed. The one word greeting read, *Bonny.*

With the first sentence, her throat began to tighten and her heart to race. *I don't blame you for hanging up on me …* Adam. Had she realized it came from him, she would have thrown it away unopened. She tossed it into the trash.

The next day, she was cleaning off her desk at home. When she dumped some old notes into the trash, she caught a glimpse of the red, white, and blue American flag on the stamp, where the envelope stood up on edge, peeking out of the trash as if to taunt her. She continued on, straightening and dusting, but the thought of the letter kept nagging at her. She turned on some Mozart as she continued dusting, hoping the music would distract her. By the time she finished cleaning out the refrigerator and put in a load of laundry, it became apparent she would have no peace until she knew what he had to say.

Retrieving the envelope, she leaned back against the plush pillows on the couch, holding it with her eyes closed, remembering. Adam's face haunted her dreams at night. But the attraction she felt for Kieran was far more than she had ever felt for Adam. Even before declaring their love, it had felt as if her heart and Kieran's beat as one, more like magnets than the polar opposites she and Adam had been.

Drawing the letter from the envelope, she slowly unfolded it. Adam's cursive scribbles, so different from Kieran's precise, mathematician's hand, created even more of a distinction between them.

The first sentence startled her and she found it necessary to read it again. Adam Lawson asking forgiveness was a first. *I broke things off with Vanessa after hearing you moved to Scotland. I will do anything to show I am worthy of your forgiveness and love. It is impossible for me to love anyone but you.*

She held the answer to her prayers in her hand, but instead of the joy she might once have felt, she found herself irritated and angry. Pulse pounding, and stomach churning, she read, *If you can offer me any hope, I will get on a plane to Scotland. God is in control of my life, and nothing will threaten my feelings for you again. Please, call. I love you still and forever.*

The autumn air carried a chill, and a fire burned in the fireplace. Bonny crossed the room and threw the letter in, watching as the flames consumed it. She now knew how true love felt. *How dare he attempt to rekindle what he so cold-heartedly destroyed? Tha gaol agam ort, my Kieran.*

CHAPTER THIRTEEN

FAITH AND EMOTIONS

Do you ever get nervous?"

Kieran and Bonny ambled down the trail leading from her house to Loch Linnhe, the day before her solo at church. A slight mizzle hung in the air, a fine day by Scottish standards. The gray waters of the loch churned and white-capped in the wind, matching the blustery mood she had been in since Adam's letter. *If Kieran had changed his mind about coming to hear her solo, why didn't he say so?*

"Of course. I've sung solos in church and at school since I was five, but I'm still nervous."

He caught her hand in his. "You'll be perfect, as in everything else." Pulling her close, he kissed the top of her head and continued down the trail.

"You haven't changed your mind?" She turned and looked into his eyes, demanding they meet her own.

"Bonny ..."

"You'll attend Dr. Cameron's church to please him, but pleasing me doesn't matter? Does one morning make such a difference?" She didn't care if her frustration showed.

"First it will be for your solo, then the Christmas program. If you want it, fine. Don't try to change me." His voice rose in volume.

"Kieran, it's the first thing I've ever asked of you." She raised her voice also.

"Can't I get away with listening to you practice?" He didn't even try to mask his exasperation. "I won't go with you every week." When she remained silent, he shook his head and said, "Just once."

She smiled up at him. "Remember when you told me how much it meant to see Janet or your mom in the crowd at the Highland Games? I want to see you out there when I sing. How can we have a healthy relationship if we can't share our faith?"

"So now you believe in a caring, personal God?" He dropped her hand, his reply laced with sarcasm, his eyes boring into her.

She pulled herself up to her full height. "I find Graeme's sermons convincing. They remind me of truths I have ignored for too long."

"Two years, Bonny. Two years of pain and questions without answers." His face flushed with anger, and he turned away. "I'll come for your solo. Don't expect anything else."

"What matters more, Kieran, your past or your future?" She held her voice steady. "I choose the future."

"Bonny, my darlin' lass." His broad shoulders sagged as he turned, pulling her into his arms, holding her close. His lips touched her forehead, wooing her, his voice softening, and the rolled r's became more pronounced. "What're you doin' to my settled life? I hate arguin' with you."

Neither spoke on the way back to her house. When she unlocked the door, she felt his uncertainty. "I need to think. Do you mind if I don't stay for dinner?"

Standing on tiptoe, she pulled him down, planting a kiss on his cheek. "If it will help, go ahead."

CR&

When she heard bagpipes from the cemetery, Bonny recognized his attempt to settle his doubts. Janet came to help her practice her solo, and they prayed for Kieran's peace.

"I tried to bring you together at first, but I didn't realize how deep his anger at God went." Janet frowned. "You're letting your heart lead you. Why spend your life second to a dead love?"

Bonny hung her head in silence. This was getting a little old. Uncle Dùghlas had been fatherly, but she didn't expect such criticism from a friend. Janet spoke the truth, but she imagined his arms around her, the warmth of his breath soft on her cheek as he whispered the Gaelic endearment she found so sweet. "More than anything on earth I want to marry Kieran MacDonell. I know what he feels. He will change."

Janet's eyes searched hers, narrowing in suspicion. "Has he proposed to you?"

"No, but he's the man I've searched for. How can I give him up? He believes in God the Creator. He agreed to come hear my solo …"

"Bonny, disagreements where faith is concerned destroy marriages every day." Janet's terse statement reminded her of a mother warning her child. "Promise me you'll pray and take your time. See how he reacts. Talk to Graeme, please?"

"Yes." Bonny nodded, images of Kieran filling her with longing. He was her soul mate, his love—a gift.

ೞ

Kieran entered the church as the service began and took a seat next to Agnes. Bonny was already on the stage, the sun shining through a window, highlighting her glossy red hair. The halo effect in burnished gold caused him to draw an involuntary breath. They had seen each other in passing but shared no conversation over the past four days. The separation was his own doing, and he regretted it.

As she began to sing, tears flowed down his cheeks. She had the voice of an angel. "Be Thou My Vision" was an ancient Gaelic hymn, and Bronwyn's favorite. The last line, sung in Bonny's lilting soprano, stung his conscience. "Heart of my own heart whatever befall, still be my vision, O Ruler of all."

When she came off the stage and claimed the empty seat next to him, he put his arm around her, pulling her close. When they were alone he would apologize and tell her how her voice had touched him.

The church atmosphere wasn't as uncomfortable as he expected. He liked Graeme, but a battle raged within him. He didn't understand why God had abandoned him. These people must have experienced loss and heartache, but He hadn't left them alone. When they reached Bonny's house, he put his arms around her and cried. She held him—waiting. "I've struggled since you started attending church. I don't want anything to steal you away from me. As

I listened to you sing, I realized what a gift you are, but I still can't believe the way I used to."

The issue placed an almost tangible barrier between them. Their future depended on him coming to terms with his past.

CR&O

With myriad emotions roiling inside, Bonny refused to answer the phone when she recognized Adam's number. The words of his apology kept coming back to her since Kieran's struggle over the matter of church.

Her hands shook as she dialed, grateful to hear the voice on the other end. "Kari, why does he keep bothering me?"

"Because he can't stand to lose."

Kari's concern was obvious, and her own voice had a shaky quality. "I stood and watched his letter burn in the fireplace. He has to realize I can't welcome him back into my life after what he did. I'm doing fine without him. His superior attitude always made me feel worthless. It grew worse after his rejection."

"Why haven't you blocked his number?" It must sound simple to Kari. She and Dan had known they belonged together since the ninth grade. She had no way of knowing how painful this was.

"It's harder than you think, but how did he get my address? Why does he torment me this way after what he did? And he expects me to take him back? I matter to Kieran." *Do I really matter? The solo didn't. Is doubt about Kieran why I can't block Adam, or do I still ... Am I angry, sad, or both?*

"You never said you felt worthless around Adam. Why didn't you say something sooner?" Kari said. "Bonny, the church secretary asked for your address. I never thought of Adam wanting it."

"I didn't realize it until he was gone. Then I was so ashamed. I should never have let my self-worth be tied to Adam Lawson. I can see my life with a new perspective from here." She hesitated. "I have new friends at work and church, and an amazing new man in my life."

"How are you and Kieran doing?" Kari's tone was wary.

Bonny was thankful she hadn't told Kari about Kieran's doubts. "We walk three times a week. At least three nights a week we eat dinner together, and on weekends he takes me sightseeing or riding at his farm. Our fly-fishing experience was fun. We enjoy being together."

"You know what I mean." Kari didn't attempt to hide her irritation.

Bonny imagined how Kari's students must feel when caught doing something they shouldn't. "We're in love. If you met him, you'd understand my feelings."

"You would stay in Scotland?" It sounded like more of an accusation than a question.

Bonny wished she hadn't called. "I don't know. I feel so right when we're together. We're two wounded people getting to know each other. He understands and cares in a way Adam never could. It's too early to discuss marriage."

Following a protracted silence, Kari said, "Bonny, you were engaged before your dad died, but he asked Dan to watch over you. Doesn't it seem odd that he would ask your best friend to watch over you rather than your fiancé?"

Bonny exhaled hard. Her dad had not been pleased that Adam only came to see him once in the hospital.

Kari continued. "Think hard before you transplant yourself to Scotland for the rest of your life."

"Don't worry, Mother Kari." Bonny regretted her sarcasm, but constant criticism grew tiring. Kari's remark about her dad left her feeling stunned. *Why wasn't she happy for her?*

"Go slow, please."

"I will." Bonny hadn't felt so chastised since her teen years.

"Bye, I love you."

"I love you, too. Give Dan my love."

"I will."

Bonny remained seated as the light faded. Things were complicated—Kieran's lack of faith, her growing desire for faith, the long distance between Scotland, and home. Adam was handsome, charming, successful, ambitious, but she wasn't certain anymore why she had loved him. It seemed like something she should know.

CR&O

When she didn't see Kieran at school, Bonny checked in the office and discovered he had requested a substitute. His battle was with himself. For the first time in a long time, she prayed, asking God to help him overcome the turmoil in his heart.

Around eight o'clock on the evening of the third day, she heard a tentative knock at her door. Through the peephole, she saw Kieran with a bouquet of yellow roses and her notebook of poems.

She opened the door, letting him in out of the cold. He was unshaven, his curls sticking out in a burning bush. His shirt was rumpled, and his eyes rimmed in red.

"These are for you." His voice sounded strained as the tired eyes met hers. "I—I needed time alone, but there's no excuse for failing to tell you where I was. Your singing touched me in a way I can't describe and your poems also."

His pain tore at her heart. She accepted the roses, burying her nose in them. "They're lovely, but you don't need to apologize, I understand. Would you like some tea? I have a fresh pot, ready to pour."

He followed her into the kitchen, where she put the roses in a vase, and he helped her carry the tea. When they sat down in the living room, he heaved a ragged breath and began. "I owe you a deep apology. I was selfish in everything I said and did from the time you invited me to hear you sing. I care too much to hurt you."

She started to speak, but he put his finger to her lips. "I spent the last four days alone in an old bothy, a shepherd's cottage on the farm, reading your poems over and over. I can't forgive God for Bronwyn's death, but neither can I deny my love for you. At first we agreed on our lack of faith in an impersonal, uncaring God, and now—ach, I can't lose you, lass. I don't merely love you, I need you."

Bonny's heart leaped, but she remained silent.

"The sight of you on stage, with the light shining down on your hair—that hymn was Bronwyn's favorite. Bonny, God isn't the Lord of my life. Perhaps He never was. If my faith slipped away so easily, maybe it wasn't real. Can you be patient with me?"

"You don't owe me an apology."

"Wait and hear me out, please? I appreciated the sermon. But I can't change overnight. If you'd prefer to break it off now, I understand."

Bonny laid her hand on his wet, unshaven cheek. "Oh, Kieran, don't you understand? I'm so familiar with your struggle. I'm the one person best suited to stand beside you now. Please, don't shut me out?"

The sole sound was the ticking of the grandfather clock. He slid to his knees, putting his face closer to the level of hers. Grasping her by the shoulders, his eyes peered into her soul. "If you're willing to walk this road with me, I accept. Nothing can change my feelings. I love you."

"I love you, Kieran. We both need an understanding friend. If you aren't ready for more than ..."

"Ach, lass, it's so very much more than friendship." The expression in his eyes sent a tingling sensation through her as he reached for her hand. "I'll go to church, and I'll sing in the Christmas program. I can't promise anything else right now."

She cupped his face in her hands. "It's enough."

ଓଽ

"You're kidding me. Gaelic must be the most confusing language there is. It's nowhere close to anything I've ever heard in my life." Bonny felt her frustration mounting after only one lesson in the Scottish Gaelic Kieran asked her to learn for their duet of "Silent Night."

"Give it another try. I've spoken it since I was a wee laddie." Kieran pointed to the words with his pencil.

He helped her syllable by syllable. It meant hours with the man she loved, well worth the difficulty of convincing him to audition. He loved to sing, and singing with her proved to be the potent persuader she hoped.

"Scottish Gaelic is unique," he explained. "It flows together without breaks between words or sentences, unlike English."

"There are sounds the American tongue just can't be trained to make." She gave it her best shot, but the lessons ended with hilarious laughter at her pronunciation.

Her heart swelled to hear his deep baritone singing of the birth of the Christ Child, "*Sàmhach an oidhch', naomha an oidhch.*" Once he made up his mind to participate, he had definite opinions on how to do it. He recorded it so she could hear the correct pronunciation. When she grew comfortable with the words, they added the harp accompaniment, creating an ethereal quality.

He left her at her door after choir practice, tilting her face up to his. "Singing together is an intimate experience, *mo gràdh*. I feel very close to you when I hear how our voices blend."

Love washed over her from deep blue eyes, an ocean tide, threatening to sweep her away. The melding of their voices made it difficult to remember he lent his voice alone. His heart was still full of anger toward God.

CHAPTER FOURTEEN

ANYTHING BUT THAT

The Afghani wind whipped the tent flaps hard, howling and sending sand sifting through the fabric. Dan sat on his bunk in their temporary headquarters, using a notebook for a desk as he attempted to compose a letter to Kari. Out here, in the open, they were so vulnerable. In preparation for launching a new offensive, the squadrons were traveling by Humvee to a different base. He hated traveling in this enemy-infested country. The desert swarmed with rebels and their improvised explosive devices, known as IEDs.

He stared at Kari's photograph on the trunk next to his cot. Once he made it home, she would be his forever. He prayed to God to keep him safe.

Becoming a Marine was Dan's childhood dream. Born the son and grandson of Marines, "Semper Fidelis" was more than a motto. His father and grandfather emphasized love of country, respect for his leaders, being faithful to do what he promised, and to give his absolute best. He believed in a loving, all-controlling God, who was present everywhere. He clung to God when fear overwhelmed him, sharing his faith with his men and encouraging them.

A young corporal stuck his head through the tent flap. "Major, the Colonel wants you on the phone in the command tent."

"Thank you, Corporal. Has the mail come yet?"

"No sir." He needed to finish the letter to Kari. Writing reassuring words to her might settle his inner thoughts.

CӠЮ

At daylight, Dan, his buddy Jeff, and the others climbed into their Humvees with an armed escort, and headed out. Half an hour later, they passed a WWII

Jeep full of locals. When they got about one hundred yards further down the road, everything exploded.

Men began yelling and the searing heat of fire grew closer. Dan struggled to surge into action. "Jeff," he yelled. "Jeff, where are you?" The heat drew closer while he lay trapped in a twisted tangle of hot metal. Everything turned black, and with the heat on his back and legs, he didn't need sight to know it was creeping closer.

"Jeff, where are you?" No answer. *Stay calm, Dan.* He shouted names and heard cries from outside, but didn't understand the words. *Lord, please, don't let me burn to death. Anything but that ..."*

CB&ED

Bonny stepped out of the shower to hear the phone ringing. "Bonny, thank God you're there. Dan's injured, he's burned ..."

"Oh, Kari, no. How bad is he?" Her heart fell to the pit of her stomach.

"It's bad." Kari's voice quaked with fear.

Bonny had experienced death and loss. Healing wasn't in her realm of experience. Her losses destroyed any hope of help. Dan was her best friend, a brother in all but blood. She willed herself to stay calm. "What happened?"

"His Humvee hit a roadside bomb. Burns, Bonny, my poor Dan. Oh, there's another call ..." The line went silent.

She dropped to her knees, praying as she hadn't done in years. At that moment, a wall came down, and she knew God heard her. She hadn't made a connection with Him in such a long time. It felt so right. She was still praying when the phone interrupted her.

There was real panic in Kari's voice now. "They hit a roadside bomb and the gas tank on the Humvee exploded. Dan's the single survivor. Guys from the other vehicle pulled him out. His buddies, closer than brothers—they're all dead. He's in critical condition with third degree burns over forty percent of his body and down into his windpipe. His eyes were damaged, but they don't know how badly yet. They're air-lifting him to Germany."

"Kari, he's alive." Bonny struggled to keep her voice from betraying her rising alarm. *Lord, I can't lose him, too.*

"His back, legs, and face. He must be in such pain." The heartbreak in Kari's voice made the miles between them unbearable.

Bonny's mind searched for scriptures, memories from long ago, and pieces from Pastor MacDholl's sermons. "Remember, Kari, the Holy Spirit prays for us with groans words can't express. He knows what Dan needs right now. How long will they keep him in Germany?"

"From Landstuhl they'll transfer him to Brooke Army Medical Center in San Antonio. He'll arrive there tomorrow evening. His dad's arranging for plane tickets. Bonny, what if …" she broke off, crying.

"Don't, I can't stand it." Bonny began sobbing, also. "He's alive. People can survive burns. Gather everything encouraging you can think of, your Bible, journal, favorite devotional books, and novels to help you relax. They'll help you through the difficult days and sleepless nights."

"Okay, I will, and Bonny, thanks. I know it's scary for you too. I wish you were here."

"If you need me I'll come, Kari. I love him too. I'm praying." For the first time in a long time, she found the promise easy. She knew God heard her.

"Thank you. I'll phone again when I know something. Will you ask people there to pray also?"

"Yes, there's a prayer chain at the church, and at school. I'll take care of it right away. I love you." Bonny prayed again and then notified the prayer chains. The words she shared with Kari warmed her cold heart the way warm winds thaw ice in the spring, and there, in place of her fear, was God. For the first time in a long time she didn't feel alone, and it had nothing to do with a person.

"Thou preparest a table before me in the presence of mine enemies," she whispered. "Take my fears, God."

She needed Kieran. The emotions she held in tumbled out the second she heard his voice on the phone. "When I hung up, I fell to my knees and prayed. For the first time since my dad got sick, I felt God's presence, Kieran. I moved away, He didn't, and now I've moved closer again."

The silence lasted so long she thought the connection was bad. "Kieran?"

"I'm so sorry about Dan, Bonny." She heard his sincerity. "What do you need?"

"Pray I don't fall apart. I have to teach. I can't cry."

"He's receiving the best of care." His words were soothing, but his voice sounded hollow, a measured tone as if holding back. "They know what they're doing in Germany. A lad from Beauly was there. Dan will be in my thoughts and so will you. My student is here. I'll see you tonight, *mo gràdh*."

"I love you too, so much." She hung up the phone, comforted by his words, but confused by the sound of his voice. For the first time, she longed for him to pray with her. A slow, creeping chill spread through her, echoes of Adam's responses when her dad was dying—a gulf opening between them. God—it began when she said she felt God. *Oh please, not Kieran, too.*

Bonny requested prayer from each of her classes. She found it too easy to slip back into the calm-on-the-surface façade she had learned to put on when her parents were ill and after Adam left. Calm on the outside, but everything on the inside was churning, turning, and crying for help.

Scotland had men fighting in Iraq and Afghanistan also. The Royal Highland Fusiliers and the Argyll and Sutherland Highlanders, nicknamed "Jocks," had recently deployed. Her students prayed and showed sympathy, lifting her spirits with their concern.

She performed her job as if everything was fine, though inside, her world was shaking. Now she carried with her the assurance of God's control, peace in the midst of the storm.

⋘⋙

Bonny ran to the car when Kieran arrived, craving his arms around her and praying for God to help him understand the change which had taken place in her heart. "I haven't heard anything more. Kari was flying with Dan's parents to San Antonio, Texas, to the military burn center. Kieran, I can't stand it if something happens to him. Poor Kari, I wanted to help, but I kept remembering when my parents died. I remembered scriptures I found helpful when my mom was sick and shared something from Pastor MacDholl's sermon last week. Then I prayed and ..."

"*Noo jist haud on.*" He wrapped his arms around her.

"What?"

"It's what my mother used to say when I was a wee laddie and speaking too fast. Slow down, lass. Your words are tumbling out as fast as water in a rushing burn." Guiding her inside, he handed her a new tissue, then brought her a glass of water and seated himself beside her on the couch. He clasped her hands between his own, the reddish-blond hairs on the back of his hands shining in the lamp light. His touch felt warm and comforting, and she inhaled his unique scent of hay, farm animals, leather, and aftershave—masculine and strong. Maybe she had imagined the coolness over the phone.

"I know being so far away is difficult." The hand he placed on her back warmed and steadied her.

"Yes." The tears began welling up again and she brushed them away.

"What will help you, *mo annsachd*?" He cupped her face in one hand, and she saw her own pain mirrored in his deep blue eyes. He understood on an emotional level, she had no doubt.

"There's only one thing—prayer."

"I'm not a hypocrite. I love you, but I won't lie." She heard it again, the hollow sound in his voice, and the corner of his mouth twitched.

"Then I'll pray, because it calms me. Do you mind?" She wasn't imagining it. The crevasse opening between them was real. He moved away from her, not much, but enough that she noticed. He bowed his head, putting his hand on her back again. It felt so warm—so reminiscent of her dad.

"Lord, I lift Dan up to you," she prayed. "Please guide the doctors to the best possible treatment. Heal him and repair his eyesight. We pray for his parents and for Kari. They're so frightened, Father. Give them courage. Give me courage also. Keep me calm and help me speak words of comfort to Kari, in Jesus' name, amen."

Solid and strong as ever, he pulled her into his arms. "Should we have dinner another time?"

"I can't be alone right now. Please?" The warmth of his hand lingered long after he removed it.

Kieran chose the quiet Crannog Restaurant on the pier. He was more quiet than usual, his words coming slow and deliberate. She knew he wanted to avoid sensitive topics, but she needed him near to distract her racing brain. "Growing up on the farm, you must have enough entertaining stories to occupy my mind."

He leaned forward in his seat, holding her hand across the table. "One time we rode our horses over to the Bolinn Hill area. Our parents forbade us to go near there. My cousin, Billy, crawled into a crevice between some stones to hide, but he fell asleep. We searched everywhere, and finally went home and confessed." His voice warmed, his taut expression relaxed, and the light came back to his eyes. "Our parents met him on the bridge as they headed for the woods. When he explained, they restricted us to pretty tight boundaries for the rest of the summer."

They drove back to her house in the midst of a story. He told her how he once let the sheep out when he forgot to close the gate leading to the road and loch. Before they realized it, the clock struck midnight again. Standing by the door, Bonny reached up, tracing his strong jawline with her finger. "Thank you for distracting me. I'll cook dinner later in the week, when I'm in a better frame of mind."

"Aye, and we'll take our hike tomorrow. *Tha gaol agam ort.*" He kissed away the wet drops on her cheeks, before brushing her lips.

"*Tha gaol agam ort,*" she whispered as he drove away. She craved the warm comfort of his arms. But even more, she desired to pray with him. *Please God, I need him so.*

CHAPTER FIFTEEN

CONFESSIONS

Janet's piercing look made Bonny uncomfortable. "Mum will be pleased her scones tempted you. Kieran said you didn't eat enough to keep a wee *cheetie* alive yesterday. Kari will call when she knows more."

They sat at the kitchen table, a fresh pot of Brodie's Edinburgh Tea between them, along with fresh-baked scones, compliments of Agnes. Janet passed the clotted cream, and Bonny smeared it on her scone.

"I can't get them off my mind. It's amazing, Janet, the barrier between God and me no longer exists. A heavy burden has lifted, and I know He's with me, as well as watching over them. I'm doing okay, considering." She popped another bite into her mouth, licking her lips.

"What does Kieran think?"

"A gulf opened between us as soon as I told him. I'll keep praying, and thank God he's still willing to attend church. I'd appreciate you praying with me though." She poured more tea for both of them.

Janet stirred milk into her tea. "Of course I will, but why the big breakthrough now? You admit tragedies pushed you in the wrong direction in the past."

"I appreciate the way Graeme explains things. Over here, removed from the past, I can allow God's word to sink into my heart in ways I refused to when anger and bitterness filled it instead." She swallowed a sip of tea and reached for another scone. "I know I'll be fine now. Your mom makes the best scones, by the way."

"You haven't wanted to discuss what precipitated your fall from faith. If it's none of my business, say so, but ..." Janet's eyes locked with her own, and Bonny realized she was foolish to hide the truth.

"You're so patient. I was too embarrassed to tell you, though what Sean did to you was worse." She stood and crossed the kitchen, reaching for the homemade apricot preserves Kari's mom sent, needing a taste of home.

As she explained how Adam had lied about Vanessa, Janet's wide-open eyes and downturned mouth displayed the understanding Bonny should have known was there all the time. "I felt ashamed. It fit into the conversation naturally with Kieran, but it still wasn't easy. Now Adam keeps trying to contact me, and I want nothing to do with him."

"You poor dear, but why now?"

"He's very controlling. Adam Lawson believes one phone call will put me on the next plane begging him to take me back." She picked up the teapot. "More?"

Janet held her cup out and reached for another scone. "I won't want anything for dinner. Those apricot preserves are delicious."

"It's girl's night, enjoy." She refilled both their cups. "Someday I want to let him have it—tell him I love someone else and see his expression. He no longer has a hold over me. He's so opposite of Kieran."

"Why did you let him control you? You seem so brave and strong." Janet set her cup down, shoving the scones away.

"He's handsome, charming, and he loves the outdoors. He wasn't so controlling until his ambition became unmanageable after law school. By then, we'd been together so long, marriage felt natural. He said I'd be a perfect wife when he was ready to pursue politics, and a perfect hostess."

Janet picked up the photos Bonny pulled out of the back of her wallet. "Aye, he's braw enough to turn any woman's head. Handsome is as handsome does, though. Has Kieran seen these?"

"No, I edited Adam out of the photos I showed him. I shouldn't still have these. In fact, I'll throw them out now." She started to tear them up, but instead tossed them in. "I refuse to let him control me now. A more tender, loving man than I ever dreamed of has taken his place."

"Slow down, lass." Janet's voice took on a warning tone as she pointed her fork at Bonny. "Your knight in shining armor is somewhat tarnished, don't you think? There's a reason I'm here praying while your best friend is fighting for his life, and Kieran's not."

Bonny carried their dishes to the sink. "He isn't tarnished. He's a strong support. He understands the feeling when someone you love is suffering and you're helpless. Listening to Graeme and singing in the Christmas program will impact him, wait and see."

Janet shook her head. "I've been with him from the day it happened. If he changed easily, we wouldn't be praying for him now. Why continue in another relationship with someone lacking the qualities you want?"

"He'll come around, Janet, faced with the right circumstances. Let's pray." She headed into the living room.

Janet put on her coat after they prayed. "Something occurred to me as we were praying. You won't thank me, though."

"You don't sound encouraging."

"Perhaps you aren't in Kieran's life to marry him. It's possible you're a catalyst to help him change." She laid her hand on Bonny's arm. "If he refuses to change, maybe it's time to move on. Don't be trapped in a relationship where you can't become everything God intends."

Bonny's heart dropped to the pit of her stomach. "I won't. See you tomorrow. Goodnight."

Janet walked out into the night. Bonny shut the door and put another log on the fire. When she turned out the kitchen light, she picked up the photos lying on top in the trash, remembering her first love. Carrying them to the bedroom, she placed them face down in the bottom of her jewelry box.

Before climbing into the big four-poster bed, she took her dad's Bible off the shelf and curled up on the couch. Thumbing through the worn pages, she stopped at her favorite passages, filling her with hunger for the word of God again.

Deuteronomy, her dad had read from chapter thirty-three to remind her where her help lay. The comforting words flooded her mind, especially where it said God was a shield, a helper, and a glorious sword. How had she forgotten?

His voice echoed in her mind. "The eternal God is your refuge, and underneath are the everlasting arms."

She longed to lay her head on his strong shoulder and feel his hands, rubbing at the knots and sore places in her neck. Just as her father had massaged her sore muscles, God's words assuaged the sore places in her mind and heart. Those earthly arms were gone, but the eternal, everlasting arms of God remained. She was right with God again, but she knew everything in her life wasn't as He wanted it to be.

Recorded in her memory, she heard her mother's voice reminding her to keep Him as the center of her life. She needed to develop her own faith, instead of relying on her parents, as in the past.

Turning to another dog-eared page, she read from chapter thirty-two, "'Take to heart all the words I have solemnly declared to you this day … They are not just idle words for you—they are your life.'"

She closed the Bible and laid it on the arm of the couch. Putting her head on the worn cover, she breathed in the familiar, leathery smell, reminiscent of her earthly father, but filled with the words of her heavenly Father. She closed her eyes and fell asleep. When she awakened, the moon shone through the open curtains, bright and full.

Janet's warnings mingled with the words of scripture, but she refused to lose hope. Kieran would change.

CB&I

The phone said, "No Caller ID." Maybe it was news about Dan.

"Hello?"

"It's me, Bon. Has someone called you about Dan?" It was Adam's voice.

"Kari called before she even knew for certain how bad he was. I blocked your number. Why are you calling?" The seething tone of her own voice shocked her. How could he miss her anger?

"I had to make certain you knew. I'm so sorry, for him, for Kari and his family, for you. I know how you love him."

"I appreciate your concern, but I have no desire to talk to you, even about Dan."

"The four of us had some good times. It's scary to think we could lose him." His voice broke. At least he had some sympathy for someone.

"Adam, please leave me alone! I am in love with another man. I am completely loved for the first time, by a man I could spend the rest of my life loving and never feel I had loved him enough. You have to accept that and move on. Let go, Adam, and let me move on."

"Bonny, please? I don't want anyone else."

"Then I guess you'll just have to live alone."

"What about all the years we spent together, the dreams we shared?"

"I have a new dream." It was time to hang up.

"Bonny …"

"Goodbye, Adam. No more tricks. I won't talk to you again."

Bonny hung up the phone, changed her number on the Internet, and called Kieran with the new one. No more Adam, ever.

Of course, when she went home, there was a box full of never-mailed wedding invitations and a never-worn dress to be dealt with. And though she hated to admit it, she felt a little sad.

CHAPTER SIXTEEN

THE NIGHTMARE

Help! Somebody help! I'm burning—get me out of here!" Dan's throat hurt every time he called out. He couldn't see the smoke, but he smelled it. Acrid and thick, it filled his lungs. When he coughed, it felt as if his lungs were on fire, as well as everything around him.

"I can't see! Please, don't let me die! Get me out of here, God, please, get me out!" He no longer felt the intense heat, but his entire body was wracked with stinging, searing pain. "God, I don't want to die!"

"Dan."

He jumped, startled. The hand that touched his was cool.

"Where am I?"

"You're at Landstuhl Regional Army Medical Center in Germany. I'm your nurse, Karen." The voice was calm and gentle. "You were injured in a roadside bombing, but you're in the hospital now."

"Please, I don't want to die." He was shaking, shivering, unable to control the terror rising in his mind. To die without Kari beside him, to leave her … "No," he felt like a little boy again. His lower lip was quivering. He had no control of mind or body. "Help me."

The hand was on the back of his neck now, circling firm and slow. "Your family and fiancée know, Dan. They'll meet you in San Antonio at the Brooke Army Medical Center. You'll all be together tomorrow night. They send their love."

"What happened?" His voice was weak and raspy. He was surprised she heard him.

"Your Humvee hit a roadside bomb, and you became trapped in the explosion and fire. They pulled you out, but the smoke you inhaled burned your trachea, your windpipe. It takes two or three weeks to heal."

"I can't see you! Am I blind?" Panic rose, like gorge in his throat.

"Dan." The human contact of her hand on his hand felt reassuring. "Your face received second degree burns, so your eyes have damage also. The bandages will come off in two weeks. We won't know anymore until then, but I promise you'll receive the best care we can provide."

Her answer caused his stomach to knot up, and he struggled against the nausea of pain and fear. He was trapped, unable to turn, and attempts at moving brought deep, torturous pain. "Why am I facing down?"

"Your back and legs received third degree burns. Your legs got the worst. The second-degree burns on your arms should heal fine. I won't lie, they're serious. We have to keep the pressure off as much as we can. But you'll receive the best possible treatment here."

"What am I lying on?"

"You're lying face down on a Circo-electric bed. It allows us to keep pressure off the burns and rotate you whenever we need to. We're using heat lights to keep you warm. Can I explain anything else to you?"

"How long before I go home?" *This dark world is frightening. If only she'd stay.*

"They're airlifting a group of you at 0600 hours tomorrow. You'll arrive at BAMC by nighttime and your family will be there to greet you. The C-17 serves as an intensive care unit, so the medical staff has everything they need to keep you comfortable. You'll travel in the bed. Can I tell you anything else?" She rubbed the back of his neck in a circular motion.

"No." If he kept talking she'd stay, but he would scream if she told him more.

"There's a buzzer next to your right hand for you to call when you need something." She moved his hand and helped him locate the button. Once again, she laid a hand on his shoulder. "I'm close by."

Tears stung his burned eyelids. As her footsteps receded, he whispered, "God, where are you? My parents and Kari—they must be so worried. What will happen to Kari and me?"

 Cᴧᴙᴏᴏ

"No!"

A hand on his shoulder startled him awake. "Dan, it's Karen, can I do something for you?"

"I—I heard screams—my buddies, what happened to them?"

Her cool hand touched the back of his neck again. "I'm sorry, Dan. The other men in your Hummer didn't get out alive. The guys from the vehicle in front of you pulled you out of the burning wreckage."

"Dead. They're all dead?" *God, no!*

The sympathy in her voice was enough to make him cry again. "I can ask a chaplain to visit if you want."

"Just let me die."

He heard a male voice from his right. "Dan MacDermott, I'm Dr. Carlisle. Does the morphine control your pain enough?"

"I hurt everywhere." Anger mixed with the fear. "I'm trapped in this bed. My buddies, they're all …"

"I know, Dan, and I'm sorry. I can increase the morphine in your IV. I've spoken with Karen. Can I answer any more questions? We want you to have the information you need."

"If I live through this, will I be scarred and deformed?"

"You're fortunate. Your face and arms received first and second degree burns, which should heal fine." Fortunate wasn't the right word for it, but the voice sounded calm and reassuring.

"Barring infection, we can take the bandages off your eyes in two or three weeks. Your back and legs received the worst."

"Will I walk again?" He steeled himself for the answer.

"There's no reason to believe you won't, but it will take a while." The voice sounded cautious and confident at the same time.

"My buddies, dead …?" Tears stung his bandaged eyes again.

"I'm sorry, Dan. I know it's difficult." He could hear the compassion in Dr. Carlisle's voice, and it calmed him for the moment.

He felt Karen next to him, still giving a comforting pat now and then. "We'll give you heavier sedation for the trip home. I'll make certain the chaplain sees you before then."

I probably look like something out of a horror movie. My buddies are dead. I may lose Kari. Heavy sedation—good idea, maybe they'll give me too much and I won't wake up. Bring it on.

⊰⊱

Kari and the MacDermotts arrived at one in the morning, not long after the C-17 carrying Dan and the other patients from Landstuhl set down, turning their patients' care over to the dedicated staff at Brooke Army Medical Center.

The majority of patients made the 7,500-mile journey from Landstuhl in less than seventy-two hours after the rescue helicopters picked them up. Once in San Antonio, teams of BAMC surgeons waited to operate on those requiring immediate attention.

The young man at the information desk pointed the way to the burn unit. "Ask for his nurse. She'll have up-to-date information on his condition and medical procedures."

After calling on the red phone, a nurse came through the over-size double doors. "Hi, I'm Becca. I'm Major MacDermott's nurse. You're his family?"

Dan's father held out his hand. "Yes, his parents." He put his arm around Kari. "And this is Dan's fiancée, Kari Anderson."

The first thing Kari noticed was the odd smell. It was unique, sickening, and she feared the source.

"Welcome." Becca's smile brought warmth to the cold hallway. "I'm certain you're tired and frightened. The major went into surgery an hour after he arrived. They will debride, or remove, as much of the burned tissue as they can. This is the first of many surgeries. The waiting room is around that corner, to your right. I'll notify the doctor to speak to you when he's finished."

Mr. MacDermott put one hand on Kari's back and the other on his wife's, guiding them to the dimly lit waiting room. He nodded toward a counter with coffee, tea, and water. "Ladies, can I get you some coffee?"

"Nothing, thanks." Kari slumped into a chair, covering her eyes as if she wished she could wake up from this nightmare. *If I feel this frightened and hopeless, how must Dan feel?*

An hour later, she jumped to her feet as a doctor wearing green scrubs entered the waiting area. "I'm Dr. Andrews. Major MacDermott came through in fine shape."

"How bad is he, doctor? What are we facing here?" With an uncharacteristic quiver in his voice, Dan's father spoke for them all. Kari was so thankful not to be here alone.

"He received extensive burns on his back and legs. We map the location, size, and severity of the burns in order to decide the best way to proceed. During the first surgeries, we debride the burned tissue. The less severe burns on his face and arms will heal more rapidly than the rest. We'll start skin grafting on his back and legs in the next day or so. It helps keep out bacteria, controls temperature, and promotes the healing process."

"Where will you take the skin from?" Dave MacDermott's eyes grew moist.

"In Dan's case, so much burned area must be covered that we'll use pigskin and cadaver grafts. There's a long road ahead of him, but barring infection, he should make a complete recovery."

CHAPTER SEVENTEEN

LOVE AND THANKSGIVING

Thanksgiving was coming, and Bonny was homesick. She composed a long email to Kari. Then, she made invitations, asking Kieran, Janet, Graeme, and the Camerons to a Thanksgiving dinner.

The day before, as she had prepared the turkey, gales of laughter had accompanied her work, thinking about the Scots calling the big birds "bubbly jock."

She explained her family's traditions to the guests packing her dining room. "We didn't have a large family, so we invited people from church or the university to share our meal. We went around the table before the blessing, letting each person say what they were most thankful for."

"I'll go first," Janet said. "My sister gave birth to a healthy baby after a problem pregnancy."

Kieran answered, "A good year on the farm."

Bonny followed his cue, and avoided personal matters. "New friends and Dan's improvement."

In the absence of American football games, they gathered around the piano in the living room, and Janet played her guitar. At one point in "Loch Lomond," as if on cue, everyone stopped, leaving Kieran and Bonny singing, his deep baritone blending with her high, delicate soprano, startling them both.

When the last guests were gone, Kieran pulled her close, whispering in her ear. "I didn't trust my emotions in front of everyone." The warmth of his arms and the love in his eyes created a giddy sensation as she turned her face upward.

"I love you, Bonny Bryant. I can't pass an hour without thinking of you. I don't understand why you chose to love an older man, lacking your depth of faith, and living so far from your home, but I am so glad you're here."

She stood on tiptoe, caressing his broad forehead and straight nose, the roughness of his cheeks, and finally his lips. She entwined her fingers in the curls at the back of his neck. "There's no choosing about it. Loving you is as natural as breathing. If you lived on Mars, I'd find a way to reach you."

He led her to the couch, where they sat close together, his eyes searching her face. "When you walked into the faculty meeting, I realized you were special, but I never dared to dream you would love me."

She leaned her forehead against his. "God brought us together. He doesn't make mistakes."

He stiffened. "Whatever the reason, I'm glad you're here. I just can't believe God has anything to do with it."

She cupped his face in her hands. "It will get easier when you're used to being loved. God hears when we cry out, but sometimes we must believe when everything in us screams He isn't there. Our difficulties should draw us closer to Him. I forgot that for a while. Tragedy put me here with you now. You'll believe in time."

"And if I don't?" His gaze held steady.

A warning bell sounded in her brain. "I love you enough to risk it."

CSEO

"We need to talk." Dan's soft voice held an undertone of tension when Kari walked in on Thanksgiving morning.

"What's bothering you?" She reached for his hand and brought it to her lips.

He gently withdrew his hand. "Kari, I love you, but I won't hold you to our engagement. There is no guarantee what condition I'll be in if I survive. I release you."

"No, Dan." She took his hand back, bringing it to her lips. "This ring stays on my finger, and I stay at your side. I knew the consequences when I promised to marry a Marine. For better, for worse, remember?"

"We haven't said our vows yet." He held her hand, rubbing her palm with his thumb. "We have to face reality. You could have an invalid for a husband. Amputating my legs is a possibility if they don't get this infection under control soon. It's conceivable I won't live. I love having you here, but if you can't handle it, you have the freedom to move on with your life."

She touched his cheeks where the new skin grew pink over the less serious burns. With the bandages off, she was able to look into his beautiful, blue-gray eyes again. "It won't ever happen, Dan MacDermott. I've loved you since the ninth grade and I'll love you until I die. God saved your life and I'm committed to you and Him. You're stuck with me, Marine. Semper Fi."

He broke into a wide grin. "Semper Fi."

When her lips touched his, he had no doubt she meant it.

cₛₒ

"His eyesight is undamaged, and his hearing is back to normal. He's very down though." Kari's call made Bonny wish she were closer, but the distance was too great unless Dan's condition deteriorated.

"What cheers him up?" Imagining her childhood friend as an invalid was impossible. They had reveled in their mountain playground, riding horses, hiking, and enjoying the outdoors.

"We pray and read scripture. When he's alone he listens to Christian music to keep his mind calm and occupied."

"Can I send him CDs or something?" Being so far away gave her a helpless feeling.

"He'd love anything you choose. He misses you."

"What do you hear from the doctors?"

The answer was so long in coming, it was obvious Kari hesitated. "The infection in his legs has the potential to become life-threatening or cause him to lose his right leg. The hospital chapel has become a refuge. I go there when I can't sleep."

"Do you have a chaplain or someone to encourage you?" It tore at Bonny's heart to hear the pain in Kari's voice.

"One chaplain has become a real friend. He understands what we're going through." Kari sounded so tired.

"Good, you need to rest or you'll be sick. Assure Dan people here are praying for him."

She sniffled. "He offered to break our engagement. Bonny, I love him. The thought of losing him frightens me. I can accept amputation. I can't accept him living without me. Our love goes back so much further than his injuries." She made a choking sound.

Bonny longed to put her arms around Kari and give her a big bear hug. Their bond of love and friendship remained strong in spite of the miles, providing a foretaste of her life if Scotland became her home.

Chapter Eighteen

Stonehaven Farm

Visiting Kieran's sheep farm was an important, and perhaps, a dangerous move. Marriage was on both of their minds, and Bonny believed their love was strong enough to surmount the difficulties of faith. Kari and Dan, even Janet and Agnes, advised against it, but she wanted to know everything about him. She had to penetrate the periods of aloof behavior, which began when she revealed her breakthrough with God.

She had been to Stonehaven Farm to ride horses and watch the men work with the sheep on weekends, but she hadn't taken pictures yet. After asking him to pull over the sixth time, Kieran suggested she wait. "We'll be late for tea. You'll have more opportunities for pictures, maybe even a clear day."

Banned from photo stops, she peppered him with questions to make the smile lines crinkle around his eyes. "You smile more than when I first met you."

"Before you, there wasn't a reason to smile." He broke into another grin and squeezed her hand where it lay on the console.

"If you smiled like that the first time we met, I would have thrown myself into your arms and declared my love." No longer shy, she reached over and coiled her fingers in the curls at the back of his neck.

"I wasn't aware I had such charm." His eyes sparkled.

"Then you're the only one who doesn't see it. Dierdre hasn't said anything, but she glares at me from the back of class."

He tilted his head back and laughed. Passing Invergarry, he continued toward Loch Oich, and soon they faced the hulk of a ruined castle. The stark granite walls loomed above them, a shade darker than the leaden hue of the clouds, their long-empty windows keeping sentinel over the narrow loch.

"My ancestral home, m'lady," Kieran stopped at the ruins of old Invergarry Castle. "My forebears weren't all good men. Alexander Ranaldson MacDonell was a cruel clan chief who drove the people from the land in favor of sheep and cut the trees in order to graze the land."

Bonny loved the way he made the stories of the Highlands come alive, sharing family history as if talking about people he knew. He leaned against a crumbling wall, damp from the heavy mist, one hand resting on her shoulder. "*Alasdair*, in the Gaelic, lived an affluent lifestyle and his son inherited such serious debt that he sold the estate to the Marquess of Huntly. The mass immigration of the Glengarrys to Canada took place in 1828, and the clan no longer held its familial lands."

"When was the castle last inhabited?" Bonny massaged the back of his hand with her thumb. She could easily picture him wielding a claymore, the *claidheamh mòr*, battling to defend his home, as his melodic voice continued.

"Oliver Cromwell destroyed the castle in 1654 during the Civil War. They eventually repaired it, and during the Jacobite rising of 1745 and 1746 Bonnie Prince Charlie himself stayed here. 'Butcher Cumberland' destroyed it following the Battle of Culloden, *Blàr Chùil Lodair*, in an attempt to force Highlanders to submit to the English."

"It's still impressive." She tilted her head back, contemplating the towering ruins. "So if the Bonnie Prince stayed here, and Cumberland destroyed it, your family was Jacobite on both sides."

He drew her into a rough, playful, bear hug, planting a kiss on her nose. "You do know your history, Professor. Both the MacDonells and MacKenzies were Jacobites."

"I will confess to reading up on the subject. I have a personal interest now." She grabbed his hand, pulling him after her. Stopping, she eyed the black volcanic rock forming the foundation. "What a formidable defense it must have made."

"Yes, Rock of Raven, *Creagan an Fhithich*, in Gaelic, was their battle cry. I'm certain the fortress provided an advantage and slowed down their attackers.

When I was a lad, I wanted to play here and climb on the walls. I wish it still belonged to the family."

Bonny studied him as he regarded the rocky remnant rising high above them. The blood of ancient warrior kings coursed through his veins. *Yes, she could follow this man anywhere.*

"It looks invincible, even as broken ruins. What a fascinating heritage. Tell me more, Laird MacDonell."

He settled back against a large stone. "The MacDonells were a rabble-rousing clan. They forfeited their lands more than once because of their rebellious ways. Alasdair was wild and rugged, as violent as the storms on Loch Garry itself. *Garu* means 'stormy and turbulent.'"

Bonny seated herself next to him, loving his way with a story. "Long before the estate was sold to the Marquess of Huntly, the MacDonells who left the islands settled here and changed the spelling of their name to the Gaelic, *MacDhomhnuill.*"

She laid her cheek against the scratchy wool of his shirt, and looked across the valley where the ever-thickening mist filled the air with the scent of rain and evergreen. "They were always fighting to keep their homes, weren't they?"

He raised her hand to his lips, caressing the back of it. "You'll be interested in this, Professor Bryant. Scotland was a representative republic five hundred years before the United States existed."

Without hesitation, she said, "The Declaration of Arbroath."

His eyes widened and he tousled her damp, tangled curls. "I thought I could teach you something. The *Sassanachs* must be right. We MacDonells are 'primitive and barbaric.' I looked it up. I didn't remember the part about the republic."

There was mischief in his grin, and she followed his lead. "So I've been swept off my feet by a barbarian?"

He gave her a rakish grin, his eyes dancing with laughter. "Oh, aye, we Scots are wild and unruly. You knew about the Declaration of Arbroath?"

She put her hands on her hips. "Of course. What kind of a history professor isn't aware of such an important historical document? Americans prefer to believe the whole idea was theirs, though."

His eyes darkened and his voice grew husky. "'… for as long as but a hundred of us remain alive, never will we on any conditions be brought under English rule. It is in truth not for glory, nor riches, nor honours that we are fighting, but for freedom – for that alone, which no honest man gives up but with life itself.' Very radical ideas for the times, and Scotland has not been independent for hundreds of years."

"Thomas Jefferson came from a Scottish-Welsh background and was very educated. He must have thought about it when he penned our Declaration of Independence. So you're in favor of Scotland obtaining freedom from Great Britain?"

"Absolutely." The rain was coming down harder, but he ignored it. He drew her closer and she inhaled the irresistible scent of damp wool and Kieran. "Set your students straight, lass. It's something both Scots and Americans need to understand. When they executed Alasdair, son of Ranald, the first Lord of the Isles, in 1427, MacDonell lands became the property of the King of England. The majority of the clans admitted defeat. We refused to submit for another forty years and eventually received the charter to Glengarry and other lands in this part of Scotland. Of course, after Culloden, we lost it all."

"When you say 'we,' you make it sound as if it were a personal affront to you."

"Aye, as it is to every Scot. My family is somewhat of an anomaly. Very few Scots own even a small portion of their ancestral lands."

"And now you carry on in their place with your farm, and these ruins are everyday reminders of your history."

He sat down, encircling her waist with his hands, pulling her to his lap. "I've now learned how to gain your complete attention—history lessons."

"There are other ways." With the overpowering sensation of his arms around her, no one else existed in the world.

"What about this?" He bent, kissing her slow and sweet.

She returned it, delighting in the closeness between them, the undercurrent of passion and love that made his touch irresistible.

"Ach, lass, don't tempt me. Did I tell you Alasdair joined a rebellion to help

Donald Gorm of Sleat attain the position of Lord of the Isles? Donald died, and Alasdair ended up in jail."

"Outlaws—how romantic." Bonny giggled. "I love the way your accent grows stronger when something is important to you."

"Wheesht, woman, you're distractin' me again." She knew he enjoyed her teasing and the interest she showed.

The rain had slackened, and he wiped a drip off the end of her nose with his handkerchief. "The Glengarrys were especially difficult to control. It must be our Norse blood, the fair skinned, redheaded Viking blood. The MacDonells and MacKenzies fought each other for years, and hundreds died."

"So your mother's clan feuded with your father's? I can't imagine there's a barbaric bone in your body." She poked him in the ribs.

"Why are you smilin'?"

"I love you, Kieran MacDonell, even if you aren't the laird of a great castle. Thank you for sharing your family history with me."

She quivered as he bent toward her upturned face, his lips brushing hers in a gentle kiss. She knew he felt it, too, from the way his arm tightened around her waist.

"You're a darlin' lass, Bonny Bryant, lovely enough to steal the heart of the toughest knight of old."

"It takes more than that little kiss to steal my heart." She took off through the thick grass surrounding the castle walls.

Catching her, he lifted her to the top of a large stone. His hug threatened to squeeze the breath out of her. "What's this? First my kisses aren't what you'd expect of a barbaric Scot, and then they won't steal your heart? You're lucky I'm restrainin' myself, or you'd call me a barbarian for certain."

"I surrender, Laird MacDonell. You've proved your point." She hopped down, grasping his hand, and pulled him toward the Land Rover. "I don't want to push a member of such a blood-thirsty clan too far. Let's get out of this rain. I'll meet Eleanor looking like a selkie."

"Perhaps you are—an enchantress who will steal my heart and then disappear back where you came from."

"I thought I'd already stolen your heart, but I'll never disappear."

⋆⋆⋆

A stab of nostalgia squeezed Kieran's heart. He and Bronwyn had chased each other around these ruins. This new love at his side was reason to feel thankful. It felt good not to travel this road alone.

Curious when Bonny remained silent, he sneaked a peek at her face. "What are you thinkin' now? I can see the wheels turnin'."

Bonny turned a lovely, bashful pink. "Imagining you as the laird ruling over the people on your land." Those eyes, the color of a Scottish hillside in spring, caused him to forget everything else.

"And what type of laird would I be?"

She leaned across the console, smoothing back his wet hair. He shivered more from her touch than his damp clothes. "Not one who threw people off the land and chopped down trees for sheep. I can imagine you making certain everyone received fair treatment, suitable houses, education, medicine, and enough food. I can't conceive of you being cruel."

With her fingers in his hair and her gentle touch on his cheek, facing life without her beside him became unimaginable.

"Kieran, can you live your whole life here and still feel in awe of it?"

He attempted to swallow the lump in his throat without success. "During the worst of my depression, nothing was beautiful, and I still struggle. Other than my time in Glasgow, I've spent my entire life on this piece of land. I love it, but I'm not building it for anyone. There's no purpose or future beyond myself."

"Feeling alone makes you think dangerous thoughts." She gave him a playful tap on the shoulder. "Look where it got me."

"Aye, and I've been alone too long. You remind me of sunshine, warm and sweet, bringing everything you touch to life. The entire world is new, thanks to you. Bronwyn was like the flowers she loved. They push their way through the ground in spring with amazing strength, but the bloom doesn't last. She left too soon, and now you're turning my world upside-down."

Their conversations held magic.

⋆⋆⋆

As the Land Rover came to a stop in the yard, the canine greeting committee surrounded them. When Kieran opened her car door, Bonny reached for his hand, squeezing it. Her eyes were glowing with excitement. "Can I see everything this time?"

Surrounded by yipping dogs, he couldn't help smiling. "Every inch if you want."

The kitchen door opened, and a woman wearing an apron came out. "Bonny, meet my second mother, Eleanor. She'll show you to your room while I carry up your bags. I'm certain she's prepared a lovely tea to warm us."

While Bonny freshened up, Eleanor caught Kieran on a trip through the kitchen. "Lad, are you gettin' carried away because she's another red-haired beauty? She's quite fragile for the demandin' life of a Highland sheep farm."

He rubbed his forehead in frustration. He didn't need more criticism. "She may be a wee biddie, but she's as hearty a woman as you or my mother any day. I must have inherited my Da's affinity for redheads. She's tough, Eleanor. Her great-grandparents were pioneers in the American West. She grew up in the mountains around horses, hunting, and fishing, and she beats me at hiking. Get to know her. You'll discover I'm right, I promise."

Eleanor turned back to preparing tea, but he noticed the china clinking harder than necessary, as she laid her tray. "Tsk, tsk, tsk."

◯◌◯

Kieran hadn't taken Bonny upstairs before. His mother had raised him with strong morals, and Bonny respected him more because of his standards. The top of the curving staircase provided her first view of the grand old house from a different perspective, creating again the odd sensation of stepping into another time.

Eleanor kept the wainscoting of dark mahogany polished to a fine sheen, and the smooth wood of the banister showed the patina of hundreds of MacDonell hands. The massive chandelier of stag's antlers, which she had admired on previous visits, spread its light throughout the large foyer. Wall sconces, each made of a single antler, lit the walls of deep green, hung with ancient portraits of MacDonells from the glory days of clans and chieftains.

Lost in her survey of Kieran's forebears, she stopped at each portrait, looking for a family resemblance until she heard him laughing. "They don't speak, you know. I realize your imagination is capable of creatin' a plausible story for each of them, but the tea's coolin' off. Come and join Eleanor and me by the fire." He held out his hand.

"They're the people from your stories. It's lovely, Laird MacDonell." When she reached the bottom, he kissed her hand, holding it high in a chivalrous manner as he escorted her into the library. A fire crackled in the huge fireplace with the head of a monstrous red stag above the MacDonell coat of arms.

Eleanor sat ramrod straight in a wingback chair, the tea in front of her, ready to pour. The welcoming, homey scene was reminiscent of another century. She stood and greeted Bonny with warmth. "So you're here at last. One would believe no other woman existed the way Kieran goes on."

Bonny chose to accept it as a compliment. "Thank you."

Kieran closed the draperies against the cold and came to where she stood near the fire. "We should drink our tea so Eleanor doesn't need to heat more." Looking at his housekeeper, he said, "Do you think this bonnie lass has the potential to breathe life into these old walls?"

She didn't miss the reproach in his housekeeper's eyes.

"Time will tell."

Sensing dangerous territory, she tasted a scone from the plate Eleanor handed her. "These are delicious. Do you share your recipes?"

"You'll know you've impressed Eleanor if she lets you into her kitchen." Kieran reached for another, smearing it with jam. "She keeps her recipes under lock and key. However, she did pass them on to her daughters, Bridget and Kathleen. They work for my mother at the Inn in Beauly."

After dinner, when the housekeeper retired, they snuggled up on the couch nearest the fireplace. He held her close, rubbing her earlobe with his finger. "What do you think?"

She grabbed his hand. "I love your home, and Eleanor is very nice. I expect to be cross-examined in-depth, though, to determine if I'm suitable for her bonnie laddie."

"Ach, you should have heard Eleanor, concerned you weren't suitable for life on a Highland sheep farm because of your delicate build. She warned me against getting carried away with 'another red-haired beauty.'" In spite of the continuing rain, they climbed into the Land Rover and headed up toward the kyloe pasture, early the next morning.

"Her welcome was warm enough. Are you certain you aren't?" When he looked puzzled, she added, "Attracted by my red hair, I mean."

He laughed, pulling her closer. "My mother's hair was the color of yours before turning white. Though, if I had to choose your most bewitching physical characteristic, I'd pick your eyes, the deep green of *Alba*. Eleanor watches over me like a lad of fourteen rather than a man of forty. When you went upstairs after breakfast, she said perhaps she was a wee bit hasty. Considering your faded jeans and worn Wellies, you must know your way around a stable."

"So worn Wellies will earn her approval? What will get me into her good graces on a more solid basis?"

"Being the sweet woman I fell in love with. By the end of the weekend, she'll tell my mother what a lovely lass I found." He cupped her cheek in his palm. "She'll love you when she sees how happy I am."

Bonny wanted to absorb everything, begging him to stop for occasional photos of the lush forest and pastureland rising above the storm-tossed loch. The scent of damp grass and evergreens filled the air with a heavenly aroma. Kieran pointed out a majestic stag, one antler lost in battle, standing at attention on the hillside above, before disappearing into the vaporous fog.

They were alone in a hushed world blanketed in mist and cloud. Surrounded by mountains and rushing burns, the enchantment cast its spell over her. Kieran and the idyllic setting called to her heart as one.

Bonny tromped through the mud with Kieran all day, ignoring the rain as he checked on the well-being of his animals. She had paid attention a few weeks earlier when she accompanied him for the sheep dipping. It was a nasty job done twice a year to protect them from fleas, ticks, and parasites. That experience might just help her show Eleanor she was prepared to face anything a Highland sheep farm might send her way.

The sheep-dipping had made it clear how Kieran kept his arms and shoulders muscular enough to compete in the Highland Games. The nasty task required manhandling the uncooperative sheep through a narrow gate leading to the trough. Once in, farmhands shoved the unwilling animals under the chemical dip. It was necessary to immerse them until their mouth, nose, and eyes burned, before allowing them to scurry up the ramp. Kieran worked alongside the others, claiming no special privileges as owner.

She had laughed at Kieran, Angus, and the others as she surveyed the dirty, stinking group, laughed so hard in fact, that Angus had suggested dipping disrespectful females. The loch laid placid, clothed in the colors of autumn, and the air echoed with the sound of stunning stags in rut, their antlers clashing and thwacking as they struggled for supremacy. Their "roaring" echoed through the dense, wet air as they announced their readiness for battle and gathered their harems for mating. Hearing their roar for the first time, Bonny jumped in surprise, expecting something similar to the high-pitched bugling of American elk. *Yes, it was a life she could live, a life with the man she loved.* The holidays were coming. Would he ask her?

Another weekend, she had accompanied Kieran and his hired men as they drove lorries of sheep to the Fort William market. On the way, he quizzed her to see how well she was learning her lessons about sheep. "Tell me what you've learned."

As serious as she could be, she replied, "Female sheep are called ewes, rams are males, and lambs are babies."

"That's all you've learned?"

She didn't waste her opportunity to prove how well she had listened. "I'll show you a thing or two, Dr. MacDonell. Castrated males are 'wether' lambs. They're easier to handle than rams. A 'tup' is a ram used for breeding or 'tupping.'" A pleased smile had spread over his face. "A lamb is less than one year old and hasn't produced offspring. Its meat is called lamb, while mutton comes from a sheep more than a year old."

Kieran's laugh made her studying worthwhile. "We'll turn you into a sheep farmer yet."

"I read up on the Internet. I'm interested."

She smiled to herself, remembering how he stopped the Land Rover, grinning from ear to ear.

"How did I find someone fascinated with everything I love?"

"I enjoy being with you, so what you care about is important." Her eyes searched the lush pastures from side to side. "Breeding season for the sheep starts in a couple of weeks. Do you plan to pair certain couples off for mating?"

She remembered how the corners of his eyes crinkled at that. "Bonny, they're not dating. It's breeding, and anxious rams will cover as many ewes as we allow. But yes, I plan to breed specific pairs to obtain the strongest offspring. Everything settles down some after tupping is over, meaning more time for you."

She reached over and squeezed his hand. "Sounds great to me, though I suspect Angus thinks you have more romance on your mind than sheep."

He reddened, shrugging. "You bet I do. A woman like you only comes along once. In the spring you'll want to be here all the time, for the lambing. My parents come down for it. Bronwyn loved to help with the lambing."

He had placed his arm around her shoulders, and Bonny leaned her head against his wool-covered arm. "I'll be back from Kari and Dan's wedding by then. I don't want to miss anything."

Things were different now that winter was coming. The sheep were in the lower pastures, divided into separate fields in preparation for tupping. "The cattle are still higher up. They can winter outside."

"Oh, I expected to see them again. They're so cute."

"Don't worry." With both of his hands back on the wheel, they bounced across a grassy meadow toward a rough trail, in a heavy sleet. "We'll find them. It's rough going."

"I love it. It's no rougher than four-wheeling with Dad in the Land Cruiser."

By the time they headed back, she longed for dry clothes, a warm fire, and a cup of tea, but it had been a wonderful day. "There's something else I can tell you."

He glanced sideways. "What?"

They hit an especially hard bump and she grabbed the handle above the door. "Cattle and sheep can't share pastures."

"And how would you know that, more reading?"

"My great-grandfather raised cattle. He had a long-running feud with neighboring sheep ranchers, partly because the sheep eat grass down to the ground, leaving nothing for the cattle. Cattle eat the tops of the grass, and it grows back better." He beamed with pleasure, making her homework worthwhile.

"You're amazing."

"You're pretty special yourself. I'll reward you with dinner."

"Reward? You're the one showing off." He reached over and ruffled the hair escaping from its knot.

"You're sharing your home and your life with me. We'll have the green-chile stew I brought, since Eleanor's in town. Should we invite her and Angus for stew when they return?"

"She'll eat with her children in town and her son will bring her back afterward. She isn't as adventurous in her cuisine as you are. Besides, I want the company of the cook to myself."

Yes, she would enjoy farm life, given the opportunity. The yearning in his eyes made her heart beat faster. This incredible man, so tender in his love, might one day belong to her.

CR80

While Kieran caught up on some paperwork, Bonny sought out Eleanor. Hoping to reinforce her down-to-earth side, Bonny wore gray sweats, her hair flowing around her shoulders in a riot of curls. "Thank you for the mouthwatering meals, Eleanor. You've been so welcoming. Can I help with anything?"

Eleanor pointed to a pile of potatoes and a peeler. "A hearty welcome is the best dish in a Scottish kitchen. He's very happy, which makes it easy to welcome you. I understand you have differences where his beliefs are concerned."

"He told you?" Bonny stopped, holding the potato peeler in mid-air.

Eleanor set down her spoon, turning to face her with narrowed brown eyes.

"I've known him since the day he was born, and we discuss almost everything. He's wrong on this. Keep challenging him, lass."

"I'm not having any success." Bonny kept her voice low. "A chasm opened up between us after I told him I felt God's presence when I prayed. He insists he can't trust God because He allowed Bronwyn and Liam to die. I've suggested his choice will decide our future, but I don't want to lose him."

"You can't lower your standard." Eleanor laid a weathered hand on Bonny's arm. "A marriage without a shared faith is destined for problems. I believe he'll return to it though."

Convinced a herd of kyloe was in the house, Bonny turned to see Kieran lumbering down the back stairs. "What are you two discussing with such serious expressions?"

Eleanor waved him away. "Wash up for dinner."

⚘

After dinner, Eleanor seated herself in a corner under a lamp with her cross-stitch, tapping her foot in time as they sang, spelling each other at the piano. When they finished "Loch Lomond," Kieran said, "Bonny, sing your solo from church for Eleanor. I'll accompany you."

She relinquished her place on the piano bench, marveling at the delicate touch with which his big fingers moved over the keys, the dense hairs on the back of his hands glowing golden in the lamplight.

"Your voice is as clear as a sunny day." Eleanor wiped her eyes with a hanky. "What a lovely rendition of 'Be Thou My Vision.' Laddie, don't let her get away."

"No one receives such a high approval rating that fast." He winked at Bonny.

⚘

"Kari." Bonny phoned on Saturday afternoon while Kieran and Angus discussed the upcoming week. "Kari, it's me. How are you and Dan?"

The answer was a choked sob. "The infection in his legs isn't responding to the antibiotics. They're considering amputating his right leg below the knee."

An icy knife passed through her heart. "Oh Kari, no …"

Kari sobbed, "I shouldn't complain. I want him alive and out of pain."

"Of course you do. What does he say?" Bonny was shaking so hard, she found it difficult to hold the phone.

"He's ready to heal and go home." She hiccupped. "The improvement is very slow. His eyesight is fine, and his arms will have no noticeable scarring. The skin grafts on his back are taking, and the doctors seem pleased with his progress otherwise."

"I can't bear to think of him having to go through this, but we'll rest easier when his life is out of danger." Bonny tried her best to sound positive, remembering how he loved to hike, climb in the mountains, fly fish, and hunt from horseback.

"The infection has gone into the bone and he's in so much pain. Overall, he has a good attitude. He doesn't believe it will improve and wants to get on with his life." She paused, and Bonny heard her blowing her nose. "It's his best chance."

The drops sliding down Bonny's cheeks kept pace with the raindrops on her bedroom window. "Call me if they decide to operate. We're praying over here."

"Thank you. What's up with you?"

Bonny pulled a crocheted blanket over her legs. "I'm so ecstatic I feel guilty when you're having such a difficult time. I'm spending a long weekend at Kieran's farm, although it's more of an estate. Kari, it's so gorgeous here. The old stone house is right on Loch Garry, surrounded by forests with meadows full of sheep, and magnificent mountains. There's fishing in the loch and the river. Bronwyn planted flower gardens everywhere. Did I tell you they filmed 'Braveheart' and 'Rob Roy' in this area?"

"You know what I mean."

She sighed at the frustration in her friend's voice. "I love him, Kari, and he loves me. My relationship with the Lord is growing stronger. Everything is more wonderful than I ever dreamed."

The irritation in Kari's voice grew stronger. "How is Kieran's walk with the Lord?"

Bonny wished she had never let it slip the last time they talked. "He's struggling, but Eleanor, his housekeeper, believes he'll come around. He needs the right circumstances to remind him of God's grace and faithfulness, the same as me. Pray for him."

Kari's voice grew stern. "I'll pray for both of you. You're so vulnerable. Being alone isn't the worst that can happen."

"You know I didn't come here to fall in love. Remember how it upset you when Dan offered to break your engagement, or the infection threatened to take him from you? Please try to understand. I've found a very special man to love. Can't you be glad for me?" She was angry. Kari had her family, and Dan and his. She had no one.

"You're on shaky ground. God set specific guidelines for marriage. Wait until the two of you agree before committing yourself. You don't need more heartbreak."

Bonny changed the subject, refusing to argue again. "What's happening with your wedding plans? Will Dan be home by then?"

Kari rambled on and on, but Bonny was willing to listen as long as she didn't criticize Kieran.

CRWO

Sunday morning, Bonny arose early and spent time praying and reading the Psalms in her window seat, overlooking Ben Tee to the south. The rain had stopped, and a heavy mist hung low over the loch, obscuring the dense woods with the mountain rising above it.

At breakfast, she suggested a ride, and they headed for a rocky hill above the farmhouse, where they looked down on the farm, the loch, and south to the forests and mountains. As a shaft of sunlight shot its way through the clouds she felt a thrill of delight. "It reminds me of the song, 'Highland Cathedral.'"

"How does farm life suit you?"

The morning sun sparkling in his eyes reminded her of sapphires, his hair shining a deep, burnished gold, as breathtaking as the view.

"I believe I'd enjoy it."

Sidepassing Storm closer to Misty, he reached for her hand. "Do you have plans for Christmas?"

Her heart beat faster. "Nothing definite. Janet mentioned including me with her family."

He dismounted, reaching up to help her down, and drawing her into his arms. "I want you to spend Christmas and Hogmanay in Beauly with my parents and me. They need to meet the amazing woman who stole my heart and turned my world inside out."

The idea of spending the rest of her life in his warm, strong arms left her speechless. She leaned her face against the solid strength of his chest. He had disappointed her again by ignoring Sunday, when Angus and Eleanor drove into Fort William for church. But there was still time for change before Christmas, so she said, "I'll consider it."

୧୨୦

"Delivery for Dr. Bonny Bryant."

Puzzled, she signed and shut the door, carrying the long box to the kitchen table. "Kieran, what have you done now?"

She removed the top from the box, revealing a bouquet of two dozen red and white roses tied with a red ribbon. Her fingers shook as she opened the card. "To Bonny, with love. Please remember. Forever, Adam."

The postscript read, "Don't miss the small box in the bottom."

She lifted the roses out and discovered the small, pink, velvet box containing her engagement ring. Memories of what seemed like a long-ago time overwhelmed her, and she sat down hard, closing her eyes. They had eaten dinner at High Finance, a restaurant at the top of Sandia Peak and lingered to ride the last tram car down the mountain, a beautiful ride with the lights of Albuquerque spreading out below them. She had been surprised that no one else was with them for the ride down until he explained he had paid for the entire car, so they could be alone.

Adam had knelt before her, asking her to marry him. And when she said yes, he placed the ring of rose-gold with a rose-cut diamond on her finger. Now, as it sparkled in its box, she tried to remember how she felt back then. The memories were eclipsed by thoughts of the day she removed it from her finger and shoved it into his hand when he confessed his affair with an attorney in his office.

She would return the ring. "Adam, you're much too late." She carried the roses out back and placed them in the trash.

CHAPTER NINETEEN

CONVERSATIONS, REVELATIONS, AND STRUGGLES

Kieran walked down High Street concentrating on his list of errands. Bonny's weekend at the farm had convinced him he wanted a life with her. It also meant he must deal with his anger over Bronwyn's death. On their tour of the farmhouse, he had skipped the room they once shared. The idea of changing it disturbed him, but he knew he must leave the past where it belonged.

The physical attraction, present since the first time he saw Bonny, grew by the day, as did their emotional attachment. He knew she felt it too, sensing her reluctance to return to Fort William. It felt so natural to have her at the farm. She made it seem like home again, a place he wanted to be.

"Hello, Kieran." A familiar voice startled him out of his private thoughts.

Looking up from his shopping list, he stood face to face with Graeme MacDholl. He shook the outstretched hand. "Hello, I need to finish a couple more errands before heading back to the farm."

"Would you join me for a cup of tea?"

Lately, he planned his errands to avoid the church, but Graeme stood in front of him, and there was no escape. "Aye."

Graeme tilted his head in the direction of a small restaurant across the street. "How about the Sugar and Spice?"

Wrested out of his musings, Kieran seated himself across from the pastor, waiting for him to begin the conversation.

"How's the sheep business?" Graeme scooted his chair forward.

Kieran turned his chair sideways, trying to create more leg room. "It's busy this time of year, what with tupping and winter coming, but it will slow down again before Christmas. Of course, now I come to town for choir practice, thanks to Bonny and Janet. I've practically taken up permanent residence at my Aunt Alice's."

Graeme laughed. "They are two energetic and persistent ladies. I wondered how you managed the drive from your farm so often."

"Aye, well, even if I had to drive, there's no point arguing with either of them." The waitress approached and he set the menu aside. "Hello Sheena, I'll have a pot of Earl Grey, please. Pastor, it's on me."

"Thank you." Graeme nodded. "I'll take the same, and it's Graeme." As Sheena walked away, he asked, "One of your students?"

"One of Bonny's, I've met her a time or two when I attended Bonny's lectures. Have you heard her teach?"

"No, I understand she's causing quite a stir though." Graeme spread a napkin in his lap as Sheena set the pots of tea down.

"Sheena, bring us a plate of my favorite scones, please." Kieran balanced the spoon on his finger. He felt more comfortable discussing Bonny than himself. "The students and faculty both love her. Are you busy around the church?" Pouring his tea, he reached for the cream.

Graeme buttered a scone. "Aye, we're busier around the holidays, especially with the musical this year. I peeked in on rehearsal the other night. Your voice adds the depth the choir was lacking."

"Thank you. I sang in the chorus at university and in the church choir before my wife died. It's lovely to sing with Bonny. She has a special gift." Kieran picked up another scone.

"Yes, she does. We're blessed by both of you." Graeme put jam on his second scone. "Where did you attend church before Bonny brought you to Faith Chapel?"

"I grew up in the Church of Scotland." He hurried through the basics. "I haven't attended with any regularity since my wife died two years ago."

"Faith Chapel must be very different for you." Graeme propped his elbows on the table, his brown eyes expectant.

Kieran shifted in his seat. "Yes, but I appreciate your preaching. You're straightforward." The moment for complete honesty had arrived, and he didn't welcome it.

The pastor poured another cup of tea, so relaxed he could be discussing the fog over the loch. "If it's not prying, how did your wife's death affect your faith?"

Unable to sit still, Kieran leaned his chair back on two legs. "The death of my wife and son caused me to doubt everything. I'll admit, I don't believe in the personal God you preach. I've spent over two years angry with God. I'm in church for Bonny."

"I see you're an *aefauld* man, such straightforward honesty is something I don't see every day." Graeme's expression remained unchanged. "To my understanding, Bonny had much the same struggle. We talked after her friend Dan's injury."

"Aye, she did." Kieran felt the panic of a trapped bird, fluttering here and there with no escape. "She's patient and understanding. She's agreed to give me time."

Graeme emptied his teapot, and leaned back in his chair. "If I can help, don't hesitate to ring me."

"I expected a sermon." The pastor's easy acceptance of his last comment surprised him.

Graeme laughed, and Kieran noticed that the left side of his mouth turned up more than the right. "I am concerned, believe me, but God will deal with you at the right time."

"I appreciate you not lecturing me." Kieran relaxed more than any time since they met. He waved at Sheena. "Can you bring me the bill, please?"

Graeme met his eyes with candor and warmth. "I don't believe in lecturing. An experience such as yours challenges many people's faith. In the ninth chapter of the Gospel of Mark, the father of the demon-possessed boy asked Jesus to help his unbelief, and Jesus didn't judge him for it. Stop in sometime, if you need a listening ear."

"Thanks. Things are becoming serious between Bonny and me. We need to deal with our differences." He was surprised how comfortable he felt talking to the pastor.

Sheena handed him the bill and both men stood, shaking hands. "I enjoyed visiting with you. I have an appointment at the kirk."

"Yes," Kieran said, somewhat stunned at the easy camaraderie. "I enjoyed it too."

CXZO

Kari's sobbing made her voicemail difficult to understand. "They're amputating Dan's right leg below the knee this morning. The infection isn't responding, and he spiked a fever again. He's come to terms with it easier than the rest of us. I'll let you know when he's out of surgery."

Once again, Bonny fell to her knees in prayer and then phoned Kieran. "He's my oldest friend. We grew up climbing trees, hiking, and riding, and now—I can't believe it. He's a superb horseman. He loves to camp and hike. Kieran …"

"Love, you've portrayed Dan as a man of courage, faith, and physical strength. Consider that. With the advances they're making in prosthetics, he should be able to do almost anything he wants, in time." His deep voice had such a calming effect.

She sniffled. "You're right, but …"

"But they're your good friends, and you feel far away right now."

She coughed and cleared her throat. "I've deserted them. They've helped me so many times."

"I'll see you this evening. You might know more by then."

She heard a muffled sound on his end. "Kieran, are you crying?"

"I hate for my bonnie lass to cry alone without me to hold her. I'll finish with Angus and come early. *Beannachd leit, mo annsachd.*"

"*Tha gaol agam ort.*" She hung up the phone and prayed for Dan, longing for Kieran to join her prayers.

CXZO

"Hey, Carrot-Top, I wanted to tell you, I'm fine."

"Dan? I can't believe you're calling me straight out of surgery. I'm so sorry I'm not there." Bonny stopped, choking back a sob.

"The morphine's working right now. Don't worry. I'll be doing tricks on my prosthesis before the wedding. No crying. I wanted to serve my country, and I'd do it again." The strength in his voice was encouraging.

She steeled herself to sound strong. "Yes sir, Major MacDermott. No more crying."

"That's my girl. Is Kieran with you?"

"Yes."

"Hand him the phone, please." He groaned, and she heard sheets rustling.

Kieran's eyes widened when she turned on the speaker and handed him the phone. "Dan, I'm so sorry. Can I do something for you?"

"Take care of my girl. Make her smile and keep her from worrying."

Dan, ever the loving guardian her father knew he would be, even from his hospital bed.

Kieran laughed, but his voice cracked as Bonny felt a quiver run through him. "Aye, I'll do my best. When you're better, we'll talk sometime. She's quite a woman."

"One of a kind," Dan said. "Thank you for taking care of her. The nurse is here. Bye."

Kieran hung up the phone, clearing his throat as he embraced Bonny.

"I guess you have your orders."

"Quite a friend you have there, thanking me for taking care of you." He wiped his eyes on the back of his hand. "He's a brave man."

Rain pelted the windows, but the glow of the fire prevented the dark from overwhelming them as they stared into the flames. She didn't need words, only the security of Kieran's arms.

◌ॐ◌

A Saturday hike in Glen Coe was usually a source of fun. Reaching a rock where they sometimes stopped to rest, Bonny gestured toward it. "Sit down. There's something I should have told you a long time ago."

Kieran sat, pulling her toward his lap, but she resisted, standing before him clasping and unclasping her hands. "What's wrong? We can deal with anything together, love."

Grabbing her hands, he stopped her from massaging her throat, unnamed fears flashing through his mind.

"I've had problems for a long time, female problems." She pulled one hand away, but he caught it again and held it tight as she continued. "I saw a doctor when Adam and I were engaged, and he suggested testing to determine the problem. Kieran, the doctors said it would be difficult, if not impossible, to have children. I had major surgery, but the problems returned. I—I thought Adam found someone else because of it."

He stared at her, unable to speak for a moment, held by the lustrous green of her eyes and the trepidation in her voice. The sudden death of his desire for a family was a shock. He felt fear in her trembling hands and swallowed hard. "I love you, Bonny. I won't treat you the way he did. All I want is your love."

He wiped her cheek with his finger. The warmth of her tears stood in stark contrast to the icicle piercing his heart as she struggled to speak. "I—I shouldn't have waited so long. You want children …"

"Wheesht, it's all right." He drew her to his lap, stroking her hair and whispering his love as sadness for her pain, and the loss of his hoped for heir, squeezed one more dream out of his heart. "*Tha mo gaol gu bràth*. My love is forever. Relax, *mo chridhe*, you're so tense."

"There's more."

He willed himself to say nothing, waiting …

"It's Adam. He keeps contacting me in sneaky ways. Envelopes with someone else's return address. Phone calls from different numbers since I blocked his. And now …"

Kieran bit his lip hard. "Now?"

"I received flowers the other day and assumed they were from you. I had to sign for them, which was odd, but in with them I found Adam's engagement ring. He included a note asking me to remember the dream we once shared. I sent the ring back the same day, with no response, and threw two dozen roses in the garbage bin."

"What do you intend to do?" He pushed her to her feet and stood up, heading down the trail toward the car. What was he supposed to feel? She hadn't kept them, but she hadn't been forceful enough to stop Adam's attention either. He turned back to face her.

"Isn't sending the ring back enough?"

He willed his voice to remain calm. This was a lot to take all at once. "How do you plan to keep him from getting in touch with you again? Will you see him when you go for the wedding?"

She stopped, staring at him with her mouth wide, tears trickling down her cheeks. "You know I don't want to see him. I've told him to stop. I've ignored him, blocked him, and changed my number. He doesn't quit."

"Bonny, I want him out of your life, unless you still love him." The pressure cooker in his heart felt ready to explode.

She shook her head. "You know I don't. There's no reason to be jealous."

"First you say you can't have children, when you've had plenty of opportunities to tell me. Then I find out you haven't stopped Adam's attention."

Rivulets flowed down her cheeks, leaving black smears of mascara behind. "I—I'm sorry, Kieran. I was afraid to tell you. You know I changed my number weeks ago. I don't know how he got the new one. I don't."

White-hot anger forced itself up, exploding before he gained control. "Afraid? Have I ever given you reason to feel afraid?"

"No." It was raining harder, and she shivered.

"I promised you I wouldn't lie, but when you leave out important details, it's the same as lying. It matters. You can't stop Adam from contacting you by mail, but I have to know you're telling the truth." He stalked down the path, leaving her behind.

"Kieran." She ran up beside him, grasping at his sleeve. "I didn't intend to lie."

"Whether you intended it or not, you said nothing when you knew it mattered. I've talked about a family, about how I long for an heir." He reached the Land Rover and swung open the driver's side door.

Her breath came in gulping sobs. "Please forgive me. I should have told you. I'm sorry, Kieran."

"Get in and I'll take you home. You nag me about God, but you let me believe we could have a family." He started the engine and backed out before she had her seatbelt on. "I have to think this over. In the meantime, let me be. When I have something to say, I know where to find you."

The ride home was silent and tense. He sat with the engine running while she climbed out of the car, heading down the street before she reached the front door.

He drove all the way to the farm, anger and disappointment chasing him down like hungry wolves and tearing at his insides. Bonny's announcement took him by surprise. He loved children and had anticipated she would give him another chance to have the family he longed for. What wounded him the most was that she had numerous opportunities to tell him and had held it back. Why was she so afraid?

She insisted that his lack of faith had bearing on the quality of a marriage relationship, yet she had been dishonest about something she knew was important to him.

The whole thing was crazy, a whirlwind romance with someone ten years younger, from another country. What was he thinking?

Following a sleepless night, Kieran took one of the farm trucks and headed for the bothy. Solitude didn't sound pleasant, but neither did the questions and curious glances of Eleanor and Angus.

During the day, he stalked the hills, his mind in a tumult of pain and longing. When he did sleep, he dreamed of Bonny—of holding her, warm and sweet smelling in his arms, and hearing her say she loved him. The memory of her face, wet with tears, and her voice pleading for his forgiveness, hurt to the depths of his being. He could live without children. He couldn't live, didn't want to live without her. She had never tried to have children, maybe the doctor was wrong. As for Adam, he wasn't worth worrying about. All that mattered was the chance to spend his life with her.

He packed up and headed down the side of *Cnocan Dubh*, a mountain northeast of the farmhouse. Traveling a little-used trail to the A87, he headed for Fort William. She should be home from class by the time he arrived.

Rain was falling hard, and it was almost dark when Kieran pulled to a stop in front of the little cottage. Bonny's face appeared at the window as he pulled into the drive. The door opened and she stood, silhouetted against the light, waiting, so small in stature but so large in heart. Scotland might have been an escape to allow her to gain a better perspective, but she didn't run from the challenges of life.

"May I come in?" It was his turn to feel uncertain. In that moment, he knew why she hesitated to tell him she couldn't have children. He had let her down by responding just as she feared he might.

"Please. Do you want a cup of tea?" she asked, as if she expected him.

"Yes, please. We need to talk."

She had the water hot, and he stood in silence while she poured it into the pot and set the tea things on the tray. He carried it into the living room for her, all the time his heart was pounding like drums at the Tattoo.

"Bonny, I have to apologize. I am so sorry I got angry. On my way down the mountain, I was so afraid you wouldn't want to see me again. My love for you is not dependent on your ability to produce an heir, like one of my prize ewes. I love you whether or not we can have children."

"Kieran—" She was twisting her hair again, and he reached for her hand.

"I'm sorry I was angry about Adam. No matter what you said, I was afraid the ring might tempt you to return to your first love."

"But why? I told you I wanted nothing to do with him. You know what he did …"

"Because a man wanted to put a ring on your finger, and it wasn't me. I was jealous. But I was wrong to be angry for something you can't control."

"I have tried to end it. But Kieran, I don't love him. I love you."

"I know that. There's one more thing. Faith in God is important to you. I will keep coming to church with you, and I will talk with Graeme. I don't want any of these things to stand between us. I love you, Bonny, without any qualifications."

Her hand was still in his, and she placed the other on his cheek. "I'm so happy you came back. I should have told you sooner. I was wrong too. But Kieran, you have to trust me where Adam is concerned. It's possible I might see him when I go for Kari and Dan's wedding, not because I want to, but because it's out of my control."

He swallowed hard. He didn't want another man to think he had a right to her love, but she was right. "I trust you."

"Thank you. I don't love him. You taught me about true love, and you're the only man I love."

"I have dreamed of holding you, your scent, your lips …" He felt her trembling as she looked into his eyes. Letting go of her hands, he wrapped his arms around her, holding her against his heart. Her lips tasted sweet as she responded to his kiss. Her love was all he needed. When he pulled back, she smiled, and it felt as if fireworks were exploding in his head. "Will you come to Beauly for Christmas?"

Light sparked in her eyes, and a smile spread across her lips. "Yes, if you still want me, I'd love to."

He kissed her again, and a tingling streamed through him. Life without her bright presence to chase away the dark was no longer imaginable. He drove to his aunt's at midnight, his lips still tasting of her kiss. *I never dreamed of loving this way again. If you're real, God, please don't make me live without her.*

CHAPTER TWENTY:

PREPARATIONS AND DILEMMAS

"Wait until Dr. Cameron hears his American professor is prejudiced against Scots." Deirdre leaned across Bonny's desk, her peculiar amber eyes reminding Bonny of a predatory cat. "I won't fail a class because you're unwilling to allow for beliefs different from your own."

Bonny's heart beat faster, her breath coming short and fast. She mustn't allow her fear to show. Kieran had warned her about being alone with Deirdre Adair, but the imposing woman had entered her office when the majority of faculty had left for the day. She must have hidden inside before the outside doors were locked. "I prefer to discuss this during normal office hours. Students aren't allowed here this time of day."

Thankful for the desk between them, Bonny slid the cell phone out of her pocket with as much stealth as possible and touched Kieran's name on the screen. If he answered, he might recognize something was wrong. He was in his office at the opposite end of the hall.

"I waited to catch you alone." The eyes narrowed, sending a chill through Bonny. She felt evil whenever Deirdre was around—didn't trust her. With the door closed, it was impossible to see if anyone passed by who could help.

"In the future, make an appointment during regular office hours. This time is for faculty to work undisturbed." Bonny's heart pounded, and her hands shook, but she heard Kieran's voice, a mere whisper with the volume turned down. She felt calmer knowing he was on his way.

"Deirdre," she spoke louder than necessary to ensure he heard. "You've refused time and time again to complete the work as it's assigned. This was to be a paper on the Christian faith of a Founding Father of the United States, not a diatribe against Christianity. I'll allow you one opportunity to complete this paper in acceptable form before Friday. Grades must be in by Monday."

Deirdre put her hands on the desk, her long nails adding to the cat-like image.

"If you fail me, I'll speak with the *Heidy.*" In her anger, she slipped into the Scots dialect, more common in the South.

Kieran opened the door without knocking. Her phone trick had worked. Deirdre's eyes grew wide in surprise as his booming voice and imposing presence filled the small office. His eyes fastened on Deirdre, though he spoke to Bonny. "Dr. Bryant, I recognized your car in the car park and didn't think you should walk out alone in the dark."

Bonny's heart slowed. "Thank you, Dr. MacDonell. I was discussing a paper with Deirdre, but we're finished. I appreciate you thinking of me." She stood, breathing deep, and forcing her voice to a commanding tone. "Deirdre, the office wing is off limits to students except during office hours. If you're here again outside those hours, I'll have to report it to administration."

The large woman stood only a few inches shorter than Kieran's six foot four and weighed close to the same. His eyes sparked blue fire as he seized her by the arm. "I heard you in the hallway. I'll not tolerate you threatening Dr. Bryant. You'll follow rules or suffer the consequences. Talk to Dr. Cameron if you will. You won't fool him."

The narrowing eyes and down-turned mouth indicated her annoyance at the interruption. She eyed Bonny with undisguised disgust, but her expression when she turned to Kieran was like an all-together different person. "Why Dr. MacDonell, I was just leaving. It's so kind of you to think of a woman walking alone in the dark. You never know what might happen these days."

"The only woman I'm concerned about is Dr. Bryant. Get on out of here before I escort you out, and don't let me see you near her again."

Deirdre continued in the syrupy sweet voice she only used when talking to Kieran. "I'm sorry I lost my temper, Dr. Bryant. I've been under some strain lately."

Forcing her into the hall, he shut the door on her heels and held his arms out. Bonny couldn't get out from behind the desk fast enough. She rushed to him, laying her head on his chest. "Thank you. She's a terrible woman. I won't coddle her. I'll fail her if she doesn't do as she's told."

"Aye, but keep your office door locked and be careful. She'll not forget this." He turned her face up to his, kissing her hard, then held her away, searching her face. "Are you all right, hen? Using your phone was brilliant."

She buried her face in his chest again. "I was frightened for a minute, but I feel safe now."

He swallowed hard, shutting his eyes. "So you are, *mo annsachd*." He buried his face in her hair. "I'll keep you safe, my precious Bonny."

♋

The note in Kieran's box in the college office was addressed to "Dr. MacDonell" in bold letters, written in pencil. He ripped it open to find a page of math problems in his own writing. Unfolding the sheet of paper, he recognized the handwriting at once. It was Deirdre's.

My Dearest Kieran. Well that was a stretch. It continued:

> *I can't continue at FWCC and face seeing you with her all the time. We could have had something special, but you have been blinded by the American. You belong to Scotland. Our nation needs men and women of Scottish blood to build our nation. When you realize you are making a mistake, I will be here. For now, I am going away, but I'll know when you're ready. Remember me, Deirdre*

> *This doesn't qualify as a secret. Bonny knows I don't care for Deirdre. No need to make waves. I'll get rid of it and be glad she won't be around making us uncomfortable anymore. He tore it in shreds and threw it away.*

♋

More than turmoil at school or rehearsals for the musical, the trip to meet Kieran's parents made Bonny nervous. Janet, resigned to the decision, reassured her. "Maggie and Hamish are special people. She's protective of her son, but once she recognizes your heart for the Lord and your sweet spirit, you'll do fine."

"Kieran warned me she's not pleased I'm from America."

Janet patted her shoulder. "Turn it into something positive, Bonny. Gifts from New Mexico could help them get to know you. Learn the Gaelic and let them know you love it here, too. Hamish enjoys gourmet cooking."

"What about a gift basket of New Mexican food?"

Janet nodded. "Perfect. Men love food. He's as gentle and kind as Kieran. He'll love you. Maggie's taste isn't much different from your own. Choose a gift typical to New Mexico that you would like."

Bonny touched the cross at her neck. "People say how pretty my turquoise is whenever I wear it. I saw a turquoise cross on the Internet the other day—simple and lovely."

"Perfect. As for Kieran, dinnae fash yoursel'. Men appreciate a picture of the woman they love. Remember the one I took of you in the heather near Ben Nevis last fall? Your eyes look so lovely with your green sweater. Have it enlarged and framed."

Bonny agreed, adding a book on American History and another on New Mexico, with the potential to provide them with hours of conversation. She suspected Kieran planned a proposal, but she still wasn't certain how to respond. He was everything she had ever dreamed of, except for one thing. It was hard to believe only one problem created a major threat to their otherwise strong relationship.

CBEO

"Mmm," Kieran licked the chili off his finger. "You should cook a New Mexican dinner for my parents."

"If your mother approves." She swatted the back of his hand as he prepared to stick his finger in the pot again.

He lifted her hair and kissed the back of her neck as she turned back to the stove. "Stop worrying. You'll love each other once you get acquainted."

"I'm not worrying, but a woman's kitchen is her domain, and I shouldn't presume."

It was useless to argue when she used that firm tone of voice and set her jaw. "I'll call them after dinner."

Hamish greeted the idea with enthusiasm, and Kieran hung up with a smile. "You're on, Dr. Bryant. My da thinks it's a super idea."

"I said to ask your mother." She set the tea tray on the table and sat down next to him.

"Da can convince her of anything. You worry too much."

"I'm not worrying."

He put his finger under her chin, turning her face. "I see those wrinkles in your forehead. Relax. This Christmas will be lovely, I promise."

ιε

"I don't believe this is Kieran's idea. It's hers."

Hamish sat next to his wife and reached into the box of Christmas decorations. "Maggie, he's found someone to love after two years of misery. We prayed for his life to change, and it has. Stop complaining."

"Ouch." She put her finger through a glass ornament. "Now see what I've done. I agreed to help with his plans for a romantic proposal because I had no choice. Agreeing to her cooking us a New Mexican meal, whatever that is, is simply a ploy to move Kieran one step closer to America."

"He's not moving to America. Don't judge her before you know her."

ιε

The phone ringing at five in the morning startled Bonny awake. "Rise and shine, Carrot-Top."

"Dan, oh Dan, it's so good to hear your voice." She turned on the lamp and sat up in bed.

"Being home again is the best feeling ever. At times I thought I wouldn't make it. A quiet family Christmas sounds perfect, but one important member of our family is missing this year."

"Oh, I wish I was there to welcome you home." The distance felt like a tangible thing.

"It doesn't seem right with you gone. Do you have plans for Christmas?"

"Actually, I had two invitations, but I decided to spend Christmas with Kieran's family, so I can meet his parents." She held her breath, waiting for his answer.

"That's a big step, Bon. Kari has kept me filled in on things. Remember what Drew taught us in the college group at church about dating relationships?"

It didn't take him long to get to that.

"Like-mindedness in spiritual matters. He warned us not to date someone we wouldn't consider marrying." She didn't attempt to hide her irritation. "Kieran isn't a non-believer, Dan. He's caught in the same struggle I went through."

His voice remained calm. "You're pinning a lot on what you think and not what he does."

"You're a dear friend, Danny Boy, but I know his heart. I can't imagine refusing if he proposes."

She knew the sound when he clicked his tongue in exasperation. "I can't say anything to change your mind, but I'd feel better if I met him."

Once he admitted defeat, she changed subjects. "You would like him, I promise. How are you doing? I worry about you."

"I'm down to one crutch already. I plan to go hiking next summer. Consider what I said, please?"

She did as she promised while she packed for the trip to Beauly. As much as she hated it, Dan was right.

CHAPTER TWENTY-ONE

BEAULY

Thick fog and blowing snow caused Kieran to concentrate on the road as they traveled north to Beauly three days before Christmas. Surrounded by the snowy silence, neither spoke for miles. When he managed to think about anything other than the road, he envisioned his grandmother's oval ruby ring encircled by diamonds sparkling on Bonny's finger.

She laid her hand on his shoulder, interrupting his concentration. "I appreciate you bringing the Bible out after dinner and suggesting we pray together the past few weeks."

His lips curved up with pleasure at her praise, but his eyes stayed on the road. "I need to put my past behind and move forward. Talking to Graeme and singing in the choir convinced me to examine my attitude."

She squeezed his shoulder. "I know you're trying."

He wanted to please her, but more than anything, he desired to make her his wife. The loneliness was too much to bear any longer.

☙☙☙

Bonny's mind strayed to a subject she preferred to avoid—the Christmas card. It arrived the day before in an envelope with the return address of an old college friend. She tore into it, eager to catch up on the news. Instead she discovered a letter from Adam. Once again, he had used an envelope with the address label of a mutual friend as the return, and used an address label for her address, rather than handwriting it. *He must be stealing address labels from people. That's pretty low.* Once again, the letter was typed.

"Dear Bonny," it read, "I find it difficult to face Christmas without you. I can't accept that you love someone else. Please give us another chance. The love I have for you will not die. I will always be faithful if you return to me. Love forever, Adam."

She glanced over at Kieran, questioning whether her love limited her visibility toward the man beside her as much as the fog limited his visibility of the road. He had watched her throw the card and letter in the fireplace, and thanked her for telling him. The adventure of being loved by him was priceless. If only …

CR&O

Kieran's eyes strayed to Bonny, asleep in the seat beside him. His throat tightened at the sight of her face, relaxed in sleep, with her long auburn lashes shadowing her cheeks. How he wanted her to be his first sight in the morning. He put Christmas music in the CD player and stroked her cheek as they drew near Beauly. Before falling asleep, she had reminded him to awaken her before they reached the Inn.

She stretched, yawned, and brought out her lipstick.

"My parents will love you whether or not you have perfect lipstick."

As she put it away and fluffed her hair with her fingers, he made a sharp left and stopped in front of an ancient and charming stone house, its steep gabled roof with chimneys, or *lums*, rising above each room.

"The Heather Hill Inn, my second home."

She gasped. "What a beautiful house. It looks as if it came straight out of a Dickens novel."

Pleased with her reaction, Kieran sounded the horn and his mother hurried out, his father following close behind. Maggie hugged Kieran, then turned her attention to Bonny. "Welcome. Come out of the cold and let the men bring in the luggage. I have a real old-fashioned tea ready." She whisked Bonny away following the briefest introductions.

His father embraced him in a firm hug. "You've found another jewel from the glimpse I got. Can I *gie ye a haund*?" He began to lift the luggage out of the back of the Land Rover.

Kieran grunted as he reached for Bonny's suitcase, weighing twice as much as his own. "Aye, that she is, Da. I inherited my excellent taste from you. Mother's still a beauty at sixty-five."

Hamish shook his head. "Your mother is a rare blessing, it's certain. Ach, I'm still amazed she chose a sheep farmer. She's pleased you're attending church and singing in the choir. Be prepared, she's not comfortable with you falling in love with an American yet." He held open the door. "Come *ben the hoose*, son."

Kieran squeezed past his father into the large entry hall. "Bonny will win Mother over. Wait 'til you get to know her."

He followed close behind his mother and Bonny as they went up the stairs, awaiting her reaction. The exquisite, antique, four-poster bed with its rose velvet bed curtains and sumptuous down comforter in a brilliant floral design had the old-fashioned elegance she loved. A round-mirrored dressing table with lace doilies, a delicate writing desk, and a giant mahogany wardrobe completed the effect.

"Take time to freshen up. Tea in twenty minutes." Maggie took off down the stairs.

Kieran stood behind Bonny, so close he felt her warmth. As she stepped into the room, her eyes rested on a bouquet of red roses on the nightstand. When she turned to thank him, he caught her in his arms, laying his forehead against hers. "At last I have you in my parents' home. I haven't looked forward to Christmas in two years."

He pulled her toward the window and wasn't disappointed with her response to the view. "Oh, Kieran, it's amazing."

"I told Mother you would love this room. Mine is right next door."

The rugged cliffs rising up behind the house weren't obvious from the front. Forest, mountains, and a picturesque round tower frosted with wet, heavy snow created an irresistible charm. Watching her face light up as she drank in the beauty of his family home, he expected to have a bride before the week was out.

☙❧

Margaret MacKenzie MacDonell was still an attractive woman. At sixty-five, she possessed a grace and depth of presence few women ever acquire. Her world revolved around her God, her husband, and her son.

The busy life of overseeing one of the premier bed and breakfast establishments in the Highlands energized her. Thanks to her well-trained staff, she was free to serve as a gracious hostess. Visitors traveled from around Scotland to attend high teas at the Heather Hill Inn.

One thing Maggie hadn't anticipated was her son falling in love with an American. Holding back tears, she located Hamish in the kitchen. "I can't do this. We'll lose our son. At the expense of breaking his heart again, I want her to go back home."

He drew her close and smoothed her hair. "Maggie, *mo bhean*, he's a grown man who's suffered more pain than most people do in a lifetime. If there's any possibility for him to find happiness, we must support him." He bent and kissed her forehead. "You can, and you will."

"I'll put up with it, but I won't be happy." She wiped her tears on her apron.

He put a finger under her chin, forcing her to meet his eyes. "You will if he's happy. Let him make his own decisions."

"And if we lose him?" She located a tissue in the bottom of her apron pocket, wiped her eyes, and blew her nose.

He leaned over, whispering in her ear. "We won't lose him."

"But …"

He stroked her hair back from her face. "He's a grown man, middle-aged. You once said you'd have a difficult time sharing your only son with any woman, but you and Bronwyn had an ideal relationship."

"After I got to know her."

"Give Bonny the same opportunity, love. You prayed for God to rescue him from his loneliness, and He has. You wanted him in church and he's there. She's lost everyone. Let's give her a family Christmas. It's wiser to win her with honey than to alienate them both with harsh words."

"You force me to see everything in a different light, don't you?" She gave him a mischievous shove. "Now, let me finish preparing the tea. I'll do my best, but it won't be easy."

"Thank you, *mo gràdh*." With a lighthearted swat on the *bahooky*, he went into the parlor to build up the fire.

"I'll try, but it won't be easy."

�⋈

"I'll give you the tour later." Putting his hand on her back, Kieran escorted Bonny downstairs for tea.

Hamish stood when they entered the room. "*Ceud mile failte, caud mile failte,* a hundred, thousand welcomes, Bonny." He motioned to a chair next to him. "Here, next to me. Maggie rushed you inside so fast, I didn't have a proper chance to greet you."

Bonny knew she and Hamish had made an immediate connection. A large, strong man, though smaller than Kieran, both father and son shared great similarities in voice and appearance. She looked twenty-five years into the future, recognizing Kieran in the large, calloused hands and jolly laugh. His coloring came from his mother. Maggie's hair was snow white now, but her deep blue eyes were the same. Being part of a family for Christmas felt good.

Bonny turned from one to the other. "It means so much to spend Christmas in your lovely home. Thank you."

"It's our privilege, lass," Hamish reassured her.

"You must miss your home at Christmas," Maggie said. "Your offer to fix a dinner intrigues me, but I question whether it's due to homesickness."

Bonny noted blue sparks flying between the matching eyes of mother and son.

"Yes, I am." Bonny recognized a test. "This is the first time I've been away from home at Christmas. My parents have been gone such a short time that I miss them very much. Kieran suggested the dinner, and I wanted a special way to thank you for your hospitality. I'd like to show you something about my home. New Mexico has some very unique traditions, and Kieran thought it would be fun for me to share them."

"We look forward to it." Hamish laid a hand on Maggie's arm. "Don't we, my love?"

�⋈

Following tea, Kieran began their tour at the front door. Ancient family portraits of the MacKenzies dotted the deep red wallpaper rising to a high vaulted ceiling. A large, round table boasted a monstrous floral display, and Bonny walked over to get a closer look.

"What an impressive flower arrangement." She leaned closer, inhaling the sweet aroma of a large, white rose.

Kieran put an arm around her waist. "Mother designs and creates them herself. You should ask to see her greenhouse."

An unusual combination of red poinsettias, white roses, pine boughs, and holly, the mixture of roses and pine together gave off a sweet, tangy scent she found irresistible. Bonny inhaled the fragrant perfume again. "She's talented. It's one of the most striking and unique arrangements I've ever seen." Perhaps the way into Maggie's good graces was by complimenting her talents.

The table stood against the backdrop of a wide, curving staircase, its banister draped in holly. An ornate stained glass window on the landing let in colored light, and the old wood floors shone from years of traffic and scrubbing. Double doors led to a large parlor filled with fine antiques and a massive white plaster fireplace. On the opposite side of the foyer was a dining room with a table of such massive proportions it seated thirty people at once.

Kieran refused to take her down one hallway. "We'll go there another day. It's special." He pointed out the window where big, wet flakes of snow whirled in the wind. Not even the nearby barn was visible. "We'll put off the tour of the grounds until tomorrow."

CRSO

Bonny snuggled under the fluffy down comforter later that night, conscious of the single wall separating her from Kieran. She had already caught glimpses of the faith he was raised with in the blessing his father said before the meal and his mother's promise to attend the Christmas Eve service whether or not the snow let up.

"Lord," she prayed, "please help Kieran return to his faith in you. Then I can have peace in my heart. Please cause him to change before he asks me to marry him. You know my heart's desire. I'll need your strength if I'm to refuse him."

She heard the bed next door creaking from time to time. She quivered, remembering the obvious longing in his eyes and hoping that he sensed her unspoken desires as they discussed home and family.

At last, aware of the slight snoring from the next room, she fell asleep, dreaming of dancing in his arms, a diamond sparkling on her finger.

◌◌

At breakfast, Kieran announced plans to help Hamish with odd jobs around the house. Helping himself to more scrambled eggs and haggis, he glanced at Maggie. "Why don't you and Bonny spend the time getting better acquainted, Mother?"

Understanding his intent, Bonny said, "I heard you mention baking, Maggie. I want to help however I can."

When the men headed for the basement, she carried the dishes to Bridget, the Inn's cook. There was a marked resemblance between Maggie's cook and her mother, Kieran's housekeeper.

Maggie brought out her cookbooks. Pouring more tea, she handed a cup to Bonny. "Before we do the baking, I think we need to get to know one another."

"Thank you." Bonny accepted the cup. "Kieran and Eleanor say wonderful things about you and Hamish."

Maggie's smile looked stiff and unnatural. "I'm concerned because your home is so far away. While I can't ignore the changes in my son, the difference in your backgrounds concerns me."

"It's surprising to learn how much we do have in common." Taken aback by Maggie's abrupt approach, Bonny was determined to remain positive. "I assure you, my heart and home will be with the man I love, wherever he is."

Maggie appeared to ignore her. "This house has belonged to my family for generations. It's not a castle or large country manor, but I grew up here. I would like it to remain in the family. Though I doubt Kieran will keep the inn open, I love sharing it with others."

This topic was one she could respond to with enthusiasm. "Both of your homes are beautiful. I fell in love with the farm, the sheep, the loch, and the mountains."

Maggie's smile showed genuine satisfaction and perhaps pride. "I love it, too. As you can imagine, living so far away from town was an adjustment, and an agricultural life is not an easy one. However, it's been gratifying to watch Kieran work the farm."

Bonny met Maggie's eyes, hoping to convey her agreement. "Kieran's heritage and his passion for the lands he will inherit is something I respect very much."

"Great responsibilities accompany both properties. The Inn and sheep farm must be different from anything you've experienced. They will prevent him from spending large amounts of time away." Maggie's voice carried a warning tone, which made Bonny uncomfortable.

"Yes, I understand." Her eyes locked with Maggie's in a challenge.

Maggie continued her narrative. "As for me, my day begins and ends on my knees and in the word of God, and Hamish likewise. Kieran did the same until the deaths of Bronwyn and the baby. He still struggles, I think." She poured herself another cup of tea.

"I start and end each day with my time in God's word. But not so long ago, I was struggling just like Kieran is." Bonny held out her cup as Maggie offered more tea. "We read a passage from Psalms or Proverbs after dinner. He's trying since he's been going to church with Janet and me."

"Thank you. I'm pleased he's attending church again." She met Bonny's eyes with a nod of gratitude.

Bonny dropped a cube of sugar into the fine china cup, stirring it with a demitasse spoon. "I'm looking forward to attending church with you on Christmas Eve. My favorite memories of Christmas include church with my parents."

"We attend Christmas Eve service as a family, except for the Christmases Kieran spent in Glasgow. Then, he and Bronwyn came here for Hogmanay, your New Year's Eve."

Bonny latched onto the family theme. "I know your family is very close. Having lost my own, that's important to me. I appreciate you allowing me to spend Christmas with you."

"I want you to enjoy your time here." Maggie poured another cup, inhaling it's aroma with a pleasure peculiar to someone with an expertise in tea.

"Kieran and I plan to share our music from the Christmas program with you. We enjoy singing together. I think it helped him decide to join me at church." She made eye contact with Maggie. "I fell away for a time when I lost my loved ones also. I've learned that the single answer to the 'whys' in life is God's sovereignty. Being in Scotland, away from everything familiar, helped me take a new look at my situation. Whatever happens between us, I pray for Kieran to return to the Lord. A heart as tender as his heals slowly."

The surprise on Maggie's face convinced Bonny she had scored. "I'm glad you recognize those qualities, considering the short time you've known each other."

At last she discovered common ground. "From the first evening together, we've talked into the wee hours of the morning. We understand each other and are discovering how much we agree on."

Maggie's voice grew softer. "Thank you. If it's not too forward, are you in love with my Kieran?"

Bonny didn't hesitate. "Yes, I am."

"I pray you both listen for God's wisdom. Love can blind you to potential problems. I do see changes in him, and I appreciate you encouraging that change." Maggie stood, her hand brushing Bonny's shoulder. "Now, we must get to our baking or the men will come upstairs and ask what we've been doing."

Handing Bonny the recipe for Kieran's favorite shortbread, Maggie began on Hamish's favorite macaroons while Bridget made Scottish Tablet, a candy that was new to Bonny. With her cookies in the oven, Bonny brought out her special Swedish Tea Ring, a Bryant family tradition. "We used to eat it for breakfast, but you can use it however you want."

Squaring her shoulders, Maggie accepted it. "We'll include it with the eggs, black sausage, and haggis, thank you."

Delectable smells filling the house drew the men up from the basement in search of sweets and their sweethearts. While taking cookies off the sheet, Bonny found herself wrapped in a warm hug with a soft whisper of, "I love you."

She considered the morning a success. In time, she believed it possible to develop a strong relationship with Maggie. The nagging voice in the back of her mind warned her to wait for signs of Kieran's true faith.

CHAPTER TWENTY-TWO:

ARGUMENT AND OPPORTUNITY

The snow had taken a brief respite, though the clouds still hung heavy and dark above the winter-white landscape. Bonny and Kieran put on boots and coats, setting out to explore the grounds. Wrapped in a safe, loving cocoon, they trod through the foot-deep snow in silence.

On impulse, she bent and formed a snowball while he moved some branches, broken by the weight of the wet snow. When he straightened up, she threw it hard at his back. He turned in surprise, scooping up a handful of snow, and they pelted one another until they fell down laughing. Giggling, Bonny made a snow angel and Kieran followed suit.

"You made an archangel. It's huge compared to mine." She laughed at him, lying like a snowman fallen over in one piece.

He rolled over, crawling toward her, and pulled her into a snowy hug. "You gave me a fair skelpin'. Where did you learn that, my wee desert rat?"

"It snows in New Mexico. It's a desert, but we have real mountains."

He kissed the top of her head where it lay in the crook of his arm. "You're amazing, hen. It's so lovely to have you here."

Lying in the cradle of his arm, she turned her face up to his. "I love you. I also love your homes, both of them, and your parents."

"Even my mother?" His blue eyes shone through snowflakes caught in red-gold lashes.

She brushed the snow off his face with a gloved hand. "Of course your mother. She wants the best for you. I dreaded my first Christmas away from home, but I never expected to find love when I looked for escape."

Pulling her up with him, he planted a snowy kiss on her cheek. "I need a lifetime to show how much you're loved." He tucked a strand of hair under her cap. "We'll be droochit. Are you cold?"

Bonny shook her head. "I'm warm as toast. I want to see the barn. How many horses do you have?"

"Four, but they're for the sleigh and carriages, no riding horses."

She took his hand, pulling him along.

"We can ride horses back at the farm, and when you come to Albuquerque someday—"

The corners of his eyes crinkled, and his face lit up. "I don't remember you inviting me. Did I miss something?"

"I—ummm," she hesitated, her cheeks growing warm in spite of the cold. "You might come sometime."

Kieran put his hand under her chin and tilted her face upward. "Perhaps when we're married?"

"Kieran …" She buried her face against his chest.

"It's possible. We've talked around the subject since we met."

She stifled a sob as he lifted her face toward his once again. "Why are you cryin', lass?"

Bonny hid her face again. "It's no secret. I'm so confused. If …"

He stiffened, pulling away. "Confused? What are you doin' here then? You think we shouldna be married, because we don't agree about God? You would throw away everything we have together because of one difference? It's not as if I lied." His voice rose in pitch as he continued. "And you say you love me? You can stop prayin' for me too."

"Kieran …"

He turned, striding toward the house.

When he looked back, his face flushed more with anger than the cold. "Ach, stop *nippin' my heid*, it's not hard to see why Adam left you. No one meets your standards. I'm done tryin'." His voice grew harsher, his eyes glinting steel below brows furrowed in fury. "I was wrong to believe we had somethin' special."

"Kieran, please?" She wiped her cheeks with a gloved hand, her heart pounding harder at the mention of Adam.

"I can't meet the standard you set. It's too high." With a defiant set to his jaw, he turned toward the house.

"Kieran, I love you." She ran after him, grabbing his arm.

He shook her off. "Ach, I'll not be criticized for the rest of my life. Perhaps you'd prefer someone like Graeme."

"Kieran, we can't ignore this. We have to be of one mind in spiritual matters." Her heart pounded, and the familiar lump grew in her throat. *Is it my fault?*

He called over his shoulder, "I intended to fool you into believin' I'd changed. Well, I can't. We will tolerate each other this week for my parents' sake. When we return to Fort William, we'll act as if nothin' happened between us. Go put on dry clothes."

She chased after him, her thoughts roiling in panic. "Kieran, wait. I was engaged to one man who lied about being a Christian. Why bother with church and the choir if you feel this way? You promised me the truth."

His anger was something new, and his Scottish burr was growing so strong she struggled to understand him. "When we met we agreed. I felt loved for myself. For my parents' sake, let's not create a scene over this. At least we found out before we made a mistake."

CうৎৎৎD

Maggie met them at the kitchen door, glancing from Bonny to Kieran's anger-reddened face and back again. "Dry off. I'll bring up tea. You must be freezing."

Bonny headed upstairs, knowing she had made an enemy where she hoped to make a friend.

"It's not your business, Mother. Leave me alone." Bonny heard his angry reply when his mother knocked and bit her lip hard enough to hurt as Maggie knocked on her own door.

"May I come in?"

She opened the door wider and stepped aside, knowing her eyes must look red and swollen.

"I brought tea to warm you." Maggie's steel-blue eyes mirrored those of her son. Setting down the tea, she walked into the bathroom and turned on the shower, speaking in a whisper. "What happened? You promised not to hurt him."

Bonny reached for a tissue. She had to make his mother see her love for Kieran. "Maggie, I love him, but we have to agree where our faith is concerned. Now he's so angry ..." She perched on the edge of the bed, but stood again, unable to stay still.

"How do you disagree?" Maggie's voice sounded as cold and biting as the wind picking up outside.

Bonny clasped her arms to stop trembling. "He claims he's a Christian ..."

"Of course he is." The maternal claws came out in defense of her son. "It's not unusual to struggle with doubt after what he lost."

Bonny repeated Kieran's words, hiccupping and sniffling. "The man I was engaged to before claimed he was a Christian, but he deserted me for another woman the day after my father's funeral. To lose Kieran would tear my heart out. I thought the time in choir and church might help him. A moment ago he admitted lying to me."

Maggie's eyes sparked with the passion of a mother protecting her child. "My son isn't perfect. I told you I saw too many differences. Perhaps you should end it now." She paused, and a shadow passed over her face.

Bonny hiccupped as she nodded. "I love him more than I ever imagined I could love anyone, but he's angry with God, and refuses to accept the deaths of Bronwyn and the baby. We can't have unity in our marriage if he won't forgive God." She massaged the uncomfortable knot in her throat. "He said to stop praying for him, that everything I thought was change was actually lies. True love can't exist without trust."

"He admitted he lied?" Maggie's jaw muscles clenched, and her hand brushed Bonny's shoulder as she passed, shutting the door with care.

CR&O

Kieran came downstairs before Bonny, and his mother pulled him into the small parlor, shutting the door. "What happened between you two? I heard a young woman say she was willing to put your relationship with the Lord above happiness for both of you. Yes, you've struggled, but I had no idea you doubted everything."

White-hot anger rose from deep inside. "Ach, *Mathair*, I won't have you sidin' with her."

She grasped him by the shoulders, blue sparks flashing from her eyes. "Kieran, if you don't believe all of God's word, you don't truly believe. Don't hurt both of you by clinging to the past and your anger." She laid her hand on his cheek.

All he needed was two of them preaching at him. "She told the truth. I have reason to doubt God, but she won't rest until I become a specimen of perfect Christianity." He slammed the door on his way out.

CR80

Bonny and Kieran sat in silence as Hamish explained the pastor's request for them to sing for the Christmas Eve and Christmas Day services. He and most of the choir had the flu. Kieran turned from the window where he stood staring into the night. "We haven't practiced since the program two weeks ago, and we don't have an accompanist, though we can accompany each other for our solos."

"Didn't you bring CDs so you could sing for us? Would they help you?" Hamish had called Kieran and Bonny down from their rooms, where they vanished as soon as dinner was finished.

"We did." Kieran turned to Bonny. "Will you do it for my parents?"

The heartbreak in her eyes was his fault, and he gentled his tone. Her struggle to maintain control was obvious.

"I can if you can. We'll have to spend tomorrow practicing."

Kieran approached her, remembering how close they had grown singing together. "Perhaps we should start now, unless ..."

Before he reached her, she turned and headed up the stairs. "I'll bring the CDs."

Taking his arm, Maggie asked, "Can you do this?"

He nodded. "She will do her best, and I'll do it for you."

Bonny headed for the grand piano in the guest parlor, her eyes on the floor. "We need to warm up our voices." She seated herself on the piano bench, flexing her fingers before playing a scale or two.

When she began warming up, Kieran saw his mother turn to his da, her eyebrows raised in surprise when he joined in. Both of them applauded the moment they ceased. Hamish crossed the room and put his arm around Bonny. "You have a lovely voice my dear, have you considered singing professionally?"

Her cheeks turned an attractive shade of pink. "Oh no, I've sung at church and school since I was five years old. I enjoy using the gifts God gave me."

"You have an exceptional gift," said Maggie.

"Thank you. Shall we begin with 'Silent Night'?" She avoided looking in Kieran's direction. He cued up the CD and began the first line in Gaelic.

Maggie and Hamish applauded as the song ended, and Bridget came in from the kitchen.

Though her face remained solemn, Kieran recognized the appreciation in Bonny's green eyes. Hamish crossed the room and placed his hands on her shoulders. "Bonny, you must have spent hours working on your accent. You sound as if you were born speaking Gaelic."

"I had a good teacher." Her voice caught, causing Kieran's heart to lurch.

"I've missed hearing you sing, Kieran," Maggie said. "Bonny's voice is the perfect complement to yours."

"We should practice at the church in the morning, so you can set the sound levels, Da."

He glanced at Bonny, but she only nodded, her eyes remaining on the floor.

The clock in the entry chimed eleven, and they headed upstairs. Hamish put his arm around Bonny. "You're a treasure, my dear. We're very blessed to have you in our home."

Kieran started after her. "Bonny…"

She kept going without looking back. He had to say something. He followed, laying his hands on her shoulders as she touched her doorknob. "Please, talk to me."

She pulled away, avoiding eye contact. "All I want to do is go back to Fort William. Since that's impossible, please let me have some time alone. We have a busy day tomorrow. I should rest."

The warmth of his hands lingered as she prepared for bed. Once in her nightgown, she curled into a comfortable chair by the small fireplace, holding her Bible as she prayed for him.

೮೫೮

Kieran never imagined he would feel so alone again, after Bonny said she loved him. Now she might as well be back in America, the gulf between them was so wide. Heading back downstairs, he slumped into a deep leather chair by the fire in Hamish's office, propping his chin on his hands, prepared for a lecture.

"I assumed you had come to terms with the Lord when you decided to ask Bonny to marry you. If not, then you're asking her to settle for something less than God's design for marriage. You suffered a huge loss, *mo balachan,* but you aren't the first man to lose his wife and child."

Kieran heard the disappointment in his father's voice. "Da, I love her, but she expects too much. I quit believing in a loving God a long time ago."

Hamish shook his head. "Asking her to compromise her beliefs is not love. As her husband, you will be responsible for her spiritual as well as her physical needs. To carry anger and loss into a new marriage will destroy it. What if she clung to her former fiancé the way you cling to Bronwyn?"

Kieran buried his face in his hands to avoid his father's eyes. "I've tried, Da, for two years. God abandoned me a long time ago. He quit listening to my prayers. She can accept me with my doubts or forget it."

Hamish shook his head. "Your behavior has forced your mother to side with Bonny. She now recognizes a bigger problem than an American background. Faith is not a feeling, *mo balachan*, it's a decision—a decision to leave self behind, to leave 'why' behind, and choose to believe God."

Unable to sit still, Kieran stood and turned his back, feeling like a lad caught in a lie. "I love Bonny, but I can't move past Bronnie's death. I can't ..."

"Then your lack of belief is nothing more than stubborn pride and rebellion. Many people have lost more than you. It will destroy you." The solid warmth of his father's arms coming around him shattered his last shred of control.

His entire body began to shake with sobs. "Da, help me. I can't lose her."

His da's hands moved to his shoulders. "Dear Father, thank you for the joy and love Kieran has brought to his mother and me. Help him as he struggles to surrender his burden of pain and anger. If it is your will for him to marry Bonny, enable him to grow into the man of God you created him to be. Amen."

"I can't …"

Hamish stepped back. "Then perhaps you're not giving it to God with your whole heart—believing. When you do, the burden will lift, and the Holy Spirit will enable you to do what you're powerless to accomplish on your own."

Hamish walked out, closing the door behind him. Kieran watched as the fire burned down to embers. The answer was clear. He must change if he expected Bonny to marry him.

He walked to the window, staring out into the snowy night, then picked up his father's Bible and read the passages Hamish had written on a notepad for him. Filled with an intense longing for peace, he asked God to open his eyes, and heighten his understanding, giving him the power to obey. He chafed at the chains of anger, rebellion, and depression, which refused to release him from their grasp.

"God, help me." The sound of his own voice startled him, and in the silence, he made a decision. He was not going to lose her. *I will continue to sit with her in church and sing in the choir, whatever it takes to keep her love. Maybe when she is mine I can believe. I won't feel so angry when I can go to sleep and wake up with her by my side.*

CHAPTER TWENTY-THREE

NOLLAIG CHRIDHEIL

O hhh"— Bonny let out a breath as they entered the church. Rich, dark woodwork and deep red carpet contrasted with the lighter gray stone walls and columns. The small amount of light that escaped the clouds filtered through two floor-to-ceiling stained glass windows at the front. A large, gold cross was suspended in between them, and rustic lanterns hung from a ceiling of rough-hewn timbers.

"It's the church I dreamed of … It's charming." She wiped her eyes with the sleeve of her coat.

"Aye." Kieran laid a tentative hand on her right shoulder. "It makes you want to stand quiet and humble before God."

Her eyes questioned as he placed his other hand on her left shoulder, turning her until she faced him. "Bonny, I've broken the promises I made to you. I am so sorry. Will you listen?"

Pulling off her coat, she moved into a pew, and he slid in beside her, relieved she didn't resist when he reached for her hand. "Da spoke to me last night, and God did too. I went to bed at three this morning. My rebellious attitude toward God caused me to hurt you and everyone I love. I was wrong and cruel when you tried to help me. Darlin' lass, I should have learned from the faith you have turned to in your own pain. Please forgive me?"

She moved closer, laying her hand on his cheek, but when she began to speak, he put his finger to her lips, feeling a twinge of guilt. He had lied about his faith once again, but his intentions were good. "Let me finish. I prayed last night, asking God to change my heart. Now I ask you to forgive me."

A gleam like sunshine on snow danced in her eyes. "I already forgave you."

He smoothed the soft, copper tendrils from her forehead. "*Tha gaol agam ort, mo chridhe.* I promise to learn to love you as God wants me to. I'll devote myself to your happiness and spiritual growth." When he put his arms around her, she showed no resistance.

"Thank you," she whispered, before hiding her face against his chest.

He was concentrating on kissing the tears from her cheeks when Hamish slammed the door and called out, "Are you ready to get busy?"

"We're ready," Kieran answered back. "We don't have much time, and we need God's help. Da, will you pray?"

He gave his parents a thumbs-up when Bonny turned to dig for a tissue in the bottom of her purse.

ᏣᏍᎣ

It was no easy task to blend their music with a choir decimated by illness. Kieran studied the music at the piano while Bonny and Maggie worked in the kitchen. "Bonny, love, I need your opinion. You're much better at sight-reading, and we need to see how it sounds."

"Go on, you belong in there with him." Maggie took the towel and sent her into the parlor.

Bonny had different ideas, but when he committed to taking the lead, she refused to interfere. Taking a seat next to him and leaning against his shoulder, she thanked God for his changed attitude.

The snow began falling again in earnest before time to leave for the Christmas Eve service. Hamish suggested they hitch up the sleigh. He drove, with Maggie in front beside him while Kieran and Bonny cuddled in the back with warm coats and heavy sheepskin lap robes. They rode through the silent, snow-covered hills, holding each other close, overwhelmed by love and the allure of a nighttime sleigh ride.

Wearing her emerald green dress as she stood next to her kilted Highlander, Bonny knew the emotion of their own full hearts came through in their music as never before.

Reverend Sinclair clapped Kieran on the back. "We're truly blessed. You two did a lovely job. Kieran, it will be a terrible mistake if you let this lass get away."

◌੩੪◌

Christmas Day dawned sunny and cold. Bonny snuggled into the warm wool of the new Fraser tartan outfit which Kieran insisted she open early. She stood in front of the cheval mirror and admired herself.

When she went downstairs, Hamish stood in the foyer waiting for the others. "What a lovely lassie you are. Merry *Yuil*, my dear."

"Thank you, Hamish, and Merry Yuil to you also. My dad would have loved this."

He put his arm around her and squeezed. "You must miss your parents today. How can we help?" His voice, so similar to Kieran's, was fatherly and reassuring.

"You've already done it, and more besides."

The snow-covered hills and silvery gray of Beauly Firth created the perfect Christmas card setting as they made their way to the church. The Land Rover was easier, warmer, and faster, but Kieran had convinced his father the sleigh had romantic benefits. Bonny snuggled into his arms as they glided through the glittering snow, the bells jingling on the harnesses.

She greeted people before the service with "*Nollaig Chridheil*," in close-to-perfect Gaelic. Once she managed, "*Nollaig Chridheil agus bliadhna mhath ur*," Merry Christmas and Happy New Year, with only minor mistakes. Her tongue was learning to cooperate with the odd sounds. She marveled at words with unpronounced letters and sounds not even spelled out in the word.

She overheard more than one suggestion for Kieran to marry her and keep her in Scotland. He flushed red each time, but she was unable to read his expression.

"Two people committed their lives to Christ following last night's service." Reverend Sinclair approached them before the service, insisting on delivering his Christmas message in spite of the flu.

As they sang, Bonny's heart filled with thanks to God for the man whose voice and heart blended so perfectly with her own.

After a stirring sermon on living Christmas every day of the year, they headed home. She and Kieran were oblivious to everything but each other's voices, the warmth of each other's arms, and the oneness of their hearts' longing.

CR80

The large parlor felt warm and cozy as they gathered around the glittering twelve-foot tree. Maggie served them generous pieces of Bonny's tea ring, along with steaming cups of tea while they sat in front of a roaring fire, trying to get warm after their chilly ride home.

Kieran held up Bonny's framed photo for his parents to see. "I'll treasure the picture of my bonnie lassie in the purple heather."

He surprised her with a diamond cross on a silver chain. "Oh, Kieran, the tartan was enough. This is so beautiful."

He caught her in his arms while they prepared for dinner, fingering the cross at the base of her throat. "It suits you. Small, delicate, and very precious." Drawing her into an embrace, he kissed her under the mistletoe until she was breathless.

Maggie swished past on her way to the kitchen with the tea tray. "Enough, you two. I've seen teenagers behave with more maturity."

"I feel like one, Mother." He kissed her again to prove his point.

"Go visit with your dad," Bonny said with a gentle shove. "I'm going to help your mother wash the dishes."

Maggie set the last china plate in the drainer for Bonny to dry, and pulled off her rubber gloves. "I apologize if I've been a wee bit harsh with you. I appreciate what you've done for Kieran. You were very gracious to help with the music. I don't know when I've heard two voices so perfectly matched."

Bonny knew her cheeks must be red, but there was a sudden rush of warmth in her heart. "Thank you, Maggie. I'm glad to help. I won't forget what you and Hamish did for Kieran last night. I don't know what lies ahead, but I appreciate you opening your hearts and home to me."

A hug from Maggie was the last thing she expected. "Having you in our home this Christmas has brought tremendous blessing. I won't lose him, if you two decide to marry, will I?"

Bonny put her hand on Maggie's shoulder. "If I have the opportunity, I promise to make Scotland my home, and the MacDonells my family."

ଓଞ୍ଚ

Kieran entered the large parlor where Bonny and Hamish sat by the fire discussing America, and took her hand. "I have one more Christmas surprise, so I'm stealing her away from you, Da."

He led her to the large wooden door he had avoided before. "My entire world changed the day you showed up at the faculty meeting. I wouldn't have believed you would be here with me now. Close your eyes, love."

Opening the door, he guided her inside. She shivered at his touch, his whisper warm on her neck. "Open ..."

The sweet scent of roses greeted her, and opening her eyes, she stood, speechless at the sight before her. They were in a room more romantic than anything she could imagine. A large fire burned in the ornate, cream-colored, plaster fireplace of a small sitting room. The table in front of a small couch boasted a bouquet of red and white roses in a crystal vase, and candles burned everywhere, providing the only light other than the fireplace. More roses graced the mantle and another smaller table.

Up three steps stood a set of double doors, intricately carved with Celtic knots. Bonny gasped as Kieran opened them, revealing a room containing an elegant four poster bed, curtained in deep red velvet and festooned with crocheted lace. Large windows in a curved wall revealed that they were in the ground floor of the tower visible from the back of the house.

Closing the doors, he said, "This is the bridal suite. Since it's too cold to be out in our mountains, I want to create a special memory here."

"It's lovely. There must not be any red and white roses left in Beauly."

He led her to the couch and seated himself close beside her. He turned to face her, taking both her hands in his. "There aren't words to describe the change in my life since the day I helped you in the car park, *mo gràdh*. I have love and hope again, and I believe my faith will grow as a result."

She was aware of nothing except the intense blue glow of his eyes and the light of the fire playing over his rugged, handsome features, and glinting off the red-gold of his hair.

"This suite has served as the traditional place for MacKenzie couples to spend their wedding night since the house was built in 1800. I want us to continue the tradition."

She caught her breath. His tight grip on her hands was as steady as the deep musical timbre of his voice, and his unwavering gaze held her spellbound. "I planned to bring you here last night, but thanks to my blundering, the timing was wrong."

The pounding of her heart increased as he slid to his knees. "My beautiful Bonny, will you be my wife? Will you marry me and spend the rest of your life letting me love you?"

She never gave her answer a thought. It seemed so right. "Yes, yes, Kieran, I will."

The sweet scent of the roses was overpowering. The light in his eyes, the warmth of his hands, and the woodsy scent of his aftershave overwhelmed her. "It's what I've longed for since our first evening together."

His expression of utter love and joy was beyond anything she ever imagined. He retrieved a small red velvet box from a drawer in the table, opening it to reveal a large, blood red, oval ruby surrounded by diamonds.

"Oh Kieran   "

"It belonged to my mother's mother. I asked for it when I discovered how you loved rubies." He slid it onto her finger, kissing it softly. "Bonny Faith Bryant MacDonell."

"It's the loveliest name I've ever heard." She gazed into the cerulean depths of his eyes. "I love you and want nothing more than to be your wife. After we argued, I prayed for God to do something special in your life, even if we never married. I prayed through the night when sleep was impossible."

"You prayed when marriage seemed impossible?"

She laughed. "I've prayed since Dan was hurt."

His expression attested to a joy and love as passionate as she felt for him. "We have so much to discuss, but we should tell my parents before it gets any later. We can come back here by the fire for as long as you want."

"Of course, we have to include them in our happiness." Her voice came out no louder than a whisper.

He stood up, pulling her with him, which led to another embrace. His kiss, gentle but confident, sealed their commitment more than words could ever do. Pausing at the open door, he brought the hand with the sparkling ruby to his lips. "Now, the whole world will know you're mine."

As they started through the kitchen door, he picked her up, carrying her into the kitchen, beaming. "Mother, Da, welcome your future daughter-in-law. She said yes."

"*Co-ghàirdeachas, mo chridhe,* put her down and let us welcome her to the family. You have the rest of your life to hold her." Hamish strode forward with arms outstretched. "Congratulations son, you've found a jewel."

Maggie followed, and Bonny found herself squeezed between the two of them.

"When and where?" Maggie asked as Kieran enfolded Bonny in his arms again.

"There's a lot to discuss. We came for tea and sweets." The ardor in his face filled her stomach with butterflies.

"Bonny, dear, you haven't said a word." Maggie touched her cheek with such tenderness it brought tears to her eyes again.

"I'm overwhelmed," she said, turning to her future mother-in-law. "I have a family, an amazing man who loves me, and parents who will be there for me. I promise I will love your son the rest of my life and make Scotland my home."

Carrying a tray with tea, sandwiches, and cookies, Kieran escorted her back to their haven. When Maggie passed the open door in the morning, she discovered them, still sitting on the couch with Kieran's head back. Bonny sat curled up with her feet under her, her head on his chest. His arm held her, and her small hand with the ruby and diamonds sparkled on his chest. The fire had burned down to glowing embers as they fell asleep, dreaming of their life together.

∝∾

"We want to be married in Beauly in early July with a reception at the inn, outside if the weather permits. I'd like to take a weekend trip over to Skye before the long flight to Albuquerque, where we'll spend a month." Kieran spooned generous helpings of haggis and eggs onto his plate.

"Bonny, are you certain you want the wedding here? What about your friends?" Maggie asked.

"No one really matters other than my best friends, Kari and Dan. We'll have a reception in Albuquerque. The miracle happened here. There's no place more perfect for our wedding."

"Will you live in Scotland all year?" Maggie asked.

"Of course. Where do you expect us to live?" Kieran moved Bonny's finger around, watching the light play on her ring.

Maggie reached across the table and took her other hand. "Can the Mother-of-the-Groom offer to help the bride prepare for the wedding?"

"Yes, please. I wondered how to manage alone." She stood and rounded the table to hug Maggie.

Kieran watched them, grinning. "Mother, you have a new daughter."

"Your mother gets excited enough when we have a wedding here for someone she doesn't know." Hamish shook his head, but his eyes were smiling. "What will you do with your home, Bonny?"

"Kieran wants to see it before we decide. The house is paid for, so my inheritance will pay for the upkeep. We'll take a vacation there each year—but of course not during lambing season."

"Every year?" Maggie's eyes grew wide.

Hamish interrupted, laying his hand on Maggie's arm. "Bonny, isn't this the day you're treating us to your New Mexican Christmas celebration?"

"Yes." She reached over and tousled Kieran's hair. "And you, Laird MacDonell, can be my assistant. Maggie and Hamish, prepare for a treat."

ৎৎৎ

"My mother handled our news with grace." Kieran peeked over Bonny's shoulder as she rolled the sopapilla dough.

She offered him a bite before he stole one. "She wasn't pleased when we mentioned keeping my house."

"She'll get used to it." After swallowing the dough, he stuck his finger in the salsa and licked it. "She offered to help with the wedding."

Bonny slapped his hand in play as he licked the spicy sauce from his finger. "Yes, and I'm very pleased."

She had prepared much of the meal ahead of time, and her future husband proved a willing pupil with the rest. Sending him out to shovel the front walk, she assembled the luminarias, consisting of brown paper lunch sacks, filled with sand and a 12-hour votive candle. When lit, they gave a soft glow, reminiscent of every Christmas of her life.

At dinnertime, Bonny led them into the parlor, closing the door while she lit the luminarias, visible through the tall dining room windows when she opened the draperies. Then she changed into her denim, broomstick skirt and a vest in a Native American pattern, with red western boots. Her silver and turquoise jewelry completed her outfit. It felt strange to think she would no longer wear them on a regular basis.

She led them out a side door and up the luminaria-lined walkway to the door. They gave a collective "Oooh" when they saw the table set with bright linens and heard the pulsating staccato of mariachi Christmas music.

"This is really good." Hamish put honey on his fourth sopapilla. "Maggie and I should visit you over there."

Maggie reached across the table for her hand. "Bonny, your dinner was lovely. I see now why Kieran insisted on you cooking for us. Your traditions are unique, and I can see why they are meaningful to you. I apologize for being less than gracious."

Bonny sighed. A victory had been won.

❦

"You pronounce Hogmanay the way it's spelled, with the accent on the first and last syllables," Kieran explained. "New Year's resolutions, fireworks, bonfires, and shooting guns into the air originated in Scotland. My favorite part is *threacht mean oiche*, midnight. After singing 'Auld Lang Syne,' it's traditional to kiss." He proceeded to demonstrate in detail.

"Hmm," Bonny wrapped her arms around his neck. "I think I need extra instruction to accomplish it in the proper Scottish way."

"Why don't you two go out for a walk?" Maggie's timing was impeccable.

"It's a lovely sunny day."

As they snow-shoed through the sparkling snow, Kieran asked, "What if we quit teaching and concentrated on the farm? We would start our new life with fewer responsibilities."

She felt at peace for the first time in a long time. "Concentrating on you sounds lovely. I will become the best sheep farmer's wife possible."

At teatime, Bridget entered carrying a two-tiered cake. Bonny turned to Kieran for an explanation, but Hamish spoke up. "It's an old Scottish tradition. The wedding cake is baked at the engagement. You eat one tier for the wedding, and save the other for the birth of the first child."

Bonny swallowed hard as Kieran squeezed her hand, remembering the secret he refused to share with his parents. "Thank you both. I can't wait to taste it."

"There's a wee one to have with tea," Maggie said. "It's a delicious fruitcake. It didn't have long to soak up the brandy, but by the wedding it will be perfect."

Kieran held up his teacup in a toast, "To my bonnie bride."

Her heart beat faster as she held her cup to his. It felt like a dream.

Chapter Twenty-four

Challenges and Surprises

Finishing his paperwork during a weekend at the farm, Kieran determined the time had come to change the room he and Bronwyn shared. He had kept the room as a shrine, and a tight feeling began in his stomach, moving to his chest. Gulping for air, his heart raced and sobs tore at his gut. Boxing up Bronwyn's possessions and hiding them away in the attic felt as if he was burying her again.

His stomach knotted with sobs as he slid to the floor beside the bed. "God, why did they have to die? I love Bonny, but I can't stop questioning why Bronnie—Liam—my son …"

Bonny appeared, as if sensing his need, crawling close to him, and pulling his head into her lap. "Bronnie, how can God take a baby before he lives?"

She rubbed his back, whispering. "Shhh, Kieran, it's me—Bonny. Bronwyn is dead, love, but I promise you won't be alone again."

"Bonny? Did I say Bronnie?"

She brushed her lips across his forehead. "Yes, it's okay."

"No, it's not. I am so very sorry. For a moment, in this room, I mistook you for her. I should have packed it all away a long time ago. I'm angry, when I should be thankful for you, and for the life we'll have together. What's wrong with me?"

She smoothed the tangled curls at the base of his neck. "You faced the hardest test and weren't ready yet. Everyone falls backwards sometimes. God will never leave you or forsake you. Ask for His help."

He wiped his eyes with his sleeve. How could he explain the fear filling his mind? "Nothing's changed."

She leaned her soft cheek against his. "Love, God understands your pain."

"If He's so all-powerful, why didn't He stop it?" He didn't realize how hard he was gripping her hand until she loosened it and held his between her own. "Please, don't give up on me? I can't lose you too."

"I won't desert you. I promise." She smoothed his forehead with her other hand, so cool and soft. "If you're not ready to change this room, you can wait."

The violent trembling refused to stop. "No, I'll not bring you here as my bride while this shrine to Bronwyn remains. It's not fair."

"You've had a struggle. It doesn't bother me to leave it for a while. Aren't there antiques in the attic?" Bonny asked. "Let's find different furniture, and I'll have Kari send my grandmother's Double Wedding Ring quilt for the bed. Then it will hold a piece of each of us."

He leaned his head against her shoulder. "I don't deserve you."

"I don't deserve you either, but what a grand life we have ahead of us." She brushed a stray curl back from his forehead.

He had thought the depression would be over with the certainty that Bonny would be his wife, but he continued to have dark episodes of brooding. Some days he skipped class, wandering around the farm with no real aim, even missing dates with Bonny. In spite of her devoted love, the fearful despair was growing worse instead of better.

⊂3&⊃

Laughing and teasing, Bonny and Janet packed snacks while Kieran and Graeme loaded their gear into the Land Rover. Graeme had suggested the weekend ski trip to the picturesque town of Aviemore and Cairn Gorm Mountain.

Bonny had visited *An Cairn Gorm*, the Blue Mountain, in the summertime, and looked forward to her first glimpse of it in winter. Janet said the name referred to a smoky quartz common in the area.

They had ridden the funicular railway which whooshed up and down the mountain, carrying visitors to the top in the summer while protecting the fragile mountain tundra. In the winter, it transported skiers at a more rapid speed. The views from the top were spectacular.

When Janet carried a box out to the Land Rover, Kieran tried to distract Bonny by kissing her while stealing a bunch of grapes. She returned his kiss and reclaimed the fruit. "I can't wait to enjoy the view from the top with the love of my life."

He popped a plump, juicy grape in her mouth. "Everything is lovely with you."

Bonny thought the drive to Aviemore might be the perfect time to draw Graeme out and get him to talk. "I haven't had the opportunity to get acquainted with you until now. Tell me something about yourself."

He blushed. "I'm thirty-eight, and I grew up in Edinburgh with one sister."

"Does your family still live there?" Kieran asked.

"No, my parents are dead, and my sister married the pastor of a large church in Glasgow, so other than an aunt, I have no real ties to Edinburgh anymore."

"Is Faith Chapel your first church?" Bonny asked.

"No, I served five years in a large church in Edinburgh, before I answered the call for an assistant pastor to the Community Church of Fort William. The pastor was aging and needed help. He retired two years ago, and the elders asked me to replace him. I know I'm where God wants me. We changed the name to Faith Chapel when we moved into the storefront location. The church has grown so much that I will soon be announcing the need for new facilities."

"Will you stay in Fort William?" Janet asked, and Bonny caught the undertone of fear in her voice.

She had already noticed that he aimed his replies toward Janet. "Yes, I enjoy the slower pace of a smaller town. I have more time for people and outreach projects to the community. Word is circulating about the strong Bible teaching at Faith Chapel."

Janet turned toward Graeme. "We always discuss church, not our lives outside of church."

"I prefer to talk about other people." He turned a brighter shade of red.

∞

No matter how fast Kieran went, Bonny held her own, beating him about half the time. She skied without fear. They forgot the others until a problem with his bindings caused him to send her on, promising to catch up.

She met Janet at the bottom, waiting to board the train to the top, her eyes flashing. "The four of us were going to ski together, Bonny. Is there a plot to make me spend time with Graeme? You know I can't get involved with him."

"The guys planned the trip. I'm sorry. Kieran and I are so absorbed in each other I didn't realize we were making it difficult for you," Bonny said. "Aren't you having fun?"

"Of course it's fun. He's a lovely person and a terrific skier, but I'd hate for him to get the wrong idea."

"I'll ski with you for a while. Kieran needed to fix his bindings. In the meantime, maybe he and Graeme will find each other. Let's go."

"Thanks, Bonny." Janet stepped on the train. "I should have talked to him a long time ago."

⊰⊱

When the two men met halfway down the mountain, Graeme was in high spirits. "She's lovely, and so easy to talk to. Would you ask Bonny to dinner so Janet and I can have dinner alone?"

Kieran clapped him on the back. "Aye, you pick the restaurant and Bonny and I will eat somewhere else."

When they met at noon, Kieran offered to bring lunch to Bonny while she guarded their table and relaxed. Graeme followed his lead, and Janet let him.

Halfway through the meal, Bonny noticed that the conversation seemed to be growing more comfortable. Janet had even lost the terrified look in her eyes.

It was fun to hear Graeme talk outside the church. He had skied at the best resorts in Europe and a couple in America and demonstrated a great sense of humor. "The first time I preached, I was so nervous I couldn't sleep. I stayed up late the night before, studying. I sat down in a comfortable chair waiting to follow the choir in, and dozed off. I awakened to the sound of the service beginning. I hurried around the back of the stage, and when someone asked if anyone had seen me. I yelled, 'Just coming.'"

Bonny noticed that his eyes stayed on Janet. "I stepped onto the stage with my tie over to one side, hot, and sweating. I had time to calm down during the prayer, but I felt so flustered I forgot half of my sermon. It wasn't the best start, but I survived. Believe me, I make finishing my sermons ahead of time and getting a good night's sleep a priority now."

Kieran brought up dinner plans during a break in the conversation. "I hope you two don't mind, but I planned a romantic dinner with Bonny this evening."

"I guess we're on our own, Janet. How about the Royal Tandoori?" The eagerness in Graeme's voice was hard to miss.

With no other choice, she agreed.

❧

The rest of the afternoon was a no-holds-barred competition, testing their stamina to the limit. Kieran fell taking a turn too sharp, and Bonny missed landing on top of him with a quick maneuver. Coming to a stop, she fell over in the snow, laughing, and found herself wrapped in two snowy arms by a big Scot who placed cold, wet kisses on her nose. They laughed until their sides hurt.

"Let's race." He tapped her on the nose with a gloved finger. "I'll beat you this time."

"Loser owes the winner a hot chocolate at the bottom." She shoved him as he reached for a stray ski pole and headed down the hill.

Graeme and Janet waited at the bottom, laughing. As Bonny came to a stop, she yelled back to them. "Hot chocolate for everyone. Kieran's buying."

"Sounds good." Janet grabbed Bonny by the arm and headed inside, leaving the men behind.

❧

Dressed in a lavender sweater, Janet met Graeme in the lobby with a heavy heart. He offered his arm as they strolled down the street to the restaurant.

"I'm glad for the opportunity to finally have dinner with you." He held the door, and the savory odors of curry, cumin, and turmeric greeted them as they entered the crowded restaurant.

"Kieran surprised me when he announced his plans for the evening." Janet plucked at a piece of lint on her sweater. The waitress called them before he answered, but discussing the menu and the day's skiing wouldn't last long.

"Janet," he said, after blessing their food, "I've watched you around the church since I came here. I'd like to spend time with you."

She shut her eyes and plunged in. "Graeme, I enjoy skiing with you, but there's something I should have told you a long time ago. I taught for a while at Edinburgh University and met a man in the military. We fell in love and married."

The color faded from his face and a serious expression entered his coffee-brown eyes. She pressed on, explaining Sean's affairs and the divorce.

"It's not appropriate for me to spend time with a minister. I have to live with my mistake, but I didn't intend to hurt you. Continuing as a foursome with Kieran and Bonny isn't right. We have to remain pastor and church member, nothing more." Her napkin had become a handkerchief, dabbing at her eyes, where the mascara formed dark puddles under her eyes.

He cleared his throat, staring at his untouched dinner. "I'm so sorry. It's my fault for assuming …"

Silence loomed loudly between them. Janet hung her head. "I should have said something. I'm ashamed of the way Sean behaved, so I've avoided mentioning it since moving back to Fort William. Can you forgive me?"

He choked with emotion. "I should have made an effort to learn more details of your life outside church. How can I help?"

She dug a tissue out of her purse. "By allowing me to continue serving without making me feel uncomfortable. We can enjoy ourselves skiing tomorrow. I'll be more relaxed now that you know, but we can't spend time together again."

Leaving their meals untouched, they walked back to the hotel, his hand putting light pressure on her back as they crossed the street. When they reached her room, he laid his hand on her arm, turning her to face him. He placed a light kiss on her hand as he said goodnight.

The next morning she told Bonny they had agreed to remain friends. Then they skied side by side, enjoying the only time they would ever have.

Three weeks later, Janet sat alone by her window staring in the direction of the church. Agnes walked in, laying her hand on her daughter's shoulder. "Why do you ignore Graeme after church these days?"

"He loves me, Mum. In Aviemore, I explained what happened with Sean. I love him, but there is no way around the problem. It's difficult to watch Kieran and Bonny. I don't see how even God can fix this."

Agnes massaged her daughter's neck. "Just because you can't see it doesn't mean God can't do it, love."

CHAPTER TWENTY-FIVE

INTO THE DEPTHS

A few weeks later, Kieran and Bonny stood atop the Nevis ski area overlooking a magnificent world, white with sparkling snow and dotted by shimmering silver lochs. Kieran drew Bonny to him in a strong embrace. "I love you, my precious wife-to-be."

"I love you, too." He stood below her on the slope with their faces near the same level.

"July is so far away. I need you beside me." Moisture puddled in the corners of his eyes, his lip quivering as he sighed.

She touched his cheek. "You're not alone. We can see each other every day. We have a busy time finishing this semester, our pre-marital counseling, and wedding plans. I have to return to the States for Kari's wedding."

He rested his chin on top of her head. "Peace and quiet—you and me, alone, sharing the rest of our lives together. I want to snuggle with you and enjoy you as my wife. Aren't you anxious?"

"Of course I am. I want it more than anything." She moved back and looked at him. "Kieran, what's wrong, love?"

"I don't want to be alone anymore." She saw a shadow behind his grim attempt at a smile.

Sidestepping, he put his arm in front of her and pushed off down the hill, beating her to the bottom, laughing as he watched her whoosh down after him.

"No fair. I want a rematch."

"I couldn't make another run if I had to. I'm wabbit. Your enchiladas sound perfect."

Bonny slapped him on the back. "No fair, I demand a rematch."

"I'd beat you again." He pulled off his skis.

Bonny stepped out of her bindings and bent to pick up her own skis. "I've beaten you before."

"Another day, Professor Bryant, another day. Will you drive home?"

"Of course." The vacant stare and hollow sound to Kieran's voice made her nervous.

They pulled into her driveway after dark. Kieran dropped onto the couch as they came through the door. "Ach, I need to sleep."

Bonny touched her hand to his forehead, but he didn't feel warm. "You're so tired lately. What's wrong?"

It was obvious that he avoided meeting her eyes. "I've had trouble sleeping."

"Then rest. I'll call you when it's on the table." She handed him a blanket from the back of the couch, and within seconds, he was snoring.

When dinner was ready, she whispered his name, placing a light kiss on his forehead.

He jumped, grabbing her arm, and pulling her down on top of him. "Bronnie, oh Bronnie, don't leave me, please?"

She stiffened and pulled away. Something was very wrong, and she felt it in the pit of her stomach. Maybe the first time at the farm wasn't a fluke. Perhaps the problem went deeper than the dreams. "Kieran, it's me, Bonny."

He sat up, shaking his head, his face pale and eyes wide, struggling to grasp his surroundings. His confusion changed to sorrow when his panicked blue gaze fell on her. "Bonny … I was dreaming." His head dropped to his hands, his voice weak and hoarse. "I'm having strange, vivid dreams. They're so real."

Her pulse quickened as she sank down next to him. "What dreams? You called me Bronnie again, love. You're scaring me."

His face turned whiter still, and he grasped her by the shoulders, fear etching lines in his forehead and around his eyes. "Forgive me, Bonny. I need you. I heard the baby crying. Sometimes, I'm not certain if I dreamed of her or you. Everything is lovely in my life now, but I feel hopeless. Bonny, I'm frightened."

She put her arms around him, rubbing his back in circles, and he buried his face in her shoulder. She had no idea what to do.

The red-blond head shook back and forth, his eyes on the floor. "In my dreams they're pleading with me, asking me for help. I should have moved her to my parents' after the doctor said she had a problem." He rubbed his eyes while gulping air.

Bonny shivered. "You turned this over to God at Christmas, remember?"

His eyes, wide and ice blue, fastened on hers. "It keeps coming back, getting worse since the day you found me in her room. I—I need a doctor." His voice sounded hollow. "I need help."

Bonny reached up, combing her fingers through his hair, her thoughts whirling in a tornado of fear and love. "We'll phone the doctor Monday. It's an illness, love. You can't help it."

"I'm so weak. Forgive me." The man who had become her rock dissolved into sobs, and her stomach knotted in reply.

She cupped his face in one hand, wiping the tears from his eyes with her fingertip. "No forgiveness is needed, Kieran. Admitting you need help shows strength. The failure to accept help is weak. I'll stay beside you."

He folded her in his arms and wept on her shoulder.

C02BO

The doctor put Kieran on strong antidepressants without hesitation. He slept at his Aunt Alice's when not teaching or preparing for classes. Maggie and Hamish drove down when they received Bonny's urgent call for help. They would run the farm until he improved, entrusting Bridget and Kathleen to handle the inn.

"Thank you." Maggie put her arm around Bonny. "He's not as bad as in the past. You did a good job of getting him help."

Hamish put his arm around her from the other side. "You and God will give him a reason to get well, *nic-chridhe*. He'll pull through. We appreciate what you've done."

"Thank you, but I think you're wrong." She didn't have a tissue, so she wiped her eyes on her sleeve. "He's so quiet and withdrawn. He doesn't touch me or respond when I touch him."

"It's the depression." Maggie reached for her hand. "He acted distant before. It will require patience, but I believe it will pass. He's not alone this time."

Bonny nodded, swallowing hard before she found her voice. "It's not difficult showing patience. He's so sweet and gentle—so very sad. I thought loving him was enough." There was one thought she couldn't bear to voice. *What if he didn't get better?*

CR80

The coming of spring brought little improvement. For two weeks he refused to see anyone but the doctor and Graeme. One thought repeated itself again and again. *She deserves better.*

The white marble headstone felt cool to the touch. Kieran laid his face against it, smoothing his hand over the names. "Bronwyn Murray MacDonell, Beloved Wife and Mother, and Liam Hamish MacDonell." He put his hand to his chest, feeling the same sharp pain near his heart that he felt every time he saw only one date below his son's name. The picture of the pale, small bundle lying on the floor beside his bleeding mother was etched in his memory.

He set the vase of yellow roses next to the stone. "Bronnie, I'm in love. She's a lovely woman, and I have a chance for happiness, but I cannot make myself move on without you. I can't pack away your belongings or change our room. My love for you and my anger at God follows me everywhere. How can I leave you behind?"

He sank down on his knees, pulling his handkerchief out of his pocket. "I want Bonny for my wife, but it's not fair to her. I can't stop dreaming of you, *mo bhean, mo chridhe.* She deserves love with nothing held back, and I can't promise it. I'm so alone. How can I live without you or Bonny, without life and laughter and love?"

With one last swipe at his eyes, he stuffed the handkerchief back in his pocket and walked the short way to Bonny's office at the college. After class, she was driving him to a doctor's appointment. It wouldn't help. Nothing did. It was impossible to fill Bronwyn's place with Bonny or anyone.

CR80

Graeme asked Bonny to to sing the songs she prepared for Kari's wedding when he taught on marriage from the fifth chapter of Ephesians.

For the first time since beginning his medication, Kieran decided he felt up to going to church. He had to hear her sing once more before she left. But as he listened, he realized what God expected of him and how wrong he had been to lie.

When she took her seat, he reached over and patted her arm, but the gnawing guilt growing inside made him fold his arms across his chest. As Bronwyn's husband, he learned from watching Hamish. Now, he realized the intervening years of anger since her death showed his faith was false. He was unable to love Bonny as Christ loved the church because he did not love Christ.

He felt restless, jittery, and unable to sit still. He had read those same words in Beauly at Christmas. Now they shouted at him—he was a farce, incapable of loving Bonny as he should.

He felt fidgety and anxious to get away from the church, away from these people, and away from the feeling of being condemned as a liar and a fake. The ruby and diamonds sparkled on Bonny's hand resting on his knee, causing his leg to burn as guilt and shame bore down on him. He loved her too much to force her to deal with his depression and failed expectations for the rest of her life.

While friends came up following the service to wish her luck on her trip, he exited through a side door and climbed into the passenger seat of the Land Rover. Bonny followed a few minutes later and scrambled into the driver's seat. "What's wrong, honey? You seem so tense."

He couldn't look at her, so he stared straight ahead, emotions roiling and churning inside him as she drove to her house for lunch. He hated himself for the angry, harsh words tumbling around in his mind. "Sit down, Bonny, we have to talk."

Tempted to run, he paced the floor with his heart hammering hard in his chest. "The entire service this morning pointed at me. Now I understand what you want."

She patted a spot on the couch. Her smile was a knife, tearing at his insides. "Kieran, I've prayed so hard. Come over here next to me, and stop pacing."

Unable to face her, he focused on a picture hanging above her head. "Bonny, my faith isn't real. You've compromised your beliefs because of me. I can't meet your deepest needs any more than Adam can. I love you too much to lie."

He saw her wince when he mentioned Adam.

"Kieran, no ..."

"I can't believe in God, and I can't get over Bronwyn." He put his finger to his lips. "You deserve complete love with no competition. You won't have that with me."

There, he had said it. With one sentence, he hurt her and destroyed any future happiness for himself. She massaged her throat until it turned red. He hated causing her pain, but to continue lying was impossible.

Tears shimmered in those green eyes, which could drive him to distraction with their love and vulnerability. "Kieran, don't you love me?"

"My faith is a farce. Arrange to return home at the end of the spring semester. It's better this way." He turned toward the door, grabbing the keys off the table.

As his hand touched the doorknob, Bonny leaped up, grabbing him by the arms. "Please, Kieran, let me phone the doctor, or Graeme. It's your depression. Listen, please ..."

He wrenched out of her grasp, almost knocking her off her feet, and walked out. *I hate this, but I have no other choice.*

216

CHAPTER TWENTY-SIX

ALONE AGAIN

A clap of thunder shook the house, and lightning streaked the sky as the Land Rover disappeared into the thick fog. A chill settled over Bonny from somewhere deep inside. She ran to her room, collapsing on her knees beside the bed. Her heart cried out for God to heal Kieran's heart. After venting her tears, she slept. When she awakened, she slid the ruby ring off and laid it in the box.

Five days later, Janet drove her to the airport. She averted her eyes as they passed the cemetery, avoiding the sight of the towering Scots Pine, blackened and split in two by a bolt of lightning the night Kieran left. At Kari's insistence, she upgraded her plane ticket to first class to allow more privacy on the long flight. Though her heart was in tatters, she felt God's presence unlike anything she had ever known. Each breath was a prayer for Kieran.

Kari met her at the airport in Albuquerque, her warm hug threatening to expose the raw emotion just below the surface.

"I can spend the night if you want me to. I thought you might need company on your first night home."

"Thanks, but I'll be fine. I haven't slept much this week. I think I can now. I'll call when I wake up."

Kari clasped her hand, her eyes narrowing with worry. "You sound calm. Is it because you're so tired?"

Bonny took her arm as they headed for baggage claim. "I feel calm. I'm heartbroken and disappointed, but God is carrying me. I'm so much stronger than when I left." Her throat tightened as she rubbed her empty ring finger. "I wanted to come home wearing Kieran's ring, knowing he was waiting for me."

"I'm so sorry, Bonny." Kari handed her a tissue and a bottle of water when they reached the car.

She rubbed her eyes with the tissue. "I prayed for God to enable Kieran to leave his past behind, no matter what happened between us. I will grow stronger because I know only God can complete me, not a person. My heart will survive."

Kari reached across the car and placed her hand on Bonny's arm. "Call Dan or me. We're as close as the phone. Don't hesitate, no matter what time it is."

"Fill me in on the latest wedding plans." She changed subjects before she lost control. "What can I do?"

"Not tonight." Kari handed her the box of tissues. "You'll have a terrible week, what with jet-lag and emotions. My wedding day is my day. We need to talk."

Bonny massaged the constricting muscles in her throat, pondering her response. One deep breath, and she dove in. "I realize you didn't approve of Kieran, but he's an incredible man. Kari, he suffers from bouts of a severe form of depression over the deaths of Bronwyn and the baby. He called me by her nickname, Bronnie, more than once, when I startled him. He's on medication now and needs our prayers."

She saw the shadow pass over Kari's face. "Oh, Bonny, I prayed you wouldn't get hurt again."

"He's worth it, and I'm convinced he will recover. He's responded well to treatment in the past. No one except his parents, Graeme, Janet, and Dr. Cameron know. It's wrong to make him the subject of gossip." She wiped her eyes. She had to stop crying whenever anyone mentioned his name.

"And you didn't trust me with this."

Bonny's tears began and ended with the intensity of a New Mexico thunderstorm, as she cleared her throat, determined to take control. "He's struggled a lot since he started to pack away Bronwyn's belongings. Do you want to know why he broke our engagement?"

Kari nodded, keeping her eyes on the road as the heavy truck traffic on I-40 rumbled past.

"Graeme preached on marriage from Ephesians five and asked me to sing the songs for your wedding." Her words tumbled out with the pent up emotion held in through the long plane flight. "Between the songs and sermon, Kieran realized what I needed. He—he said he was no better for me than Adam was, and he wouldn't marry me under those circumstances. He did it out of love." She sat in silence as Kari exited onto the quieter North 14 running along the east side of the Sandia Mountains.

"I'm so sorry. How can Dan and I help?" Kari turned off onto the dirt road where she, Dan, and Bonny had grown up, then into the gravel drive winding up to Bonny's house.

"I'm fine, dear friend. Unlike when I left for Scotland, I know God is helping me, and I will recover. I'll phone you when I wake up." They carried her suitcases into the house.

Kari hugged her, leaving two damp circles on her shoulder. "I can't thank you enough for coming when I know you left your heart in Scotland."

The next three days kept them busy to the point of exhaustion. Bonny fell into bed as soon as she prayed and slept through the night. She was grateful Scotland was so far away. No one knew Dr. Cameron had asked her to remain another year. She had refused.

Bonny rounded the curve in the driveway two nights before the wedding. Her guard went up when she spotted a car in front of the house. It sat in an isolated spot, out of sight and hearing of her closest neighbors.

She shifted into reverse when a man began walking toward her, but she heard her name and recognized something familiar—Adam. Her heart dropped to the pit of her stomach. To face this man who came close to destroying her, and to admit Kieran also sent her away, was grinding salt into a fresh wound. Earlier in the day, she took her never-worn wedding dress, the last reminder of the cancelled wedding, to a consignment shop. Now, with him here in her driveway, she had nowhere to run.

She stepped out of the car, determined not to let him control her. Drawing closer, she realized the man approaching her was not the confident attorney capable of holding an entire courtroom under his spell. This man was tentative and ill at ease.

"Hello Bonny." His voice lacked its usual confidence. "I didn't mean to frighten you. I knew you'd come for Kari's wedding, but you wouldn't see me unless you had no other choice."

Though her heart thudded hard against her ribs, she felt unusual confidence. For the first time she held the upper hand. "What do you want, Adam? It's late, and I need rest. I have a busy day tomorrow."

She intended to unnerve him even more by her icy, unemotional tone.

"I need to explain, if you'll let me."

With her nerves on edge and her emotions raw, she didn't care how she sounded. "There's not much to explain. You left. I moved on."

He shut his eyes and the corner of his mouth twitched. Adam cry— impossible. He stepped aside and allowed her to go up the porch steps ahead of him. "Will you stay in Scotland long?"

"I love it. I plan to stay for a long time. What do you want?" His uneasiness energized her with a sense of control.

"Please, sit with me. I need to explain my behavior." His face appeared blurry in the dim light of the porch, but she heard the pleading in his usually confident voice.

Unlocking the door, she set her purse inside and turned on more lights. "I have nothing to say to you. But since my feet are tired, we can sit on the porch a minute." She motioned to a couple of wooden rockers, determined to stay in control.

His uncertainty gave her control for the first time. "I'm asking you again to forgive me. I deserve your disdain. I turned my back on the Lord, on you, on everything. There is no excuse. I love you, Bonny."

She measured her words for impact. "I'm glad you're right with the Lord again. I read your letters, threw them in the trash, and deleted your voicemails."

Adam's face paled beneath his tan. "I heard you were dating a farmer in Scotland." His eyes searched her face. It was difficult to hide anything from him. He had known her too long.

Her jaw tightened at the mention of Kieran. She resolved not to encourage him. "Yes, Kieran is a math professor whose family owns a large sheep farm." Keeping her composure was a challenge. "I didn't know how true love felt until I met him."

He recoiled at her words, his eyes shifting from her face to her hands. "I—you're not wearing a ring."

She took a deep breath, choosing each word with care. "I would marry him in a minute. Now, I need to rest." She stood and opened the screen door.

"Is there any hope?"

She realized a victory in forcing him to accept the consequences of his actions. "I owe you nothing, Adam. You destroyed my trust. It's over."

She stepped inside and closed the door, leaving him standing alone on the porch. Reminiscent of a scene from long ago, she leaned against the door, waiting to hear him drive away. As the car crunched down the gravel drive, she burst into tears.

ౡ౪

Kari demanded an explanation for her tired, swollen eyes the next morning. "I found Adam waiting at the house last night."

"He has a lot of nerve. What did you say?" She placed her arm around Bonny's shoulders.

"I said I had nothing left for him, that I intend to marry Kieran. I restrained myself from saying I got rid of my wedding dress and everything else relating to him. I cried when he left, but not for him, for Kieran."

"You've closed the door on a huge part of your past and your future, too. I can't imagine how it must hurt." Kari wrapped her in a hug.

Bonny pulled away, straightening her shoulders. "It's a special day. We have decorating to finish and a wedding to prepare for. Keeping busy, even with a wedding, will help occupy my mind." Soon, she found herself laughing and enjoying helping Kari create her dream.

Separating their joy from her own situation proved difficult at times, yet she could not begrudge what they had come so close to losing. Kari and Dan entered marriage having already faced one of the more difficult challenges of their lives. The ordeal of Dan's injury, amputation, and recuperation had forged a powerful bond of love and commitment.

Oh, Lord, will I find what they have some day?

CRSO

Dan found Bonny sitting alone under a large aspen before the wedding rehearsal. "Hey, Carrot-Top, we need a brother-sister chat." He sat down next to her, rubbing the thigh muscles of his amputated leg. "I remember a thing or two your dad taught us. I'm willing to talk to Kieran."

"Thank you, Dan." Bonny reached for his hand. "My heart says to leave him alone. If God wills, He'll resolve it. If not, then there's a better plan for us both."

He pulled her into a brotherly hug. "Now you're talking. You didn't have this confident, trusting faith before."

Bonny laid her head on his shoulder, the way she would have with her dad. "We've been forced to grow in ways we never imagined this past year, haven't we?"

Dan lifted his prosthetic leg. "God won't give us more than we can bear, no matter what we think."

"It's more than we can handle on our own but not more than His strength enables us to bear." She leaned back, looking him in the eye. "Graeme taught from Ephesians chapter one, where it says believers possess all the power of the Spirit which raised Christ from the dead. What an awesome power. He gives me strength when I want to fall apart. This is between Kieran and God. I may have prayed it into happening. Now I need to wait and have faith."

"Way to go, Carrot-Top." Dan gave her a bear hug as Kari came through the door.

She put her hands on her hips, tapping her foot in mock irritation. "What do we have here—the groom and maid of honor caught in a compromising situation?"

They burst out laughing as Dan held an arm out to Kari. "We're three friends who have faced the worst and triumphed through the grace of God. We're friends for life, wherever it leads us."

Kari reached for Bonny's hand. "Thank you for putting your pain aside to stand with us tomorrow. It means so much to have you here."

They wrapped their arms around each other, joy mingling with the pain.

CHAPTER TWENTY-SEVEN

BLACKNESS

Anger and depression overwhelmed Kieran as he drove away from Bonny's house. When he reached the turn-off to Invergarry Castle, a lump developed in his throat for the first time. He got out of the Land Rover, heedless of the heavy downpour and the thunder echoing through the mist-shrouded mountains. Visions of his lost loves lingered among the old stones. Ruins—his entire life lay in ruins. Far away on another continent, Bonny was as lost to him now as Bronwyn.

Reaching the place where he first showed her the farm, he remembered her enthusiasm, and a warm sensation passed through him in spite of his wet clothing. He recalled the warmth of her beside him, her hand in his and the sweet brush of her lips against his cheek, her whispers of love in his ear.

Pushing it to the back of his mind, he reflected on tasks he had neglected or left to Angus. He needed to return to his full responsibilities on the farm. He would not quit teaching. Silence and loneliness were fierce enemies. He needed purpose, if nothing more than helping struggling math students.

"You're the last person I expected to see." Eleanor turned from the stove as he came through the door, stomping his muddy feet and dripping on the floor. "Put on something dry while I get the tea."

He headed up the stairs. The face in the mirror unnerved him. Vacant, anguished eyes stared out of a face as pale as death, a ghost from two years ago—angry and empty. He was amazed that Eleanor said nothing. Changing clothes, he exited through the front door, avoiding her questions.

He planned to discuss farm work with Angus in the morning, work half a day, and then return to the farm after class as he did before Bonny entered his world. Working until he was exhausted every day allowed minimal time to dwell on what would never be.

He left Fort William in such an angry rush he forgot his belongings at Aunt Alice's house. He was no more anxious to answer his aunt and uncle's questions than those of Eleanor or his parents. He headed back to the house, resigned, but his motherly housekeeper said nothing throughout the meal.

Disturbed by her silence, he knocked on the door to her sitting room an hour later, and she welcomed him, motioning to a chair near the fire.

"I broke my engagement to Bonny."

Eleanor closed her book, turning her full attention on him. "I knew you'd tell me in time. You look like *death oan a pirn stick*, lad."

"I love Bonny, but my faith died with Bronwyn. It's not fair to her." He rubbed his forehead. He was drained and sick.

In a steady voice, she asked, "What did the lass say?"

"She wanted to call Graeme and the doctor, as if anyone can fix what's wrong inside of me. She grabbed my arms, but I shook her off, and she watched me leave without a word. It's better this way."

"How can you be so cruel?" Her response served as a preview of his mother's reaction.

He studied the pattern on the rug. "I'm not what she needs. I'm still angry about the deaths of Bronnie and the baby. I lied when I said I believed in God in order to convince her to marry me. It's over. She can return to America at the end of the semester."

"Did you wait to hear what she wants?"

His gaze shifted to the fireplace. "Aye, a wee bit, but I didn't want her to change my mind."

"Kieran, you're wrong." Her words stung, with no attempt to disguise her disappointment. "Can you imagine how the poor, wee lass feels right now? She's God's gift to you, the answer to your lonely life, and you've broken her heart."

Eleanor leaned forward, her silent insistence forcing him to meet her pale blue eyes. "You're not falling short of Bonny's standards, but God's. You cannot blame her for your failure to accept the normal problems in life and to believe God. Those times grow us if we seek God's help."

He stared at the carpet.

"Have you told your parents?"

"No."

"You're driving to Beauly and telling them in person. Listen to them, Kieran." He expected her to shake a finger at him. "I've said more than I have a right to, but you're no different than my own son. I care about Bonny too, so I won't apologize. You may go now." She stood to dismiss him, and he headed to his room, chastised.

CRWD

Maggie stared up at him, her eyes wide in disbelief. "You threw away your one chance for true love. Why? I saw your love for Bonny even when I didn't want to."

"She expected too much." Kieran balled his hands into fists, wanting to hit something.

Hamish led him into his office, sitting down in his old leather chair before the fireplace. "Son, you don't treat someone you love with such callous cruelty."

Angry, Kieran slumped in the deep chair. "I love her, Da, but I can't share her faith, and I've lied too many times. Even if I change, she can't forgive me after what I said."

"Did she say anything?" His father's eyes probed for answers.

Kieran stood, turning his back and staring out the window. "I didn't give her time. Now she's in America for Kari's wedding. A husband who can't forget the past is the last thing she needs."

"She loves you, and you love her. Stubborn pride has no place in a true love relationship." His father's calm disturbed him.

"Don't meddle in my life. My decision is final." He walked out, slamming the door behind him.

Returning to the farm, he began inspecting the herds. He left no time to think between the farm and school. The lights in his office burned late into the night, and he rose with the sun, worked hard, and stayed away from everyone as much as possible.

Something deep inside of him died, and the blackness closed in.

ᜣ৪ᜣ

"Kieran." Footsteps pounded behind him, and a hand clapped him on the shoulder. "Didn't you hear me, man?" Graeme MacDholl breathed hard from chasing him down. The pastor topped the list of people he preferred not to see.

"Hello." He didn't slow his pace.

"I heard you and Bonny broke up. Can I help?"

"No."

Graeme gripped his forearm hard. "Something major happened for you to break your engagement to Bonny. If you need to talk, I have time."

He had to face the pastor sooner or later, but not on High Street at noon. "All right, but in your office."

"Of course. I'm headed there now." Graeme removed his hand and headed for the church.

As the office door closed, Kieran sunk into a chair, his face in his hands. "Your sermon made it clear, along with those bloody songs. I couldn't mislead her any longer."

Graeme set a bottle of still water on the desk next to Kieran. "Ohhh, Ephesians five, loving your wife as Christ loved the church …"

"Aye, I pretended to believe when I don't. I love her too much to …"

When Kieran raised his head, he saw Graeme watching him, waiting. "So you misled her."

"You're not angry?"

"Of course not. I know you've struggled."

He reached for his handkerchief, settling into a more comfortable position in the too-small chair. "I'm not what she needs. Ach, I didn't intend to hurt her, but I did."

Graeme leaned forward. "I'm truly sorry, *a charaid*. She's a lovely woman."

"You think I'm a hypocrite?"

"You said it, not I. How can I help?" Graeme's eyes bored into his. Kieran stood and moved to the window. He expected condemnation from the pastor. "It's not long until the end of the semester. She'll return to Albuquerque, and I'll go on alone as before."

"The depth of love you two shared is a rare thing." Graeme moved to his side at the window. "It's possible to change. Unbelief is a choice, you know."

"I tried. I appreciate your time, but I need to finish my errands and head back to the farm." He crossed the room and reached for the doorknob.

Graeme called after him. "If you need me, I'm here."

Kieran paused. "You're different than the pastors I've known. Thank you for not beating me over the head."

"You must be doing enough of that yourself. Bonny is a tremendous loss. I admire your honesty." He stretched out his hand.

Kieran shook it and left in silence. When he climbed into the Land Rover, he pounded the steering wheel hard enough to hurt, and rubbed the heel of his hand. The physical pain allowed his emotions to explode and he wept for the first time.

Chapter Twenty-eight

The Accident

Kieran sat at his desk at 3 a.m., eight days after Bonny left for America, two weeks with misery and self-chastisement as his unrelenting companions.

The phone rang, and he grabbed it on the first ring. "Bonny?"

The male voice on the other end sounded surprised. "Uhh, hello, is this Kieran MacDonell? I'm Dan MacDermott, Bonny's friend."

"This is Kieran." If Dan was angry over Bonny ...

"Forty-eight hours ago, Bonny was in a car accident. Kari's bro ..."

He felt as if a cannonball from Mons Meg hit him in the stomach. "She's dead ..." *God, I cannot stand the death of another woman I love. Why?*

"No, but she's in critical condition—on a ventilator. She ..." Fatigue and worry laced every word.

Kieran's chest grew tight, his mind whirling out of control as Dan continued. "Kari's brother was driving her home after the wedding when a drunk driver hit the passenger side. Bonny took the full brunt of the impact. She may die."

"No." His stomach churned, and his heart beat a rapid tattoo. There would be no chance to work it out or hold her in his arms again. "No, please, not Bonny." *I cannot stand over another grave.*

Dan was gulping for air, struggling for words. Kieran remembered Bonny agonizing over Dan's injuries, how she referred to him as a brother. There was no doubt Dan felt the same as he continued. "She has eight fractured ribs, a lacerated liver, and a bruised spleen. One lung collapsed, but they managed to re-inflate it, and she has a chest-tube. Her right leg is broken in three places and her right arm in two. They have her in a drug-induced coma for a severe concussion, and she's on a ventilator. The drunk driver died. Kari's brother is in ICU with fractured ribs and a punctured lung, but he will recover."

There would be no waking up to discover it was a nightmare. The rote recitation of facts stopped with a choking sound. "The car—it's demolished. It's a miracle anyone survived. Kari and I spent our wedding night in the waiting room of the hospital. We've stayed here since then."

"So it ends with the death of the last woman I will ever love."

"If the swelling in her brain responds to the drugs, she has a chance. The liver is a major concern, but the other injuries will heal. Since we haven't met, this is a little awkward, but …" Dan paused. "I'll be honest. Kari insisted I call you. If you truly broke the engagement for Bonny's spiritual well-being, then I respect you for it. But she loves you and her emotional state affects her ability to survive."

"Ach, man, I love her too much to live a lie. She deserves more than I can give. Kari's wrong. I would make it worse." He was going to be sick.

Dan's voice quivered with exhaustion. "Kieran, we discussed it with her before the wedding. She hoped your differences would be resolved. Please consider it. Call if you change your mind."

"No, I'm not what she needs …"

"Maybe she only needs your love."

Breathing grew difficult. "I can't …"

"She could die."

"I'm sorry." Fear knotted his stomach, and filled his mind with terrible images.

"Me, too." The line went silent.

Kieran fell to his knees, tears dropped on his hands, his chair, and the floor as he prayed. "Dear God, heal her from these terrible injuries. Don't let her die. Please?"

Two days later, Kari phoned. "I don't believe she has the will to live. Kieran, Bonny loves you. If she heard your voice, she might try. Please come."

"You're wrong, I can't help."

"We know why you broke the engagement. No matter what you think, she still loves you. A couple of nights before the wedding, she sent Adam away, saying she would marry you in a minute." She made a soft hiccupping sound and a sniffle.

Disbelief, so stunning he had difficulty speaking. "She—she still wants to marry me?"

"Yes, she told me. She told Adam too." Kari was pleading.

"I promised not to hurt her, and I let her down. She doesn't need me." The blood pounded in his ears until he had difficulty hearing.

Kari's ragged breaths and stifled sobs grew louder. "Bonny told Adam she learned what true love was from you."

His heart lurched. "I can't watch her die. I can't ..."

Kari's crying changed to anger. "I won't accept your fatalism. If you won't try, maybe you're right, she's better off without you."

Dan took the phone and put his arm around her, pulling her close as they stared out the window into the night.

CB&O

Kari and Dan occupied long hours in the waiting room outside the Intensive Care Unit at the University of New Mexico Hospital by watching people. The swelling in Bonny's brain was subsiding, but the longer her liver function remained abnormal, the smaller the likelihood she would survive.

When Adam stepped off the elevator, they stood to meet him. Kari knew Dan was angry with Kieran, but he had no respect whatsoever for Adam. She laid a cautioning hand on his arm, his muscles hardening as he glared at Adam, his blue eyes narrowing to slits.

"You don't belong here." Kari recognized the tone of a weary, battle-hardened Marine in Dan's words.

"Hello to you too, Dan," Adam countered with his smooth courtroom voice. "I know you're protective of Bonny. Even if she doesn't love me, I still love her."

Kari squeezed her husband's arm. "We can't let you see her, Adam. We know what she told you."

Adam's brown eyes filled with tears, the handsome face pale and drawn. "Please—will she live?"

Dan's demeanor didn't soften. "They're doing everything possible, but it's not promising. She takes a breath on her own now and then, and is conscious for short periods, but her liver function is not improving. She's in God's hands. If you still pray, I suggest you do."

"I do and I'll continue." Adam turned to leave. "You'll see me again, soon."

As he headed for the elevators, Dan called after him. "Don't hurry."

CB80

Kieran sat behind his big, old desk, staring out the window. Hearing someone, he turned to discover Angus at the door, shaking his head. "Have you received a new report on the lass then, *a charaid*? How's the *puir* wee thing gettin' along?"

"They're still not certain she'll live." He remained focused on an unseen point far from Scotland. "She's breathing on her own and wakes up for short periods. She's developed a kidney infection, and her liver function isn't normal."

The older man pulled off his cap and smoothed his damp hair. "Ach, it's beyond me what you're doin' sittin' on this side of the ocean. If you love her, go to her, *mo duine*."

"I don't belong there, Angus. Why would she still care? I don't deserve her."

The older man walked toward the desk, his tone softening. "A woman doesn't look at a man the way she looked at you unless she loves him heart and soul."

He pounded his fist on the desk. "Did you come to meddle in my life or talk business?"

Angus turned toward the door. "I'm goin' to the high pastures to check on the beasties."

It irritated Kieran when the foreman referred to his kyloe as beasties. "Ach, get to it, man. I prefer your reports on the stock to you telling me how to manage my personal life."

Angus walked out muttering. "Aye, I'll be goin', though it's nothin' I wouldn't say to my own sons. You're wrong. You belong at her side."

As soon as the foreman left, Kieran headed to the barn and saddled the gray gelding. He needed a hard ride to clear his mind.

Chapter Twenty-nine

Re-enter Adam

Bonny was alone while Kari and Dan went to lunch. Hearing a noise, she turned and saw a face at the door which brought back vivid, if not pleasant memories.

"So the 'sleeping beauty' has awakened at last." Adam approached the bed with a bouquet of roses. "What happened to your watchdogs?"

"What—why are you here?" The sight of him created uncomfortable feelings. She wanted Kari and Dan.

"You're not very welcoming, but I don't deserve better. I came to see you in ICU, but they kept me away." His short, brown hair and deep suntan stood in complete contrast to the handsome face with a light complexion and mane of red-gold curls she remembered well.

"I don't—love you." She remembered loving arms, but they weren't his.

He dropped into a chair by her bed. "Bonny, I still love you. I want to prove I've changed."

"I—I love someone else." A smiling face remained vivid in her memory. She struggled to remember his name.

Adam's disarming grin was familiar, but she also remembered the manipulation and deception behind it. "Where is this Scotsman of yours? If you've discussed marriage, why isn't he here?"

"I—he has a—a problem. We—love each—other." She did not appreciate the way he referred to Kieran. Her mind retrieved his name as she realized she had twisted a strand of hair into a knot.

"If he can't put his problems aside when your life is in danger, maybe he doesn't love you." The insinuating tone was too familiar.

Dan appeared in the doorway, barking like a drill instructor. "You don't belong here, Lawson."

Adam focused on Bonny. "Let her decide for herself."

"She's crying and it's your fault. It's wrong to expect her to deal with emotional issues now." Kari pushed past Adam to her side. "There's a long road ahead of her. She has a difficult time putting thoughts together and can't remember everything yet."

Adam placed his tanned, muscular hand over her small, white one. "Think about what I said, Bonny. I'll come back unless you prefer not to see me again."

"I—I love—Kieran." If only she could stop trembling.

"But does he love you?" He used that tone again. "I'd have gotten on the first plane."

CR80

Adam's visit left Bonny feeling upset and agitated. With Dan at the Veteran's Hospital, she and Kari were alone.

"When Dan was hurt in—over there." Finding the right words was such a struggle.

"In Afghanistan, fighting in the war," Kari prompted.

Bonny nodded. "You—stayed with him?"

Kari laid a warm hand on her shoulder. "I didn't want him to die without me at his side. Why?"

"You spoke with—Kieran. W—won't he come? Doesn't he—love me?" Her throat tightened.

"Did he say he didn't love you?" Kari scooted her chair close to the bed.

"No. He loves me. I would—go if …"

"Adam upset you, didn't he?" Kari picked up a brush and smoothed her hair, making her head hurt when she tried to unsnarl a knot.

"He asked me—to forgive." The tears tumbled out in a flood. "I need Kieran."

Kari smoothed a curl away from her face. "He says he doesn't deserve your forgiveness. Honey, he was crying. I told him you love him."

"Let me call ..."

Kari handed her the cell phone. "What if he says no?"

Her hand was shaking. "I'll know."

The phone rang and rang. When he answered, she said, "It's me."

"Bonny?"

"I need you—please?"

"I'm sorry. You deserve better."

The line went dead. She laid the phone down and closed her eyes.

"What did he say?"

Bonny turned her face to the wall. The pain in her heart hurt more than the pain of her injuries.

CO&O

Kari jumped for the door to head Adam off. Once again, he ignored the sign asking visitors to check at the nurse's station. He had confidence, a defiant air, feared in the courtroom and difficult on a personal level. "May I come in?"

Bonny looked from Kari to Adam. "Yes."

"But ..." Kari began.

"I won't upset her, I promise." Adam held his hand up warning Kari, and pulled a chair close to the bed. "You seem so much stronger, 'Bunny Rabbit.'"

Bonny's father was the only one to use that nickname. Putting her right hand to her throat, she shut her eyes. "Exhausted—hurting."

Memories of his warm, strong arms assailed her. However, the warm exterior still hid the same cold-hearted attitude which caused him to break their engagement. Those memories were too clear, but he said he loved her. He was here.

"You don't have any trouble remembering me, do you?" Adam's voice was gentler than she remembered.

"No ..." His tall, athletic build, the deep brown eyes, flecked with gold, and his movie star looks stood in stark contrast to Kieran's rugged and fair features.

"Don't you have a smile for me? I've missed it." He leaned toward the bed and grasped her hand. His manicured nails and soft palms felt so different from Kieran's chapped, rough callouses.

236

Dear God, what is happening? I want Kieran.

His lips parted in a smile. She had grown used to the tender expression in Kieran's sky-blue eyes. Adam's expression suggested possession and conquest.

"How much longer will they keep you in traction?" His question brought her back to the present. She freed her hand and straightened herself in the bed.

"Two weeks?" She turned to Kari for confirmation.

"Yes, they'll put your leg in an external fixation device, and take your arm out of the cast also."

"I can't wait to move—around." She shifted position, attempting to ease her weary backside.

He laughed. "I'll bet. You're not one to sit still for long."

"They say I have …"

"Pneumonia." Kari spoke up. "Nothing serious yet. How's your law practice, Adam?"

He answered Kari, his eyes remaining on Bonny. "I'm pleased, considering I've been on my own for such a short time."

"You're on your own?"

He squirmed, turning his eyes to the window. "They, uhh—they fired me for dating a co-worker. I lost very few clients, which helped."

"They fired you because of Vanessa?" Kari asked.

He reddened. "Yes, I—uhh, ruined the best thing in my life. I kept my land, but I lost the Beemer. I'm living with my parents, attending their church, and getting biblical counseling. I work with the high school youth group. I needed to slow down and get my priorities straight. It hasn't been easy."

"Those are—big changes." Adam's intensity made her uncomfortable. When Kieran's eyes met hers, she felt like melting, melding together, becoming one in thought and emotion.

"I lost everything important. God, you, and my self-respect. It requires a lot of changes to get right with God when you make as big of a mess as I did." He stood to leave. "Thank you for seeing me, but I won't overstay my welcome."

"Thank you," Bonny said.

"I want to visit again."

"I tire fast."

"I'll come back soon." He smiled at Bonny, bowed his head toward Kari, and left.

"Bonny ..." Kari warned.

"I need to talk to Kieran." The emotions roiled inside her. Kari had to understand.

"Bonny, are you certain? He wasn't willing ..."

"He needs to—believe I still love him."

"Bonny ..."

"Now."

Kari dialed the number, waited for the international call to go through and handed the phone to Bonny, who motioned her to remain close enough to hear. He answered in a voice laced with panic. "What's wrong?"

"It's me, Kieran." She waited as the sound of her voice registered.

"Bonny?" How she longed to hear his deep Scottish burr. Her heart began fluttering at his first word.

"I need you. *Tha gaol agam ort.*" She waited for her words to sink in.

"You're doin' better then?" Joy, concern, and love were all there.

"I have pneu—pneumonia. Kieran—it's not—right without you."

"I'm sorry. You deserve more." His words sounded tentative, and his voice too soft. She heard ragged breathing, and a sob.

"I need you. I'm afraid." She said it slow so he understood she meant it.

Silence again.

She struggled to make the words come out right. "I want you, *mo gràdh.*"

"No, I can't ..."

"Remember ..." Tears streamed down her face, clogging her throat. "Please."

"*A bheanachd, mo chridhe, mo gràdh.*"

She must be rubbing her throat red. She forced herself to stop, but he hung up. She handed the phone to Kari as the gut-wrenching sobs began. "Shhh, hush now," Kari said. "We're still praying. God's still in control."

"He won't let God or me in, Kari. You —hear."

"Was that Gaelic?"

She rubbed at her eyes with a corner of the sheet, and turned her face to the window. "*A bheanachd, mo chridhe, mo gràdh.* It means—a blessed farewell, my heart, my dearest love. Kari, it can't—be over."

CHAPTER THIRTY

CRISIS

Why didn't you call? I deserve to know they put her back in ICU." Adam rushed out of the elevator, his face pale, eyes wide with alarm.

Before he finished tongue-lashing Kari and Dan, Dr. Clark came through the double doors. "It's serious. She has a blood clot, or pulmonary embolus, in her right lung, and the pneumonia is worse in both lungs. The kidney infection isn't responding to the antibiotics. Infections in two major organ systems and an immune system compromised by the trauma and her poor liver function create a very bad scenario."

"How bad?" Dan loosened Kari's grip on his arm, rubbing the dents made by her fingernails.

"Any embolus is life-threatening. With the infections it's doubly so. She's at high risk for developing a systemic infection, something we call sepsis. We're using two of the strongest antibiotics we have. The next thirty-six to seventy-two hours are crucial." His pager beeped and he silenced it, focusing on Dan and Kari. "You should notify everyone important. I'll let you know when we get the test results."

They stood in stunned silence, until Kari straightened, pulling the phone out of her pocket. "I'll have to phone Scotland again, though if Bonny couldn't convince Kieran she needs him, I doubt I'll succeed." Adam stopped her.

"She called that Scotsman?"

"She loves him, Adam," Kari said. "She wants him here. He thinks he hurt her too much but …"

"He hurt her? She didn't say …" He grew red in the face, and clenched his fists as if ready to punch his rival in the nose.

"It's between them." The anger she harbored toward both men felt like it would be boil over. "Forgiving and loving aren't the same, Adam. Now, if you'll excuse me, I have to make these calls." She kissed Dan on the cheek and headed for the elevators.

"Why tell them? If he doesn't love her, be done with them."

"They're her friends, Adam. She teaches at the college. They have to know."

Kari and Dan began to let Adam rotate shifts with them. They were exhausted but trying to concentrate on the healing power of God. Bonny's face, pale against the sheets, her mouth obscured by the ventilator tubing once again, forecast a bleak outlook. During the infrequent moments when her eyes opened, she gave no sign of recognition.

Adam whispered he loved her and made grand promises, but she responded to nothing. As her kidney function decreased, she began to retain fluids. With her frail body growing bloated, the doctors warned of the possibility of heart failure. She was slipping away.

CRBO

The day was as dreich as Kieran's mood. The college building juddered as if it were a medieval castle battered by Mons Meg, the medieval siege cannon in Edinburgh. Sheets of rain lashed the windows, running down like tears. *If Bonny dies, they will never stop for as long as I live.*

A knock on his half-open office door jolted his mind back from the hospital in far off Albuquerque, where his love lay dying.

"Kieran, I heard the news."

Deirdre.

"May I come in?"

"I was just getting ready to go home. I'm tired."

She walked around to his side of the desk, her fingers running up his arm. "You could come to my place for dinner. I heard about you and Dr. Bryant."

"Deirdre. I thought you left school." He shoved the stack of papers he had been grading into his briefcase, and stood.

"I'm back. I told you I would know when you were ready." Her voice was smooth as steel, but it irritated his raw nerves like winter wind down the chimney. Why would no one leave him alone?

"No Deirdre, I'm not interested. I love Bonny. She's dying, but I'll never love again."

She rested her hand on his, caressing, and squeezing. "You say that now, but a man shouldn't be alone."

He extracted his hand and moved toward the door. "Go home, Deirdre. I just want to be alone."

"I'll leave you alone for now, but I'm available anytime you change your mind."

She headed down the stairs, and he stepped back into his office. He was not going to risk running into her between his office and the car.

He closed his eyes, leaning his head against the back of his chair.

There was a knock at the door, and Janet stuck her head around the door. "Can I come in?"

"Of course." He nodded, pushing back from the desk, and gripping the arms of his office chair, ready for her scolding.

She came around the desk, standing beside him with her hands on her hips. "Kieran, without a miracle, Bonny will die in the next day or two."

"Kari phoned me."

He stood, moving past her to the window, turning his back. The thunderclouds in Janet's eyes were almost as threatening as the storm raging in his heart. "She let Adam visit, but she also asked me to come."

"You spoke to Bonny?"

He kept his back to her, grasping the pencil in his hand so tightly it snapped in two. "Twice."

She grabbed his arm, and he turned around to find her eyes blazing with fire. "You blamed yourself for not being with Bronwyn when she needed you. Now, you refuse when Bonny asks you? I'm fed up with your self-pity, Kieran. If you cared about anyone but yourself, you'd get on the next plane, beg her to live, and tell her you love her."

"I can't …"

"Ach, Kieran, you're daft. One of those stones you throw must have hit you in the head. I've coddled you when I should have walked away a long time ago." Her face grew red as her voice rose with anger. "You broke her heart for self-righteous, stubborn reasons. Surely you won't let her die without telling her you love her, or let her recover and turn to Adam, believing you don't care?"

Fatigue and fear descended on him, and he sank into his chair, cradling his head in his hands. Janet moved closer, putting her arms around him. "My heart breaks for you, *a charaid*, but you have to shake your depression and do something for Bonny."

He kept his head down as the pain tore at his gut and traveled up to his throat. "It's too late. If I had gone when Dan first called … If she's willing to see him, she doesn't need me. Shut the door on your way out."

Janet brought one rounded fist down hard on the desk. "*Eejit*, if you love each other, it's never too late." She slammed the door behind her, leaving him staring at the desk.

⊂∂⊃

"Kieran, Bonny's worse." He recognized Kari's voice and held his breath. He had just decided to go downstairs for a cup of tea, but slumped back into his chair.

"She has pneumonia and a blood clot in one lung. They put her back on the ventilator. She loves you. Please come."

"I told you, I'm not what she needs." He felt as if his heart had stopped.

"Can you forgive yourself if you don't try and she dies? Fight for Bonny if you love her."

He hung up without saying a word, laid his head on the desk, and sobbed. Then, putting on his raincoat and Wellies, he whistled for the dogs and hiked up into the hills behind the house. He stopped at the place Bonny once called a highland cathedral. They had planned such a full life. *How can it end this way? Dear God, please?*"

He returned to the house after dark, chilled from the pain in his heart as much as from the biting wind and driving rain. Sleep eluded him with emotions churning in his heart and mind. Going into his office, he turned on the computer, searching for the earliest flight out of Inverness, anything with a connection to America—to Bonny.

Kari's last words replayed in his mind. "Can you live with yourself if you don't try and she dies? If you truly love Bonny, fight for her."

He knew the misery of living with regret. If she did still love him, he had to try. He had the long trip to Albuquerque to work it out with God.

At daybreak, he called Janet. "I can't live with myself if I don't go. My plane leaves at nine."

"Finally, *go mbeannaí Dia duit.*"

♋

Kieran leaned forward, his face in his hands. At last, he settled for leaning his head back against the seat with his eyes closed. Though he kept his eyes shut, he was not sleeping, but instead praying. The first available flight out of Inverness stopped in Dublin and forced an airline change in New York. He could only pray he was not too late.

A hand on his shoulder made him jump. He glanced up at a young flight attendant with dark hair and deep brown eyes. "Sir, you seem upset. Can I do anything to help?"

He shook his head. "No, no one can."

"You're obviously distressed." Her hand still rested on his shoulder, warm, tangible humanity, with a comforting voice and eyes soft with concern.

"Someone I love is dying. I'm not certain I'll make it in time." He didn't recognize his own voice, it sounded so weak and shaky.

"Would you let me pray for you?"

Her words were an answer to his prayers. "Yes, please."

She led him to the galley. "My name is Christen, what's yours?"

"Kieran, Kieran MacDonell."

"How can I pray for you, and for your loved one?"

He felt so strange, standing in the galley of a plane with a young woman near Bonny's age, letting her pray when he didn't know if he believed. "Her name is Bonny. She was involved in a terrible car crash. She …"

"Do you mind if I take your hands, Kieran? I think it's good to have contact with people you're praying with." Her voice had a comforting quality.

"Is she a friend or relative?"

"My former fiancée. We argued before she left Scotland for her friend's wedding. I hope she's still alive. I have to tell her I love her." It was strange how it helped to voice his fears, even to a complete stranger.

Christen bowed her head, and he followed. The prayer was simple, for Bonny's healing and their relationship. The words were nothing special, not so different from his prayer, but she believed.

Unexpected, and startling, like a riptide, dragging and pulling, then sending him bobbing to the surface for a breath of exaltation, the knowledge of God's love and care washed over him in a way he had never experienced before. God had already answered by sending someone to pray with him.

When Christen finished, he prayed. "God, I have doubted and wavered in my belief. There is no reason for you to listen to me, except for your grace. I ask your forgiveness for my anger and unbelief. Create a new and clean heart in me. Please, help my unbelief. Heal Bonny's terrible injuries and forgive me for hurting her. Bring her back to me—at least let me see her alive again. Amen."

The weight of guilt and self-loathing lifted and the warmth of God's love continued to flow through him in an overwhelming wave, unlike anything he had ever known. Along with it came a certainty Bonny would be healed and God willing, agree to marry him.

He felt as if he was in another world, but he managed to find the words. "Thank you, Christen. I appreciate it more than I can tell."

"You're welcome. I'm not usually on this flight, but I traded with a friend. When I saw your eyes, I knew what I had to do. I'll continue to pray for you and for Bonny. God bless you."

He walked back to his seat, knowing his heart had changed. *Dear God, let Bonny live long enough to know.*

C33880

The red-blond giant getting off the elevator outside the Intensive Care Unit drew Kari's attention. Rumpled and unshaven, his curly hair was disheveled and standing on end. She leaped out of her chair, darted across the waiting room, and threw her arms around him. "Kieran, thank you for coming. She'll get better now, I know she will."

He sounded bewildered. "Kari? How did you recognize me?"

"Bonny emailed photos to me. She calls you her 'Highland hunk.'" Pulling on his arm, she dragged him through the double doors to Bonny's bedside. "I'm so glad you came. I don't know how much time she has left."

He stood in stunned silence, his eyes roving from one machine to another. The ventilator, two IV lines, a chest tube, and heart monitor. His face froze in fear as he processed the reality of Bonny's impending death.

Kari had become accustomed to the strong odors of a hospital—illness, disinfectants, medications, and fear. From the way Kieran rubbed his nose and eyes, the hospital was far from routine to him. His eyes had the panicked appearance of a horse about to bolt.

Bonny's face and hands were puffy, her eyelids translucent. Her skin had a disturbing, yellow pallor. The continual "Beep, beep, beep," of the heart monitor and rhythmic "click-whuhhh," sound of the ventilator, offered the only reassurance that the small, motionless figure still lived.

⊂੩੭ʊ

Kieran's legs gave way and he sank into a chair. One word escaped from his lips. "No."

With his heart kathumping in his chest, he remembered Christen's prayer. God would not let Bonny die. He had been so certain of that on the plane.

"Talk to her, Kieran. Let her hear your voice. Encourage her to fight. You must have private things to say, so I'll leave you alone."

As Kari pulled the curtain around the bed, he leaned forward. Timidity gave way to emotion and he grasped Bonny's hand, wet droplets scattering across the back of it and spattering onto the sheets. "Bonny, I'm here at last. I needed to tell you how wrong I've been. God has changed me. He has forgiven me, and I believe He will heal you. Live. I love you. I need you."

⊂੩੭ʊ

Dan's military bearing was undiminished by the slight limp from his prosthesis. He spoke straight as an arrow. "Right after the accident, I wanted you to come. As time passed, your procrastinating proved I was right in warning Bonny not to rush it. When Kari said you were here, it made me furious."

Kieran met his eyes. Dan had a right to say worse. "I put her through so much pain out of my own stubbornness and guilt."

Dan shook his head in frustration. "I'm worried enough, without having two rivals vying for her hand. In my mind, neither of you deserves her. I don't relish mediating between the two of you."

He nodded in understanding. "I know my behavior has puzzled you. It will be different from now on."

Dan motioned toward a corner where he and Kari had set up their post and offered him a bottle of much-appreciated water. After two hours, Kieran already understood Bonny's fascination with large bodies of water and humid air.

"Your presence creates a difficult situation. Adam won't be polite or understanding. I'll lay the ground rules and expect you both to follow them. Please, join us in prayer? I expect him any time."

Kieran bowed his head as Dan prayed. "Lord, we ask for your wisdom. Enable each of us to honor you first and to treat each other with respect. Help us remember our primary concern has nothing to do with our relationships but with Bonny's life."

When Dan finished praying, Kieran realized Kari was regarding him with a curious expression. "Why did you come now, when you refused so many times?"

He chose his words with care. "You said if I loved Bonny, to fight for her. I made a terrible mistake in waiting this long, but I hope I'm not too late. I hurt her the same way Adam did, but I have to try."

"No, it wasn't the same." Kari laid a comforting hand on his arm. "Bonny prayed for God to save you, whether or not you were together again. She loves you. She's leery of Adam."

"She didn't send him away."

Pulling the wrapper off a granola bar, Kari said, "A couple of nights before the wedding, he was waiting when she came home. She sent him away, telling him she wanted to marry you. You know, new shoes are better than old ones, but when they hurt your toes, you want the old ones back. Adam is the old shoes. When you refused to come, it hurt, and he was available. He's not who she wants."

"Here he is."

Kieran followed Dan's eyes to the tall, dark-haired man getting off the elevator. Studying the athletic man in the expensive business suit, he didn't find Kari's analogy of old, worn shoes very accurate.

Following an uncomfortable introduction, they shook hands like adversaries in a prizefight. Complete opposites, Kieran still recognized a formidable opponent.

Dan cleared his throat, the sound bearing striking similarity to "Atten-hut." He assumed a military bearing, feet apart, arms crossed, eyes narrowed, and voice firm. "We have an unusual situation here, gentlemen. In my mind, neither of you deserves Bonny. We are Christians, and I expect each of us to conduct ourselves in a manner honoring to our Lord. Bonny is our sole concern. Nothing else matters."

Kieran noted Adam's somber expression, meeting Dan's eyes and nodding. There was no doubt as to who was in control. "We need someone with her around the clock. Kari suggested a schedule. I have therapy at the Veteran's Hospital daily. Kari substitute teaches, so she's flexible. Adam, you have a complicated schedule, while Kieran has total flexibility, so he will fill in around everyone else. Kari and I make Bonny's medical decisions because we have her Power of Attorney. However, we'll discuss it with you if necessary."

Listening to Dan, Kieran developed a stronger respect for raw recruits in the Marine Corps. "You will behave with respect for each other and for Bonny. Now, let's pray." Without waiting for a response, he began. "Father, we come to you asking for healing for Bonny. We love her and believe in your power to heal. Help us to honor you, and unite us in our common goal. Amen."

Dan relaxed his stance. "You will come into contact with each other. Any future either of you hope to have with her depends on your conduct toward each other. I won't tolerate anything other than complete cooperation."

"I respect your authority, Dan, but I've travelled a long way, in both a literal and spiritual sense." Kieran avoided looking at Adam. "I will remain here at the hospital until and unless Bonny says otherwise. The rest of you do as you want."

"Now wait a minute, Scotsman." Adam's tone made it a slur, not a nationality. "Dan explained his routine. Why should you be different?"

Kari stepped between them. "Perhaps he can rest and eat when you're here, Adam."

As Kieran headed to the men's room, Adam caught Kari's arm. "In spite of anything I did to Bonny, that Scotsman doesn't belong here. They had a romantic fling, nothing else."

"She called him herself, before she got so bad. Maybe he can help her regain the will to live." She pulled free and walked away.

Chapter Thirty-one

The Rivals

A dam's anger reminds me of a lava flow, a cool crust on top and red hot underneath. He won't make it easy." It was only the second night Kari and Dan had spent at home together since their wedding.

Earlier in the day, she discovered Kieran singing a Gaelic lullaby to Bonny in his deep baritone. When she returned later, he was reading scripture. Over and over, he said, "I love you, lass, with my whole heart. God is helping me change. He replaced the anger and pain I felt for so long with hope and peace. Please, love, come back to me."

Watching him, they recognized in his anguish his deep love for Bonny. Eventually he explained why he broke the engagement and what happened on the flight over to change his life. Dan clapped him on the shoulder, congratulating him.

Kieran rubbed one eye. "I'm a new man, thanks to God. I pray she'll live to know I've changed."

CREO

On the seventh day following his arrival, as Kieran prayed aloud at her bedside, Bonny squeezed his hand. It continued throughout the day and started again the next morning when he returned. No one else experienced it.

He phoned Kari. "I awakened from a catnap to increasing pressure on my hand. When I opened my eyes, Bonny was staring at me—she sees me."

He kissed her forehead and wet her face with tears of joy. "I'm here, lass. *Tha gaol agam ort.* Please pull through, Bonny? We can have a life together."

♥

Bonny was out of Intensive Care and could sit in a wheelchair. The pneumonia and kidney infections were showing improvement. Her liver function studies trended toward normal, and her spleen showed signs of healing.

Kieran leaned on the arm of her chair, stroking the shimmering red curls, so thin since her accident. Meeting his eyes, she asked, "Why didn't you come?"

Her unrelenting, green gaze challenged him, and he swallowed, gathering courage to answer. "I'll regret failing you until the day I die. It took a while to admit I was wrong, but my love never wavered. I can share your faith and commitment now."

She wiped her eyes on the corner of the sheet as he cradled one small hand in his.

"I felt trapped, Bonny. You and God stood on one side and on the other, my own pride and anger. I don't deserve anything, but I ask your forgiveness."

Bonny brought his hand to her cheek. "I forgave you the second you left my house and prayed for you to commit your life to God, no matter what it required. If it meant my death, I would consider it worthwhile. You went back on your word too many times. I need to see changes proving your faith is real."

He put his hand over hers. "You will, I promise. God put a Christian flight attendant on the plane. She saw me crying and prayed for me. She traded with a friend or she would never have been on that flight. Bonny, I believe God has forgiven and healed me. Don't say this is the end."

"Kieran, you don't stop loving someone." She paused. "I sent Adam away a couple of nights before Kari's wedding. However, since the accident, he reminds me of the man I once promised to marry. It's tearing me to pieces. I can't make important decisions now."

It hurt to see the anguish in her eyes. "I understand, and I'll stay here unless you ask me to go. Adam will arrive soon. I prefer not to see him, so I'll leave now. Take your time, but believe me, I won't wander away from God again. *Tha mo gaol gu bràth.*"

Tears filled her eyes, and she clutched her throat as he touched her hand and walked out.

CRITICAL

"How's my best girl today?" Adam carried flowers and a box of chocolates. "Why do you keep coming when I don't love you?"

He pulled a chair nearer, leaning over the bed rail. "I lost my way for a while, let my priorities slide. When I discovered you moved to Scotland, I panicked. When you refused my attempts to contact you, I understood for the first time how much I hurt you. It devastated me when you sent the ring back. After your accident, I was afraid I wouldn't be able to ask your forgiveness."

He sounded believable. "Can you keep missing work to sit here with me?"

He laid his hand on hers. "I'll stop at nothing to prove I love you."

She put her hand under the sheet to avoid twisting her hair into knots. "Regaining someone's confidence doesn't happen overnight. You betrayed me and destroyed my self-worth. I wasn't thinking right when you first showed up or you wouldn't be here now. You have to give me time."

CRITICAL

The conversations with her ardent suitors made Bonny so upset she accepted when Kari insisted on spending the night. At three in the morning, she awakened in pain and remained awake after her shot. "Kari, would you stay with me for a couple of days and ask Kieran and Adam not to come? I need to pray and talk with you and Dan."

The next day she moved to a room with a view of the Sandia Mountains. The majestic mass of towering cliffs and jagged peaks reminded her of God's power to make everything beautiful.

Bonny spent the time away from her suitors, reading her Bible and praying. She could voice the tumult of thoughts and feelings roiling through her heart and mind to Kari and Dan. "I spent ten years with Adam. We have a history, and he admits he made a mess of things. On the other hand, Kieran is the sweetest, most gentle man I have ever met. He seems sincere in his new faith. I can see the changes in him. His whole demeanor is different."

"Bonny," Kari said, "I like Kieran. Dan and I both do, but Scotland is so far away from everything you've ever known."

"Hold on," Dan interrupted, "you shouldn't let your feelings about her moving far away enter into things, Kari. This isn't about what we want. It's about God's will for her life. Bon, I could trust Kieran with your heart and your life. He's an honest man, simple and straightforward. Only you can decide if moving 4000 miles away to become the wife of a sheep farmer is a change you can make. Give it some time. You're not going anywhere for a while."

Three days later, Dan called both men. "Bonny says you may keep her company, but not mention the future. She won't discuss love or marriage right now."

CR80

They celebrated Bonny's move to rehab with a dinner from La Placita, a restaurant in Old Town.

It required effort, but Bonny convinced Kari and Dan to take their long-delayed honeymoon to Hawaii. "I can handle them. Please have them both here at the same time to listen to my plan. Then take your wife on your honeymoon and enjoy each other."

They all gathered in her room that evening, Kieran and Adam standing in opposite corners like boxers.

"I'm not a prize with you two as competitors. You'll treat each other as Christians should, and if you press me for decisions, I'll banish you both."

Listening to her, Dan put his hand on her shoulder. "That's my Carrot-Top. Now I can leave in peace."

"You go, girl." Kari kissed her cheek before she left.

Bonny closed her eyes, praying the time with her two sparring knights would reveal her heart and God's will. She was anxious to go home, to her own home in the mountains.

CR80

The first day Kari and Dan were gone, Adam arrived with flowers and food from Chez Bob, a small French restaurant they had enjoyed together. He walked straight to her chair and kissed her on the cheek.

In a stern voice, she said, "No more kisses."

"But Bonny, I used to greet you with a kiss." He sounded both puzzled and pleading.

"Everything's different now." She was determined to hold them both at bay.

"And about the nickname, no one but Dad has ever called me 'Bunny Rabbit.' Don't use it again. Please act like a friend and allow me to recover."

His eyes widened in surprise, and the corners of his mouth turned down. "Come on Bon, with you back home I should have home-turf advantage."

"This isn't a courtroom or a football game, Adam, and there is no advantage."

The next day he arrived with a Scrabble game and a couple of movies, and she recognized his reluctant acceptance of her terms.

⊗⊗

Kieran was the complete opposite of Adam. He offered to pray, and she heard power in his prayers. He attended church alone and spent hours shopping for books and studying. "The Christian book store was lovely. I bought books to read and a Bible study to do at the hotel. It's not very green here, but the weather is amazing, and Sandia Peak is incredible. I see why you love it."

"I told you it had a beauty all its own."

He laughed, and his hand brushed hers, but then, as if remembering her request, he pulled it back and continued his stories of life outside the hospital walls. "I understand now why you complained about learning to drive on the wrong side of the road. I remember you telling yourself to look right and turn left, so I tried it in reverse. It helps."

Bonny laughed. "I was so scared to venture into traffic. I considered staying in the parking lot."

When he left, she closed her eyes and tried to calm her thoughts. His eyes drew her, and his voice enthralled her. When Janet called the next day, Bonny said, "His love is as wild, adventurous, and romantic as the mountains, glens, and rushing burns of the Highlands. A quiver flows through me when he enters the room, but can I trust that his wavering belief and deception will resolve after a life-changing encounter on the plane? How can I know he's really changed?"

"Take it slow, Bonny. Make him prove he means it. You're right to be leery. This is your future you're talking about."

The next morning, Kieran arrived with a copy of *Great Expectations*, a box of Scottish toffee, a bottle of sunscreen, and two big straw hats.

He knew her so well, it showed in everything he did, and she laughed out loud. "What do you have in mind? The therapists hardly give me a break. "

"At the first opportunity, I plan to escort you to a lovely, wee patch of grass for a bit o' sunshine to put the bloom back in your cheeks." His accentuated brogue made her laugh. "You need fresh air. I can't believe this dry, sunny weather."

"Oh, *hou* lovely." She mimicked his accent, making him laugh also. "I'm so thin and pale. The therapist said you can come along and learn the right way to help me in and out of the wheelchair."

His eyes narrowed, his lips set in a serious expression. "I don't need lessons. I'll lift you. Why, you weigh less than one of my sheep." He flexed the muscles in his work-hardened arms.

With mock irritation, she said, "Kieran, I need to do this myself. Until my arm gets strong enough for crutches, I'm bound to this wheelchair. I refuse to stay trapped in it one minute longer than I have to."

The corners of his shining blue eyes crinkled—the well-remembered predecessor of the smile she loved. "My plan is better. It's been too long since I've held you in my arms." His eyes hinted at far more than the words themselves.

A quiver ran through her at the enticing thought of being in his arms, but ... "Too much has happened. I need time to see where God and my heart lead. You have to accept it."

His blue eyes clouded as she spoke, revealing the depth of guilt and pain her words evoked. "I'll wait as long as necessary. It's my fault."

After an hour of reading Dickens under an umbrella on the patio, she grew tired and relented, allowing him to lift her back into bed. He held on longer than necessary. But, it felt right to be in his arms, even for a moment.

෩෨

The two men avoided each other with a plague-like abhorrence. Kieran departed before five, finding the sight of Adam so repugnant he left plenty of leeway. They alternated on the weekends.

One day, Adam arrived with flowers and began describing his weekend outing with the high school boys at church. "I thought of you when we climbed Battleship Rock on Saturday, Bon. We had a lot of fun. I know how you love the

Jemez Mountains."

Pleasant memories flooded her mind. "I had a lot of fun as a kid at church camp there. How I would love to climb Battleship Rock and see the river flowing below again. I remember climbing a hill up behind Camp Shaver and holding a communion service with hotdog buns torn into bite-size pieces and small cups of grape juice. Fun times."

Old memories came flooding back as he spoke.

This new Adam held a fresh appeal. "You've changed during our time apart."

He leaned forward in his chair, a spark in his eyes and new eagerness in his voice. "God's changing the way I handle my law practice and everything else in my life. Sometimes it's not crucial to win the case. It's more important to help the parties reconcile, because it's right, not for the fee."

It was surprising to find herself enjoying his visits. He represented her first love, home, and old friendships. The pleasant memories, suppressed for so long, returned in vivid detail. Even if she did still love him, was he worthy of it?

◌🙖

Seeing Adam striding right toward him in the parking lot jolted Kieran out of his musing. He should have remembered that the last time Adam flew back from Phoenix, his plane landed early. The days when Adam was out of town were ideal for Kieran and Bonny. He stayed later than usual, talking with freedom and unrestrained enjoyment as they had in Scotland, before their world fell apart.

He said a polite hello without stopping, but Adam grasped his upper arm. "Why don't you go back to your sheep, Scotsman? You're not needed here."

"I received a personal invitation from Bonny." Quelling the impulse to jerk his arm away, Kieran measured his words with care. "We're getting on rather well."

"There's no way a sheep farmer can hold a candle to the life I offer." Adam sneered.

He was treading on dangerous ground. If Adam intended to bait him with sarcasm, he refused to step into the trap. "I have far more than a sheep farm to offer. If you mean quantity, I can provide anything she needs or desires. As far as quality, she knows I can fill those needs."

With the attitude of a schoolyard bully, Adam said, "Bonny and I have a long history together. She has friends here, and it's home. Romantic flings happen, but when you return, reality sets in. Why prefer your smelly little sheep farm when she has me close to home and friends?"

Kieran knew he should walk away, but an irresistible force made him continue. "I can assure you, what lies between us is real. We helped put each other's world back together and developed a strong love and respect for each other. She didn't get respect from you, and I didn't humiliate her when she was hurting and vulnerable. One other thing, I'm proud of my heritage. Referring to me as a Scotsman as if it were a slur, is equivalent to me putting you down for being an American, or a lawyer."

Adam's lips curled into a sardonic grin. "I made a mistake—you made a mistake, but when it comes to offering her a life, she's better off here. Leave her alone, Scotsman."

Kieran turned and walked away. *Dear God, keep her from doing something she will regret.*

೫೦

"How's the patient today?" Adam walked in with roses and Mexican food takeout from an airport franchise. "You're beautiful even when they say you're sick."

"Thank you." She straightened up in the bed. "How did your trip go?"

His eyes glinted with pride as he shrugged his shoulders. "A piece of cake. People will sue over anything. I met Kieran in the parking lot. Was he in a foul mood with you?" He turned toward the window. "Nice view."

It was easy to see he was avoiding her eyes. "Kieran, angry? You started something, didn't you?"

Adam's voice took on the smooth tone he used when surprised by unexpected testimony in court. "You set the ground rules, Miss Bryant, in no uncertain terms. He doesn't want me near you."

She pointed her finger at him as if chastising a child. "I know you, Adam

Lawson. Did he say he doesn't want you near me?"

He glanced toward her, but not at her. "Something about me not respecting you and how much he has to offer—garbage. He's only a sheep farmer, Bon. What do you see in him?"

She felt the nudge of suspicion. He was too nonchalant. "Kieran doesn't behave that way. What difference does it make that he's a sheep farmer? He's worthy of my love. He knows how to give of himself and ask nothing except love in return."

Adam touched her cheek with his fingertip and lowered his voice. "You haven't known him long. Didn't Kari mention he had mental problems?"

That insinuating tone was so annoying. "He experienced some depression related to the death of his wife and baby, which is normal. Adam, he wouldn't confront you unless you provoked him. You do love to bait people."

He set the Styrofoam container of Mexican food on the table. "You're quite the cross-examiner. Watch yourself. You've known me far longer."

"So I know what to watch out for." She tried to sound as firm as possible, pulling the plastic utensils out of their package and pointing them at him. "Evade my questions if you want, but I can imagine what happened. It's upsetting for you not to keep your promise to behave as a gentleman. I prefer being alone tonight. Now leave, please."

She waved him away.

Adam reminded her of a spoiled child straining to avoid punishment. "Why blame me for your Scotsman's jealous temper?"

"Quit calling him 'Scotsman.' I explained the rules, and I don't appreciate your attitude. Now leave." She turned away and Adam stamped out.

⁂

Kieran arrived carrying a bouquet of daisies while Bonny was eating breakfast the next morning. Dark circles under her eyes, pale cheeks, and a listless manner gave evidence of a sleepless night. Kneeling at her chair, he laid one hand on her upper back. She was a wee rickle of bones. It was amazing she had the strength to hold herself upright. If Adam appeared now, he wasn't certain what he might do. "What happened, hen? You're all peely wally."

Her eyes filled, and she reached for a tissue. "What happened between you and Adam?"

Icy hands wrapped themselves around his heart, his mind racing for the right words. He preferred not to say anything unkind, but he had to tell the truth. "We ran into each other in the car park—parking lot. Jealousy got the better of us both. A wee stramash, nothin' more."

"'A wee stramash?' Kieran, we once promised each other honesty."

He pulled a chair close beside her, reaching out to brush a bright curl from her eyes. "He suggested I return home since you're out of danger. He says you deserve better than a sheep farm and 'a romantic fling.'"

"Who started the conversation?" Her voice sounded tired and weak.

"He did." Kieran guarded his words. "He questioned why I waited so long to come. I admitted to my mistake, and then I became angry."

She sighed. "What did you say?"

"I said at least I didn't humiliate you at the lowest point in your life."

She closed her eyes, making the dark circles more noticeable. He could throttle Adam.

"To which he said?"

He caught her hand on the way to her throat, but she pulled away, tucking it under the blankets. "Kieran, he said you confronted him, saying he didn't respect me."

He felt the warm flush of anger moving up his face. "I walked away, Bonny. I got into the car and left. I didna want to argue." He strode to the window and then turned to face her. "You have to decide who to believe."

"He's tough on people sometimes. It's intimidating in the courtroom, but difficult in real life. If I believe you, it means Adam lied." She reached her good hand toward him and he took firm hold of it. A tear slipped down one cheek, and he reached over to wipe it away. In a voice as gentle as a Scottish mist, she said, "I believe you, Kieran."

He lifted her chin with his finger. "I tried to respond in a way I could be honest about. I won't accuse him of lying. It's how he sees it."

"Thank you." Her face took on a pinched appearance, and wet drops rained down on his hand.

"In his opinion, you belong here, where you have friends and familiar surroundings." He handed her a tissue and scooted his chair even closer. He might as well remind her of the truth and see where it led. If God wanted them together, He would settle the questions in her heart. "My life is so different. You have friends in Fort William, but your life-long friends are here. If you want me to leave, I will."

Bonny's touch was cool as she removed his hand from her face. "Sooner or later something was bound to happen between you two. I won't be a rope in a game of tug o' war."

He shook his head. "I won't pressure you."

"Seeing you both every day ..." She pulled him down to where his eyes were level with hers. "Kari and Dan have sacrificed so much. They are my family, Kieran. This is my home, and since the accident, I find it difficult to think about leaving."

The icy hands squeezed his heart again. "Bonny, you can come home anytime."

She turned away, letting loose of his hand. "Life happens, and what we plan with the best intentions doesn't. The farm is an important responsibility and we agreed your parents and the farm are priorities. We can't foresee the future."

His heart in his throat, he knelt, putting all his love into his words. "I won't keep you from your home, Bonny. Dan and Kari are too important."

Her voice grew quiet. "I need to clear my mind. Will you push my wheelchair out in the sunshine? Tell me stories or give me a history lesson on Scotland. I can't decide this now."

She's not sending me away. "Of course."

CHAPTER THIRTY-TWO

THE CHOICE

Bonny's crisis of the heart had reached its peak. Adam was out of town again, so Kieran came early and stayed long into the evening. She relaxed as the day wore on, letting him remind her of the special times when their love was first beginning.

She saw Scotland mirrored in his eyes as he said, "Remember the rainbow from the top of Grant Tower—the two of us sharing it alone, in spite of the crowds? The best day, except for when you agreed to marry me, was the first time I took you to the farm."

When his firm grip surprised her, she realized she had taken his hand. The warmth of his touch was too comforting to pull away. "The first afternoon when you changed my flat and ate chili at my house was so special. We had a lovely time getting to know each other. That night at the ball —all the women envied me."

His smile reminded her of the day they sat on horseback and watched as an opening in the clouds let the sun stream through in fingers of light, reflecting off the waters of Loch Garry far below them. "The men envied me."

They remained hand in hand, letting their thoughts return to happier days. Then she pulled away, straightening herself in the bed and tucking her hands under the blankets. "I broke my own rule."

"Perhaps you should listen to your heart." His soft voice paused before he continued. "Bonny, the depression and medication sent you away. I need you."

"No, please ..." The lump forming in her throat felt the size of a golf ball.

He looked out the window toward the mountain and changed the subject. "I'm reading a book about missionaries killed in the jungles of Ecuador. Later, a couple of the wives returned and helped the same Indians come to the Lord. I want faith that makes a difference, Bonny." She heard new fervor in his voice, his face alight with excitement. "I pray for a faith worth dying for—a faith impacting every aspect of my life and everyone I meet."

"This is the conversation I dreamed of having with you. Adam and I talked this way until I discovered everything was an illusion. Kieran, time is the sole revealer of true change."

He leaned closer, his warm, masculine scent surrounding her. "Self-control comes from the Holy Spirit. I didn't knock him out when I had the chance. Walking away is not my natural inclination where he's concerned, hen."

"True." She laughed, but the lump in her throat grew larger.

CR80

Bonny didn't fall asleep until daylight shone through the blinds. She awakened to the sight of clouds forming mare's tails above the towering mountains to the east. Kieran's words had made her realize what she needed. She had missed her life-long friends while in Scotland. Now, weak, hurt, and confused, Albuquerque was home once again.

Adam's touch didn't make her long for his arms around her the way Kieran's did. Perhaps she had willed things to succeed where God did not intend, based on the magnetism of his presence and her own loneliness. She had prayed for the opportunity to marry him when it was not right in God's eyes, and she had lost him.

She had dreamed of Adam returning to her life for so long. They had special memories of their own and years of history. He had his faults, but less of the unknown related to him. It seemed logical to remain near her life-long friends, her church, and her home.

Hurting Kieran, with his newfound faith, was comparable to stepping on a tender, young plant. But for now, she needed the familiarity of home and friends. If God willed something else, he would let her know.

CR80

Kieran brought Bonny's hand to his lips as they enjoyed the sunshine of the hospital courtyard. "The hours I spent in the hospital chapel praying for your life included healing our relationship. I cannot separate them. God saved your life for a purpose, and I believe it involves me."

He drew the small velvet box out of his pocket and revealed her ruby ring. "Bonny Faith Bryant, will you marry me?"

She wanted to talk and pray with Kari and Dan, but in the end, the decision was hers. Janet's words came back. *It's possible you're not in his life to marry him.*

Her heart was pulsing in her throat. "Kieran, I need more time. It was wrong to relive those old memories."

The color drained from his face. "They're ours. They watered the seeds of our love. I never intended to hurry you. I thought remembering ..."

"Kieran ..." The touch of one calloused finger wiping her tears caused her to cry harder.

"You're going to marry Adam." There was defeat in his voice. How could she hurt him?

She saw her own pain mirrored in the blue pools of his eyes. The hand holding the ring—her ring, dropped to his side. He walked across the courtyard, standing with his back to her, snarling his fingers through his hair.

"I haven't said I'd marry anyone. I can't make such life-changing decisions when I've only now reached the point where I still have a life."

When he turned and walked toward her, she saw agony etched in the lines of his forehead, the stern set of his mouth, and the gray cast in his eyes. "Why, Bonny? We knew we belonged together from the first night we talked. You love me—I know you do."

He stopped in front of her and stood, looking down at her before dropping to one knee at her side. She reached out to brush a curl off his forehead—but pulled her hand back, feeling as if her heart would break. "Kieran, I've been hurt by you both. I love you—but part of me still loves Adam. You're a wild, romantic dream, a Scottish knight in shining armor. You swept me off my feet and helped me live again. I love you, but for right now, I choose home and familiarity. I—I'm sorry."

"Don't choose now, Bonny, please. I can wait as long as it takes."

How could she hurt him? "I can't keep you here forever while I decide. Go home to your Highland cathedral and grow in your walk with God. Then my presence in your life will have meant something. If God wants more, He will show us in time."

Kieran put the ring box back in his pocket, where it formed a lump the size of the one in her throat. His voice grew husky with emotion. "I'll help you to your room."

Looking at him was impossible. "No, tell them you left me outside. It's—it's easier this way."

He stroked the tangled curls on her shoulder. Reaching underneath to separate a bright strand, he pulled his knife from his pocket, and cut it, tucking it in his shirt pocket. "If you decide you're wrong, I'll be waitin'." His muted voice signaled emotions held in check with enormous difficulty. "There will never be another woman—ever. *Bidh gaol agam ort gu sìorraidh. Beannachd Dè Rìgh Alban.* I will love you forever. God's blessing."

With the dull thud of the door closing behind him, a door closed in her heart, sealing off a place, which would belong to Kieran forever.

☙❧

Bonny saw the look of alarm on Kari's face when she walked in the next morning, the first day back from her honeymoon. The mirror had already revealed how her red-rimmed eyes stood out in her pale face.

She knew they believed Kieran was a far better match for her than Adam. His gentle spirit and passionate new walk with the Lord touched their hearts.

"Does Adam know?" Kari asked.

"No, ask him to stay away today, please?"

When Kari called, Dan came straight from therapy, striding in with such a confident gait no one would know one leg was prosthetic. "Bonny, your dad said not to marry someone you can live with but to marry someone you can't live without. Is Adam someone you can't live without?"

"Too many questions, you guys. I didn't say I wanted to marry Adam. I am alive and going home when I expected to die. For right now, I need home. With

Kieran, this would never be home again. I have to know I'm doing God's will, not mine."

"Bon, I—uh, tried to call Kieran," Dan rubbed his hand across his eyes. "He's gone."

☾☽

Bonny sat close to the window, wearing pale, pink warm-ups, which complimented the glow in her cheeks. She was so lost in her reverie, she failed to hear him. Adam watched the enchanting woman he longed to claim for his wife with an unfamiliar feeling, the fear of losing. He suspected she had made her decision, but assumed Kieran suffered the same banishment. She turned, and a smile lit up her face. *How was I foolish enough to leave her?*

"You're looking pretty." He measured his words with caution.

She motioned toward a chair. "Thank you. Come sit next to me. I asked you to stay away while I prayed and talked to Kari and Dan. It's only a partial decision, but following your encounter with Kieran, I realized it was wrong to keep you both waiting. Coming to understand what God would have me do for now is the hardest thing I've ever done."

He was drowning in the emerald sea of her eyes, his insides tying themselves in knots. "Forgive me. I reacted out of fear when I saw you together."

She was staring out the window again. Her silence did nothing to diminish his anxiety, but then she looked him in the eye. "I appreciate your apology. I sent Kieran back to Scotland. We will wait for God to lead. For now I need home."

He was on his knees, emotion threatening to overcome him, a feeling he hated. "I've dreamed of this moment. Can you forgive me for the pain and humiliation I caused?"

She placed her hand on his shoulder, warming his heart with feelings he was afraid to voice.

"The confident Adam Lawson, kneeling before me. I'll remember this. I forgave you in Scotland once I let the Lord have control of my life."

He swallowed hard, his mouth suddenly dry. "I want you to marry me, but it sounds as if you have something different in mind."

"I didn't say I would marry you, Adam. I didn't tell Kieran it was over between us either. I need to heal, physically and emotionally. I don't know when I can decide."

"Bonny, I'll wait."

Her voice was firm, stronger than the Bonny he remembered. "I won't rush things. I'm going home tomorrow. Jeni and Jake will continue caring for the house, and women from the church will bring meals and help with personal things. Dan and Kari are nearby, though I've stolen enough attention from their marriage."

He gripped her hands, small and delicate compared to the strength of her voice. "I'll help on evenings and weekends. I can fix meals and help around the house, anything you need."

She extricated her hands from his grasp. "Thank you. Nurses will visit three times a week and I have therapy every morning, I won't lack for much. Jeni will help me with bathing and dressing."

He restrained his enthusiasm. "I'll come after work and on weekends. We can walk in the evenings. My sister, Christy, will be home for the summer. She can stay with you at night. You two enjoy being together. She threatened to kill me when I broke off our engagement."

Bonny laughed, her distracting eyes lighting up. "I would have applauded her for it. I still don't know if I trust you."

CB&O

Adam and Bonny stood on the balcony of her mountain home watching the sunset four months after she left the hospital. The clouds glowed in glorious hues of pinks, oranges, and purples, amid the silence of nature pausing in preparation for the night's rest, and a quiet hush settled over the forest. The birds and crickets ceased their singing, and the coyotes were not yet on the move.

"I love this time of day."

She shivered as the evening air cooled, and he wrapped his arms around her tight and secure, his breath warm on her neck. "I love you, Bonny. Will you marry me and let me watch the sunset with you every day for the rest of our lives?"

She stiffened. "We traveled this road once before, Adam. I'll consider your proposal, but I can't answer you now."

His arms loosened, but then he drew her tight against him. "I'll wait, but this is the last time I'll ask."

They watched as the sun dipped below the mountains. He turned her in his arms and kissed her, when an unexpected image flashed through her mind. Clear and unmistakable, she saw a snapshot of a piper, high on a misty hill surrounded by sheep.

CHAPTER THIRTY-THREE

LONGING

A heavy Scottish mist greeted Kieran as he headed for Fort William, much more appropriate to his mood than the New Mexico sunshine. On the flight home, he made a promise to Bonny, to himself, and to God. Pain would not separate him from the God who brought him back to life. If life was without Bonny, he would serve the Lord with his whole heart, blessed for having loved her.

Deirdre Adair was already waiting outside his office when he arrived. "Kieran, I was afraid you had forgotten. You've never been late before. I've missed you so much."

"I'm sorry. I had a lot on my mind. This will be our last tutoring session." He unlocked the door and motioned for the tall brunette to precede him into the office.

She set her books on the desk and turned to face him. Her amber-colored eyes were wide with disappointment and surprise. "Kieran, whatever is wrong? You didn't say anything about quitting." She sat down, shaking her head. "What am I supposed to do without you?"

He sat down behind the desk and opened his college algebra book. "It's nice of you to say so, but you'll do fine with Fergus McClanahan."

She took hold of his arm, picking at the tweed of his jacket. "I didn't learn as well from Fergus as I do from you. I really struggled while you were in America—and I was so lonely."

Something about the way she said it rattled his thinking. "I made some plans, and I'm anxious to get started on them. I'm quitting teaching to pursue other things."

Her hand traveled up his sleeve, resting on his shoulder for a moment before she cupped his cheek in her hand. "Maybe this is the answer to my prayers."

"What are you talking about?"

"I heard Dr. Bryant isn't returning. If you're no longer teaching, there's no reason for us not to see each other."

His face felt hot and his collar too tight. She had always been flirtatious, even when Bonny was around. Her smile was really quite stunning, but—

The thought of a woman other than Bonny was disturbing, almost to the point of making him ill. Deirdre was attractive, but not to his taste. "I'm not ready for a relationship, Deirdre. I have a lot of things to take care of after being gone so long."

She leaned in close, still cradling his face in her hand. What had Bonny said her cologne was called? Midnight something?

"Maybe I could help you out. My grandparents had a farm. It would give us a chance to become better acquainted." She leaned closer, her face almost touching his.

He shifted in his chair. "Deirdre, I'm flattered, but I've been through a rough time."

Her finger traced around his ear, stopping at the lobe, and she leaned in close, whispering, "I always felt we could make a great team. She was an American, Kieran. She could never understand you the way I do."

His heart was racing and so was his brain. "I can't." He shoved his chair back and stood. "I'm flattered you feel that way, but my heart is in America. Bonny may not have chosen me, but my heart chose her."

She stood, gathering up her purse and books. "I understand you needing some time. I can wait, but when you're ready ... I care about you, Kieran. Call me?"

She kissed his cheek and walked out.

Deirdre was pretty. It wasn't going to be easy going on alone. Her home was already in Scotland.

He took a deep breath to clear his head and slow his heart. Her cologne still lingered, but … No. He would have Bonny or no one.

かね

Janet's door was ajar, and she glanced up from her computer when he knocked. "Kieran, what's wrong? You're all peely wally."

He sank into a chair, still clutching his computer bag. "Can we go somewhere to talk?"

She raised her eyebrows, but smiled. "Sure. Is something wrong?"

"I need your opinion, help—I don't know what."

"Mum's in Glasgow with my brother. How about lunch at my house?"

"Yes, perfect. I owe you one."

Janet stood and grabbed her purse out of the closet. "Let's go then. Are you coming back after lunch?"

Peeking out into the hall, he let her precede him. "Yes, I have an appointment with Dr. Cameron."

"Sounds good, I'll ride with you then."

Now that he had someone to listen, he didn't know how to bring up the subject. When they reached her house, he decided to dive right in. "Have you heard from Bonny?"

She put her arm through his, leading him toward the house. "Aye, last week. She's still seeing Adam, but she misses Scotland. She wanted to know how you're doing."

He opened the door when she unlocked it, allowing her to precede him into the house. "I'll be fine. God is showing me a purpose. If I stop tutoring, I can spend more time on it. Graeme is the one person I've told."

"What's going on, Kieran? You didn't pester me for details about Bonny, and if you're not sharing your secret with me, there has to be something else."

"You ken Deirdre Adair, aye?"

"Yes, of course. Is she still after you, then?" She pulled an assortment of sandwich meats out of the refrigerator and began fixing lunch.

"Aye, she keeps pushing me to date her. She's not bad, but I still hope Bonny will change her mind. She's making a mistake, Janet. He'll hurt her again." He took the plate she offered and sat down, meeting her eyes across the table. "Do you think she's serious about marrying him?"

"No, I don't. She still loves you. You haven't eaten a bite."

"Sorry, no appetite. The problem is, as much as I love Bonny, I was tempted to accept Deirdre's invitation out of loneliness."

"There's no reason not to." She paused, tapping her finger on the table. "I could manage to tell Bonny you were seeing her."

Kieran relaxed and laughed. He had done little of that since coming home. It couldn't hurt.

The appointment with Dr. Cameron over, he finished his errands and returned to Stonehaven. Throwing the hammer helped work through his anger at the thought of Bonny with Adam. The experience with Deirdre increased his longing for the one woman who would hold his heart forever.

০৪৮০

Kieran asked Deirdre to meet him at the Nevis Bank Inn on Belford Road, which seemed like a public enough place to have dinner. It kept him from any awkward scenes that might occur if he had to drive her home. The dark wood paneling and large windows made for a pleasant atmosphere. But, being in a hotel, it didn't have a dimly lit, romantic atmosphere that could be misunderstood.

She got out of her car as soon as he drove into the car park. That she was there first, waiting, was no surprise. "Kieran, I was so pleased you called." She gripped his arm and laid her cheek against his sleeve as she spoke.

He had expected her to move fast. He pulled his arm free and put his hand on her back, pushing her through the door ahead of him. This was a mistake. He knew he would regret it already. *Lord, I miss Bonny. I don't want another woman in my life.*

He pulled her chair out and seated himself across the table from her, picking up the menu and concentrating on the contents to the point he failed to see the waiter approach the table until he heard Deirdre speaking.

"Champagne, don't you think, love?" she crooned, nudging his boot with her foot.

"If you want a glass, that's fine." He looked at the waiter. "I'll have sparkling water, please."

She reached across the table, placing her hand on his. "But love, you need champagne for our toast."

"Our toast—to what?"

"To us—what else? We've waited a long time for this moment." Her long, dark lashes veiled her eyes as she smiled at him.

"I—uhh, I prefer not to have champagne when I'm driving back to the farm."

"Two glasses of champagne, please," she said to the waiter. When she turned back to him, the corners of her red lips turned down in a pout. "You disappoint me, love. This is the start of something big. We should toast."

"We're just getting acquainted. Don't you think a toast is premature?" *What have I let myself in for? I didn't think she would be this forward.*

"Of course not. We're both adults. We don't have to play a game any longer. I'm not a student, and you're no longer a professor. We can do as we please, and no one will be reporting on us to Dr. Bryant." She had taken off her shoe and was running her toes up beneath the hem of his pants.

He jerked his leg away, tucking it, with some difficulty, underneath his chair. "I think of us as friends. We really have no relationship beyond that, and I'm not looking for anything else."

"Kieran, I never took you for being shy—"

The waiter returned with the champagne and his water. That was a relief. "Are you ready to order, Deirdre?"

"I've been too distracted to think about the menu. Would you order for me?" Her tone was seductive, teasing even, and he felt the warmth rushing to his face.

"I'll have the Highland venison casserole. Deirdre, do you like venison?"

She turned up her nose and opened her menu. "No, I'm in the mood for something lighter. How about the fillet of salmon, please."

She excused herself to go to the ladies room when the waiter walked away, and Kieran breathed a sigh. *I can't do this. I need Bonny. Even if she never returns, I won't try this again. It's better to be alone.*

He listened to Deirdre chatter all through the meal, only answering when necessary. The woman never stopped talking. She had made only the slightest progress with her meal when the waiter removed his empty plate. Eleanor would have said it was licked so clean she didn't need to wash it. Minus his meal, he had no choice but to listen to what Deirdre was saying.

"My great grandparents on my mother's side went to Canada during The Clearances."

That caught his attention. "Adairs?"

"Of course not, that would be my father's side. On my mother's side, I'm a Greenfield MacDonell, so we're distant relatives. We have more in common than you thought, don't we?"

He pulled his legs back as her toes began creeping up his leg again. "Yes, I guess we do, though that is so far back it doesn't mean anything." He remembered telling Bonny how their clans had feuded, implying that meant a special closeness, but he was in love with her.

She finished her salmon, much to his relief, and when the waiter took her plate, he asked for the check.

"So soon? Would you like to come back to my place for a while? It's not as public, if you know what I mean." She captured the hand he had been careless enough to leave on the table.

"No. What I mean is I need to make an early night of it. Something came up right before I left home. I need to get some sleep. I'll have a long day tomorrow." He extricated his hand and placed them both in his lap.

There was the pout again. She really was a terrible flirt. He found it very unbecoming, especially compared to Bonny's sweet, almost shy, demeanor.

"How would it be if I drove out to your farm tomorrow?"

"No, I'm sorry, I have a lot of business and will be up and gone early. Deirdre, I'm not ready for the type of relationship that a young woman like you is interested in. I'm afraid I won't be asking you out again. This was a mistake. I'm sorry." Taking his credit card back from the waiter, he stood and turned to walk away.

"Kieran, how can you do this to me? You led me on for months. You made me believe you cared. The American is gone. She's not coming back. We're Scots, you and I, we understand one another. The same blood flows in our veins." She came after him, grasping at his sleeve.

"She bewitched you. I never trusted that little American. We'll be together yet, you'll see."

"I never gave you a hint of anything between us, and I never will. I'm sorry if you misunderstood. I'm almost old enough to be your father. I was wrong to ask you to dinner. Goodnight." He increased his stride across the car park, stepped into the Land Rover with her on his heels, and locked the doors as soon as he was inside.

As he drove away, he saw her shaking her fist and stomping her foot.

That's the end of that. I'll stay alone until the day I die, unless you send Bonny back to me, Lord.

Chapter Thirty-four

My Heart's Home

Adam, I haven't said I would marry you, but I don't want to live at San Pedro Creek. It's lovely here." Bonny shoved the casserole of green chili chicken enchiladas into the oven and banged the door shut, turning to face him.

"Aww, Bonny, you know I've owned land out there forever." He took hold of her, massaging her upper arms. "I want a new house, something of our own, more contemporary than this overgrown cabin of your parents. It's old." *Why can't he keep his word?*

She heard his irritation and pointed out the window. "This house has some of the most spectacular views in the East Mountains. We've talked about living here before. I have the barn for the horses and the lawn my dad planted. You have pinons and cedar, not the tall pines, firs, and ponderosas I love."

"You didn't mind leaving it behind for a dirty old sheep farm before you succumbed to my superior charm." He wrapped his arms around her, leaning his forehead against hers.

She jerked away and then walked out the door onto the deck. He was back to his old, domineering self. "You act as if it's a Third World country. It's a Highland estate on a scenic loch with forests, wildlife, and a two-hundred-year-old farmhouse, but we weren't discussing Scotland. We talked about how much fun it would be to have Kari and Dan as neighbors."

"San Pedro Creek isn't as far as Scotland. I want privacy after waiting so long for my bride, and twenty-five acres should provide it. I'll build your dream barn, I promise. Come on, honey?" He took her in his arms, turning her, and kissed her, while tangling his fingers in her hair. His arms wrapped tight around her, his lips demanding.

She liked her old home. Contemporary and mountains did not belong together in her mind. "Quit bringing up Scotland whenever we disagree. Your land is further from church and town. When we have children, it will be difficult to keep them involved in church activities."

"I'm in no hurry for children." He nuzzled her neck when she turned to avoid his lips.

She squirmed, but he held her fast. "Adam, I want our children to grow up involved in church."

"I don't know about the kid thing, Bon. I'm not sure about adoption. If it's only you and me, we can travel and live however we want with no other responsibilities." He kept her tight against him, caressing her face with one hand.

"But you—we agreed…" He pressed his lips to hers, but she shoved him hard, raising her voice. "Does anything I want matter? I haven't agreed to marry you. We discussed living here, and we discussed children. Now you're changing everything."

"Hush and tell me you love me." He held her around the waist, his breath warm on her forehead as he crushed her against him again. "I've waited for a month."

When she tried to protest, he captured her lips again, demanding submission. It wasn't right to have thoughts of Kieran when she was in Adam's arms, yet he appeared with increasing regularity. Gentle, easy-going Kieran, laughing, with a random curl on his forehead, hiking a mountain trail, riding horses, all with an expression of ardent love in his cobalt blue eyes.

Adam loved her in the only way he was able, but he needed to win. There would be consequences in choosing to marry him as there would be if she made Scotland her home. Kieran said Adam didn't respect her. He was right.

Bonny put her hands on Adam's shoulders and shoved him backward. "Okay, you'll get your answer. I can't marry you. I was wrong to let it drag on so long. I needed to know I was choosing God's best for my life and you've made it clear. We don't want the same things."

His face reddened, and he stepped away, the gold flecks in his eyes sparking. "I should have known—swept off your feet by an accent and a kilt. Go back to your Scotsman and his smelly sheep farm." He crossed the deck, surveying the three mountain ranges visible to the north, each a lighter shade of blue than the one before it.

She followed. "A commitment of a lifetime requires more than safety, familiarity, and long-lost dreams. I need someone who loves me more than himself. My needs never mattered to you."

He grabbed her upper arms hard enough to bruise. "Bonny, I love you. What is so lacking?"

She put her hands on his shoulders. "A depth of love greater than I ever imagined possible. Kieran is as much a part of me as breathing—our thoughts—our feelings, have been one since the first night we talked. We've never had that Adam. We never would."

"One question. What took you so long?" His face showed surprise and confusion.

She waited, willing him to meet her eyes. "I've loved you for a long time, but I see our differences in a new light after our time apart. I never promised that by staying here I was saying I would marry you. I said I needed to be near home to heal and pray. I need someone who considers my feelings and sometimes who sets his own aside."

Striding to the door, he turned back with his hand on the knob. "When I walk out, it's too late."

The door slammed behind him. Bonny followed and watched from the window as he gunned the engine, skidding around the curve in the driveway, rocks flying as he sped away, clueless.

☙❧

The next morning, Kari sat with Bonny at the kitchen table overlooking the valley below. The pleasant aroma of Mary Twining's Spiced Tea and fresh apple pie filled the room. "I told Adam I won't marry him. I haven't slept well for weeks. Kieran fills my mind twenty-four hours a day. In spite of his struggles of faith, we had something special. I miss him. Kari, I love him."

"You're serious aren't you?" Kari put one arm around her still thin shoulders.

Someone knocked at the door, and Kari hurried to open it, turning her face up for Dan's kiss.

"I read your note and hurried over as soon as I got home. Hi, Bon, what's up?" Dan was red in the face and out of breath.

"She refused Adam's marriage proposal." Kari clasped his hand, pulling him into the kitchen.

Bonny turned to meet Dan's questioning eyes. "I shouldn't have refused Kieran's proposal. I still love him. God never says the safe and familiar is His best. Sometimes the greatest blessings come when we leave the familiar behind and take a step of faith. He deserved a chance to prove his commitment to the Lord. I want to feel safe, loved, and valued for myself, not as an extension of someone's ego."

Dan accepted the pie she offered him. "You'll live with this decision for a lifetime."

She leaned her head back, closing her eyes. "At the time, I chose home and time to heal and pray, but home is also a feeling. With Kieran, I always felt at home. I can't live with someone who doesn't respect me."

"Bonny, honey, you're willing to make Scotland your home, to say goodbye to your life here?" She heard the hint of resignation in Kari's voice.

Reaching for a tissue, she dabbed at her eyes. "When you dream of one man while in the arms of another, the one who dominates your thoughts is the one you can't live without. My heart can't be at home apart from Kieran."

Dan reached for her hand. "Kari and I wanted you to choose him. You've taken time, prayed, and considered the consequences." He pulled her close in a brotherly hug. "Your dad would choose Kieran."

Kari joined the hug. "So when will you call him?"

Bonny shook her head. "I planned to leave for Scotland as fast as—but I can't. I don't want any more broken hearts. I can't wait to hear Kieran's voice, but it has to be in the Lord's timing."

✿

Guilt overwhelmed her. Bonny began to understand what kept Kieran away after her accident. She had two broken engagements, a cancelled wedding, and two refused proposals behind her—not a good track record.

She filled her days with long-neglected tasks, cleaning and painting, and working outside. She redecorated the master bedroom and moved into it. Joining two Bible studies and helping with Kari's for the middle-school girls kept her busy.

Kieran filled her dreams. Riding horses, hiking, skiing, singing, watching him throw the hammer, and tending to the sheep. A lifetime of experiences filled a few short months.

"I love him, Kari, but I won't chase after him. It isn't my place. I'm open to God's leading, preparing my heart and mind for His will. I'm not certain I want to teach again."

The two friends were enjoying tea at the St. James Tea Room in Albuquerque. Bonny sat on the red velvet couch sipping her Pumpkin Pie scented Black Tea, dressed in a purple silk blouse and well-fitting black skirt, hemmed just above her knees, with turquoise jewelry.

Kari bloomed like a morning glory in her blue dress, her eyes narrowed in confusion. "I don't understand. Why prolong your misery? Janet said he still loves you. One of you needs to swallow your pride."

Bonny swallowed the last bite of her Cucumber and Roquefort tea sandwich. "He's been in church and active in a Bible study since he returned home. Sometimes I think I should just stay here with the horses. They don't demand anything and won't disappoint me."

Kari set down her teacup, throwing up her hands in surrender. "I give up."

Bonny tried to describe her uncertainty and frustration. "I have a knack for choosing the wrong men. When I went to the grocery store yesterday, I ran into Christy. Adam quit church and is already dating again. He would have broken my heart. Janet says Kieran is expanding the farm and stays away from women. Maybe we're all better off alone."

Shopping and church activities provided safe conversation as they finished their tea, avoiding upsetting topics. "Let's head home before the traffic through the canyon gets bad, since it's Friday." Kari stood, picking up her purse. "Ready?"

Bonny followed, sticking her finger in the last dollop of clotted cream on her saucer and licking it off. "I love Kieran, but I think it's best if he comes to me."

They rode home in silence. She kept her face to the window, wiping her eyes and sniffling. She was no longer afraid of being alone. She refused to rush in where God didn't lead her.

CHAPTER THIRTY-FIVE

RIGHT PERSPECTIVE

Dressed in old, grubby jeans and an old flannel shirt, Bonny was heading for the vegetable garden when the doorbell rang. She laid down her dirty gloves and opened the front door. Kieran stood there smiling, unshaven, with a stray curl hanging over his forehead. His eyes, the deep blue of the Scottish flag, crinkled at the sight of her. She felt the old, familiar tingle of excitement.

"I've come to take you home, *mo gràdh*—to Scotland." He spoke with a strong burr, his voice cracking with emotion, musical in its deep timbre. He reached for her hand as his lips broke into a wide smile.

"Kieran, what …" Finding herself at a complete lack for words, she backed into the room in surprise, but also by way of inviting him in.

"Janet said you refused Adam's proposal. We belong together, Bonny." The love in his voice, the hope in his eyes, and the power of his presence overwhelmed her.

She freed her hand and continued to back further into the room. "You still want me?"

He reached her side in one long stride, enfolding her in his arms.

No logical words came to mind, and she gazed up at him, helpless. "Kieran, I …"

He laid a finger on her lips. "Shhh." Scenes from her dreams moved in slow motion as his face lowered toward her own. Without hesitation, her arms went around his neck, her face turned upward, and the earth turned upside-down.

When he pulled away, she searched his eyes, feeling she was floating through a dream. "You're certain?"

"Aye, and how did you treat me worse than I did you?" His incredible eyes remained fixed on hers, drawing her into their bottomless depths, his love sweeping over her in an ocean wave. "Why did you refuse Adam?"

"I'm a possession to him. What mattered to me meant nothing." Dizzying electricity crackled through every nerve in her body as his lips touched hers again. Her fingers tangled his hair and caressed his cheek. She reveled in the reality of his presence, heightened by the scent of his aftershave—Eau de Quinine, she remembered.

When he stopped, he cupped her face in one hand—those rough yet gentle hands. "Now, why can't you marry him?"

"I—I missed you, this ..." She laid her finger to his lips, trembling.

His mouth claimed hers again, soft and sweet. One hand rested around her shoulders, the other around her waist, lifting her from the floor. He whispered, "Why?"

"I can't live without you." She was quivering.

He moved his hands to her shoulders, holding her at arm's length, and a flicker of a smile moved across his lips. "Why could you not live without me, Bonny?"

"Because I love you."

"Ach lass, why didn't you come to me?" She heard the burr of the Highlands strong in his beloved voice. He kissed her again, pressing her against him so tight their pounding hearts beat as one.

"There have been too many mistakes." She felt the warmth creeping up her neck and cheeks.

His eyes glowed with a tender light. "Didn't I tell you I would never love another woman? I have loved you every moment of every day. I never dared to imagine I would hear you say you loved me again."

"I never stopped." Overwhelming emotions made it difficult to speak. *He's here, and he loves me.*

"Then promise me ..." His voice was so soft the blood pounding in her ears threatened to drown it out.

"Anything …" She laid her hand on his rough cheek.

He moved one hand to the back of her head, his breath soft against her face, his voice tender and sweet. "Promise you'll return to Scotland with me. We'll start over, dating and talking about how we've changed. One day, you'll be my wife."

"I promise …" Her words were lost in his kiss, communicating the love only complete commitment to another creates.

⚬⚬⚬

Kieran and Bonny drove to Ribs, a nearby restaurant, for barbecue. "You only have a slight limp." He offered his arm as they climbed the steps. "Will it improve with time?"

"It's much better than it was." She held his arm for reassurance as much as for balance. "I still take walks, but not as far as I used to."

"When I think of what you survived—God has such purpose for your life." His grip tightened.

They chose to eat on the patio, enjoying the warm September evening. When the hostess led them to a table, they moved their chairs close together. "The purpose is becoming clearer by the moment." She lifted his hand to her lips, feeling its strength, the skin roughened by work, and the thick golden hairs against her cheek. "I've seen the devastating effects of acting before seeking God's will. It means so much for you to forgive me."

There was such love in his smile and light in his eyes. "I forgave you before I reached the airport. I prayed you would be blessed, whoever you chose."

"I told Adam you were as much a part of me as breathing."

"You did?" His eyes crinkled, his words ringing with laughter.

"Yes, when I told him I couldn't marry him." She gauged the effect of her words by the surprise on his face. "I didn't tell him I saw pictures of you flashing through my mind when he kissed me. I would see you in your kilt, standing on a misty hillside with your bagpipes, surrounded by sheep. I had to push him away because I realized where my heart truly lay."

He threw his head back and laughed until tears ran down his cheeks. "You saw me in your mind when Adam kissed you? Ach, lass, what a lovely answer to prayer. What goes through your mind when I kiss you?"

"Nothing, except that you love me. I want to do it again and again for the rest of my life." Her answer earned her another, without regard for the waitress bringing their meal.

"I prayed for you to remember me."

The pulse pounded in Bonny's ears as the undeniable truth overwhelmed her. "That would explain the nagging doubts, perhaps even the images of you with your kilt and bagpipes …" She stopped, hesitant to explain.

The corners of his eyes crinkled as if he read her mind. "God did exactly what I asked."

Her cheeks grew warm. "You'll gloat over it for the rest of your life won't you?" She followed up with a playful poke in the ribs.

"Aye, I will, but because God did it." His lips curled in a broad smile. "Adam doesn't understand what we have, does he? Poor chap."

"Not even close." She shut her eyes, savoring his unique scent of soap, aftershave, and the outdoors. "I dreamed of you, felt your presence, and heard your voice. Seeds of doubt began to grow, and I couldn't sleep. The more controlling Adam became, the more I remembered our easy-going relationship, your calming presence, how you protect me, and how happy and loved I feel when I'm with you."

"Bonny, when was our relationship ever easy-going?" He caressed her hand between his thumb and forefinger. "We had differences over my faith, my deception, and my depression."

"When we first fell in love, whether hiking in the mountains, talking until the wee hours of the morning, or riding horses at the farm, I knew I was safe and loved. I never felt safe with Adam, because he wasn't honest with me. You were gentle and understanding. I knew you would believe someday."

He shook his head. "I'm still in shock. I prayed for you to remember me, but I never imagined such a powerful answer."

"God is amazing, and our story is only beginning."

⚮

Cuddled up on the glider, with her head resting on Kieran's shoulder, Bonny relaxed into the warmth of his arms.

"You had no reason to believe it at the time, but God changed me on that airplane. When you asked me to leave, my faith didn't waver. I'll serve Him, no matter what."

She tilted her head back to see his face. "I've prayed so hard for you."

"God was my one hope." His voice grew quiet. "At first I thought you'd change your mind. I lay awake, longing to hold you. As time passed, I did my best to forget and turn my love for you into love for God. It was impossible to go back to the anger and emptiness I lived with before. I had lost you, but God would not leave me alone. I've tried to honor Him. I help Graeme lead a Bible study and I'm taking seminary classes."

"Really? What a delight to see his laughing eyes, to inhale the woodsy scent she still connected with him, and to know he loved her.

"After what God has done in my life, I will be only what it pleases him to make me." His voice carried an undertone of passion, throbbing in the strong arm resting on her shoulder, and in his chest beneath her cheek. "It's difficult for many of the farmers and crofters around Stonehaven to attend church. I'm building a chapel, just north of the single-track, near the bridge over the loch. It will be white with a steeple holding a cross so high it's visible for miles. It has to stand out, not hide the way the farmhouse does. I'm calling it Hope Chapel, because God's hope fills my heart in place of the anger and doubt. It's an outreach of Faith Chapel. Graeme and I feel there's a lot of potential."

"Kieran, that's amazing. I wasted so much time."

He placed one finger under her chin, raising her face until her eyes were level with his. "Aye, but a sovereign God doesn't make mistakes. He will bless us because we waited on His time."

"What an exciting life, to work alongside you on the farm, and also for the Lord." She reached up to caress his cheek.

His voice grew softer. "My precious, wee Bonny, we'll explore those old hurts before I put my ring on your finger. You will see my faith in action. I've spoken to Graeme. He'll guide us through the healing process."

"You discussed us with Graeme?"

"He's become a close friend and helped me put things in perspective. Our life won't be easy, hen. Sheep farming is difficult. The wife of a pastor in a rural area won't be easy either. Our people will be scattered far from the church, and at times, they'll have no one else to ask for help."

"I'll thrive on the work as long as we have the Lord and each other. You've still never said how you came to be here." She brought the hand lying on her shoulder to her lips.

"After Janet told me you had refused Adam, I tried to ring you up. I became worried when you never answered your phone, so I tried Dan. He said you wouldn't come to me, but I knew my time had come."

"I changed my number to keep Adam from calling. I was determined to place my future in God's hands, even if it meant I spent the rest of my life alone."

He laid his forehead against hers. "What did we pray for when you agreed to marry me before?"

"God's blessings."

His lips brushed her hair. "We didn't pray for His will, His way, or His timing. They were our plans. We both knew we should wait. This time the Lord made it right."

"And my Scottish knight in shining armor came for me."

"The bridegroom came to claim his bride." He wrapped both arms around her, exhaling a deep breath she interpreted as contentment.

"What now?" This new Kieran would give her the right answers. His breath tickled her ear.

"There's an old Scottish saying, 'The only cure for love is marriage.'"

She snuggled closer, enjoying the well-remembered comfort of his embrace. "Old Scottish sayings are very wise."

"Aye, I'm a wise man. The moment I saw you, I knew you were the woman I had waited for. When can we leave? Do you still want the wedding in Scotland?" He caressed her cheek with his fingertip.

"I can be ready in a week, two at the most. As for the wedding, Scotland, of course, where we first fell in love." She shook her head, still overwhelmed. "I can't believe we're together again. For a Marine, Dan doesn't follow orders very well. I told him I needed time."

He brought the hand she laid on his chest to his lips, kissing the finger which would one day wear his ring again. "Oh, aye, he does. I asked where you were and he told me. He picked me up at the airport and invited me to stay with them. Are you sorry?"

"No, nothing felt right after I sent you away."

It grew dark. The crickets were chirping and cicadas singing. Before she drove him to Kari and Dan's, they prayed together for the first time, thanking God and seeking His will for their future. "It's hard to let you leave me again, even until morning."

"I'll see you in the morning, *mo chridhe*. Dream of me."

"You're my most precious dream. *Tha gaol agam ort.*" Her tongue had no trouble with the well-remembered words.

"*Tha gaol agam ort-fhèin.*" He closed the car door, standing and watching as she drove away.

Entering the house, she fell to her knees, thanking God for bringing them together at last.

CHAPTER THIRTY-SIX

GOD'S PERFECT TIME

Bonny stared out the window, clutching Kieran's hand as the plane set down in Inverness. Once he retrieved the Land Rover, they headed straight for the farm. With Eleanor and Angus as chaperones, Stonehaven offered the solitude they craved.

He stopped at the exact spot where he had pointed out the farmhouse on her first visit. Resting her head against his arm, Bonny surveyed the dense forests, heathered hills, and the shining loch below with a sense of home. "The land of my dreams ..."

He leaned closer. "What did you say, love?"

"I call Scotland the land of my dreams. I came here longing for escape and peace. Then it looked as if I might never see it again. Now the land of my dreams will be my home with the man of my dreams."

The electricity in his eyes sent pins and needles spiraling through her.

Six dogs tumbled out from behind the house in woofing, tussling excitement as they drove up. Angus and Eleanor came running to welcome them, the latter enveloping Bonny in a warm hug. Angus led them inside, where dinner for four was waiting.

After dinner, Bonny and Kieran retreated to the library, where a fire roared in the fireplace to ward off the autumn chill. Snuggling on the couch felt so right. Yet, in another way, it seemed as if a lifetime had passed.

When he left her at the door to her room, she inhaled the sweet scent of the rose bouquets he had Eleanor place there. "If only I hadn't left."

"God used it all for good. You'll see how much good, starting tomorrow."

CRISO

At Graeme's suggestion, Kieran and Bonny began dating again. They drove out to the east coast one weekend, where an old college friend of his lived, not far from Dunnottar Castle. Sitting on its massive rock, the magnificent *Dun Fother* connected to the mainland by a single narrow strip of land. They watched the sea waves crashing against the black volcanic rocks over 160 feet below, sending white spray high into the air as gulls circled above and below, their cries filling the air. Dunnottar possessed a wild beauty all its own.

She shouted above the battering wind. "Defense-wise, the location would have been valuable, but what a difficult place to live. You would be in danger of blowing off into the ocean if you ventured too close to the edge. Each trip to the mainland for the barest necessities of life would have been an adventure."

He pulled her against him as an especially hard gust caught her off guard. "Isn't that life? We're always in danger of going over the edge unless we stay at the center of God's will. Safety can be found nowhere else."

"I guess we both learned the tough way." They spent the entire day roving over the castle grounds, delighting in the beauty of their surroundings and each other's company.

"You belong here, lass, on this wee bit o' land." They headed up the steep path to the car park. "The day you sent me home, you said something I've wondered about ever since."

"I felt so tired and confused back then. I don't even know what I might have said."

He held tight to her arm as they climbed, then held her away, letting the sinking sun shine on her face. "You said I was a wild, adventurous, romantic dream. What did you mean?"

The tweed of his jacket was soft against her face. She laughed at his baffled expression. "You are."

"What makes a forty-one-year-old sheep farmer adventurous and romantic?"

"You're Scottish, with a musical accent, an academic sheep farmer in an idyllic setting. You live in an ancient house filled with antiques and family history. You wear a kilt, play bagpipes, and compete in Highland Games. Kari agreed you were a hunk after she met you, by the way." His face turned a delightful shade of red. "There you have it—masculine, foreign, wild, romantic. Life has been one gigantic adventure since the day we met."

With a deep belly laugh, he grasped her under the arms, holding her close and turning around in a circle. "You know I lead a quiet, boring life. Kari told me about your 'Highland Games hunk' comment. It's flattering, and I'm glad my future wife is attracted to me, but I'm just a sheep farmer, Bonny."

"In my eyes, you're a wild, adventurous, and romantic sheep farmer."

He winked. "It's the kilt, aye? Women do go weak over a man in a kilt."

She poked him in the ribs and then pulled him closer. "Adam seemed to think so."

She remained silent the rest of the way to the car. He opened her door to let her into the Land Rover. When he climbed in, he asked, "What's on your mind?"

"It's, well, we haven't visited your parents, and …"

"You're wondering what my mother thinks?"

"Yes."

"She wasn't pleased about you staying in New Mexico. She didn't want me to get hurt."

"Did it upset her when you decided to come after me?" She stroked the red-gold hairs on the back of his hand lying on the console.

"She knows it's impossible for me to love anyone else." His eyes glowed with a tender blue light. "We have her blessing."

⋐⋑

"Kieran, you've never ridden a horse in your kilt before. Where are we going?"

"You'll find out soon enough."

Kieran's answer did nothing to quell Bonny's suspicions. He had told her to dress in the outfit he called her "Lady of Loch Garry" outfit, a long, flowing skirt of filmy, red plaid, with a black velvet jacket, lacy blouse, and black riding boots.

They headed up the mountain behind the farm, riding Storm and Misty. Across the valley, shafts of sunlight streamed through the clouds like bits of heaven, lighting the mountain peaks and turning the loch to a shimmering silver mirror.

They rode in silence until he stopped in one of their favorite places. She sat still until he reached up to help her dismount. In the long skirt, she needed him to lift her down, and for him, holding her close as he set her on the ground was too lovely.

"My highland cathedral." Her heart filled with eager contentment. "I wondered when you would bring me here again."

"Spread out the blanket and get comfortable while I get something." He handed her the blanket tied behind her saddle, turning back to his horse, and the mysterious, blanket-wrapped object she had stared at all the way there.

"Your bagpipes, Kieran …"

"Can a man have a wee bit of silence, please?" She smiled at his mock irritation and the sparkle in his eyes.

She wasn't dreaming this time. The man filling the bag with air and adjusting the tuning slides until the pitch of the drones suited him was very real. She felt as if he could see into her soul while he played the majestic strains of "Highland Cathedral." It was a big concession on his part. He had told her over and over how he disliked the song, which was written in the 1980's by Germans. But there he stood—surrounded by sheep with mist swirling around them, preparing to play it for her—true love. She remembered her first day in Scotland, imagining a kilted piper on a hillside, and here he stood in the flesh, the man she loved more than her life. She shivered as the sun broke through the clouds and shone on their special place.

He laid his pipes down, kneeling and reaching for her hand. "Bonny Faith Bryant, will you marry me and let me love you for the rest of our lives?"

She brought his hand to her lips. "Yes, Kieran, I will marry you."

Reaching into his sporran, he pulled out the velvet box. He removed the ruby ring and slipped it onto her finger. "You'll be Mrs. Kieran MacDonell at long last."

Her answer was lost in his kiss.

"Ooof." He moved from his knees to sit beside her. "It sounds romantic, but kneeling on rocky ground isn't for forty-one year old men. Shall we set the day?"

"Soon, and you're not old, my braw and bonnie Highlander. I can't wait for our adventure to begin." The world turned beneath her, spinning, whirling, and rocking as life changed forever with his precious words.

He took the long end of his tartan which wrapped around his shoulder and placed it around her shoulders also as the wind began to blow. "The church in Beauly is easy to schedule. We can't have the reception outside though. The weather in late fall is too unpredictable."

She cupped his face in her hands. "I only need you."

Chapter Thirty-seven

Fear

Someone is poaching deer at Stonehaven Farm, Constable … Yes, the biggest red stag on the farm is dead, its head cut off, and the rest left to rot …Yes, I'd say earlier today … I heard a shot a couple of hours ago …Tomorrow or the next day. Can't you get anyone here sooner … Thanks, yes, I understand."

Kieran slammed the phone down, turning to Bonny, who was standing on the bottom step of the back stairs. She, Maggie, and Eleanor were cleaning the farmhouse from top to bottom, putting away early wedding gifts, and putting female touches on the guest room Kieran had created from the room he once shared with Bronwyn.

"A poacher at Stonehaven? And they can't come any sooner?" She ran to his side, putting her arms around him as he stood rubbing his jaw, his eyes flashing with anger.

"I found the big stag dead on the lower slopes of *Cnocan Dubh*." She felt his tension, but sensed something else, a desire for revenge.

"You won't do anything until the police come, will you?"

He headed for the stairs.

"I'm getting my shotgun and going to see if I can find more signs of poaching. They're down lower this time of year, easier to find. I won't have poachers on my land." He stomped up the stairs with her close on his heels.

Footsteps signaled Maggie's arrival at the top of the stairs. Looking from one to the other, she asked, "What's wrong?"

Bonny jumped in before he answered. "Someone killed the old stag. He's

293

going after them before the police get here." His indignant expression as he turned to her was no deterrent. "Talk to him, Maggie."

"Ach, it's my land, and I'm the gamekeeper here. I'll do what I have to." He pushed past both of them and up the stairs.

"Bonny's right, *mo mhac*, you need to let the authorities handle this. It's too dangerous." Maggie headed after him with Bonny on her heels.

"The carcass is a few hours old. No one comes onto my land and steals my deer. The sheriff has a large area to cover and can't get here until tomorrow or the next day. I'm not letting them get away if they're still in the area." He unlocked the safe, grabbing his shotgun and ammunition as he spoke.

"Then I'm coming with you." Bonny gripped his arm again. "I can shoot, and you're not going after them alone."

He set down his gun, cupping her face in his hand. "I know you're capable, but you're not coming. The ATV tracks indicate they used the trail between Loch Loyne and Tomdoun. I have to make casts of the boot prints and tire tracks before the snow covers up the evidence. I'll be back soon."

"Kieran, it's too dangerous. I can be changed in a couple of minutes." Bonny headed for her room, when he grasped her arm and turned her around.

"I said no, and I meant it. Now stay here." Snatching up his gun, he strode down the stairs and out the door, mounting Storm, who was standing saddled right outside.

Bonny went to the map on the kitchen wall, tracing the route to the base of the mountain with her finger, then finding the trail he said the poachers had used. "I'm calling the police back," she said. "They need to know he's out there alone. Maybe they'll come sooner."

"I'll call Duncan in Tomdoun," Maggie said, taking her cell phone out of her purse on the sideboard. "Maybe he can intercept him. He has ATVs."

When neither phone call proved successful, the women sat down at the kitchen table with a pot of tea to wait.

⁂

"I can't sit here and do nothing." After two hours of nervous anticipation, Bonny came downstairs dressed for a ride, and headed for the door.

"Where do you think you're goin', lass?" Maggie turned from the window as Bonny stepped out the door, shotgun in hand.

"To find Kieran. Anything could happen to him out there alone." She shut the door, but Maggie followed, running to catch up.

"What good is it to have two of you out there? Angus should be back soon, and he'll go after him."

"Maggie, what if he's hurt? You stay here and keep trying the police. I'm going after him."

Misty's hooves slogged through the mud and wet grass as fast as Bonny could make her go. Four days of heavy rain left everything dreich and drookit. The gray clouds hung low and heavy. The snow had begun. Heavy, wet flakes, sticking to the ground as the temperature dropped. A blustering wind raced across the pasture, rippling the grass and heather in its wake. The sheep turned their backs to the impending storm.

She stopped, wondering which trail he followed, when a gunshot sounded from due north. Stifling her fear, she headed up a hill where they had seen the old stag a week ago. Within a mile, she saw blood in the fresh snow and the signs of a large man dragging himself.

"Kieran! Kieran! Where are you?" She began to call his name, frantically, the shotgun ready in case the poacher still lurked in the area.

She stopped to listen, hoping, hardly daring to breathe.

The mist-shrouded hills were silent. The snow fell harder now, and she knew that soon any tracks would be covered. She walked further up the trail where they had spotted the stag a few days ago.

At last, she heard a weak voice calling her name. Rounding a thick stand of trees, she saw him lying in the snow at the end of a trail of blood.

"For once I'm thankful you don't follow orders." His voice sounded weak, punctuated by quick, shallow breaths. "It's in my abdomen, love. I grazed his leg as I fell to the ground. He scared Storm away and headed east on an ATV toward the A87. I need help fast."

Running to his side, she unzipped his coat and opened his shirt to see the wound, her stomach turning as she realized how much blood he had lost.

"Don't you die on me, Kieran MacDonell. We have a wedding in four weeks and nothing will stop me from marrying you this time." She ran to her saddlebags for the first aid kit.

"Can you ride?" She noted the ashen gray of his skin. He was shivering, whether from pain, shock, or cold, she wasn't sure. If only she had remembered a blanket.

He shook his head. "I can't get up. I used my strength shoutin' to get your attention. How did you find me?"

Bonny tore open the packages of gauze and pressed them against the wound, propping him against the rock to wrap an ace bandage around him. "When I reached the big rock where the trail splits, I heard a shot and began looking in this direction. I followed the trail we were on the other day. I'm going to bring Misty over and see if we can get you up on her back."

"I shot into the air—I think I'm going to pass out."

He felt stronger after she urged him to take deep breaths. With her help and a large stick for a cane, they succeeded in getting him up on a large rock, enabling him to drag himself onto Misty's back.

"Hold onto my saddle horn. You'll be grateful for my Western saddle." Bonny took the reins and led Misty back toward the house. With his strength ebbing fast, his eyes were sunken, his stare blank, and he had trouble staying on the horse.

"Honey, we're getting close, hold on tight." When he made no sound, she turned, horrified to see him lying forward on Misty's neck. *What would I do if he falls off?*

Bonny exhaled with relief when the house came in sight, with the constable's car in front. "Call for the rescue helicopter. He's been shot in the abdomen."

One constable came running to help as the other got on the radio. By the time the copter arrived, Kieran was unresponsive, his breathing shallow. The constable took over putting pressure on the wound after Bonny packed it with as much sterile gauze as Maggie and Eleanor had. She didn't know how much blood someone could lose and still live, but he must have reached a critical point.

The paramedics struggled to get an IV going, saying his blood loss made it difficult to find a vein. After multiple tries, they resorted to an intra-osseous line going straight into the bone. When they told her it was reserved for the worst cases of shock and circulatory collapse, she sat down with her head between her knees. No medical background was necessary to see that his life was ebbing as his blood seeped through the bandages, slower now, but every drop brought him closer to death.

Angus had returned in Bonny's absence, and insisted on driving her and Maggie to Inverness. Eleanor remained at the house where the constables set up their command post for the manhunt. Hamish would meet the helicopter at the hospital and sign the surgical permit, having stayed behind in Beauly.

Bonny clutched her future mother-in-law's hand. "What if …"

Maggie wiped the tears which were streaming down her cheeks like waterfalls on the Sisters of Kintail, putting her arm around Bonny as she called Graeme and the Camerons. "I need you to call the prayer chains at your churches and the college."

She could hear Graeme struggling to keep control, his voice sounding choked and unnatural. "I'll call Janet. We'll come as fast as possible."

Constable MacFadyen stayed in touch, but there was no sign of the poacher. "If he had a car waiting at the A87, it will be difficult to find him."

◌℘

A solemn-looking Hamish met them as they came through the doors of the emergency room, and reported the medical staff was pumping blood into Kieran as fast as he was losing it. "If you hadn't found him when you did, he would have died. The surgeon says it will be touch and go."

Bonny felt all the strength leave her legs and collapsed into his arms. "I can't lose him. What will I do?"

"He will make it, Bonny. A lot of people are praying, and the three of us should also." Maggie took her hand and between them, she and Hamish led her to a couch in the waiting room.

The last time she had felt so afraid was standing beside her parents' grave. "You don't understand. The people I love don't get better, no matter how I pray.

I love him so much, and I'm going to lose him."

"Your friend Dan didn't die. You've done everything possible to keep Kieran alive. I'm proud of the way you took charge and bandaged the wound. You're the perfect wife for him. In a short time you'll be on your honeymoon, and this will be a bad dream." Maggie stroked the hair away from her face and pulled her close.

Kieran was still in surgery when Graeme and Janet arrived. Acknowledging their presence with a nod, she continued her silent pleas for a miracle.

"What have they told you?" Graeme asked.

Hamish took Bonny's cold hands in his warm ones. "Before surgery they said he was doing better than expected, considering the massive amount of blood loss. According to the doctor in the ER, the pressure dressing Bonny put on saved his life."

"See, my dear," Hamish kissed Bonny's cheek. "The doctors are doing their job now. The rest is up to God."

When Dr. Wallace came out four hours later, they gathered around him in stony silence. Hamish introduced Bonny and Maggie, and the doctor took Bonny's hand. "Good job. You kept him from bleeding to death. Don't be surprised if we give more blood tomorrow. The bullet did serious damage. We have more than replaced his blood volume, and I removed a third of his large intestine. He will be weak and his recovery slow. We'll keep him in recovery for at least three or four hours. You can see him when he wakes up."

"Will he live a normal life with so much of his intestine missing?" Bonny asked.

"He'll do fine," Dr. Wallace said. "Once he recovers, he won't notice. We'll have him up walking by tomorrow if his blood work is good. He needs lots of rest, no lifting, regular hours, and a lot of sleep. Being the active man he is, you have your work cut out for you keeping him quiet."

"You know Kieran, Dr. Wallace?" asked Bonny.

"Call me David. We became acquainted as undergrads in Glasgow. His reputation as a champion in the Highland Games still follows him. Everyone in the operating room knew of him. I see him occasionally in Fort William, where I have a summer home. He's going to be in ICU until he stabilizes. You can have family or friends donate blood. Get some sleep. You're going to need your strength." He squeezed Bonny's hand and walked away.

The constant beep, beep, beep, of the heart monitor haunted Bonny whether she sat at Kieran's side or not. He would wake for brief periods, but say nothing, sometimes taking a sip of water or trying to smile, but then drop back to sleep. She was afraid of him dying when she wasn't there to say good-bye.

৫৪৩৮

Kieran attempted a smile when Bonny and Maggie walked in. Bonny rushed to his side, kissing him on the cheek while Maggie did the same on the other.

"What happened?" He turned from one to the other in confusion.

"The poacher shot you," Bonny answered. "Don't you remember me helping you onto Misty?"

"No." He shook his head with a bewildered expression.

His hand felt heavy and failed to give her the strong squeeze she was used to. "You passed out, and I was afraid you'd fall off, but Constable MacFadyen had arrived by the time we reached the house, and then the helicopter came. They removed a third of your large intestine, and you have blood in your veins from all the people you love."

He shook his head in disbelief. Maggie said, "We almost lost you, *mo balachan*. You gave us a terrible scare."

"The poacher?" He glanced from one to the other.

Bonny wiped his face with a cool cloth from the bedside stand. "The manhunt is continuing. No sign of him yet, but the constable says they'll get him. When I found you, I saw tracks from his ATV heading toward the A87."

He rubbed his eyes as if awakening from a dream. "How long have I been here?"

"Three days, dear," Maggie answered. "You've been unconscious the whole time. Janet is here, and Graeme is coming back. People in three churches are praying for you."

"Four," Bonny said. "Don't forget the church in Albuquerque."

"The farm?" His brow furrowed in concern.

Bonny squeezed his hand for reassurance. "Angus and Seumas can handle it. Your da talks to them a couple of times a day."

He began to doze again, but Bonny refused to leave his side.

CRBO

Overnight, Kieran's temperature spiked to 39.5° Celsius, and he lapsed into a stupor. Dr. Wallace entered the ICU with the chart in his hand, his eyes narrow as he studied it. "I need to examine the wound."

Bonny's stomach knotted at the grim look on his face, watching while he poked and prodded at the wound. "How bad are you hurting?" Aroused by the painful exam, Kieran grimaced.

Dr. Wallace sat on the edge of the bed. "The blood tests show a marked increase in white blood cells—signaling an infection."

A CT scan confirmed the presence of an abscess, and they began new intravenous antibiotics.

Bonny sat beside him, wiping his forehead with a cool cloth. "Kieran, you have to fight this so we can be married."

His lips moved, and she bent over him, picking out the words, "*Mo gràdh*."

Right before he went into surgery, Sheriff MacFadyen called. "We caught the poacher on MacDonell land, butchering another stag. He's a local troublemaker who has been in jail numerous times, Brennan Adair. This time he'll have attempted murder added to his record."

"Brennan Adair?" Bonny turned to Janet, whose face reflected her thoughts. "Constable, see if he has a sister named Deirdre who attends Fort William Christian College? We've both had problems with her in the past."

CRBO

Bonny roused from sleep to find two nurses bending over Kieran. Uncurling from the chair, she was appalled at the change which had come over him in the two hours since she fell asleep.

"His heart rate is weak and thready, and his respirations are becoming labored." One nurse drew blood while the other checked the IV and peeked under the bandage. "Oooh, I found the source of that odor. The wound is draining."

"Is that good?" Bonny peered around her to see for herself. One look told her it wasn't.

"No. Mairead, call Dr. Wallace and get those blood cultures sent to the lab STAT." She peeled off her gloves and washed her hands. "He'll probably take him back to surgery. His temp is 40.3°. We expected it to be falling by now."

Bonny did the conversion to Fahrenheit on her phone: 104.3 degrees. Within the hour, he was in surgery.

By morning, his temperature was down, but his pasty white skin with dark circles around his eyes and shallow breathing frightened her. Maggie and Hamish made certain someone was with her all the time, forcing her to eat small bits of things, and trying to take her into the hall for walks. She refused to leave his side, always listening for the change in breathing she remembered all too well.

"*Nic-chridhe*," Hamish took her arm and coaxed her toward the door. "Walk with me while Maggie stays with him."

She let him lead her out of the ICU. The big hand on her back was so like his son's. "I believe he'll recover, but you'll be sick if you don't take care. He will need you once he's home, so you must eat and rest."

"I won't leave. He's all I have, Hamish." She dabbed her eyes with a worn tissue.

"With the abscess drained, he should start improving. No matter what, you have Maggie and me. You're not alone." The big hand began to work at a knot in her neck.

"You have God, *mo nighean*. If He leaves you with no one and nothing, you still have God, and therefore, you have hope. Kieran came to believe that after he returned from America. You must believe it also. He would want you to." He took a handkerchief out of his pocket and handed it to her.

She nodded as they re-entered their small world. The wise and loving words from Hamish changed something within her heart. If Kieran had accepted losing her to Adam, she must accept losing him to God.

CRBO

Dr. Wallace was smiling as he walked into Kieran's hospital room a week later. "The infection has cleared up. The wound is healing. You can go home and get ready for that wedding."

"That is the best news I've heard in a long time." Bonny leaped from her chair to kiss Kieran and hug the doctor.

Kieran held his hand out. "David, thank you. I owe you my life."

"I did my job. Bonny is the one responsible for your life, and I can't think of anyone better to owe it to. I don't know many women with the courage, much less the skill, to do what she did."

Kieran held her hand against his cheek. "God has given me far more than I deserve. You'll come down to Beauly for the wedding, won't you?"

David stopped with his hand on the door frame. "I wouldn't miss it. Thank you. Bonny, keep an eye on him. Nothing strenuous."

"Will I be better by the wedding?"

Bonny turned bright red, and David chuckled out loud. "You'll be fine. The pain will let you know if you overdo anything. A long rest in the US should do you good."

As David walked out, Kieran turned to Bonny, who was still a lovely shade of pink. "How many days until the wedding? I've lost track of time."

"Kari and Dan arrive two weeks from today. The wedding is a week later. Thanks to Eleanor, Bridget, and Kathleen, with some help from Janet and Agnes, everything is ready. I couldn't have done it better myself."

"The only thing I need is you. I'll be fine by then. He's not talking to some office worker. I work hard every day of my life. I'll heal fast."

Bonny cupped his face in her cool, soft hands. "You'll be careful. I'll see to that."

She bent down, her kiss making three weeks seem like forever.

"I am a very blessed man. A wife that will take the risk you did to save me is something I never expected to find. Do you remember when Eleanor thought you were too small and delicate for a sheep farmer's wife?"

"Hmmm." She gave him another soft kiss. "I guess I proved her wrong. The only thing in my mind was that no one was going to take you from me."

"Did they find out if this Brennan Adair is related to Deirdre?"

Bonny sat on the edge of the bed, cradling his hand between her own. "He's her brother, but it gets even weirder. Brennan Adair is Brennan Grant, your hired hand."

Memories of footprints, sounds in the bushes, the sight of someone disappearing into the woods played through his mind. "He was spying on us. You know, I had dinner with her when I returned from Albuquerque alone. I was miserable. She was flirty and presumptuous. She would have had me married before the evening was over if I hadn't told her that I made a mistake and would remain alone."

"You never told me that."

"It was the loneliness, but when it came right down to it, I couldn't stand the thought of there ever being anyone but you."

"She's disappeared, Kieran. No one knows where she is. They do want to question her." She settled herself against his shoulder, the bright curls brushing his chin smelling so sweet and fresh.

"Brennan was in an old bothy in Greenfield one day, before you ever came to the farm. He was asking a lot about the Greenfield MacDonells. Deidre told me her mother was a Greenfield MacDonell. They're up to something."

"You mean you think she'll come back?" He couldn't miss the worried quiver in her voice.

"I have no idea, but after this, I know that the two of us can defend our home. No man ever dreamed of a more perfect help-meet." He kissed the top of her head.

"I'm not going to worry. God has surmounted every obstacle that has come against us. Prayer will always be our first line of defense."

"Amen to that, now go talk to the nurses and see about getting me home."

CHAPTER THIRTY-EIGHT

GOLDEN BANDS

The night was still and perfect. A full moon shone in the cloudless sky, lighting their way to the gazebo where they sat holding hands, lost in private dreams.

Kieran still tired easily, so instead of a trip to Skye, they planned to rest at the farm for three weeks before heading to America for a quiet month at Bonny's house.

He drew her close, savoring the sweet smell of her hair and her warmth against his chest. "One more night, *mo gràdh*. I can't wait. There were so many times when I thought you would never be mine. Who would have thought we would both almost die?"

Bonny sniffled. "I was so afraid I would lose you."

He took her hand, examining it in the moonlight. "When I helped you with your flat tire, your hands looked so small and delicate they reminded me of my mother's china. When Kari took me to see you in ICU, I was afraid to touch you. You looked so fragile."

She reached up, touching his cheeks. "Kieran, you're crying."

"It's the happiness overflowing. I don't plan to ever spend a day away from you after tomorrow. Whatever we do, we'll do it together. Kiss me, Bonny."

She tasted like summer sunshine, mountains, and wildflowers, and she was his.

"I know a little bit of what our life will be like, but I have no idea how it will feel to be your wife. Does it sound strange to say I don't regret what we've been through because of how we've changed and grown?"

It was getting cold, but once they went back to the inn, his mother would make certain he didn't catch a glimpse of her until she started down the aisle. "No, it's not strange. We're so much stronger than before."

"All things become beautiful in His time." Bonny cupped his cheek in her hand. "I promise to never take you for granted."

"You will, and I will do the same with you, but I promise to love you more every day. Tomorrow, our wild, romantic adventure begins a new chapter, my Highland Games hunk. Let's go inside before you get too cold. I did promise David I would take care of you." She jumped up, pulling him to his feet.

"A little cold isn't going to hurt me." He stopped before opening the door to hold her one more time before his mother banished him to the other wing of the house. *"Oidhche mhath, mo chridhe.* Sleep well, my Bonny."

She put her arms around his neck, running her fingers through the hair at the back of his neck. Did she know that drove him crazy?

"When we first met, Janet told me women envied the love you and Bronwyn shared. She said, 'A love like that is worth waiting for.' The only thing I need is your love."

He stooped to kiss her lips one more time. "And I yours, *a beannachd,* Bonny."

"*A beannachd,* my love. I'll see you in church."

"Aye, you will." With one more quick kiss, he headed to his room for the night.

Ɑ☙

Dozens of red and white roses filled the church as winter sunlight streamed through the stained glass windows.

Kari and Janet walked up the aisle as Angus piped "Mairi's Wedding."

The doors opened when he began "The Highland Wedding," and Kieran beheld his bride. Wearing her grandmother's ivory lace wedding dress and the veil worn by his great-grandmother, Bonny moved toward him wrapped in an ivory cloud and a cascade of curls, bright against the creamy skin of her neck and shoulders. A more exquisite sight was impossible to imagine.

ॐ

Bonny closed her eyes for a moment, longing for her daddy. She took a deep breath, meeting Dan's eyes with a smile, and gripped his strong arm tighter. He squeezed her hand, and they started down the aisle. She still had a slight limp, and Dan's prosthesis showed beneath his new MacDermott tartan. She looked up at him, realizing the perfect picture of God's grace and healing they presented. Added into the equation of grace was her precious Kieran, the giant of a man in the MacDonell tartan beaming from the front of the church as tears flowed down his cheeks without shame.

She clutched her bouquet of roses and white heather, surprised to find she was shaking. It seemed as if they reached the front in an instant.

When asked who gave her in marriage, Dan placed her hand in Kieran's. "Her friends who love her, by the trust placed in them by her father."

Kieran's touch sparked a current of electricity thrilling through her. Meeting his eyes, she knew he felt it too. Their moment had arrived. They spoke their wedding vows in Gaelic as a sign of her complete devotion to her husband and his home, providing a translation for the non-Gaelic speakers.

Graeme, attired in his own kilt, gave the traditional Scottish Wedding Blessing, *"Mile failte dhuit le d'bhreid, Fad do re gun robh thu slan. Moran laithean dhuit is sith, Le d'mhaitheas is le d'ni bhi fas."*

A thousand welcomes to you with your marriage.

May you be healthy all your days.

May you be blessed with long life and peace.

May you grow old with goodness, and with riches.

He explained that the obstacles, which they had overcome by God's grace, had strengthened them and taught them to depend on the Lord. Then, he outlined the Bible's plan for marriage, quoting scriptures, and giving practical advice on fulfilling the responsibilities of husband and wife.

With a tight grip on Bonny's hand, Kieran repeated his vows after Graeme, his deep voice stilling Bonny's nerves with its steady certainty. "*Tha mise Kieran a-nis 'gad ghabhail-sa Bonny …*"

The tender love, so undeniable in the shining pools of his eyes, held her mesmerized. She spoke her vows to him alone. "*Tha mise Bonny a-nis 'gad ghabhail-sa Kieran …*"

As Graeme pronounced them man and wife, Kieran encircled her in the gentle strength of his arms, their kiss—a tender beginning to their new life.

In an old Scottish tradition symbolizing Bonny's acceptance by the clan, Maggie stepped forward, pinning a rosette of MacDonell tartan to her gown with a clan badge of sterling silver. "Welcome, my daughter," she said, kissing her cheek.

They walked down the aisle, to the joyous strains of "Jesu, Joy of Man's Desiring," their lives entwined for life.

As the bells in the church tower pealed in celebration, one of the toddlers belonging to a member of the church handed Bonny the traditional horseshoe for good luck. Wrapped in a cocoon of happiness, they climbed into the horse-drawn carriage to return to the Inn for the reception and *Ceilidh*, a traditional evening of Celtic dances and singing.

As he held her, Bonny whispered in his ear. "Kieran, love, you're squeezing me so tight, I can't breathe."

"God gave you to me, to protect and care for, my precious jewel. You're glowing." He kissed her again, drawing cheers from the people on the street.

"Because I know nothing but death can ever separate us."

❧

Kieran held Bonny tight as they danced the first waltz. "Do you remember this tune?"

She rested her head on his chest. "'The Rosebud of Allenvale.' You requested it at the ball the night you first said you loved me."

"The skin on your shoulders felt as soft as rose petals."

A man who remembered such small details after such a long time was capable of keeping her heart safe for the rest of their lives. She turned her face up to meet his.

The celebrating and feasting at Highland weddings lasted long into the evening. They ate the brandy-soaked fruitcake, remembering their first one, and how many turns and twists lay between the two.

Kieran said, "We've come full-circle, love. Nothing will ever part us again."

Dan and Kari joined them, Kari creating a stunning sight in the deep red gown. "What a beautiful wedding."

"She's mine forever. How can anything be lovelier?" Standing, he offered his arm to Kari. "Would the matron-of-honor care to dance?"

"I'd be delighted, if you're up to it." He led her onto the dance floor, moving with unusual grace for a man of his size. "I promised three waltzes, one with my wife, one with my mother, and one with Bonny's dearest friend. I promise to take care of her."

Dan took Bonny's hand. "Hey, Carrot-Top, care to dance?"

"Of course." She put her hand on his shoulder as he encircled her waist.

"We're not bad for a couple of gimps. Are you happy, Mrs. MacDonell?" Dan asked, as they moved around the floor.

She leaned her cheek against her friend's shoulder. "The only thing more perfect would be to have my parents here. We're not gimps, Danny Boy. We're walking miracles, along with my handsome husband over there. What do you suppose he and Kari are discussing with such serious expressions?"

"My guess is he's promising to treat you right to avoid the wrath of my wife." He kissed her cheek as the music stopped. "Be happy, Bonny."

Dùghlas and Mairi Cameron strolled up, arm in arm. "This is a lovely wedding, Bonny. Your parents would be so very proud of you and pleased with the man you've chosen."

Tears filled her eyes, and she wiped them with the lace-edged handkerchief Maggie had insisted she stuff up her sleeve. "Thank you, both."

"God bless you, dear." Mairi kissed her on the cheek, and they walked away.

She walked over to her husband, who wrapped her in his arms, warm and solid, bestowing a sense of peace and contentment greater than she ever imagined.

CR80

At eight o'clock, the guests assembled to escort Bonny and Kieran to the bridal suite in the tower, where Graeme broke the traditional oatcake over Bonny's head and passed it around. Following the blessing, they stepped across the threshold into the anteroom of the tower chamber, since Dr. Wallace wouldn't allow him to lift her. Giving her a quick kiss, he went to the room next door, allowing her to prepare for their first time alone as man and wife.

Kari unfastened the pearl buttons down the back and helped Bonny out of her wedding dress. "I hope the joy I see in your eyes lasts throughout your life together."

Janet hugged her. "If ever a marriage was ordained by God, it's yours. Your life has taken many detours since we first met, but God fulfilled your dreams. It's a miracle. *A beannachd*, Bonny."

Tears welled up in Kari's eyes as Bonny hugged her.

⋘⋙

Bonny opened the door to Kieran's knock, and he barely closed it before taking her in his arms. She gazed up, feeling him quiver as she laid her hands on his shoulders.

"Were you listening for them to leave?"

"Aye, I've waited a long time for this night." She stood before him clad in delicate white lace. "You're so lovely ..."

She tilted her head back and smiled in spite of her shyness. "Are you ready for our adventure, my wild, romantic sheep farmer?"

He cleared his throat. "Absolutely. Are you ready, Mrs. MacDonell?"

Reaching up, she pulled his face down to hers. "I'm ready, Mr. MacDonell."

⋘⋙

The carved doors stood open, and both rooms flickered with candlelight. Warmed by the fires, the sweet scent of rose bouquets and white heather filled the room. The down comforter was turned back to reveal creamy, lace-trimmed sheets of the finest satin. Her heart quickened at the idea of lying next to him, but he motioned toward the sitting room couch where he had first proposed. Taking a small box from the table, he lifted out a necklace.

"Oh, Kieran ..." He held up a delicate gold cross with two wedding rings entwined in the center.

The deep rumble of his voice came as a whisper. "This will remind us to keep our marriage and our lives centered in our God. And because tonight is about new beginnings ..." He reached over and retrieved an elegant wrapped box from the table.

She opened it to find a new Bible with her new name inscribed on the front. "I'll use it tomorrow morning."

He loosened his hold while she retrieved a new Bible for him from the dressing room. Her gift also included a poem, written the day before during her prayer time.

After thanking God for His past guidance and future blessings, Kieran said, "Bonny, I promise to give you reason to bless this day as long as I live."

Placing his arm around her, they climbed the steps, and he closed the doors.

൚൏

Kieran picked up the poem Bonny had read to him the night before. It smelled of roses, like the petals embedded in the hand-made paper. He read the words once again, overwhelmed by the blessings of God.

Golden Bands

(For Kieran)

Such was my trust

That I gave you to hold

My fragile heart in your hands.

God blessed us so much

He placed us within

A circle of golden bands.

I ever will thank

My dear God above,

So carefully He watched over me.

He gave me to love

Such a precious heart,

No other will ever compete.

Through all of our years
I will have no regret,
If I searched a thousand lands.
So gently you keep
My own tender heart,
Within our golden bands.

He wondered once again at the amazing gift of the woman preparing herself for their honeymoon as he waited. For her to write such words with him in mind was beyond his comprehension. No matter what lay ahead, he felt confident of God's presence in their wild, romantic adventure, and he committed himself to holding her heart gently, all of their days.

The End

DISCUSSION QUESTIONS

1. What is your impression of Bonny Bryant's reaction to the losses in her life? How does the way she handles loss affect her relationships, her decision-making, and her personal peace?

2. How do the deaths of Kieran's wife and infant son cripple him? What is necessary for him to move forward with his life?

3. Describe the basic difference in the way Janet and Bonny handle hurt and betrayal. Which are you most like and what can you learn from comparing them?

4. Describe how you see the relationship between Bonny and Kieran. What strengths do they exhibit? What weaknesses?

5. Describe what is taking place in Bonny and Kieran's minds as they get to know each other better. Are they being honest with themselves? What do you think they would discover if they really examined the motives of their own hearts?

6. Is it possible to have true and lasting love without agreement in spiritual matters? How does Kieran's decision to deceive Bonny make you feel? If you were Bonny's friend, how would you advise her?

7. Are the problems in Kieran and Bonny's relationship insurmountable? What do you think needs to happen for them to have a successful marriage? How do you see Bonny's struggle over Kieran's faith? Is she right to be concerned? Are Bonny's friends right in warning her? What would you do in her place? What would you do if she were your friend?

8. How have you seen lies and anger affect marriages? Why is telling the truth and offering forgiveness so important?

9. How do you see the situation involving Bonny and the two men who love her? What do you see as the answer to the dilemma? What is missing from the situation that could make a big difference?

10. What details give evidence of the changes in Kieran and Bonny's relationship when Kieran comes to take her to back to Scotland? What proves to them that God was answering prayers all the time?

11. What do you see as the strongest theme of this book?

12. What made the strongest impression on you? Did your thinking change in any way? If so, describe how.

GLOSSARY

A bheanachd – Gaelic, a farewell blessing; goodbye

A charaid – Gaelic, my friend

Alba – Gaelic name for Scotland

A leannan – Gaelic, my sweetheart, lover

Aefauld – Scots, sincere, honest, faithful, single-minded

Aff yer heid – Scots, You're crazy

A'm sairy – Scots, I'm sorry

A sair fecht – Gaelic, a sad or sorry fact

Awrite – Slang, Hi

Bahooky – Slang, bum, behind

Beannachd – Gaelic, blessed

Beannachd Dè Rìgh Alban – Gaelic, God's blessing

Beannachd leat – Gaelic, goodbye, singular

Beannachd leibh – Gaelic, goodbye, plural

Ben, Beinn – Gaelic, mountain, or also through, inside, or within

Biddie – a woman

Bidh gaol agam ort gu sìorraidh [bee guhrl akum ohrsht goo sheeree] – Gaelic, I will love you forever

Biscochitos – Spanish, a cookie made with lard and seasoned with anise and cinnamon developed in New Mexico from recipes from the Spanish colonists

Bonnie – Gaelic, pleasing to the eye, pretty, attractive

Boot – Slang, trunk of a car

Bothy – A small shepherd's hut or rough holiday cottage

Braw – Scots, fine, grand, superb

Bubbly jock – Slang, turkey

Burn – Gaelic, stream

Can I gie ye a haund? – Scots, Can I give you a hand?

Canny – Scots, shrewd, crafty

Cya anon – Scots, goodbye

Ceana – (Kenna) Gaelic, fair one

Ceòl Mór – The "great music," as opposed to marches, dances, reels, and strathspeys, which are known a as *Ceòl Beag*, or "little music." *Ceòl Mór* for bagpipes goes back at least 400 years.

Ceud mile failte, cuad mile failte – Gaelic, a hundred, thousand welcomes

Cheetie – Scots, cat, kitten

Chile – hot peppers, especially used in New Mexican and Mexican food. Chile is the uncooked variety. They are eaten either green or left on the plant to ripen to red.

Chili – The cooked variety of chile peppers

Claymore – A late medieval (15th-17th century) Scottish great sword, or *claidheamh mòr*, intended for use with both hands

Co-ghàirdeachas – Gaelic, Congratulations

Colcannon – Gaelic, a dish from boiled cabbage, carrots, turnip and potatoes, seasoned with salt and pepper and served hot.

Come wi's – Scots, come with me

Come ben the hoose – Scots, welcome, come into the house

Crabbit – Scots, bad-tempered or grumpy

Dafty – Scots, harmless crazy

Dinnae fash yoursel' – Scots, don't worry or stress yourself, calm down

Dreich – Scots, dull and rainy

Drookit – Scots, soaking wet

Duine – Gaelic, man

Dunderheid – Scots, fool or idiot

Eejit – Scots, fool, idiot

Enchiladas – Spanish, a corn tortilla usually filled with meat or cheese, and covered with red or green chili

Empanadas – Spanish, a stuffed bread or pastry, similar to a turnover, filled with spicy meat or fruit and fried

Fàilte - Gaelic, welcome

Fàilte gu Alba – Gaelic, welcome to Scotland

Fàilte don Ghaidhealtachd – Gaelic, welcome to the Highlands

Feasgar math – Gaelic, good afternoon

Forfar bridies - an oval pastry with crimped edges, filled with minced meat and baked until lightly browned

Gaidhlig – the Gaelic language

Gleann – Gaelic, glen, a narrow valley, used in lands that Scots have settled

Go mbeannaí Dia duit – Gaelic, may God bless you

Guid – Scots, good

Guid cheerio the nou! – Scots slang, goodbye

Handsome is as handsome does – a man who is so good looking he thinks he can get away with anything

Haud yer wheesht! – Slang, be quiet or hold your tongue

Heidy – Scots, Headmaster

Hen –Scots, Term of affection for a woman you have a close relationship with

Hotch-potch – a stew made from mutton stock, chopped vegetables and barley to thicken it

IED – Improvised Explosive Device

It's a *sair fecht* – Scots, it's a sad thing

Keeper – a gamekeeper in charge of the wildlife on a large estate; also called a stalker, or ghillie

Kelpie – Water horse, similar to the Loch Ness Monster

Ken – Gaelic, to know

Loch – Gaelic, body of water either a lake or a bay, literally "arm of the sea"

Lochaber - P-Gaelic aber - mouth (Q-Gaelic inver) –"the loch where rivers Lochy & Nevis meet"

Luminarias – Spanish, originally a small bonfire, which has evolved into a candle placed in a paper sack with sand in the bottom, lit on Christmas Eve in New Mexico to light the way of the Christ Child

Mairead - Margaret

Mariachi – Spanish, a group of street musicians playing stringed instruments and music which originated in Western Mexico. The music can be instrumental or accompany vocalizations.

Mar sin leat (singular/informal) *Mar sin leibh* (plural/polite) – Gaelic, goodbye

Mathair – Gaelic, mother

Merry Yuil – Scots, Merry Christmas

Mhòr or mòr – Gaelic, big

Mizzle – Slang, a misty drizzle

Mo annsachd- Gaelic, my sweetheart

Mo balachan – Gaelic, my boy

Mo bhean – Gaelic, my wife

Mo chridhe – Gaelic, my heart's desire

Mo duine – Gaelic, my man

Mo gràdh – Gaelic, my love

Mo mhac – Gaelic, my son

Mo nighean – Gaelic, my daughter

Mons Meg - medieval siege cannon, now located at Edinburgh Castle, once able to propel a 400 pound ball 2 miles

Munro – Any mountain taller than 3,000 feet. Some people make it a hobby to see how many they can climb, calling it "Munro bagging"

Nic-chridhe – Gaelic, a term of endearment for a female; my dear lassie, my dear lady

Nippin – Slang, nagging

Nollaig Chridheil – Gaelic, Merry Christmas

Nollaig Chridheil agus bliadhna mhath ur – Merry Christmas and Happy New Year

Noo jist haud on – Scots, now hold on, slow down, take your time

Oidhche mhath – Gaelic, goodnight

Peely Wally – Slang, pale and unwell

Piobaireachd – Gaelic, piping

Posole – Spanish, a stew or soup made from kernels of corn which have been

Gaelic

soaked in lime and hulled, cooked with pork or beef and seasoned with chili and other spices

Pure dead brilliant – Slang, exceptionally good.

Rickle a bones – Slang, very thin or skinny

Roamin' in the gloamin' – Scots, a walk in the evening

Sassanach – Gaelic, Saxons, the English, usually used as a swear word.

Saor Alba – Gaelic, Free Scotland

Sileas – Gaelic, (Shee-lus) – Cecelia

Skleping – Slang, a thrashing

Snaps – Slang, photographs

Stramash – Gaelic, a disturbance, racket or crash

Tha gaol agam ort – (Ha gool akam orsht) - Gaelic, I love you

Tha mo gaol gu bràth – Gaelic, My love is forever

Thole – Scots, put up with, endure

Vigas – Spanish, large wooden beams in the ceiling, in traditional southwestern adobe, or mud brick, structures, they helped to hold up the roof. These days they are usually ornamental.

Wabbit – Slang, tired, worn out

Wellingtons or wellies – high rubber boots often used on farms

Wheesht – Scots, quiet

You look like death on a pirn stick – Slang, You don't look too well

Made in the USA
San Bernardino, CA
07 April 2014